It is the Year of Our Lord 1453, and Sir Clegg de Lave, a battle-scarred English knight, begins his search for a life that will bring him glory and riches...

After years as a mercenary in France, Spain, and the Holy Roman Empire, Clegg returns to Scotland to establish the most powerful and profitable gambling guild the world has ever seen, modeled on the gladiatorial schools of ancient Rome.

The Ludus Caledonia quickly becomes the center of battles for entertainment, but also for opportunity—if a warrior wins, a lord may offer him a lucrative military position.

The lure of money and position makes men from all walks of life into fighters and some into winners, and only a rare few find something beyond the love of a fight.

The love of a good woman.

This rare few will know their happily ever after.

This is the world of the Ludus Caledonia...and business is booming.

THE SACRAMENTUM

I faithfully swear to do all that is commanded of me,
All that is required of me,
And all that is asked of me.
May I live both to fight and to protect my brethren.
May God smile upon me and grant me courage
So that I may not fail myself nor those around me.
Thus it is spoken, thus it shall be done.

—*Fionnadh Fuil (Blood Oath)*
of the Ludus Caledonia

HIGHLAND DEFENDER

KATHRYN LeVeQue

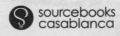

FEB 09 2021

Copyright © 2021 by Kathryn Le Veque
Cover and internal design © 2021 by Sourcebooks
Cover design by Dawn Adams
Cover art by Allan Davey/Shannon Associates

Sourcebooks and the colophon are registered trademarks of Sourcebooks.

All rights reserved. No part of this book may be reproduced in any form or by
any electronic or mechanical means including information storage and retrieval
systems—except in the case of brief quotations embodied in critical articles or
reviews—without permission in writing from its publisher, Sourcebooks.

The characters and events portrayed in this book are fictitious or
are used fictitiously. Any similarity to real persons, living or dead,
is purely coincidental and not intended by the author.

All brand names and product names used in this book are trademarks,
registered trademarks, or trade names of their respective holders. Sourcebooks
is not associated with any product or vendor in this book.

Published by Sourcebooks Casablanca, an imprint of Sourcebooks
P.O. Box 4410, Naperville, Illinois 60567-4410
(630) 961-3900
sourcebooks.com

Printed and bound in Canada.
MBP 10 9 8 7 6 5 4 3 2 1

Redford Township District Library

3 9009 0021 5893 5

PART ONE

An Principio
Inopinatus

(An Unexpected Beginning)

CHAPTER ONE

Edinburgh, Scotland
Year of Our Lord 1486

IT SOUNDED LIKE A FIGHT.

But, then again, everything in this seedy section of Edinburgh sounded like a fight.

Men fought, women fought, dogs fought. Sometimes even old people fought. There was a couple in a corner lodging at the end of the alley who regularly took to each other with clubs and shovels.

The problem was that they were so ridiculously old, and the weapons so heavy, that they could never really lift them. They ended up lugging them around and shouting at each other. Then they would drag their weapons inside and share the cheap ale that made them so belligerent in the first place. And then it would start all over again.

But this wasn't the quarrelsome old couple.

This was different.

A scream filled the air, but it was more a cry of rage. He'd been sleeping in a nook in this old alley for a few hours, ever since he stumbled his way out of the Sticky Wick. He wasn't exactly drunk, but he'd had plenty to drink of that cheap ale with chaff in it. Depression and sorrow had brought him to the nook to sleep, too unmotivated to make it back to the loft he rented from a greedy livery owner.

He simply didn't care anymore.

But the sounds of a fight had his attention.

Sitting up, he put a hand to his throbbing head, listening to sounds of a struggle and once again hearing that angry scream. The sounds were coming from a smaller alleyway that branched off from the one he was languishing in. One more scream and he was on the move.

Instinct took over.

It was early morning so people were beginning to go about their daily business. The alleyway was slick with mud from both the rain the night before and the piss tossed out of the homes. He almost slipped as he made his way toward the sound of the struggle, taking a turn and gripping the corner of the house he was next to so he wouldn't slide in the muck.

Then he saw it.

A woman was being assailed by at least three men. She had something in her arms, something they were grabbing at and she was unwilling to relinquish. She was fighting them off as much as she was able, but it was one woman against three grubby old men. They weren't really touching her as much as they were simply grabbing at whatever she was carrying, but when one man got behind her and tripped her, the fight escalated.

Most people in this part of Edinburgh wouldn't get involved in something like this. They were people who lived in poverty and filth and without the wherewithal to involve themselves in someone else's troubles. But he was different—he knew he couldn't just stand there as a woman was assaulted. It wasn't in his nature, though there were times when he questioned his nature. He wasn't even sure what it was any longer. But what it *wasn't* was passive when someone needed assistance.

Bane Morgan had never been passive in his life.

Reckless, yes.

But not passive.

Wiping a hand over his face to clear his vision, he charged headlong into the fracas.

The woman was on the ground now as the men grabbed at her.

She was kicking and scratching, unwilling to let go of whatever she was holding in her arms. Bane came up behind one of the men grabbing at her, driving a punch into the back of his head that sent him crashing into the stone wall.

The woman was in a panic. She was scrambling to get away and, in the process, dropped what she was carrying. Sausages, carefully wrapped, rolled out onto the dirty alley. That brought more people, those who had been observing the fight with disinterest until the food started to fly.

Now they came running.

The brawl became a melee.

Unfortunately, Bane was right in the middle of it. He found himself surrounded by people grabbing at the sausages rolling in the dirt, fighting over them, punching and kicking one another for the privilege of rescuing a dirty meat roll. Hands, feet, and pieces of meat were flying as the hungry and desperate fought for their very existence. It wasn't a matter of greed.

It was a matter of survival.

The fight was lost already, only the woman on the ground didn't realize it yet. She still thought there was some hope of regaining what she'd lost. She was struggling to her feet, slapping hands and shoving people, trying desperately to regain her lost meat. But when Bane managed to confiscate a couple of sausages, she thought he was stealing them and grabbed the nearest weapon, which happened to be a dented copper piss pot near a doorway. Swinging it with all her might, she brained him with it.

Piss went flying in all directions.

"Bleeding Christ, woman," he gasped as he crashed into the wall behind him. "What in the bloody hell was that for?"

She was still wielding the pot like a club. "Give me back my sausages!"

"I was going tae," he said, shaking off the bells in his ears. "Give a man a chance before ye're beating his brains in."

"Give a man a *chance*?" she repeated, aghast. "A chance tae do what? Rob me blind? Look around ye. Everything I had is lost because of ye and yer thieving friends!"

"I am many things, but a thief isna one of them."

"I saw ye help those men who were attacking me!"

He shook his head again, wiping the piss from his eyes. "What ye saw was me coming tae yer aid. I heard the screaming and came tae help." He opened his hand and let the two sausages in his grip fall to the ground. "But ye can fend for yerself now, wench. Best of luck tae ye."

He was woozy from the hit, staggering off as the woman stood there, piss pot still in hand, watching him go. As she stood there, confused and upset, the two sausages he'd dropped were picked up by children, who ran off with them.

And then there were none.

Almost as swiftly as it started, the fight was over, the crowd was gone, and she had nothing left. With only the empty burlap the sausages had been wrapped in, the expression on her face was one of despair. Hanging her head in defeat, she turned to walk away, heading in another direction, when she heard a crash behind her.

The man she'd struck with the piss pot had tripped and fallen against a rain barrel. As the woman watched, he tried to hold on to right himself but he ended up pulling the barrel down. Water gushed all over him.

Clearly, her hit to the head had done some damage.

The woman watched him struggle and her despair turned to guilt. Considering the fact that he hadn't run off with the sausages when he very well could have, perhaps he'd been telling the truth. Perhaps she'd been too hasty in her judgment and now he was suffering the consequences.

Retracing her steps, she reluctantly went to help him, but Bane saw her coming.

He braced himself.

"Are ye back tae brain me again?" he asked. "If ye are, I canna give ye much of a fight."

From his position on the muddy ground, he gazed up at her warily. She was standing a few feet away, looking at him as if debating whether or not to help him. Or kill him. It could have been either choice in her case. She'd already accused him of being a thief, so perhaps she'd come to finish what she started.

"I've not come tae brain ye again," she said after a moment. "It looks as if I already knocked ye sufficiently."

"Ye did."

She cocked her head as she looked at him, studying him as he wallowed in the mud. "I was thinking that ye could have run off with the sausages, but ye dinna," she said. "Given that everyone was grabbing for them, I hope ye can understand my reaction. I thought ye were stealing them, too."

His gaze lingered on her before he leaned back against the wall. Exhaustion was setting in and his head was killing him.

"What were ye doing with those sausages, anyway?" he asked. "I've not seen ye around here before."

She lifted the empty sack in a helpless gesture. "M'lady sent me tae the butcher's shop," she said. "This was the shortest route back home. She's expecting them for her morning meal and I was trying tae hurry, so I cut through this part of town. That was my mistake."

"Who is yer lady?"

"Lady Currie," she said. "We live in Meadowbank, tae the east, north of Holyrood. Do ye know it?"

He blinked as he processed what she'd told him. "Ye're a fair way off from Meadowbank," he said. "What in the world did ye come tae this side of town for? Surely there are butchers closer tae Meadowbank."

The woman shrugged weakly. "Lady Currie likes this butcher," she said. "Usually, she sends the menservants, but no one was available at this hour so I offered tae go."

"And ye lost yer sausages for it."

She turned in the direction she had come as if to see the butcher. "I dunna suppose he'd give me more," she said wistfully. "It was foolish tae come this way. I dunna relish telling Lady Currie that I lost her meal."

"I canna imagine she'll be happy about it," Bane said, taking a second look at the woman. She was a pretty thing, with chestnut hair and eyes the color of the sea. In fact, she was damned fine. *Too* fine to be a maid. "Are ye her maid?"

The woman turned to him. "I am whatever she wants me tae be," she said. "Today, it was a messenger."

That was an odd answer. "What's yer name, lass?"

"Lucia."

"Do ye want me tae go with ye and tell Lady Currie that ye were set upon by a thousand thieves and the sausages stolen?"

A ripple of surprise washed over her features, shocked that he would make such an offer. But quickly, she shook her head and turned away.

"Nay," she said. "Though I thank ye for the offer. I'll face her on my own."

It seemed as if there was nothing more to say. Truth be told, Bane had only made the offer because he thought she was a pretty lass and he wasn't quite sure he wanted to part ways with her yet. Not that he had any designs on her; he'd never had designs on a woman in his life.

But this lass... There was something about her that caught his eyes.

"Then I wish ye well," he told her, struggling to stand up. "I hope ye have an understanding mistress."

As he reached his feet, the world began to rock unsteadily. Perhaps it was the lack of sleep, the heavy drink, or the knock on the head. Or all three. These days, it was difficult to know what, exactly, ailed him because there was so much. He turned to walk away but he ended up staggering into the wall. Lucia reached out to steady him.

"Are ye well?" she asked.

He nodded, trying to push her away so he had some room to move and not topple over on her.

"Fine," he said. "I'll be on my way."

Two more steps and he lost his balance and went to one knee. She was on him in a flash. "This is my fault," she said. "I hit ye in the head and now ye canna walk. Where is yer home? I'll help ye there."

She sounded repentant, not at all like the defiant and frightened woman he'd tried to help moments earlier. The remorse in her voice made her sound softer, much more in line with her beauteous looks. But he thought on her question—*Where is yer home?* He didn't want her to see where he lived, a shoddy loft filled with old straw and the ghost of his life that once was.

He didn't want this pretty lass to know how low he'd fallen.

"I dunna need help," he assured her, trying to get to his feet again. "Ye'd better be on yer way."

He all but yanked his arm from her grasp, laboring to move on, gripping the stone walls as he moved. But his legs felt like jelly and he'd barely taken a few more steps when he came to a halt and simply leaned against the wall for support. But it wasn't because he couldn't make it any farther.

He wanted to see if she was still watching him.

As luck would have it, she was.

"Please," she said, coming up beside him. "Let me take ye home."

"I have no home."

She eyed him. Given that he was wearing rags and smelled of piss, it wasn't difficult to believe. The man looked as if he'd been wallowing in the sty with the rest of the pigs.

She grabbed him by the arm.

"Then ye'll come with me," she said firmly. "Can ye at least walk?"

Bane was intrigued. So she was inviting him to go along with her, was she? That was the best invitation he'd had in months. Feeling the least bit naughty that he wasn't refusing her invitation, he pretended he was worse than he actually was.

He hadn't had a woman's pity or attention in quite some time.

"I can walk," he said quietly. "But…but yer help would be appreciated."

With Lucia holding his arm tightly, as if she could support a man of his size, Bane let her lead the way.

Perhaps his terrible day was going to get brighter after all.

At the very least, it was going to be more interesting.

CHAPTER TWO

MEADOWBANK, HOME OF LAIRD AND LADY CURRIE, WAS A magnificent manse to the east of Edinburgh, outside the city walls. Out here, just north of Holyrood Palace, there were several estates dotting the land, great stone sentinels of wealthy Scottish lairds. There was a great deal of land out here, used for farming or for keeping small herds of animals.

Meadowbank was an impressive sight. Three stories in height, it had a massive curtain wall built from the pale sandstone so common to the area, stone that would eventually turn black with age and the elements.

Not strangely, Bane's walking had become steadier as they made their way back to the house, but he let Lucia hold on to him because she was convinced that she was being of some service. More than that, he let her hold on to him simply because he liked it. He couldn't remember when last he had a pretty girl on his arm.

If Lucia knew who, and what, he really was, he was quite certain she wouldn't be holding him so tightly. It was a fantasy world Bane was living in at the moment, one he hadn't realized he needed until Lucia took his arm. He'd been her hero and she was treating him like one.

God, it felt good.

Lucia took him around to the rear of Meadowbank where a postern gate led them into a vast stable yard. Hit by the smell of animals, Bane allowed Lucia to pull him through the yard until they came to the rear where a few tiny outbuildings lined the wall. Lucia shoved open the last door in the row, kicking it because it stuck.

She let go of Bane's arm.

"There," she said. "Ye can use this cottage. I know it's not much, but ye can rest here until yer head is better. Go in and sit down, and I will return as quickly as I can."

Bane looked at the tiny chamber, which was much better than the accommodations he had now. In fact, he began to see an opportunity—a lady with some guilt, an empty room, and he would have a better roof over his head. Putting his hand to his temple, he pretended to be weakened still.

"Thank ye," he said. "Yer kindness is greatly appreciated."

Lucia helped him in because he seemed to be staggering again. Bane lowered himself into a corner of the cluttered cottage as Lucia began to grab the implements lining the walls, like pitchforks and shovels.

"I'll remove these so ye willna have tae keep company with farm tools," she said. "Sit quietly, now. I'll return."

Bane had no intention of doing anything other than sitting quietly. Something else might see him get thrown out on his ear, and this was too good a situation to pass up. When Lucia departed, dragging the shovels and rakes with her, Bane leaned back against the wall and thought he might actually have found a better situation for himself. He was a hard worker, so he could offer his strength at the manor. He was sure they could use a strong hand.

And he would be where Lucia was.

A foolish thought, but one he couldn't shake. He didn't know what it was about the woman that attracted him so, but he wasn't beyond finding out.

Hearing that fight in the alley this morning was quite fortuitous.

Perhaps things were finally starting to look up.

☙ ☙ ☙

He was handsome.

Lucia had noticed that from the outset. It was difficult to tell beneath all of that grime and hair, but once she got a good look at his face, she could see just how handsome he was. And young; he wasn't old at all. Well, *relatively* old. At ten or more years than her twenty and one.

He was a man in his prime.

But he was also living on the streets, and in addition to the smell of piss from the pot she'd slung at him, she thought she could smell ale. After the chaos of the sausages had died down and she realized he was injured, she still couldn't explain what made her go back to see how badly he was hurt. Perhaps it was the fact that something in his eyes conveyed utter defeat.

He was a man who had given up.

Perhaps that was why she'd insisted he come back with her to Meadowbank. All she knew was that something in his eyes had pulled at her, something that captured her curiosity and natural empathy. Certainly, she'd seen her share of the destitute in Edinburgh. But what made this man different, she didn't know.

Something...

But first, he needed a bath and food. That was the least she could do for him, considering his attempted act of valor during the sausage disaster. But she didn't want her mistress to know she'd brought a man back to the manor, so she went to the stable master and explained the situation.

The stable master, being a very old man with a kind disposition, assured her that he would help the man. In little time, a big copper pot, clean straw, and blankets were heading to that tiny storage cottage. Everything needed for a bath was being brought in, and Lucia confiscated soap from the laundress along with clean drying linens. A trip to the kitchens had her carrying a basket filled with bread, cheese, and several apples. With all of it balanced in her hands, she headed back to the cottage.

By the time she reached the rear of the stable yard, the sky had clouded over and it was starting to rain. Fat droplets pelted the ground as she stood at the cottage door while the servants with the hot water buckets finished filling the old copper tub. Once they vacated, she entered the cottage and shut the door behind her.

"Here," she said as she turned around. "I've brought ye…"

Her words were cut off as she found herself looking at the rear view of a naked man. His filthy clothes were in a pile at his feet, and he was standing next to the tub. Startled, she tried to turn around quickly to block her view of the man's nude arse, but she ended up dumping the soap and the linens, barely saving the food in the basket. She heard a laugh behind her.

"Ye sent me a bath, lass," he said. "Am I not supposed tae use it?"

Lucia could hear water sloshing behind her as he climbed into the tub. "Of course ye are," she said, feeling her cheeks flame with embarrassment. "Ye should have told me… That is, I could have waited outside while ye removed yer clothing."

"I suppose it dinna occur tae me," he said. "It doesna matter now, anyway. Ye can turn around. My modesty is protected."

Timidly, she turned around to see that he was, indeed, sitting in the copper tub. She could see him from the waist up, which in truth wasn't a better view than his naked buttocks had been. She should have been permanently traumatized by that sight but, somehow, she wasn't.

It had been unexpectedly tantalizing.

Setting the basket of food down on the ground, she went to collect the linens and soap that she'd dumped. She extended the soap to him and he reached out, taking it from her.

"Do I smell that bad?" he asked.

"Bad enough that ye'll start attracting flies if ye dunna wash up."

He grinned, splashing water over his head and upper body, going to work with a soap that smelled of mint and rosemary. It was hard soap, rare in these times, and produced a good deal of white, slick residue. He scrubbed his head and face with it vigorously.

"What kind of soap is this?" he asked, foam all over his face.

"*Savon d'Alep,*" she replied. "Soap from the Levant. Have ye not heard of it? Lady Currie has it sent all the way from Rome. Everyone here uses it because she says she canna stand the smell of anything else."

Satisfied, he continued to scrub, smelling at the frothy bar. "Nay, I've not heard of it."

"How does yer head feel?"

He splashed water all over his face and hair, rinsing out the soapy residue. "Better," he said. "It was kind of ye tae bring me here. Ye dinna have tae."

"I know," she said, watching him splash. "But as I said, 'twas my fault ye couldna walk. I had tae make amends."

"Ye have a big heart, lass."

Lucia watched him use the soap on his arms, hands, and chest. Thoughts of the glimpse of his naked buttocks filled her mind again but instead of chasing them away, she lingered on them. Muscular buttocks that had been smooth and white, something that made her feel the least bit heated to recall. She had to lick her lips to moisten them because thoughts of the man's nude form dried out her mouth as she sucked in air. She found herself standing back by the door because it was safer that way.

Safer for whom?

Lucia had to ask herself that question. In truth, as she watched him, she could see the diamond emerging from all of that filth. The man had enormous shoulders and arms, muscular and beautiful, and beneath that growth of hair on his face, she could imagine that he was truly handsome. He had a square jaw and a profile that looked like it came from one of those Greek gods on the vases that Lady Currie had on display.

Why *had* she brought him back here? Was it really because she felt guilty?

Or was it something else?

"Ye never did tell me yer name," she said after a moment. "Ye already know mine."

"My name is Bane."

"Where do ye come from, Bane?"

He was busy splashing and washing. "The Highlands."

"Then why are ye in Edinburgh? Ye said ye had no home."

He didn't answer her for a moment. He continued scrubbing his body, now with a big leg on the side of the tub. "I dunna," he said. "Not here in Edinburgh, anyway."

Lucia watched that big leg as he washed it. "Then ye came tae Edinburgh tae do nothing but live in alleys and save women from sausage thieves?"

He smiled weakly. "I suppose I came here for the same reason most men do," he said. "Tae find an opportunity."

"What kind of work do ye do?"

He put his leg back in the tub. "I can do most anything," he said. "I can read and write. I'm not a blacksmith, but I can shoe a horse. I can build a wall or a cottage."

Those few words told Lucia he was more than just another drunk in an alley. "Then ye've been educated."

"Aye."

"Who's yer clan?"

"Morgan."

"Ah," she said. "They're a warring bunch, I hear. Can ye fight, then?"

The question caused him to avert his gaze. "I was the best warrior in my clan," he muttered. "But that's over now."

There was something in his voice as he said it, something that had her interest. It wasn't exactly rage or anger, but something... dark. Sadness, perhaps?

Or regret?

The mystery about the man was growing.

"So ye've come tae Edinburgh tae seek yer fortune, then?" she asked.

He shook his head and started in on the other leg with the soap. "Nay," he said. "Not my fortune. And ye've asked enough questions about me. I want tae hear about ye. How long have ye served here?"

Now that the focus was on her, Lucia didn't like it very much. She wasn't finished interrogating him, and she certainly didn't want to talk about herself. Standing up, she went to the pile of filthy, torn rags that he'd been wearing and gingerly held up the tunic he'd had on.

"These clothes are nothing more than rags," she said, ignoring his question. She quickly picked up the breeches he'd been wearing, peering at those as well. "I'm surprised they covered anything at all. How did ye expect tae survive the winter in these things? Finish cleaning yerself and I'll return."

With that, she bolted out of the cottage before he could say another word, rather pleased that she'd avoided his question. It would probably come up again, and when it did, she'd have to face it. But not now. Not when she was so busy trying to figure out why she wanted to see his naked buttocks again.

"Lucia!"

Someone was calling her name. Lucia turned to see one of the servant lads who worked in the house, a boy who spent his days scrubbing floors from morning to night. His name was Tynan, the son of one of Lady Currie's servants. The lad had hair like straw— blond and standing up on end, and he had a perpetually sunny smile on his face. He ran toward her across the yard.

"M'lady is asking for ye," he said. "She is demanding her breakfast!"

The sausages. Lucia's heart sank. She knew she was in for a good deal of trouble. She'd been so preoccupied with Bane that she hadn't even let anyone in the house know she'd returned yet. Somehow, tending Bane had seemed more important, but now...

Now she had to face it.

"Here," she said, handing Tynan the ruins of Bane's clothing. "Burn these. And go find Old Roy and tell him ye need clothing for a man his size. A tunic and breeches. When he gives them tae ye, take them tae the stable yard. There is a man in one of the cottages who needs them. Hurry, now."

Tynan looked at her in confusion, but not before he got a whiff of the clothing and held it away from him.

"Och!" he said, wrinkling his nose. "Where did ye get these?"

"From a man who helped me," she said, her thoughts lingering on Bane when she should very well have been thinking of the punishment she was about to face for her dereliction of duty. "Go, now. Find clothing for him."

Tynan nodded, darting off on his long, skinny legs. Lucia watched him go before squaring her shoulders and heading into the house.

She had some explaining to do.

CHAPTER THREE

LUCIA.

Bane was sitting in the remains of the cooling bathwater, thinking on the chestnut-haired lass who had provided him his first real bath in months.

Loo-cee-uh…

A beautiful name for a beautiful girl. He thought it was rather fortuitous that she'd asked him what talents he had. He had many, and hopefully one of them would fill a need at Meadowbank. If he could simply stay in this cottage, he would be willing to work hard for it. He wasn't lazy by any means, but depression had a way of destroying a man's motivation.

Somehow, Lucia had turned that around.

Therefore, he sat in the bathwater and waited for her to return. But time passed and the bathwater grew downright cold before he forced himself to climb out and wrap up in the drying linens she'd brought. An old man had brought him dry straw and blankets, and he managed to fashion an acceptable bed out of them. Much better than the bed he had in that stuffy loft.

Clean for the first time in months, he sat down on his straw bed and wolfed down the bread and cheese. He was chowing down on the apples when the door opened, producing a skinny lad with matted hair.

He looked at Bane with a great deal of uncertainty.

"Are ye…?" He stopped, swallowed, and started again. "Are these clothes for ye?"

Bane could only guess that they were, considering he had nothing to wear. "Lucia took my clothing," he said. "Where is she?"

The boy timidly entered. "She's with m'lady," he said. "She told me tae bring ye these."

He extended the wad of clothing and Bane took it. Curious, he held up the tunic. It was made for a large man and was perhaps a bit roomy for him, but he didn't care. It was in good condition, as were the breeches.

"Thank ye," he said. "Who do these belong tae?"

The child threw a thumb over his shoulder. "Old Roy," he said. "He's the smithy. He also pulls teeth if ye have a toothache. Do ye have a toothache?"

Bane shook his head, grinning. But the lad continued to stand, an intensely curious expression on his face. He couldn't have been more than eight or ten years old, and already Bane could see that his hands were chapped and callused from hard work.

He was a child who was used for labor.

"What's yer name, lad?" he asked.

"Tynan."

"Where's yer mam?"

The boy pointed toward the manse. "She's a servant tae m'lady," he said. "She brushes m'lady's hair and cleans her chamber."

"I see," Bane said. "And what do ye do?"

"I wash," Tynan said, making scrubbing motions. "I wash the floors and stone. Sometimes I even wash the horses."

"Oh."

"What's yer name?"

"Bane," he said. It seemed to him that the lad was a bit chatty, and realizing that, he thought he might be able to find out a little more about Lucia from the boy. "Ye said yer mam works for m'lady?"

"Aye."

"M'lady is Lady Currie?"

"Aye."

"She has a lot of servants."

The boy nodded firmly. "My mam and others," he said. "Even Lucia."

That was the exact subject Bane wanted to speak on. "Do ye know much of Lucia, then?"

"She and my mam are friends," he said. "I've known Lucia since she came here."

"When was that?"

The boy scratched his head. "Two winters, I think," he said. "She came tae Laird Currie after her da died."

That sounded curious to Bane. "Why would she come tae Laird Currie?"

The boy plopped down on the ground in front of him as if settling in for a nice, long chat. "I heard my mam say it was a debt," he said. Then he whispered loudly, "Her da owed Laird Currie money and Lucia came tae pay it."

He said it as if it were a secret, but more than likely a well-known one if a child knew of it. The entire manse probably knew of it. But something now made sense to Bane; when he asked Lucia what her duties were for Lady Currie, she had told him whatever the lady wished. Now he understood that comment.

She was working off her dead father's debt, any way she could.

Which was rather sad considering the woman's beauty. She should have been married years ago to a fine husband, but instead she found herself a servant in a wealthy home. It was little wonder that Lucia didn't want to talk about herself.

No doubt it was a sensitive subject.

"I see," he said. "Is the debt almost paid now?"

Tynan shrugged. "I dunna know. Lady Currie likes Lucia as a companion. She makes her sit with her for hours."

"Do ye know where Lucia used tae live?"

"Selkirk. Her family name is Symington. I heard her tell my mam that."

Lucia Symington. As Bane pulled the tunic over his head, his focus was on the boy who seemed to be a wealth of information.

"Tell me everything ye know about her."

Tynan did.

CHAPTER FOUR

THE SLAP HAD SENT HER REELING.

Lucia stumbled into the wall, catching herself from falling, as Lady Currie's nurse went in for another blow. Lady Currie had kept her nurse from childhood, a bully of a woman who liked to slap around all of Lady Currie's servants, but as she came in for another strike, Lucia lashed out a foot and caught the woman in the knee.

She went down like a rock.

"Enough!" Lady Currie cried. "Stop fighting! I will not tolerate it!"

The nurse, old and heavy as she was, was sitting on the floor struggling to breathe as Lucia stood against the wall, preparing to kick the woman again if she came at her.

"I willna let her beat me, m'lady," she said, angry and fearful. "I'm sorry for the sausages. I beg yer forgiveness that they were stolen. But there were three men against me, and I couldna stop them. I willna let Colly strike me for something I couldna help."

The former Lady Blanche Ireby, now Lady Currie, rose from her dressing table to stand between her nurse and Lucia, holding out her hands to prevent them from moving against each other. She was only a few years older than Lucia, plump and pretty, married to a man who was old enough to be her grandfather. She was also English and spoke in the Sassenach fashion.

"I am sorry you were set upon," she said. "Were you injured in the attack?"

Lucia was still against the wall in a defensive position. "Nay, m'lady," she said. "They pushed and grabbed, but I was not injured. I am very sorry for yer sausages. If ye wish for me tae go back and get more, I will."

Lady Currie shook her head. "Nay," she said. "It would take too long. Next time, I will send a male servant."

"That is wise, m'lady. I am sorry tae have failed ye."

Lady Currie looked Lucia over before dropping her hands and turning back to her dressing table. "You did not, not really," she said, picking up the cup of wine on the table. "I should not have sent you so far away for the sausages without an escort."

"May I work off the cost, m'lady?"

"That is not necessary," Lady Currie said, draining the cup and licking her lips. "But please do not kick Colly again. She will understand not to strike you again, but I do not wish to see her injured. She is old and damages easily."

Lucia almost laughed. Colly was as tough as a horse. Lucia knew it wouldn't be the last time she and Colly had a go-around, because it certainly wasn't the first.

"If she willna strike me, I willna fight back, m'lady," she said, but before Lady Currie could reply, she quickly changed the subject. "May I fetch yer riding clothes? 'Tis a good morning tae ride in the hills."

Lady Currie sat down at her dressing table, and a maid resumed dressing her pale-red hair. "I think not," she said, pouring herself more wine from a fine crystal decanter. Wine was her constant companion. "And I want you to dress well today, Lucia. We are going to the Ludus Caledonia again tonight. It seems that they have new novice warriors to look over. I am eager to see their stock."

The Ludus Caledonia. That was a name spoken frequently at Meadowbank and mostly by Lady Currie. It wasn't a place for singing or for a fanciful dinner, nor was it a merchant who sold exotic things from across the sea. It was a secretive place where the wealthy of England and Scotland gathered for gladiatorial games of the most brutal and entertaining nature.

The Ludus Caledonia, simply put, was a fight guild.

It was also a place where Lady Currie found men to do things to her that her old husband no longer had the energy or wherewithal to do. Lucia had been introduced to the place the very first week she had come to Meadowbank when Lady Currie took her along to the mysterious arena hidden in the hills south of Edinburgh. There, she sat with Lady Currie in the lists, watching men beat each other bloody while bets were placed on the winner.

The Ludus Caledonia was not only a fight guild; it was also a school where men were trained to fight in the ancient ways. The candidates were chosen well, and treated well, and expected to fight for money or honor, or both.

On Lucia's very first visit, Lady Currie had paid for the company of a gladiator who had won one of the many battles that night, and Lucia had waited outside the warrior's cottage as Lady Currie went inside to visit him. She stood there, listening to Lady Currie's gasps of passion as the man pleasured her.

That was Lucia's experience with the Ludus Caledonia. She had no use for it, to be truthful, but Lady Currie was fond of the place and Lucia could look forward to another cold, late night of bloody fights, screaming crowds, and a mistress who drowned herself in wine before she sought the companionship of a champion warrior.

"Of course, m'lady," she said, feigning interest. "What will ye have me wear?"

Lady Currie was looking at herself in the mirror, turning her head slightly as her maid put pins into an elaborate hairstyle. "The gown of blue satin that I gave to you. Wait…not that one. I do not want you to outshine me. Wear the gown the color of amber."

"Aye, m'lady."

"You may go now. Make sure the horses are prepared to take us to the Cal. I should like to leave an hour before sunset."

"Aye, m'lady."

With that, Lucia fled the manse, making her way out into the kitchen yard and then into the stable yard beyond. She considered herself fortunate that she hadn't been punished for the sausages, at least not truly punished. It could have been so much worse.

Thank God it wasn't.

On her way back to Bane's cottage, she paused to tell the old stable master about Lady Currie's plans, to which the old man simply shook his head reproachfully. Lady Currie's activities at the Ludus Caledonia were an open secret to all at Meadowbank but her husband. The older servants in particular, like the old stable master, resented her for it. She was off to fornicate while her husband sat with his books.

It was a sad state, indeed.

But thoughts of Lady Currie faded as Lucia reached Bane's cottage. Her heart was racing just a little, making her realize she was eager to see him. He was something new, and God only knew there was never anything new or exciting at Meadowbank. Remembering what happened the last time she entered without knocking, however, she rapped softly on the door.

Or perhaps I should have just opened it...

"Bane?" she called, realizing she'd ruined her chance for another glimpse of naked buttocks. "May I come in?"

The panel flew open and Tynan was standing there, his eyes wide. "Bane needs a razor!" he said, bolting past her. "I'll find him one!"

Lucia watched the boy dart across the stable yard. "Has he been in here since I left ye?" she asked.

Bane came to stand next to her, watching the child run off. "The entire time," he said. "He likes tae talk."

Lucia smiled faintly, knowing that to be true. "He's a good lad," she said. "He is a hard worker."

"He's a bit young for such hard work. His hands tell the tale."

Lucia turned to reply to him, but the words caught in her throat. Bane was dressed in the smithy's tunic and breeches, in clean clothes for the first time since they met. The breeches were a little snug, and the tunic a little roomy, but he looked clean and handsome.

Quite handsome.

She nodded her head in approval.

"It would seem that a bath and clean clothes have done wonders for ye," she said.

Bane folded his big arms across his chest and leaned against the doorjamb. "More than ye know," he said, rubbing the hair on his face. "I havena shaved in a very long time. It's quite possible that my beard has become a nest for rodents."

Lucia laughed softly, flashing straight and white teeth. "How cruel ye are tae destroy their home."

"It was *yer* idea that I should bathe."

"Are ye complaining?"

His eyes lingered on her, glittering. "Nay."

As he looked at her, Lucia felt something she'd never felt before—a charge, like a bolt of lightning coursing through her body. The longer she looked at the man, the stronger the feeling became.

"Now ye might be able tae secure a position somewhere," she said, trying to ignore that trembling feeling. "Ye said ye could shoe horses or build something. Now that ye dunna smell like piss, someone might give ye a job."

He looked out into the yard. "What about here?"

"What do ye mean?"

"I'm good for many things," he said. "Surely there's something I can do around here?"

She looked at him in surprise because that idea had never crossed her mind. "Ye want tae stay *here*?"

"Why not? Ye're here."

There was something in his tone as he said it. Coupled with that glimmer in his dark eyes, Lucia was feeling quite…giddy. Men didn't flirt with her; she was strong and independent, and perhaps never gave them the chance.

Therefore, this was quite new to her.

Truth be told, she didn't know how to flirt. She was terrible when it came to the games that men and women played. She so wanted to respond in a way that would suggest she found him a wee bit attractive, too.

But she had no idea where to begin.

"I…I'm not here by choice," she finally said. "I'm here because I must be here."

"Is it such a terrible place, then?"

She shook her head. "Nay," she said honestly. "Laird Currie is a good man. He's very old and hard of hearing, and mayhap a bit mad because he keeps a family of pet rats, but he's very kind. And Lady Currie…"

"That is the lady ye serve, is it?"

"Aye," she said. "Lady Currie is young and pretty and full of life."

He cocked his head curiously. "Laird Currie is very old and his wife is very young?"

Lucia nodded, thinking of the sad marriage of Laird and Lady Currie. "She is his second wife," she said. "He wants a son very badly, enough that he married a young English woman after his wife died. But if she bears a son, it will not be his."

"Why would you say that?"

Lucia leaned back against the wall. Perhaps she was about to say things that she shouldn't, but Bane seemed easy to talk to. God knew she didn't have many people to talk to in this prison of a place. Standing in close proximity to a man who made her feel strange and wonderful things had her tongue loosening.

"Because Lady Currie wants nothing tae do with her husband," she said quietly. "Can ye imagine marrying someone and not even being friendly with him?"

Bane shook his head. "Nay," he said honestly. "My parents were affectionate tae one another. That was the example set for me. I always hoped I would know the same, someday."

"Ye've never been married?"

He shook his head. "Nay," he said. "Ye?"

She grinned. "Do ye think I'd bring a stranger back tae my home if I was?"

He smiled because she was. "Nay," he said. Then he sighed heavily, looking out over the rainy yard. "But I'm glad ye did. God knows, ye took a man ye dinna know and helped him. Mayhap it was just a bath, and just a basket with some bread and cheese, but ye dinna have tae do it. It is a kindness I can never repay ye."

She looked at him seriously. "Ye said ye've been in Edinburgh for months," she said. "Did ye ever have a position or a way tae make money? Or have ye been living in the alleys all this time?"

He looked at her, the glimmer in his eye dull. "I never had a position," he said quietly. "I never even tried. I came tae Edinburgh... That's not right. I dinna come. I *ran*. I ran tae Edinburgh."

"Why did ye run?"

"Tae escape."

"What were ye escaping?"

He exhaled softly. "Myself."

It didn't make much sense to Lucia. Perhaps it wasn't meant to. A man had a right to his secrets, after all, and it wasn't her place to pry. But it seemed to explain why she sensed sorrow and defeat from the man. She had since the moment they'd met, and she felt a good deal of pity for him. Even if she didn't know the root of his problems, she felt as if she wanted to help him.

This man who made lightning course through her veins every time he looked at her.

"Mayhap ye'll stop running sometime," she said quietly. "Until then, I'll see what I can do about securing ye a position here. 'Tis better than living in the alleys of Edinburgh."

He nodded, looking at the clean clothing he was dressed in, before turning his attention to her. "I'd be grateful," he said. "Ye've been an angel, Lucia. I suppose we all need guardian angels, and right now ye're mine."

She smiled bashfully. "I've been called many things, but never an angel."

"That's what ye are tae me. *My* angel."

She was both flattered and embarrassed. They were still standing in the doorway together, but it seemed to Lucia that he was moving closer to her somehow. He unfolded his arms, and his fingers casually brushed against hers.

Heart pounding, she was attempting to figure out how she should respond when a shout broke the spell. They both looked up to see Tynan running in their direction.

"I've got it!" he shouted, waving something in his hand. "I've got a razor for ye!"

Bane stepped back as the boy ran between them. "Stop waving that razor around, lad," he said, grabbing the child by the wrist and plucking the sharp razor out of his hand. "Ye're going tae slash people tae ribbons running about like that."

"Can I watch ye shave?" Tynan asked. "I can help ye!"

Bane lifted an eyebrow, glancing at a flushed Lucia, as he turned back into the cottage. "I'm sure ye can," he said. "But I think I can manage by myself."

Tynan wriggled about as if incapable of sitting still as Bane lathered up the *savon d'Alep* and thoroughly saturated his beard. Using the reflection in the cold bathwater as a mirror, he began to carefully shave away at the bush on his face, with Tynan giving him expert advice from a young man with no beard at all.

But it was an endearing moment. Bane had compassion and patience, something that Lucia could see in just those few brief moments. In fact, as she watched, she decided to speak to the stable master or the smithy to see if they could use Bane's help. She'd offered to help him find a position and find one she would.

She decided at that moment that Bane Morgan was not leaving Meadowbank.

He was here to stay.

CHAPTER FIVE

ONE WEEK.

Bane had been at Meadowbank exactly one week, and in that week, it seemed to him that he'd never known another life. Something about hard work and a pretty lass who came to visit him daily had him believing that his fortunes might have finally turned around.

The old stable master's name was Angus Peele, and Bane had quickly made himself indispensable to the old man. He only had two grooms working under him, men who were so lowborn that they could barely speak intelligently, but they were hard workers and did all the cleaning and feeding of the horses.

There were fourteen horses, in fact, mostly belonging to the small group of soldiers that Laird Currie kept for protection. Bane didn't interact much with the men, but he saw them as they made their periodic rounds. Rumor had it they spent most of their time at the gatehouse, drinking. But they were well-armed, and the horses fat and expensive, to protect all that Meadowbank had to offer.

Bane had been taking care of grooming the horses himself and repairing their tack, which Angus tried to keep in good repair, but his fingers were twisted with a painful affliction that involved his joints and made it difficult. Bane had therefore taken over the chore and spent his days repairing the worn harnesses and saddles, listening to Angus chatter nonstop while he chewed pieces of fat, green grass. He'd chew up one and start on another, which had turned his teeth a nice shade of green over the years.

They'd sit in the open door of the stable, watching the rain fall and speaking on any subject that struck their fancies. Angus would tell Bane such stories as having invented the horseshoe or being personally responsible for the creation of whisky, and Bane would listen as if he believed every foolish story out of the stable keeper's green mouth.

He was coming to like the quirky old man.

But his focus wasn't only on his duty. It was on Lucia, hoping for a glimpse of her as she went about her duties for Lady Currie. No one from the house seemed to make it back into the stable block except for Lucia, and it was always with requests from Lady Currie. The woman liked to ride her snow-white palfrey through the woods, and every night she also demanded her carriage, which was prepared and then driven up to the house to collect her.

Bane had never met Laird or Lady Currie in the week he'd spent in his new position, the first week in months that he hadn't been sleeping off too much drink in an alley and wallowing with the dregs of society. These days, he was clean, he was fed, he had a place to sleep.

And he owed it all to Lucia.

Truthfully, he was coming to feel the least bit guilty for tricking her into taking him to Meadowbank in the first place. He'd seen an opportunity to play on her pity and he took it. He had a better life now than he'd had before, but his intention to take advantage of Lucia had quickly turned into something else the very first day he knew her. He was still trying to figure it all out, but he knew one thing—she was a lady he was growing increasingly fond of.

Even now at the dawn of a surprisingly bright morning, he was looking forward to seeing her. She always seemed to make it back to the stable yard at some point every morning, and he was planning on that. He'd even shaved with the razor Tynan had brought him and washed his hands and hair with the remains of the *savon d'Alep*. It was ironic that he hadn't felt like cleaning up since he'd arrived in Edinburgh, since leaving his shame behind.

Since leaving that life he was no longer a part of.

Bane's breath hung in the air in foggy puffs as he left his cottage and made his way over to the stable. A leggy black gelding needed his attention, a magnificent horse that belonged to Laird Currie but was never ridden. The horse was quite excitable and frisky, and Bane was planning on taking the animal out himself to give him some exercise. He was an excellent horseman, or at least he had been in his past. He was nearly to the stable when he caught sight of someone moving into the stable yard.

It was Lucia.

She was far earlier than expected but he didn't care. He couldn't keep the grin from his face as he changed course and headed in her direction.

"Good morn tae ye, m'lady," he said. "How may I assist ye today?"

Lucia smiled, biting her lip in a gesture that was both sweet and bashful. "Lady Currie wants tae go intae Edinburgh today," she said. "Today is market day."

Bane looked up at the sky, noting the position of the sun. "Isna it a little late tae go tae market?"

Lucia shrugged. "Not for her," she said. "She stays up most of the night and doesna rise until noon."

"I know," Bane said. "I am here when the carriage comes in. It has come in nearly at dawn every morning since I've been here. Where do they go, anyway?"

"They?"

"Laird and Lady Currie."

Lucia shook her head. "Laird Currie doesna go with her."

Bane's eyebrows lifted. "He lets his wife go out alone at night?"

"It's not as if he has any say over it. She simply…goes."

"Where?"

"Angus hasna told ye?"

"Told me what?"

Lucia looked around to see who might be near to overhear her.

Deeming it safe, she answered. "Lady Currie seeks entertainment at the Ludus Caledonia," she said quietly. "Have ye heard of it?"

Bane's brow furrowed in thought. "Is that the place where men fight?"

Lucia nodded. "Aye," she said. "It's a secretive place in the hills south of Edinburgh. Lady Currie has been going there since I came tae Meadowbank, and I've been tae the Cal more times than I can recall."

"*Ye've* gone?"

"Lady Currie doesna like tae go alone," Lucia said. "She takes me along with her and one or two of her other ladies."

"And she watches the fights?"

Lucia sighed faintly. "Remember I told ye that if she bore a son, it wouldna be the laird's?"

"Aye."

"That is because she finds company with anyone else but him, and particularly at the Ludus Caledonia." She watched surprise spread across Bane's face. "Lady Currie is a rich woman who can pay for the company of any man she likes. She pays a good deal of money for the company of the winners of the fights at the Cal."

Bane frowned. "It sounds like a brothel."

"Nay," Lucia assured him quickly. "It's not that, but the Cal is a place of many functions. Visitors gamble on the fights and sometimes the winners are offered positions with armies. I've seen men in the lists bid for their services. They also teach men tae fight, and I've heard the winners can make a lot of money. But there are women who go there, too, and they're not allowed tae gamble. But they are allowed tae watch and pay for the company of the winners. Lady Currie isna the only one."

He eyed her. "And she makes ye go with her?"

"Aye."

He didn't say anything for a moment. He simply looked at her as thoughts rolled around his head. That was clear from the way his eyes were glimmering; there was a good deal going on behind them.

"Does she make ye…" He paused before continuing. "Do ye find company with them, too?"

Lucia's mouth opened in outrage. Suddenly, she was pushing past him into the stable, and Bane charged after her. She had barely made it into the dim, musty structure when he grabbed her by the arm, stopping her. Furious, Lucia yanked her arm from his grasp.

"Dunna grab me," she snapped. "And how dare ye ask such a question!"

Bane put up both hands in a soothing gesture. "I'm sorry," he said. "I just… I dunna know why I did."

Lucia wasn't eased in the least. She jabbed a finger at him. "Ye know I'm not married, yet ye ask me if I keep…keep *company* with men like Lady Currie does? What kind of woman do ye think I am? I should slap the snot right out of ye!"

"Go ahead and slap me if it'll make ye feel better."

Whack!

Lucia did just that. It wasn't a hard slap, but it surprised Bane. He looked at her in astonishment even though he'd told her to do it.

He was fairly certain he deserved it.

"I dunna know why I should answer ye, but I will," Lucia said. "Of course I dunna keep company with them. Lady Currie only wants me tae keep her company for the journey tae and from the Cal, and if she thought I was interested in the men there, she wouldna take me. She's a jealous one, she is."

"She should be," Bane said quietly, afraid she might slap him again if she didn't like what he said. "Yer beauty surely outshines hers."

"How do ye know if ye havena even see her?"

"I dunna have tae see her tae know ye're the most beautiful woman I've ever had the privilege tae look upon."

That gentle flattery cooled Lucia's anger rapidly, like blowing out a candle. Her eyes, so recently filled with fury, now looked upon him in astonishment. Astonishment turned to pleasure, but it was tempered with doubt.

"Ye say that because I gave ye a place tae stay," she said quietly. "Ye dunna have tae flatter me, Bane. I helped ye because ye needed it, not because I wanted ye tae praise me."

They were standing near a stall, a half wall that she was backed up against. Bane took a step in her direction, moving closer to her.

"Is that what ye think?" he asked softly. "That I'm flattering ye because ye helped me?"

The fact that he was moving closer didn't escape her. "I dunna mind," she said, taking a discreet step back for every bold step he took forward. "I dunna hear much flattery. It was nice."

"Nice?" he repeated. By this time, she'd backed up into the wall of the stall and he was so close he could feel the heat from her body. "It wasna simply meant tae be nice, my angel. It was the truth."

Oh, but there was a storm churning inside of Lucia, and the lightning she'd come to associate with Bane was flying in all directions. His close proximity had started a firestorm, and she was struggling to stay on an even keel.

Gazing up at him, she could feel his hot breath in her face as his right arm went up, casually bracing himself against the support beam of the stall over her head as he looked down upon her. The closer he loomed, the more the lightning sparked.

"I...I dunna hear it often."

"From the men around here?"

"Never from them."

"Then they're fools."

"Or mayhap they know their place."

A grin spread across his lips. "I've never been accused of knowing my place," he said huskily. "Even if I did, in yer case, I'd ignore it."

God, he was so close. Lucia was having difficulty breathing and she turned her head, looking away from him because she was thrilled and intimidated at the same time. Looking at him made her feel as if she were losing control of herself. She could see him in her periphery as he leaned in, taking a long, deep smell of her hair.

It was enough to turn her bones to jelly.

"Bane..." she said breathlessly.

"Shush," he murmured. "Let me smell ye. I want tae know what an angel smells like."

It wasn't just her hair he was smelling, but her skin. He sniffed her neck, moving to her shoulder and smelling that as well. All the while, he didn't touch her. He didn't make a move to make contact. But his face, his nose, was close enough that Lucia could feel him brushing against her. His heated breath spilled over her skin, blowing against her like the bellows of a smithy's forge.

It was intoxicating.

"What *does* an angel smell like?" she managed to ask.

He moved so his face was next to hers. He was looking at her profile at close range as she looked away.

"Beauty," he muttered. "Strength. Honor. It smells like everything a man needs in life."

She sighed in utter delight as his words filled her ears. When his lips gently kissed her cheek, her jelly bones gave way and she slumped back against the wall. Bane swiftly moved forward, slipping his arms beneath hers and bracing her against the stall so she wouldn't fall. As she turned to him, opening her mouth to speak, his mouth slanted over hers in a deliciously tender kiss.

The lightning exploded.

Lucia could hear little gasps as he kissed her, hardly aware they were her own. For all of Bane's size and strength, his kisses were so very gentle, like the touch of a bird's wings, something so delightful yet something that filled her with awe and wonder. She'd never been kissed before.

Not even close.

It was as if the sun suddenly burst out from behind the clouds.

Her arms went around his neck, holding him firmly against her as she responded to his heated kiss. Enfolded in his embrace, she was vastly aware of his body pressed against hers, the heat from his big frame filling her with a comfort she'd never known before. She could hardly breathe, but she didn't care. She welcomed the giddiness. He was overwhelming her with the virile masculinity that had been buried beneath that street filth.

His scent filled her nostrils, too.

Glorious.

And then it was abruptly over.

Someone opened the barn door and Bane released her so quickly that she stumbled back against the wall of the stall. He moved with the speed of a cat, now standing on the other side of the stall with a horse brush in his hand as Angus shuffled into the barn, mumbling to himself.

Realizing the old man hadn't seen them in their clandestine embrace, Lucia simply went about her business, pretending to check on Lady Currie's white palfrey before speaking to Bane, who was bent over a horse that he'd already tended earlier in the morning and trying to make it look as if he were actually working.

"M'lady will want her carriage again tonight," Lucia said to him before turning to Angus, who was over near the tack, still muttering to himself. "Did ye hear me, Angus? We'll need the carriage again tonight."

Angus simply waved at her, unimpressed with the usual request. Passing a lingering glance at Bane, Lucia slipped from the stable, heading out into the stable yard. But thoughts of Bane were heavy on her mind as she passed through a shelter where some of the hay was kept. It was no more than a roof held up by four posts and as she passed through it on her way toward the manse, someone grabbed her from behind and pulled her behind a pile of hay.

It was Bane.

His mouth was on hers again, his big arms around her. Lucia was much more adept in responding the second time around as a thrill swept through her. Her arms wound their way around his neck as they fell back into the hay, lips fused. The hay made a convenient hiding place, a nice little cave to shield them from the world in these precious moments of discovery.

But that didn't mean they would not be seen.

"Bane," she said even as he kissed her. "We must be…careful. Someone might see us and it'll get back tae m'lady."

She was starting to sit up, fearful they might be spotted, but he pulled her back down onto the hay, his hand on her face, thumb caressing her cheek.

"Not tae worry," he said. "Angus is still inside the stable and no one can see us here. Unless ye dunna want me tae kiss ye anymore. I'm presuming a great deal that ye're enjoying it as much as I am."

His hand against her face was tender, like nothing she'd ever experienced. "No one has ever wanted tae kiss me before," she whispered.

"Lucky me."

She laughed softly, but quickly sobered. "Lady Currie doesna like her maids tae be associated with men. That's what I meant when I said we must be careful."

He lifted an eyebrow. "Tynan's mam is a maid."

"Aye, but her husband is dead."

Bane nodded in understanding. "Will she punish ye, then?"

Lucia shrugged vaguely. "I dunna know," she said. "I've never had an association with a man before, but I told ye that Lady Currie is the jealous kind. I dunna want tae end up in the kitchen scrubbing floors because I've upset her."

Bane thought on his response. Though he knew why Lucia lived at Meadowbank, thanks to Tynan, she had yet to tell him. He felt the overwhelming need to know everything about her because he'd never felt this way about anyone in his life. It was true that Lucia had saved him from the streets, so it was natural that he felt an obligation toward her. But what he felt at the moment went beyond obligation.

She was quickly getting under his skin.

"Why do ye serve her?" he asked. "Is it a family tradition?"

He thought he was rather clever the way he had asked her and Lucia was none the wiser. "In a way," she said hesitantly. "My da used tae serve Laird Currie before he married Lady Currie. He served him and his father for many years. When my da became ill, Laird Currie paid for the physic. My da died and couldna repay him, so I came tae work off the debt."

It was a simple, straightforward answer. "How long have ye been here?"

"Nearly two years."

"Then the debt should almost be paid, I would think."

Lucia didn't look too pleased. "Laird Currie told me two years," she said. "But Lady Currie wants me tae remain with her beyond that, so Laird Currie told me once that being a servant is the best life I can hope for. He made it seem as if this is the best I'll ever have in life, but I know it's not true."

"What else will ye do if ye dunna serve here?"

Her eyes took on a warm glow. "Bane, do ye not wish for something more in life? A home of yer own, a wife, mayhap children. I wish for those things, but I want more—I can make the most beautiful clothing ye've ever seen, given the proper fabric. I want tae make clothing for fine ladies and sell them for a good price."

He smiled faintly. "'Tis a noble goal," he said. "Does Lady Currie know?"

Lucia nodded unhappily. "She has me make her a new garment every week," she said. "She doesna pay me for it—I work hard for nothing. I had hoped that would help pay off my father's debt faster, but it makes Lady Currie want tae keep me with her forever."

"I can imagine so," he said. "When I asked ye what ye did for her, ye told me almost anything. Ye never mentioned ye were her seamstress."

Lucia sighed heavily. "What does it matter?" she said. "She'll not let me leave. I've made myself too valuable tae her."

He was looming over her, propped up on an elbow. She looked so unhappy that he reached out, gently stroking her cheek.

"Ye're very valuable," he said softly. "So valuable that ye dunna belong here. Ye deserve tae be a seamstress for fine ladies and get paid for it, and have yer freedom, too. An angel with clipped wings canna fly."

She smiled at his insightful words. "I hope tae," she said. "Someday."

"Would ye come with me if ye could?"

Her smile faded. "Come with ye where?"

He shifted so he was lying on the straw beside her, looking up at the roof of the shelter. "I'll find a proper position," he said. "I'll earn money for the both of us, and ye can sew tae yer heart's content."

She turned her head, looking at him curiously. "What are ye talking about, Bane?"

He didn't answer for a moment, pondering what he'd suggested. It had purely been on a whim, but even as he thought on it, nothing had ever seemed so right. He hadn't known her very long, but that didn't matter.

His heart knew hers.

He knew he didn't want to be without her.

"I want ye tae marry me," he said quietly. "I know we havena known each other very long, but we've got the rest of our lives tae know one another. I dunna want tae stay at Meadowbank the rest of my life and neither do ye. Why not live our lives together?"

Lucia watched him as he spoke, shocked by the proposal but also wildly flattered by it. "I've never had a man ask tae marry me," she said, awe in her voice. "But…when I found ye, ye were living in the street. How can ye think tae support a wife?"

"I told ye that I can do almost anything. I'll find a job."

"Then why have ye not found a job before this?"

"Because I had nothing tae live for until I met ye."

She sat up, looking at him with a great deal of confusion. "'Tis a heavy burden tae put on me, Bane Morgan," she said. "When I met ye, ye had the smell of ale on ye. Why were ye living in the street with nothing else tae live for?"

"Do ye want the truth?"

"If ye're proposing marriage, I think I deserve it."

"Are ye actually considering my proposal?"

"That depends on what ye tell me."

She grinned. He grinned. But quickly, his smile faded. "I've not spoken of it since it happened," he said. "'Tis…difficult."

Lucia could see that he was struggling. He was reverting back to that man she'd first met, the one with utter defeat in his eyes. She didn't like that look on him, not when he'd come so far in so short a time.

"Then not now," she said. "When ye're ready, ye'll tell me."

That seemed to bring him some relief, but he was still struggling with the question. It was true that he hadn't spoken of it since it happened, the event that shaped his life and cast him out of his clan.

The event that saw him living on the streets.

Perhaps the time to talk about it *was* now before he lost his nerve.

"My da is the chief of a small Morgan clan," he said. "We come from a small village called Ledmore in the Highlands. 'Tis so far tae the north that there are villages around us that still have the way of the Northmen, from the times when their princes ruled our lands."

"It must have taken ye a long time tae come tae Edinburgh," she said.

He nodded. "It took me almost a month. Traveling from the Highlands isna a simple thing."

"Go on."

He sighed faintly, reaching out to take her hand and hold it against his broad chest as he lay there and stared up at the roof of the hay shelter. Thrilled, Lucia let him.

"The English were swarming Berwick and border villages," he said. "The call went out for men from the Highlands tae help defend Scotland from the Sassenach raiders. Even though my clan is small, we had many excellent warriors, including my da."

"And ye?"

"And me," he said softly. "Once, they called me the Highland Defender. So much of my life was spent defending the Scots against the English. I know about warfare and I know how tae fight them. Therefore, when the call went out for Berwick, my da answered. He took me, my cousins, and fifty of our best lads, south tae the borders. By the time we got there, the English had burned several border villages, like Jedburgh and Hawick. My da and I were—"

"There ye are!"

Suddenly, there was a big, round woman standing at their feet, pointing accusingly to Lucia, who immediately leapt to her feet.

"Colly!" she hissed. "What are ye doing here?"

The old nurse had blood in her eye as she looked at Lucia. "Ye shameful hussy," she said, jabbing a finger at Bane. "I came tae tell ye that Lady Currie no longer wants her horse, but I find ye cavorting with…with a *man*. Lady Currie shall hear of this!"

Lucia moved toward the woman, trying to keep her attention off Bane, who was now on his feet and watching the situation with a good deal of concern.

"Hear of what?" Lucia said, trying very hard to keep her temper in check. "We've done nothing. We were talking."

But Colly would have none of it. "Ye're a sinner, 'tis what ye are," she said. "Ye disgraceful little wench. Come with me right now and confess yer actions tae Lady Currie!"

Lucia stood her ground. "But I've done nothing," she said firmly. "I came tae the stable tae tell Angus tae have Lady Currie's horse prepared."

Colly's attention turned to Bane and she looked him up and down as one did when sizing up a prize stallion. "Ye came here tae sin," she hissed. "Ye're a filthy cat, come tae mate with more filth. Ye come tae the stable too much as it is, and now I know why. Come with me now!"

"I willna," Lucia said. "Tell Lady Currie what ye must, but it would only be yer own lies. All ye do is lie and beat m'lady's servants and then ye lie tae Lady Currie's face about it. We all know it."

Colly lunged at her, grabbing her by the shoulder and tearing her garment at the seam. Lucia, defending herself, shoved at the old woman, who stumbled back but charged again.

This time, however, Bane was there.

He stood between Lucia and the large old woman, who plowed into him. He didn't do anything more than put up a hand to prevent her from grabbing at him, but with her momentum and unsteady balance, she ended up falling back onto her buttocks.

She howled.

"A brute!" she screamed. "He is going tae kill me! Help me!"

She began screaming and Lucia looked at Bane in a panic. "Go," she hissed, pushing him away. "Ye must go!"

Bane was moving, looking at her in confusion. "Why? I've done nothing."

Lucia was pushing him away from Colly, who continued to scream. "Ye dunna understand," she said anxiously. "The woman is determined tae hurt everyone. She willna rest until she has ye punished. Bane…ye must leave Meadowbank. Get out of here, or she'll make ye wish ye had. She's evil, that one. Please—go!"

Bane realized she meant he had to leave Meadowbank

altogether. "But I canna leave ye," he said. "If she's out tae punish me, she's out tae punish ye. I *willna* leave ye."

Lucia looked at Colly, who was now rolling onto her knees, crying loudly, as people began to take note. Angus had come out of the stable and servants in the kitchen yard were beginning to come through the gate that separated the kitchens from the stables. Lucia grabbed Bane by the arms and turned him toward the postern gate.

"Ye must go," she said. "Please, before Laird Currie's guards come. Run back tae where ye came from. I'll find ye there when the situation calms down. But for now, ye must go!"

"Come with me," he begged, even as they both moved toward the gate. "Please, Lucia...*come*."

Her eyes were filling with tears as she rapidly blinked them away. "I canna," she said hoarsely. "My debt for my father isna paid yet. I canna dishonor him by leaving before it's settled. As much as I want tae go with ye, I canna do it."

"But—"

"Please, Bane, *go*! I will find ye when this dies down, I swear it."

He could see the anguish in her eyes and it tore at him, but more people were now coming to Colly's aid as she wept and pointed at Bane. He knew it was time to leave but the sorrow he felt, and the disappointment, was immeasurable. Just when his life seemed to be going well, just when he'd found a woman he couldn't stop thinking about...now this.

He was coming to think that nothing in his life was ever meant to go his way.

"Very well," he said. "I'll go. But find me in the alley tomorrow, the alley where we met. Swear tae me ye'll come."

"I'll try. But if not tomorrow, as soon as I can."

That wasn't good enough for him. "Soon," he insisted. "If ye dunna come tae me soon, I will come for ye. Do ye hear me? I will return for ye, Lucia."

She simply nodded, the tears spilling over that she quickly wiped away. Bane's last look at her as he bolted through the postern gate was of her miserable, sad expression. Even as he raced back to Edinburgh as fast as his feet would take him, all he could see were the tears in her eyes.

All he could feel was the hole in his heart.

I will return for ye.

He meant every word.

CHAPTER SIX

"COLLY SAYS THE MAN BRUTALIZED HER," LADY CURRIE SAID. "She has a bruise on her buttocks to prove it."

Lucia had known this moment would come.

In Lady Currie's fine bedchamber, she was facing off against Lady Currie and Colly, who was feigning great injury. Ever since Bane had fled earlier in the day, the woman had been pretending he'd beat her, infuriating Lucia greatly. But it was her word against Colly's, and as she knew, Colly would always be believed. It was nearing the twilight hour and Lady Currie was already heavily into her wine, as evidenced by her semislurred words.

It wasn't an ideal situation.

"May I tell ye what really happened, m'lady?" she said steadily. "I fear ye've gotten yer information from a woman who lies tae ye constantly. She lies about everyone and everything, and every servant here can tell ye that."

"Ye little toad!" Colly exploded, bolting up from the chair she had been sitting on and exhibiting signs of a woman who wasn't as ill as she wanted everyone to believe. Quickly realizing that, she suddenly put a hand to her head in a feeble gesture. "She is guilty, m'lady, *guilty*. She is trying tae cast the blame on me!"

Lady Currie put her hand up to ease Colly, who shuffled back to her chair, nearly doubled over. It was a good act, one she'd used on her mistress many times when things didn't go her way.

It usually worked.

But Lucia wasn't going to let the woman bully her or lie about her. "Yer nurse has been trying tae sully me in yer eyes since I arrived at Meadowbank, m'lady," she said. "She doesna like it when anyone gets too close tae ye. I know she raised ye, but surely ye can see that she tries tae control ye. She shames ye and lies tae ye. I know ye're a bright woman. I know ye can see what she does."

"Enough," Lady Currie snapped softly. "I will not hear you speak ill of Colly, Lucia. The unfortunate relationship you two share is becoming a burden upon me. I cannot do without her and I do not want to do without you, so what am I to do? And who is this man she speaks of?"

Lucia eyed the old woman who was sitting in the chair, doubled over with contrived agony. "He is the man who saved me from harm when the sausages were stolen last week," she said. "He was kind tae me and helped me, so I brought him back tae Meadowbank and put him tae work with Angus. We were speaking and nothing more when Colly came across us in the stable yard. She tried tae attack me like she always does, and he stepped in between us. She hit him and then fell back on her own fat arse, and that is the truth. I will swear upon the Bible that he never touched her."

Colly started to wail, as was usual with the woman when things weren't going her way. Lady Currie passed a concerned glance at her nurse before collecting her cup of wine and going to Lucia, taking her by the arm and leading her away so the nurse couldn't overhear their conversation. Whether to keep the details from her or whether not to cause the woman any further stress was anyone's guess.

"Lucia, you know I want to believe you, but Colly said she saw you fornicating with this man," she said quietly. "What were you doing?"

Lucia sighed heavily. "I'm not so foolish that I'd be fornicating with a man for all to see, m'lady," she said. "We were in the hay shelter next tae the stables when Colly came upon us and started screaming at me. She called me names and tried tae hit me. Ye have seen her do this before, many times, so ye know I'm telling ye the truth."

Lady Currie listened closely. It was clear from her expression that there was some doubt, but the way she kept glancing at Colly told Lucia that the doubt was in Colly's story and not her own. She took another swig of her wine, too weak to make a decision.

"Colly raised me," she said after a moment. "When my mother would not, it was Colly who raised me."

"I know, m'lady."

"I cannot and will not send her away."

"I know, m'lady. But she is not a good woman."

Lady Currie looked at her with pain in her expression. *She knows*, Lucia thought. It made her feel sorry for Lady Currie, who was in a strange land with a man who was old and crusty and diseased. She was young and beautiful and smart. Keeping Colly with her was the only thing she had to remind her of where she'd come from, her only measure of comfort. The lovers, the lavish spending…that was simply to forget the situation she found herself in.

Even Lucia could see that.

"Lucia, if you could just try to get on with her, I would be grateful," she finally whispered. "But I must punish you for this."

Lucia tried not to show her surprise and fear. "If you feel you must, m'lady," she said, lowering her gaze. "But I swear tae ye, I've done nothing wrong."

Lady Currie took another drink of wine. So much of her existence involved the bottom of a wine jug, especially in moments like this.

"I will think of a punishment," she said. "Meanwhile, make sure the carriage is prepared. We are going to the Cal tonight."

That wasn't what Lucia wanted to hear, but it was better than immediate punishment. Or, in her mind, that *was* the punishment, given how she felt about the place. Still, she couldn't quite let the subject go because Bane had been wrongly accused by Colly, and Lucia was genuinely worried about him. He'd come such a long way in the week he'd been at Meadowbank, and she didn't want to see him revert to that ale-smelling pile of filth she'd first met.

"M'lady, may I first speak of the man I was with?" she said. "As I told ye, he saved me from being assaulted by those who stole the sausages, and he was doing good work with Angus. I sent him away when Colly fell because I was afraid for him, but he dinna do anything wrong. Could I please bring him back?"

Lady Currie eyed her. "A reward for him, is it?"

"Aye, m'lady. He was very brave."

"And you like this man, do you? No need to deny it because I can see it in your face. You are more concerned for him than you are for yourself."

Lucia lowered her gaze, trying desperately not to flush. "I...I feel a responsibility toward him because he protected me, m'lady."

"Is he handsome?"

There was something in the woman's questions that seemed rather pointed, beyond the usual inquiry, that gave Lucia pause. Lady Currie was known to be a purveyor of male flesh the way some people were experts on prize horses or sheep. If she told Lady Currie that Bane was handsome, undoubtedly she would allow him to come back...

But more than likely for her own purposes.

The thought turned Lucia's stomach.

"Nay," she finally said. "I would not call him that, m'lady. He is a man who saved me and nothing more."

Lady Currie's gaze lingered on her, possibly to determine if she was lying or not, but she didn't press. Finally, she shook her head.

"He will not come back," she said. "That is your punishment, Lucia. Your friend is not permitted at Meadowbank, and you are not permitted to see him again. This will be the end of it. Now go, and make sure the carriage is prepared. I want to leave soon."

Lucia didn't argue with her. If it was a punishment, it wasn't much of one, nor was it one she planned to obey. As she moved to quit the chamber, she happened to see Colly as the woman sat up in her chair, surprisingly healthy-looking now that she thought

Lucia was being punished. Even if she didn't know what form that punishment was to take because she hadn't heard the conversation, she still knew that her nemesis would see some retribution from Lady Currie.

When their eyes met, a sinister smile spread across Colly's lips. In response, Lucia drew a finger across her throat, indicating what she'd do to the old woman if given the chance. As Colly began to wail again, Lucia fled the chamber. She wasn't going to let that old woman get the better of her.

But it wasn't the last volley in the battle of wills.

That came later in the evening.

As Lucia headed up a dark stairwell to tell Lady Currie that her carriage awaited her, Colly was waiting for her in the shadows. Just as Lucia reached the top of the stairs, a blow to the face sent her tumbling all the way back down to the bottom. As she shook off the stars in her vision, she happened to see Colly's dark form at the top of the stairs, moving away before any words were spoken.

That told Lucia that the battle between them had just turned into a war.

CHAPTER SEVEN

SHE DIDN'T HAVE MUCH TIME.

In order to make up for losing the sausages last week, Lucia had begged to go to the butcher's again. When Lady Currie denied her and sent one of the stable grooms instead, Lucia offered to gather wildflowers for Lady Currie's bedchamber. The woman was particularly fond of blooms called "treasure flowers," which had pale-purple petals, and others called "everlasting flowers" because they never seemed to die. The colors were very bright and Lady Currie loved them.

Therefore, Lucia was given permission to gather flowers for her lady's chamber, and she headed out on a bright, cool morning, her destination the hills to the north. At least, that was what she told Lady Currie, and in truth, she did manage to make it there.

Briefly.

There was a heavily forested area surrounding a small loch, and she picked her way through the bramble, cutting flowers with her knife and quickly tossing them into the basket. Anything with color, she cut.

But she had another destination in mind and flowers weren't the focus.

Bane was.

It had been three days since she'd seen the man, and she could hardly sleep for the thought of him. With her basket full of colorful autumn flowers, she hurriedly made her way into Edinburgh. She returned to the alley where it all started and felt some apprehension. It was a dangerous place, but she doubted men would ambush her for flowers.

At least, she hoped not.

The alleys were dark and angled because Edinburgh was built on crags, so everything was sloped. That familiar smell of urine and human despair filled her nostrils as she entered the alley where she first saw Bane.

Lucia didn't want to spend too much time alone, walking up and down the alleys, because that was asking for trouble, but she wanted to give Bane enough time to find her if he was anywhere near. She was about to head down another alley that had a livery when someone grabbed her from behind.

Terrified, Lucia swung the basket with all her might at the person behind her, hitting him in the head as the flowers went flying.

"*Och!*"

Bane had his hand up on his head where she'd hit him, and Lucia's eyes widened.

"Bane!" she gasped. "I dinna know it was ye!"

He was grinning. "That's the second time ye've hit me in the head," he said. "I should have known better than tae surprise ye, but I've been watching the streets for three days. God's bones, it's good tae see ye. I've missed my angel."

She grinned, a sweet and dreamy grin because his words brought back that familiar giddy feeling he was so capable of bringing about. But she put her hand on his head, rubbing the spot she'd struck.

"And I've missed ye, too," she said softly. "I'm so sorry I hit ye. Will ye live?"

"Barely."

"Good. Then ye can help me pick up these flowers. They're for Lady Currie."

Bane did as he was told, picking up the flowers, which had fortunately missed the sewage-filled gutter. Everything ended up back in Lucia's basket, and he took her by the hand.

"Let's leave this place," he said quietly. "Come with me."

She did.

⚭ ⚭ ⚭

Bane's destination was a loch south of Edinburgh, a surprising oasis in the midst of the filth of the town. It was just a small body of water, with waterfowl swimming beneath the branches of big willow trees, but it was quiet and seemingly a million miles away from the hustle and bustle of the city. The moment they reached the banks, Bane pulled Lucia into a crushing embrace and kissed her deeply.

The basket fell to the ground again.

His kisses were fierce and passionate, a testament to his longing for her over the past few days. He pulled her down onto the ground with him, his hands in her hair as he moved from her lips to her cheek, her ear. He kissed her gently, inhaling deeply of her scent once again, until he suddenly came to a halt.

He was fingering a greenish mark on her forehead.

"What is this?" he asked huskily.

Lucia, dazed and breathless from his attention, had no idea what he was talking about until she put her hand to the spot and realized that was where she'd hit her head when Colly had pushed her down the stairs.

"I fell and hit my head," she said. "It will heal."

"How did ye fall?"

She wasn't going to lie to him. Not only had she always been a forthright person, but she felt something for Bane and she wasn't in the habit of lying to people she cared about. Faintly, she sighed.

"Do ye remember the woman who found us in the stable yard?" she asked.

He nodded, tucking a stray piece of hair behind her ear. "I do. The entire reason I was forced tae leave Meadowbank."

Lucia nodded. "She and I have a…history," she said. "Her name is Colly and she was Lady Currie's nurse. She's a vile, terrible woman. She beats the servants and tells Lady Currie that they're lying when they complain. She has a particular hatred for me because Lady Currie likes me and she's jealous of anyone Lady Currie likes. That is why I told ye tae leave—she has a grudge against me and I was afraid she would take it out on ye."

"That still doesna tell me why ye have a bruise on yer head."

"Because she pushed me down the stairs," she said quietly. "I fear her grudge against me has taken a nasty turn. I'm the only servant of Lady Currie's who fights back, and she doesna like that."

He frowned. "She *pushed* ye down the stairs?" he repeated, aghast. "She could have killed ye."

"But she dinna," Lucia said quickly. "The old hag canna get the better of me, but she'll try. 'Tis a daily battle with that one."

Bane didn't say anything, but it was clear that he wasn't pleased. He sat back on the grassy bank, his brow furrowed as he thought of the old cow harassing Lucia.

Nay, he didn't like that one bit.

"Ye might not be so lucky if she does it again," he said. "Have ye told Lady Currie?"

Lucia nodded. "She knows that Colly fights with me."

"And what does she say?"

"She asks me tae not fight with her. I believe she knows that Colly is wicked, but she tolerates it because the woman raised her. She willna send her away."

Bane's lips pressed into a flat, unhappy line. "So she lets the woman do as she pleases?"

"Aye."

He grunted and looked away, his gaze moving out over the loch. "Ye canna remain there, Lucia," he said. "That old woman will kill ye if given the chance."

Lucia knew that but she didn't like to think about it. She believed she was strong enough to protect herself, but incidents like the one on the stairs concerned her. Colly could easily catch her off guard and do some damage.

"I have no choice," she said quietly.

Bane lay back on the grass, pulling Lucia down with him. He found himself looking up at the sky as she nestled against him, her head on his shoulder and his big arm around her. It seemed like the most natural position in the world.

"I told ye I want tae marry ye," he said, his lips against her forehead. "But I willna wait, not if this woman is on the prowl tae kill ye. I must get ye out of there."

Lucia was deeply contented, curled up against him. She closed her eyes, feeling his warmth against her and letting the sound of his voice flow through her.

"Not until my da's debt is paid, Bane," she said. "I willna change my mind about that. I willna simply leave."

"I am going tae pay it. I told ye I would find a job and make enough money."

She didn't say anything for a moment. He'd said the same thing before, but she didn't feel comfortable for the man to pay a debt that wasn't his. That was the truth. But given how badly she wanted to be with him, and truly not knowing how long Lady Currie might try to keep her, perhaps paying off the debt was the only way she and Bane could be together while they were still young.

If he was serious.

"If ye mean it, then ye'd have tae speak tae Laird Currie," she said. "'Tis a debt owed tae him and he will tell ye how much."

"Do ye not think I mean it?"

She opened her eyes and sat up, looking down at him as he lay there in the damp grass. "I've known ye less than two weeks," she said honestly. "I dunna know all about ye, Bane. I know ye come from Clan Morgan, and I know ye fled from the Highlands and ye've been living in the streets of Edinburgh. But beyond that...I know nothing about ye. Ye could make me promises and then disappear. How do I know ye willna?"

Bane folded a big arm behind his head, lying on it as he looked at her. She had a point; he'd seen plenty of men make promises they never intended to keep, but he wasn't one of them.

But she was right.

She didn't know that.

"Because I am a man of honor," he said quietly. "At least, I used tae be."

"Then why did ye flee the Highlands?" She jumped on his comment because it was one he'd made before. She wanted to know why this kind, handsome, and clearly capable man had been living in such self-imposed hardship. "Ye told me ye were a great warrior once, so great that they called ye the Highland Defender. *What* happened, Bane?"

"Before the screeching hag found us in the hay, I was going tae tell ye," he said. "Do ye know anything about the wars against the Sassenachs?"

She shook her head. "Not much," she said. "My da never fought, and I dunna have any brothers or menfolk that have."

He lifted his eyebrows. "Then ye're fortunate," he said. "Three years ago, the call went out tae fight for Berwick because the English had overrun it. They brought mercenaries with them by the thousands and launched a campaign along the border that destroyed many villages. My da took me, my cousins, and fifty of our best lads and we joined up with Clan Munro. We went south tae the borders but by the time we got there, many villages were in ruins. It was war like I'd never seen before."

Lucia was listening intently. "But why did the English attack?"

"Because the Scots held the city of Berwick and the English wanted it back," he said frankly. "The Duke of Gloucester led the charge. Once we reached Jedburgh, we settled in with Clan Kerr, whose numbers were decimated. They told us that they heard tell of a group of Sassenach knights heading for a stronghold known as Wolfe's Lair. It's near the border, a great English fortress that has belonged tae the Norman de Wolfe family for two hundred years. The Kerr wanted tae intercept the knights, but they were too few, so I told my da we needed tae go in their stead."

"What did he say?"

His somber expression foreshadowed his response. "He told me not tae go because the English would overwhelm us. But I went anyway. Being foolish and believing that no Sassenach could defeat me, I went and took about thirty lads with me."

An ominous feeling crept over Lucia. "What happened?" she asked.

Bane gazed up at the sky, remembering that horrible day, the one that had changed everything. Now Lucia was going to know the truth about him. Part of him had hoped to preserve her opinion about him, that he was a man who had saved her from the assault in the alley. But he couldn't hold back the truth; if he wanted to marry her, to share his life with her, then she had to know everything.

He wasn't so heroic, after all.

"It was a trap," he said after a moment. "There was no lone group of Sassenach knights, but an army lying in wait. The day was bright, with clouds scattered about, and the smell of pines was strong. We used the trees for cover until we neared Wolfe's Lair. Then they struck. Arrows were flying and my men were falling. The English backed us against a loch not unlike this one, attacking us from all sides. I was able tae swim across it, but some of my lads couldna swim. Those who werena killed by the sword drowned in the loch. I made it back tae my da, but out of the thirty lads I took with me, only six returned."

Six out of thirty. That was a horrible loss and Lucia could see how badly it pained him. There were lines on his face that hadn't been there before, a hard set of his jaw that conveyed devastation.

"I'm sorry, Bane," she said softly. "But ye canna blame yerself for it. Blame the Sassenachs for setting the trap."

He looked at her. "They set the trap and I fell for it," he said. "My cousins were with me, lads I grew up with. I watched Doogie take a sword tae the gut, and Cauley couldna swim. He held on tae me as we fled across the water, but he panicked. I tried tae drag him along, God knows I did. But in the end, he swallowed too much water and he went down for the last time. I'll never forget the look in his eyes when he did… He knew he was going tae die and I couldna help him. Not if I wanted tae live."

Lucia's hand was over her mouth in horror. "Oh…Bane," she murmured. "I'm so sorry for ye. Ye did all ye could."

Bane sat up. "Aye, I did," he said. "But I disobeyed my da by going. He warned me not tae go but I dinna listen. When I returned tae him and told him what I'd done…he sent me away. But I dinna go home."

"Where did ye go?"

He shrugged. "I couldna tell my clan what I'd done. I'd killed their sons and fathers and husbands. So…I came tae Edinburgh."

"And ye've been here ever since."

"Aye."

"Then yer da doesna know where ye are?"

He lifted his big shoulders. "Probably not," he said. "I havena seen him since I left him in Jedburgh. I hope he's told everyone that I died in the ambush. I'm sure that's what he would prefer."

Now Lucia understood why the man had such defeat in his eyes the day she'd met him. She remembered thinking how utterly crushed he looked. By life, she presumed, but now she knew the truth behind it. Bane was a man with a horrible burden to carry.

An arrogant mistake that had cost him everything.

"I canna imagine a father would wish his son dead," she said. "Mayhap someday ye'll find the desire tae return home and see him. Mayhap time will heal the wounds of the past."

Bane's gaze drifted over her and a warm glimmer returned to his eyes. "Mayhap," he said. "But until that time ever comes, *if* it comes, I need tae find my own way in life. I hadna done a very good job of it until I met ye. Ye give me hope, Lucia. Hope that life can be good again."

She smiled. "And ye give me hope that I'll not be serving Lady Currie forever," she said. "At least, I'll have something tae look forward tae when it's all over. I can look forward tae ye."

He nodded, stroking her cheek sweetly. "Ye will, indeed," he said. "But first, I need tae find a way tae make enough money tae pay yer father's debt."

They were back on the subject of buying her freedom, and she put a hand on his arm. "Ye dunna need tae pay the debt of a man ye dunna even know," she said. "I'll work it off, eventually. I think ye have enough on yer mind without having tae worry over me, too."

"But this is something I want tae do," he insisted. "With Colly out tae kill ye, it's more important than ever. I'm not sure how I can explain this, but I couldna protect my men in that ambush. I felt so...helpless. Mayhap that is why I want tae protect ye at all costs. I canna stomach the idea of ye remaining where an old woman stalks ye."

She lifted her eyebrows. "Nor can I," she said. "But until the debt is repaid, I have little choice but tae remain and be cautious of her. In fact, I should leave now. Lady Currie wishes tae go tae the Ludus Caledonia again tonight so I must hurry back and prepare. I told her I was going tae pick flowers, so she doesna expect me tae be gone so very long."

She stood up and he followed, helping her brush the grass off her skirt. "The Ludus Caledonia again, is it?" he said.

There was something in his voice that sounded displeased. "Ye know I have no choice," she said, putting a hand to his cheek. "Ye needna worry, though. I may have tae watch those brutes, but I only have eyes for ye."

He smiled weakly. "Swear it."

"I do."

"I wish ye dinna have tae go at all."

"As do I. But that is the way of things. They have a new group of recruits and Lady Currie is eager tae look them all over, one at a time."

He knew what she meant and unhappily so. He hated the thought of Lucia being around men and women who viewed intimacy, among other things, so loosely. More than that, he simply didn't like the thought of her around other men. The woman didn't even officially belong to him, he knew that, but they had an understanding. She only had eyes for him, and he for her. Surely she knew how he felt even if he couldn't exactly tell her yet.

But he would as soon as he could figure it out for himself.

They started to walk away from the loch, hand in hand. He took her basket from her and carried it.

"Yer Lady Currie visits so frequently," he said. "One would think her husband would realize what she was doing."

Lucia lifted her skirt as they walked through the wet grass so it wouldn't drag in the water. "If he does, he doesna stop her. I dunna think he is a very happy man."

"Ye have tae feel pity for a man whose wife does as she pleases with everyone but him."

Lucia couldn't disagree. "We were at the Cal last night," she said. "There were several fights and the winner of the very last fight of the evening was awarded a very big purse, but there was a laird from Saxony who wanted tae purchase his services. The man who runs the Ludus Caledonia let the warrior pick between serving the Saxony laird or keeping his big winnings. Usually, the men have no choice, but this warrior seemed tae be very popular. I've seen him before. They call him the Eagle."

Bane was mostly stewing on the fact that she seemed to be a fixture at the Ludus Caledonia but something in what she said caught his attention.

"Big winnings?" he said. "How big?"

She shrugged. "I'm not sure, but the purse they gave him was heavy. Many coins, at least."

That had him thinking. "Men fight for purses?"

"Aye."

He came to a halt and looked at her. "*I* can fight," he said. When she cocked her head curiously, he explained. "I want tae pay off yer debt quickly, but any job I find will be whatever I can get. It could take me years tae save up enough money. But if I can fight for a big purse…"

Now she knew what he meant and her eyes widened. "But these men beat each other tae a pulp, Bane," she said. "Ye'd have tae fight for blood."

"I've fought the English," he said as he resumed walking. "I can fight anyone for blood. But I've never been paid for it."

Lucia was both shocked by what he was considering and curious. "Ye should go tae the Cal before ye contemplate such a thing and see what it is about. 'Tis a place like nothing ye've ever seen before."

He nodded, thinking he was on to a potentially great idea. "I will," he said. "How do ye get there?"

She shook her head. "I dunna know," she said. "The driver from Meadowbank goes intae Edinburgh tae a tavern, and then a man from the tavern drives the carriage from there. He makes us stay inside with the shades drawn so we canna see where we're going."

"What tavern?"

"That I do know. It's called the Sticky Wick."

He looked at her in shock. "*That* place?" he hissed. "I've been there a hundred times and I've never seen Lady Currie's carriage."

"She goes tae the alley behind it."

Now Bane understood, and of all the good ideas he'd had in his lifetime, this was one of the best. He wanted to go to the mysterious fight guild and find out what he could about joining, or volunteering, or doing whatever it took to fight for money. A few good purses and he could buy Lucia's freedom.

They could start a new life.

But he didn't say anything more about it, mostly because she seemed opposed to it, so he didn't want to upset her. But he was confident she wouldn't be upset when she saw how much money he could earn.

The Highland Defender would make a return.

"Mayhap I will be at the Sticky Wick tonight tae catch a glimpse of ye," he said as they reached the path that would take them back into Edinburgh. "Any opportunity for a peek at ye and I'm a contented man until the next time we can be together. Will ye come tomorrow?"

She nodded. "If I can," she said. "I'll have tae think of another excuse tae leave Meadowbank. I'll find ye in the same alley."

"I'll be there."

They continued to walk in silence, drawing close to the city walls, until Lucia came to a halt. When he looked at her curiously, she pointed off to a small road that skirted the walls, heading east.

"I must go that way," she said. "It will be faster than going through the city."

"May I walk with ye?"

Lucia shook her head. "It would not be safe," she said. "Ye never know who might see us together. If Lady Currie found out…"

He got the message. Since they were out in the open and there were a few people about, nearer to the city, he didn't want to make a spectacle out of kissing her, so he lifted her hand to his lips, kissing it sweetly.

"Someday, we willna have tae meet in secret," he said softly. "Someday, we'll be together for all tae see and I'll be the proudest man in Scotland."

Her fingers brushed against his hand. "I hope so," she said. "I do hate tae leave ye."

"I miss ye already."

Throwing caution to the wind, Lucia impulsively kissed him

on the lips, a lingering gesture that had him grabbing for her, wanting to pull her into his embrace, but she pushed his hands away, quickly taking her basket from him and moving off. She was already heading toward the east where Meadowbank wasn't more than a half hour away with a brisk walk.

Bane stood there and watched her walk away until she was nothing more than a dark spot against the green of the land. When she finally faded from his view, his attention turned toward that hive of human stain and corruption, the Sticky Wick.

He'd been genuinely surprised to hear that she had been there so many times and he hadn't noticed her, or at least noticed the carriage, but if the carriage pulled into the alleyway behind the tavern, he wouldn't have seen it.

Tonight, however, he was going to see it.

And he was going to find out what he could about joining the Ludus Caledonia.

Chapter Eight

"SHE WAS OFF FORNICATING AGAIN," COLLY HISSED. "M'LADY, ye *must* punish her. She's lied tae ye!"

It was another face-off in Lady Currie's lavish bedchamber that smelled of stale wine and exotic perfumes. Lucia had no sooner stepped into the chamber with her basket of flowers than Colly was shouting at her.

Startled by the shouting, but not entirely surprised, Lucia ignored Colly as she went to Lady Currie with the basket full of autumn blooms.

"Look what I found for ye, m'lady," she said. "See these pink flowers? I had tae go tae the north of Edinburgh tae find them, but they're very pretty. I thought ye'd like them."

"Lies!" Colly shouted. "She went tae find *him*!"

Lady Currie was genuinely delighted with the flowers as she took them out of the basket, but Colly's shouting had her holding up her hand to silence the woman.

"Colly, please," she said. "Lucia has come back with some beautiful flowers. Will you not look at them?"

Colly was in a huff. "I was down in the kitchen yard when she came in," she said. "Why was she gone so long?"

Lucia pulled out a long, perfect stalk with small pink flowers on it. "I told ye," she said. "I went tae the fields north of the city tae find these. I thought m'lady would like them."

"And ye went alone?"

"Of course I went alone."

"Prove it!"

Lucia looked at the old woman with limited patience. "If ye're so convinced I was with someone, *ye* prove it. I've nothing tae hide."

Colly's mouth was working as if she wanted to argue, but she wisely backed off because she had no proof for her accusations. Lucia was thankful of that but in the future, she knew she'd have to be very careful about meeting Bane.

Colly wasn't beyond sending one of her minions out to follow her.

With the old woman corralled for the moment, Lucia turned back to the flowers she'd brought Lady Currie, who asked for something to put them in. There were two beautiful vases that Lady Currie had brought from her father's home, porcelain pieces that had come from Paris, and Lucia quickly filled them with water from a bucket that was kept in a servants' alcove. She gave them over to Lady Currie, who took delight in arranging the flowers.

As the woman shuffled the flowers around, the servants in her chamber watched. She always had at least six in the room at any given time because she didn't like to be alone. Tynan's mother, Amy Dalry, was in the chamber, a tiny woman with reddish-blond hair.

She was the one who created the elaborate styles for Lady Currie's hair and Lucia caught her gaze from across the room, appreciating the woman's gentle smile. When so much of the chamber was hostile when Colly was there, it was nice to have someone who wasn't shouting at her.

"Is there anything else I can do for ye, m'lady?" Lucia asked. "I can go back and find more of those pink flowers if ye'd like."

Lady Currie was nearly finished arranging the flowers. "Mayhap tomorrow," she said. "These are quite lovely, Lucia."

Lucia smiled proudly, noting that Colly was glaring at her from across the room. She ignored the woman. "Thank ye, m'lady," she said.

Lady Currie put the last flower in place and then had Amy and another maid move them to various places around the chamber. Without much to occupy her time, and boredom a real threat, the placement of the flowers was an ordeal. When the vases were finally in the correct place, Lady Currie sighed with satisfaction.

"Excellent," she said. "They brighten the chamber a great deal. That reminds me. Lucia, I was thinking on having you create another gown for me, a bright and beautiful creation made specially to wear to the Ludus Caledonia."

Lucia cocked her head curiously. "I'd be happy tae, m'lady," she said. "What did ye have in mind?"

Lady Currie went to her overstuffed bed, lying back on the mattress. "Since the Ludus Caledonia emulates ancient Rome, I was thinking on a gown that looks like something a woman from Rome would wear," she said. "Don't you think that would be stunning?"

Lucia wasn't so sure, but she nodded. "I'm sure it would be beautiful, m'lady," she said. "But…but I dunna know exactly what they looked like."

Lady Currie waved a hand at her. "Laird Currie has pieces from ancient Rome in his solar," she said. "Ask him to show you. Tell him I want you to make me a dress in that fashion."

"Aye, m'lady."

Lady Currie's gaze lingered on her a moment before turning away. The woman seemed to be out of sorts on this day, looking a bit pale. Even Lucia could see that. In fact, she curled up on the bed, which was unlike her in the afternoon.

"I do not think we shall go to the Cal tonight," she said. "I am feeling too weary to travel this evening."

"Then ye should rest, lamb," Colly said, moving over to the bed and already fussing over her. "Ye dunna need tae go out again tonight. Ye go out too much as it is."

Lady Currie frowned as Colly pulled the coverlet over her, trying to swaddle her like a babe. "I am not ill, merely tired," she said. "But your concern is sweet. Dear Colly, what would I do without you?"

Colly smiled at her but made sure to glance around the chamber, especially to Lucia, to make sure everyone had heard the praise.

"Rest, lamb," Colly said. "I will chase everyone out so ye may sleep."

"Nay." Lady Currie grabbed hold of Colly's hand. "Please... They may stay. I do not want to be alone. But I would like something to eat."

"I'll go," Lucia said, quickly moving for the chamber door. "What would ye like, m'lady? Wine? Cheese?"

"Broth," Colly barked at her. "Did ye not hear? She is feeling poorly. Bring her broth and watered wine."

"And bread," Lady Currie said. "If Cook has any sweets, I want those, too. Thank you, Lucia."

As Lucia scurried away, Colly seemed to be paying an inordinate amount of attention to the door that Lucia had just passed through. Those dark eyes were contemplating something, undoubtedly to do with Lucia. She patted Lady Currie's hand.

"I'll go with her tae make sure she brings ye back something tae tempt yer appetite," she said. "Be still, lamb. I'll return shortly."

She moved away from the bed, but Lady Currie stopped her. "You'll not fight with Lucia, Colly," she said. "Please. No fighting."

Colly forced a smile and nodded her head, but she didn't reply. The moment she was certain Lady Currie couldn't see her face, the smile vanished.

She headed out the door.

Unaware that Colly was coming for her, Lucia scurried through the servants' passage that led to the kitchens. She thought she'd escaped unscathed from the situation, relieved that Lady Currie really hadn't questioned why she'd been gone so long. Lucia had come back with a basket brimming with flowers, and that seemed to be all Lady Currie was concerned with.

The kitchens of Meadowbank were part of the vault, chambers

with low barrel ceilings that could become quite warm when the hearths were going full bore. As Lucia came down a small flight of stairs into the kitchen, she saw Tynan lugging a full bucket of water. The child's face lit up with a smile when he saw her.

"What's wanting, Lucia?" he asked.

She smiled in return, putting her hand on his straw-like hair affectionately. "M'lady is hungry," she said. "I've come tae see what Cook has for her."

Tynan set the bucket down and the water sloshed out of it. "Cook is in the yard," he said, rushing over to the hearth. "But there's broth. I saw her boil the bones."

Lucia went over to the hearth, getting her face steamed as she peered into the bubbling pot. "M'lady will want some of that," she said. "Is there bread?"

Tynan wasn't really a kitchen servant, but he spent enough time there that he knew a great deal about it. He began rushing around, finding bread and a half wheel of tart white cheese.

"Here," he said, ripping off chunks and handing them to Lucia. "I think there's pie left from last night. The pie with the apples and onions in it."

Lucia nodded. "If you can find it, I'll give it tae m'lady."

Tynan banged around, looking in the larder that was off to the side of the kitchen. As Lucia found a tray for the food she was collecting, she called over to him.

"Did ye find the pie?"

"Nay!" he called in return. "But I found stewed sausages!"

"Bring them."

He did, trotting over to her with his hands gripping a covered wooden bowl. He carefully gave it over to Lucia. As she peeled back the cloth to take a look at the contents, he watched her closely.

"Can I ask ye a question?" he said.

"Of course ye can."

"Where's Bane?"

She paused. "What made ye think of him just now?"

The child cocked his head curiously. "He's not in the stables anymore. Angus said he had tae go."

She smiled. "Ye like him, don't ye?"

The boy shrugged his skinny shoulders. "He's nice tae me," he said. "He lets me watch him shave."

Lucia chuckled. "Aye, he's nice," she said. "But Angus was correct—he had tae go."

"But why?"

Lucia wasn't sure she could really explain it because the child didn't need to know the details with Colly and the hay shelter. She knew that Tynan had visited Bane during his stay, and given that the boy didn't remember his own father, perhaps there was some father-figure adoration for Bane in that sense. Someone for a lonely little boy to look up to, because God only knew there weren't any men of Bane's quality at Meadowbank.

She put her hand on the boy's head affectionately.

"He had tae go because he's a busy man," she said simply. "He could only stay with us a short while. But he may come back someday. Now, what else can ye find for m'lady? Are there any sweets?"

She diverted the child's attention and he scurried off again, hunting for more food. He found little red apples and a rice porridge with apples, raisins, and honey that Cook had made for supper.

The porridge was sweet and Lucia began spooning it into a wooden bowl as Tynan found more wine for Lady Currie's meal. Whatever alcohol that was in her chamber was usually exhausted by this time of day. As she arranged the tray and he went to hunt for a clean bowl for the broth, a figure entered the kitchen. Glancing up, Lucia could see that it was Colly.

She braced herself.

"I found broth for m'lady," she said before the old woman could utter a word. "There is also a rice-and-raisin porridge that is sweet. She asked for sweets."

Colly, surprisingly, didn't answer. She made her way over to the table where Lucia was collecting the food, a move that made Lucia uncomfortable because the hearth was right behind her. She wouldn't put it past the woman to try to shove her into the fire. As Colly moved in to inspect the tray, Lucia moved away.

She didn't want to be in striking distance.

Behind Colly, Lucia caught sight of Tynan as the boy appeared with a bowl. When Tynan's eyes widened at the sight of Colly, Lucia faintly shook her head at him, and he sank back into the shadows.

She didn't want the child to become a target of the old woman's vitriol.

"Where is the broth?" Colly asked, looking up from the tray.

Lucia pointed to the hearth behind her. "There," she said. "I was looking for a bowl."

"Then find it quickly. Dunna make Lady Currie wait."

Lucia didn't move. She wasn't sure why Colly was there, but she knew she didn't like it. "Why did ye come down here?" she asked. "Did m'lady send ye for something else?"

Colly shook her head, but her dark-eyed gaze was riveted to Lucia. "I came tae ensure ye brought her the right food," she said. "Ye canna be trusted, Lucia."

Lucia fought off her natural reaction to Colly, which was to argue with her. But it wasn't safe to do that in a kitchen with sharp things around. In fact, Lucia glanced around quickly, looking for the knives which fortunately were closer to her than they were to Colly. That made her feel a little better.

But only marginally.

She was on edge.

"At least I dunna lie tae m'lady like ye do," she said. "Why do ye do that? Don't ye know that the servants would respect ye more if ye were simply fair and honest with them? Ye dunna need tae frighten everyone half tae death."

Colly lifted a bushy eyebrow. "Ye foolish chit," she muttered. "Ye willna last long here. Ye'll be gone soon enough."

Lucia shook her head sadly. "Colly, I've been here for nearly two years, and ye've done nothing but vex me since the day I arrived," she said. "Did ye not stop tae think that if ye dunna bother me, I willna bother ye? I have no choice but tae be here. Believe me, if I could leave, I would. We have tae make the best of it."

Colly stepped away from the tray as if contemplating what Lucia was saying. "Ye dunna belong with Lady Currie," she said. "I know that yer father gave ye over tae Laird Currie tae pay off a debt."

"That is true. Everyone knows."

"But ye should serve Laird Currie, not his wife."

Lucia threw up her hands. "I have no choice," she said. "I go where I'm told tae go, and ye know that Lady Currie likes for me tae accompany her tae the Ludus Caledonia when she goes. I wish I dinna have tae go, Colly, believe me. None of this is my choice."

Colly continued to move away from the tray, heading in her direction. "Ye set a bad example for all of the servants," she said. "Ye're bold and ye have an unruly tongue. Lady Currie is too fine a lady for the likes of ye. Ye should have never come here."

Lucia had nothing more to say to a woman in this increasingly circular argument. Even though Colly understood that Lucia was here against her will, she seemed to expect her to flee or hide or otherwise make herself scarce. But it simply proved to Lucia that the woman wanted to control everyone around Lady Currie.

Was Lucia a bad influence? Not at all. But she was invited to go to the Ludus Caledonia with Lady Currie, and Colly was not. Colly was always left behind.

Lucia suspected that might be the root of the jealousy.

Without another word, she turned around and began hunting for a bowl for the broth even though she knew Tynan had one. But the child was hiding, so she fumbled around until she came across a big wooden bowl.

Bent over a series of stacking shelves, she was just putting her hands on the bowl when she heard something behind her. She caught sight of a foot, Colly's foot, before a sharp pain to her head knocked her to her knees.

In a panic, she knew that Colly was trying to kill her, and she cursed herself for turning her back on the woman. It had been a mistake.

A mistake that was going to cost her.

Another blow to her head and the world went black.

CHAPTER NINE

IT HAD BEEN THREE LONG DAYS SINCE BANE HAD SEEN LUCIA, and as the sun rose on the fourth day, something told him this day, too, would pass without seeing her.

It was just a feeling he had.

Something was wrong.

He'd been to the Sticky Wick three days in a row, remaining from morning until very late in the evening, watching the alley behind the place for Lady Currie's fine carriage to roll in. But it never did. Meanwhile, he'd asked the tavernkeep about the Ludus Caledonia and was met with stony silence. Either the man didn't know or didn't want to answer.

Bane suspected it was the latter.

He'd therefore spent those three days asking anyone he could strike up a conversation with about the Ludus Caledonia, hoping to glean some information. Bane had spent enough time in the place that he knew the regulars, men who drank hard and sometimes fought harder.

What he was told was what he already knew—that the Ludus Caledonia was a secretive fight guild where men gambled on the bouts. A couple of the regulars had become irritated with his questions and had thrown punches to silence him, which only earned them a hammer-like fist to the side of the head.

The Sticky Wick was not for the faint of heart.

Bane had had his share of fights in the place over the past two years. Mostly, the fights weren't directed at him and were things he simply found himself caught up in, but he had a devastating blow and the regulars knew not to tangle with him. Bane would come in, sit in the corner, and make his ale last as long as he could because he didn't have the money for more.

But today, things were different.

He wasn't going to spend another day and night at the Sticky Wick, watching for a carriage that would never come. A storm had rolled in and rain was coming down in sheets as he made his way through Edinburgh, heading east.

He was going to Meadowbank.

He knew that Lucia didn't want him near the manse, but he simply couldn't stay away. He knew the place well enough to know that he could probably sneak in through the postern gate because Laird Currie's guards were lazy.

He'd learned that from his brief time there. Men that Laird Currie paid to protect his home would gather up at the main gate in the guardroom and drink until they could hardly stand. As Bane made his way to the great stone bastion in the driving rain, he was certain the guards would not be out in this weather in any case. He had to take that chance.

As he expected, the postern gate was unguarded.

The stable yard was vacant as he made his way inside, rushing to the stables where he knew he would find old Angus. He was as nervous as a cat as he ducked and dodged all the way to the stable, terrified that the screeching old woman would see him. The last thing he wanted to do was cause trouble for Lucia, but he felt very strongly that something was amiss.

He had to discover what it was.

Ducking into the stables, he mercifully had cover so he could watch the kitchen yard for someone he recognized without fear of being seen. He had no idea where Angus was, because the old man was usually somewhere around the stable. The seconds ticked away and Angus didn't make an appearance.

But someone else did.

Bane could see Tynan as the lad entered the stable yard. He had a bucket in his hands, but he was evidently hunting for something from the way he was swinging his head about. When he came across another bucket, he picked it up, looked it over, and then swapped it out with the bucket he'd been carrying. He turned around to leave the stable yard, and Bane knew he had to act.

Quickly, he stepped out of his hiding place.

"Tynan!" he hissed.

The lad came to a startled halt, looking over at Bane with big eyes. Bane motioned him over and the lad trotted toward him, the bucket banging against his legs. When he reached the stable, Bane stuck out a big hand and pulled him inside.

"Bane!" the boy gasped. "Ye came back! She said ye might come back and ye did!"

The child was clearly glad to see him, but Bane didn't have time for a happy reunion. Every moment was valuable. He grasped the lad by the arms.

"Do ye know where Lucia is?" he asked.

The child's joyful expression morphed into a grimace. "Aye."

"Where?"

"Colly took her away," he said, suddenly fearful. "I saw it."

Bane felt as if he'd been hit in the gut as his fears were confirmed. "I knew it," he hissed. "I knew something was wrong. What happened, lad? What did ye see?"

Tynan looked around anxiously, making sure no one was listening. At the very mention of Colly, he looked like a frightened rabbit. It was clear to Bane that this woman Lucia had spoken of as a vile creature had some kind of hold on Tynan, too.

The child was terrified.

"Lucia was bringing food tae m'lady," he said quietly. "I was helping her when Colly came tae the kitchen. She hit Lucia on the head and put her in the vault until Lady Currie told her tae let her out, but Lucia isna allowed tae leave the house now."

Bane frowned. "Hit her on the head?" he repeated. "Is she hurt?"

Tynan shook his head. "I dunna know," he said. "I've not seen her very much since it happened."

"*When* did this happen?"

The boy counted his fingers. "Three days ago."

"But ye have seen her since?"

"I saw her sewing something in m'lady's chamber when I went tae bring my mam hot water." Tynan's little hand grasped Bane's big hand. "Colly says that Lucia lies and m'lady believes her."

"And that's why she's not allowed tae leave the house?"

Tynan nodded seriously. "She stays inside and Colly watches her."

"Does she not even go out with m'lady when the woman leaves in her carriage?"

"M'lady hasna left the house, either."

Bane loosened his grip on the child. At least he knew Lucia wasn't horribly injured, but she was evidently being kept as a prisoner. Lady Currie hadn't gone about her usual nightly visits to the Ludus Caledonia, which was why he hadn't seen the carriage, and all fingers pointed to the old witch, Colly. Clearly, the woman had some kind of a grip on the inhabitants of Meadowbank, Lady Currie included.

Bane was relieved that Lucia wasn't badly injured, but it was an effort to keep his fury at bay as he realized what was happening. He knew that anger wouldn't do him any good.

It wasn't as if he could help her.

At least, not yet.

But the puzzlement in what had happened tore at him because he had a hunch that somehow he'd delayed Lucia's return on that sweet morning in Edinburgh and she had been punished for being gone too long. Was that what Colly had meant by Lucia's lies? Perhaps she'd lied to cover up her actions with him.

It had been his fault.

"Bane?" Tynan asked, breaking into his thoughts. "Are ye here tae stay now?"

Bane looked at the lad. Above all of the turmoil he was feeling for Lucia, he still had the capacity to feel some compassion for the child who was clearly lonely. It seemed to Bane, and had since the beginning, that Tynan simply wanted to be loved. He was a kind, openhearted child who had been forced to grow up quickly in harsh servitude. He put his big hand on the boy's head, dwarfing it.

"Nay, lad," he said. "In fact, I'm not supposed tae be here. Ye mustna tell anyone that ye've seen me. Do ye understand?"

Tynan nodded, though he really didn't understand. "But why must ye leave?"

"Do ye know why I left in the first place?"

"Lucia said ye had tae go because ye were a busy man."

He realized she hadn't told the child the truth. Bane would leave it that way. "I am very busy," he said. "But I want ye tae tell Lucia something for me and it must be a secret, Tynan. Ye must be very careful that no one sees ye when ye tell her. Can ye do that?"

"I can." Tynan nodded eagerly. "What do I tell her?"

Bane paused as he thought of something simple yet meaningful. Tynan probably wouldn't remember a long message, so he had to make it short.

"Tell her that I will return for her," he said. "Can ye remember that?"

Tynan nodded again. "Will ye really?"

"Really what?"

"Return for her?"

Bane nodded. "I will," he said. "But ye mustna tell anyone that. Only Lucia. Tell her…I'll find a way, I swear it."

Tynan nodded solemnly. "I will."

Bane smiled at the boy, patting his head. "There's a good old man," he said. "Now go about yer business and remember… Ye dinna see me. I was never here."

With that, he slipped from the stable, leaving Tynan to run after him, stopping at the stable entry only to watch Bane as he flew across the stable yard, staying out of sight until he managed to slip from the postern gate.

The boy watched him with the naked admiration that only a child could give, admiring a man he'd not known long, but someone who had left a mark on him. Kindness to a young boy who'd not known much of it in his short life.

When Bane was finally out of sight, Tynan headed for the manse. He had a message to deliver and he would not fail. Bane had entrusted him with a special task, and he felt important as he ran back into the gray-stone house.

Being small and a child, Tynan was often ignored in the house. He knew that, and this time he would use it to his advantage. It wasn't unusual for him to retreat to the upper floors where his mother served Lady Currie, so he slipped up the servants' stairs and into the dim block of chambers that belonged to Lady Currie and her servants, including Colly.

Colly...

The name struck fear into the child even though Colly never gave him a second look. Still, he was terrified of the big, strong woman who prowled around the manse all in the name of Lady Currie. Tynan knew what the woman was capable of, as he'd seen time and time again. The incident with Lucia three days prior had only been one event in a long line of many.

Tynan knew where Lucia's bedchamber was and that was his destination, but there seemed to be something going on in Lady Currie's chamber. It was bright and warm, and women were moving about, including his mother. He could see Amy with Lady Currie, massaging her forehead as she lay in bed, eyes closed.

Colly was there, too.

The big woman was standing on the other side of the bed, holding Lady Currie's hand. Even as Tynan stood in the doorway, he could see that Lady Currie wasn't feeling well. Everyone seemed to be trying to comfort her in some way. Peering around the chamber, he caught sight of Lucia sitting against the wall, stitching a long, white piece of fabric by the light of several fat tapers on the table next to her.

Tynan didn't want to tell her of Bane's message with everyone around, but he also didn't want to fail Bane. It seemed to him that Bane wanted his message delivered to Lucia immediately, so Tynan made his move.

Nervously, he went into the chamber and headed straight for a table that usually held food and drink for Lady Currie. He knew this because often he would bring the food and wine to the chamber himself. At the moment, the table only held wine, and most of that in the crystal decanter seemed to be gone. Tynan poured the last of it into a matching crystal cup.

Carefully holding the cup so it wouldn't spill, he made his way over to his mother. He had to pass by Lucia in order to reach his mother, and he kept looking at her to see if she would notice him, but she didn't. She kept her head down, embroidering the white fabric with methodical stitches. Tynan was forced to walk by her as he went to his mother.

"Would m'lady like some wine, Mam?" he asked politely.

Amy glanced at her son. "That is kind, Tynan, but Lady Currie must rest," she said. "Ye may put it on the table next tae the bed."

Tynan moved to do it but at the mention of wine, Lady Currie abruptly became lucid.

"I'll drink it," she said.

Amy took the cup from her son, handing it over to Colly, who helped Lady Currie sit up to drink. As the old nurse was occupied with her charge, Tynan made his way over to Lucia.

He was stealthy about it, as stealthy as a child could be. He kept glancing at Colly, who was fully occupied with Lady Currie.

"Lucia," he whispered. "I've a message for ye."

Lucia looked up from her stitching. She had a bruise on her cheek from the fight with Colly three days earlier, and her eyes were dull with sorrow. But his words had her looking at him curiously.

"Message?" she repeated. "What are ye talking about?"

Tynan put a finger to his lips. "From Bane," he whispered, terrified Colly would hear. "He was here. He says tae tell ye that he'll return for ye."

Lucia's eyes widened. "Is he still here?"

They were speaking so softly that they were essentially only mouthing the words. Tynan shook his head. "He left," he said. "He says tae tell ye he'll return. That's all he told me."

Lucia stared at him, her eyes filled with emotion until she happened to glance over Tynan's head to see that Colly was looking at her. Startled, and terrified the woman might demand to know what she and Tynan were speaking of, she dropped her head and returned to her sewing. Tynan, realizing that the wicked nurse had her attention on him, quickly shuffled from the chamber.

But he'd delivered his message. He'd done what he told Bane he would do and that was all that mattered.

Lucia knew.

As Tynan raced down the servants' stairs, all the young lad could do was smile. He found himself wishing that when Bane took Lucia away, he'd take him away, too.

CHAPTER TEN

"M'LAIRD? I AM SORRY TAE DISTURB YE, BUT LADY CURRIE HAS asked me tae come tae ye."

Lucia stood at the doors of Laird Currie's solar, enormous oak doors that had been carved into figures from Celtic mythology. Fantastic dogs and creatures were on the panels along with exaggerated warriors. The doors were quite legendary in Edinburgh, and scholars came from all over to get a look at the detail.

Greer Gordon Hume-Currie, Baron Currie, was a man of great learning. He came from a long line of noble-born warriors who had discovered that their lust for money was greater than their lust for war. Wealth superseded bloody battles, and somewhere in the last century, they had become importers of fine goods from the Continent.

The products were high-end commodities, but there was no merchant stall in Edinburgh to ply their wares. All business was conducted out of the manse, and there was no shortage of customers. Laird Currie could sell an ancient crystal bowl to a wealthy lord and make enough money to sustain Meadowbank for an entire year.

Wealth was something the House of Currie had.

When Laird Currie saw Lucia standing at the doors to his solar, he set aside the book in his hand and waved her in.

"Ah," he said. "'Tis Colm's little lass. Come in, child."

Lucia did. She genuinely liked the somewhat eccentric Laird Currie and she smiled as she came into the chamber.

"Forgive me for disturbing ye, m'laird," she said. "Lady Currie has asked me tae look at one of yer Roman vases. She wants me tae make her a gown like the ancients wore."

Laird Currie was out of his chair, very interested in showing her what she sought. As he moved toward a rack of shelves against the wall, he reached into his pocket and pulled forth a big, gray rat, putting the little beastie on a nearby table and giving him a crumb to eat from the remnants of the meal there.

"This," he said as he reached up to grasp a vase. "This will show ye what the Roman women wore. Magnificent, is it not?"

He handed it to Lucia, who took it timidly. In truth, she was still eyeing the rat eating bread crumbs on the tabletop. Laird Currie was known to walk around with rats in every pocket. Pet rats that all had names like Achilles and Diogenes and Clyde.

Laird Currie and his rat family were well known.

She pushed aside thoughts of rats to focus on the vase. It was a beautiful piece, about a foot tall, with scenes depicting women all around it. The colors were white and brown and a faded red, showing women lounging and eating. More important, it showed their dress and she looked at it closely.

"Aye, m'laird, 'tis," she said. "May I ask how old?"

Laird Currie was beaming as proudly at the vase as one would beam at a firstborn son. "Two thousand years, I should think," he said. "These garments were only worn by the noblewomen, ye know. See the embroidery around the edges?"

Lucia nodded as he pointed it out. "Was it white?"

He shook his head. "Nay, lass," he said. "Gold. The gown itself must be white, mind ye. A very fine white fabric, and ye embroider the edges in gold. My wife asked for this, did she?"

Lucia nodded. "She did, m'laird," she said. "I must go tae the fabric merchant and purchase it specially for her."

The old man nodded, his movements thoughtful as he took the vase from her and carefully set it on the shelf. Another rat slithered out of his robe pocket and fell to the floor, scurrying away as he moved to another small bowl nearby and picked it up, returning to Lucia so she could take a look at it.

"She will look very fine in it," he said, stepping away as Lucia looked over the bottom of the bowl where women in fine clothing were painted. "She will look like a goddess."

Lucia sensed something wistful in that statement. Everyone knew that Laird Currie stayed to his solar all day and all night, rarely leaving. He slept here most of the time in the company of his rats, over on a leather couch that was gouged and worn. It was his sanctuary and, Lucia's father had said, also his prison.

Laird Currie was a lonely man.

"When it's finished, I'm sure she'll be proud tae show it tae ye, m'laird," she said. "She asked specifically for a Roman dress. I'm sure it was tae please ye."

Laird Currie smiled, but it was without humor. "It isna tae please me, Lucia," he said. "But it is nice for ye tae say so. I'm sure she wants a new dress tae wear tae the Cal. And why should she not want one? Everyone shows off their finery there."

Lucia couldn't dispute him but she wasn't comfortable with the turn of the conversation. Surely the man knew where his wife went nightly; how could he not? Everyone else knew, so why not him?

But that was the first time she'd heard him speak of it.

"My...my da was very fond of ye," she said to change the subject to *any* subject. "He used tae speak so warmly of ye. I never had the chance tae thank ye for what ye did for him before he died. Ye did all ye could tae heal him."

"Yer da was a sick man," Laird Currie said, though he didn't seem to be pleased with the change in focus. He looked at her pointedly. "When ye came tae work off his debt, I was pleased with the honor ye would show yer father, but now I know it was a bad thing. Ye should never have come here, Lucia. I know what happens tae ye. I hear things. I heard ye were attacked by that cow who tends my wife. I heard she locked ye in a chamber."

Lucia's cheeks flushed and she averted her gaze. "It was nothing, m'laird."

"It dinna sound like nothing tae me. What happened?"

"Colly and I dunna get on," she said. "But I dinna provoke her if that's what ye mean. I try tae behave myself, but that woman is—"

He cut her off with a snort. "I know what she is," he said. "She's a devil who tries tae rule my home. I'd like tae send ye home, but my wife likes tae have ye here. She likes the garments ye make for her."

Lucia's heart was in her throat with what he'd said. *I'd like tae send ye home.* God, how she wished he would!

"I dunna mean tae be bold, m'laird, but when *do* ye think ye can send me home?" she asked. "What I mean tae ask is when my da's debt will be paid?"

The old laird looked at her. "Soon, I should think. Where will ye go?"

Lucia was vague in her reply. "I'm not sure," she said. "I have an aunt who lives in Selkirk. Mayhap I'll return tae her, though it will seem strange not seeing my da in her home. That was the only home he ever knew next to Meadowbank."

Laird Currie nodded, somewhat sadly. "Yer da was a great help tae me when he was here," he said. "He was my friend. Not many men say that about a servant, but I do. Colm Symington was a good friend. I miss him."

Lucia smiled. "As do I, m'laird."

She was still holding the bowl with the women painted on it and Laird Currie moved to her, carefully taking the bowl from her. His movements were slow, pensive.

"I'll bring it up tae my wife about sending ye home," he said after a moment. "Mayhap after ye make her Roman dress for her. No promises that she'll agree, but I'll ask."

Lucia felt more relief than she could express. Was it really possible that the end of her servitude was in sight? "Thank ye, m'laird," she said. "But...but if I'm able tae pay off the debt myself, could I do that?"

"Do ye have the money?"

"I dunna know. How much would it be?"

He cocked his head thoughtfully. "Yer da cost me a good deal when he was ill," he said. "Truthfully, I wouldna consider it a debt, but my wife does. That's why we took yer service in payment—because she said I should. I would say two pounds should satisfy the debt. But if my wife wishes tae keep ye on, it may be more difficult than that."

Lucia knew that and she tried not to get her hopes up. "I dunna wish tae be a servant the rest of my life, m'laird," she said. "I have dreams, too."

"What dreams?"

"Tae become a seamstress and sew for fine ladies. And...and mayhap tae marry."

His old eyes crinkled. "Do ye have a lad picked out?"

She was coy, fighting off a grin. "'Tis possible, m'laird."

Laird Currie chuckled at her girlish charm, something that was so different from his own wife. She didn't have charm—what she had was purely opportunistic seduction. Perhaps if he'd been wiser when he'd met her...

But no.

He could not look back. He'd done that too much as it was.

"Off with ye, lass," he finally said. "We'll speak on this another time."

Lucia rushed off, but not before she caught a glimpse of Laird Currie as he sat at his fine table cluttered with books and more rats and a writing kit, and rubbed at his forehead as if greatly troubled.

Of course he was troubled. With a wife who only wanted to dress for her studs at the Ludus Caledonia, he had a great deal to be troubled over. He may have been the lord of the manse, but he had no say in what went on there and Lucia felt a good deal of pity for him. He was a nice man, after all.

And he'd spoken of her freedom.

Struggling to keep optimism from consuming her, she headed back up to the small, neat sewing room to sketch out an example of the dress she wanted to make for Lady Currie.

CHAPTER ELEVEN

The Sticky Wick
Edinburgh

"USUALLY, HE'S HERE IN THE MORNING," THE TAVERNKEEP SAID. "I would wager he'll be here sometime."

He was speaking to two men, one enormous and bald, and the other big, blond, and handsome. They were both well fed and well dressed, making them something of an oddity in a pit of despair like the Sticky Wick.

The blond spoke up.

"And ye said he's been asking about the Cal?" he said. "If it's the man ye've described tae me, I've seen him before. He was here when I started coming tae this place years ago, though I dunna much know him. But I do know his name—Bane."

The tavernkeep nodded. "Bane Morgan," he said. "He's much like ye were once."

"At least I found my way out of it."

The tavernkeep looked him up and down. "Ye surprise me each time I see ye, Lor. Time was when ye were a fixture here, too, living in filth and drink until those from the Cal took ye away. Ye dunna look like the same man."

Lor Careston's eyes glimmered. "That's because I'm not," he said. "The Cal can do for Bane what it's done for me, although I'm surprised it's taken this long for the man tae ask about it. He's a fighter. I can remember seeing him in the past. He's a beast when it comes to a brawl. Surely he'll make a good candidate for the Cal."

The tavernkeep nodded. "The regulars stay away from him,"

he said. "I dunna know Bane's story, but he seems...lost. There's something inside of him that's hurt and dangerous. He's a man with secrets."

"How do ye know?"

"Because I've seen enough men hiding their pasts tae know that."

The tavernkeep tapped his head knowingly as he walked away, off to help a group of men who had come in out of the rain. Lor turned to the man next to him.

"I'm sure ye've seen this man, Luther," he said. "Ye've been coming around tae the Sticky Wick for a long time. Bane Morgan is a regular here."

Luther Eddleston scratched his bald head. "I'm not sure," he said in his proper English speech. "Describe the man to me."

Lor cocked his head in thought, leaning forward against the table they were sitting at. "He's a big man, about my size," he said. "Brown hair that is badly in need of a cut and a beard. He always sits in one of the corners, out of the way."

Luther pondered that. "Walks with his head down?"

"I suppose so. I've never really noticed."

"Then we'll simply have to wait until he makes an appearance, but we cannot wait too long."

Lor knew that. Like Lor, Luther was a *doctores*, or trainer, at the Ludus Caledonia, but he was also a scout. Often, the *doctores* made trips into Edinburgh to find new blood for their fight guild. On this afternoon, it happened to be him and Lor at the Sticky Wick because they'd received word that a possible candidate had been asking about the Ludus Caledonia.

That was usually how it started. The tavernkeep received a bounty for every fight guild candidate he referred to the Cal, so he would send word if anyone was either asking of the Ludus Caledonia or if a man seemed to be a viable prospect. The other trainers were busy on this day, so Luther and Lor took the short journey into Edinburgh to check on the information. There were fights at the Ludus Caledonia tonight, however, so they couldn't spend too much time on the hunt for the elusive Bane Morgan.

During their wait, it was an interesting afternoon.

At least three fights broke out in the tavern, including one between two very old men who could barely stand, trying to brain each other with their wooden cups. That was entertaining, bringing chuckles from Lor and Luther, but one of the fights had ended in a man being stabbed.

His friends had dragged his body away, leaving a trail of blood.

The pair was about halfway through their cup of cheap ale when the rainstorm outside let up and men began to filter out, going about their day until the next bout of rain began. But as men departed the tavern, more came in. Lor recognized one of them.

He tapped Luther on the arm.

"There," he said. "Over by the door, the tall lad with the hair to his shoulders. *That's* Bane Morgan."

Luther peered at the man Lor was indicating. He was a little taller than Lor with a slender torso and ridiculously broad shoulders. "I thought you said he had a beard?"

Lor shrugged. "He's clearly shaved it off," he said. "But I recognize him. That's definitely Morgan."

Luther took a closer look, although his eyesight wasn't what it used to be. Age and a rough lifestyle had seen to that.

"I think I recognize him," he said. "Aye, I do believe I've seen him before."

Lor nodded. "As I said, he was here when I first came tae Edinburgh," he said. "He kept to himself and I kept to myself. I dunna think I've ever spoken a word to him. Do ye want tae—?"

He was cut off when one of the friends of the man who had been stabbed earlier abruptly charged back into the place, ramming the door into Bane, who lost his balance as he crashed into the nearest table.

The three men sitting at the table didn't take kindly to the intrusion. As Lor and Luther watched, the first man reached out to Bane, who deftly avoided the clawlike hands and grabbed the man by the back of the neck, tossing him across several tables until he crashed to the floor.

The second man at the table had a cup of ale in hand, and gripping the cup, tried to smash it into Bane's face. Bane was faster, however, and punched the man in the throat, instantly disabling him.

As Bane tried to move away from the table, the third man launched himself at Bane, grabbing him around the torso. Bane didn't hesitate; he grabbed the man by the hair, pulling so hard that the man loosened his grip as he started to yell. Once his grip was broken, Bane kneed him in the chest, which knocked the wind out of him. A second blow to the face sent the man to the floor, unmoving.

Knocked cold in one punch.

Luther grunted. "So that's your Bane Morgan, is it?" he asked. "Impressive."

Lor's eyebrows rose in agreement. "I would say so."

"I cannot believe I have not noticed this man before. Mayhap I wasn't looking in the right place."

"Now ye know."

"Indeed, I do."

Luther rose to his feet and Lor knew what was coming. The same thing had happened to Lor when he'd been asking about the Ludus Caledonia, hoping to make contact with men who could change his destiny. Luther had tested him before he ever spoke to him.

Bane was about to meet with a similar test.

Lor watched curiously as Luther skirted the room, watching Bane as the man backed away from those he'd just pummeled. He was making his way to the other side of the room, to one of his preferred corners, but he wasn't paying attention to where he was going as much as he was watching his back.

Luther could see that. He made sure to be in the right place at the right time as Bane backed right into him, stepping on his foot. Luther roared angrily and the fight was on.

Bane was on the defensive even though he clearly had no idea what he'd done wrong. Luther grabbed him by the neck and would have tossed him had Bane not done the same thing to Luther that he'd done to one of the other men—he threw a punch right into Luther's throat that staggered him.

By this time, Lor was up, moving for the pair before the fight turned ugly.

"Wait," he said, holding up his hands in a gesture of surrender. "Bane, wait… Look at me. Do ye know me?"

Bane was ready for battle. He had a wild-eyed look about him, but he managed to focus on Lor. He was puzzled at first until recognition dawned.

His brow furrowed.

"I've seen ye," he said, but his balled fists were still up. "Ye used tae come tae this place."

"I did."

"Who are ye?"

"My name is Lor," Lor said evenly. "Ye and I never spoke to one another, but I knew of ye. I saw ye often."

Bane was confused. He looked between Lor and Luther, his fists still raised. "Do ye want a piece of me, too?" he asked. "I'm ready for ye."

Lor shook his head. "Nay," he assured him. "I'm told ye've been asking about the Ludus Caledonia."

That drew a reaction from Bane. His puzzlement was magnified tenfold. "Do ye know about the place?" he demanded. "What can ye tell me about it?"

Lor glanced at Luther, who was coughing and rubbing his throat, before crooking his finger.

"Come with me."

Bane hesitated a moment before complying, but he kept turning to look at Luther, who was bringing up the rear. It was clear that he didn't trust the bald man, and his fists were still up, but his curiosity about the Ludus Caledonia was stronger than his mistrust.

Still, he kept a healthy distance from the man as he followed Lor to a corner of the tavern. When Lor sat down, Bane continued to stand until the bald man sat, too. Lor indicated an empty chair.

"Please sit," he said. "I want tae talk tae ye."

Warily, Bane lowered himself into the chair, lowering his balled fists for the first time. "Tell me what ye know about the Ludus Caledonia," he said. "Is it true that men can make money there?"

"Fighting or gambling?"

"Fighting."

Lor nodded. "It is true."

"Then I want tae volunteer tae fight. I want tae make money."

Lor looked at Luther, who had been with the Ludus Caledonia far longer than Lor had. "This is Luther Eddleston," he said. "He can answer yer questions better than I can."

He deferred to Luther, who took a big gulp of ale, clearing his sore throat before responding.

"Why?" he asked simply.

Bane couldn't think of anything to tell him other than the truth. It was the truth. "Because I want tae buy the freedom of a woman in servitude," he said. "She's working off her father's debt. If I can buy her freedom, we can marry."

Luther looked at him closely as he contemplated his answer. "Do you have any experience in fighting? It seems to me that you have some aptitude for it from what we've seen."

Bane nodded. "I've been fighting the Sassenachs as long as I can remember."

"Have you seen action?"

"When the Sassenachs sacked Berwick, my clan was called

upon tae reinforce the borders," he said. "I've been in many a battle, I assure ye."

"Then you have a warrior's background."

"Aye."

"What happened?"

"What do ye mean?"

Luther indicated the tavern. "A seasoned warrior finds himself here, at this place, living with the filth of society? I want to know why. What made you come here, Bane?"

Bane's jaw began to tic. He couldn't tell him the truth, as complicated as it was. Surely those from the Ludus Caledonia wouldn't want a man who had led his men to disaster. Though Bane was honest to a fault and lies did not come easily to him, he found that he simply couldn't tell them the whole truth. He was afraid they would reject him.

And he desperately wanted to be accepted.

"Because I need money," he said. "I canna find that in the Highlands. My brethren used tae call me the Highland Defender because I'm an excellent warrior. But each man must find his way in life and must do what is important tae him. Right now, making money tae pay my lady's debt is important tae me."

Luther didn't have any cause to disbelieve him because Bane made a reasonable argument. "I see," he said. "I suppose your reasons are as good as any. But let me be clear—we do not take volunteers."

"Then how does a man come to the Ludus Caledonia?"

"He gives his life over to it."

Bane looked between Luther and Lor, confused. "His entire *life*?"

Luther put up a hand. "Before we proceed any further, there is something you should know," he said. "If you are looking for quick money, this is not the place for you. If you are looking for something temporary, this is not the place for you. But if you are willing to work hard and pledge your life and your time to the Ludus Caledonia, we can change your life. Ask Lor."

Bane's attention shifted to Lor, who nodded his head slowly to confirm Luther's words. "When I first came tae the Sticky Wick, it was because I was told the Ludus Caledonia was a place that could teach me tae fight," he said. "Unlike ye, I had no real experience in it. I was told that those at the Sticky Wick could connect me with the Cal, and I was determined tae learn tae fight for one very good reason—vengeance. Like ye, I had my own wants. I wanted tae seek vengeance on those who had destroyed my village in the Highlands. But the Cal isna for opportunists. It's for men who know how tae make a vow and keep it."

Bane thought carefully on that. "What kind of vow?"

"If ye want the Cal tae provide ye with opportunities, then ye need tae pledge seven years of yer life," Lor said. "Usually, the man who owns the Cal would tell ye that, but since ye seem tae think ye can fight for quick riches, ye should know what is expected of ye before ye waste yer time and ours. We look for fighters who can commit tae training and will hold true tae that commitment. If the Cal is going tae spend money training ye, then ye must understand there is a commitment on yer part as well."

Seven years. That gave Bane pause. He didn't want to commit his life to something for seven years when he desperately wanted to pay for Lucia's freedom and marry her sooner rather than later.

But he was a realist—as he'd told Lucia, it would take him years to save enough money to pay for her freedom, were he to find any number of low-paying jobs in the city. It might take him more than seven years. But if he could earn the money faster at the Ludus Caledonia, he supposed that was worth it.

But he had one question…

"If I commit for seven years, can I bring my wife?" he asked.

"Do ye have a wife?"

"I will when I buy her freedom."

Lor nodded. "Wives live at the Cal. My wife lives there with me."

That settled it. Now that Bane had his most important questions answered, he was ready to move forward.

For Lucia.

"As long as I can make enough money tae buy her freedom, I can commit seven years of my life," he said. "What do I need tae do?"

Luther stood up, followed by Lor. "Come with us," Luther said. "If you have any belongings, go and get them. We will wait for you in the alley behind this tavern."

Bane shook his head. "I only have what you see," he said. "But...but I would like to do something before I go. I'll meet ye in the alley in a few minutes."

Luther and Lor departed the tavern, slipping out through a side door that led to the dark alley where their horses awaited. Meanwhile, Bane went to the tavernkeep as the man used a bucket of water to wash away the vomit from a patron who had imbibed too much of the cheap ale. He tapped the man on the shoulder.

"I need tae get a message tae someone," he said. "Can ye help me?"

The tavernkeep looked at him, empty bucket in hand. "I can find someone for ye," he said. "What's the message?"

"I dunna have anything tae write on."

"Tell me and I'll remember it."

Bane scratched his head thoughtfully. "I need someone tae go tae Meadowbank House," he said. "It's outside the city walls, tae the east, the home of Laird Currie. There's a servant there named Lucia. I need tae get a message tae her without letting her masters know. Whoever ye send needs tae be careful."

The tavernkeep nodded. "I understand. Give me the message."

"She needs tae be told that I've gone tae the Cal. She'll understand."

The tavernkeep held out his hand, and Bane gave the man his last pence. He tucked it into his pocket as Bane headed out into the alley. The tavernkeep intended to find someone to send to Meadowbank, but a fight broke out and a man was killed, and in cleaning up the aftermath, he forgot about his promise.

When he found the pence in his pocket the next day, he couldn't remember what it was for.

PART TWO

THE LUDUS CALEDONIA

CHAPTER TWELVE

BANE HAD A SHARP MIND AND A SHARP SENSE OF DIRECTION, and even though Luther had put a sack over his head to confuse him, he still had a fairly good idea of where he was. He was able to get his bearings before leaving the Sticky Wick, and even with the turns the horses took, he was still marginally oriented.

It had helped, of course, that Lucia had told him that the Ludus Caledonia had been in the hills south of Edinburgh, so when the horses finally came to a halt and Luther removed the sack on his head, he could indeed see that he was in the hills.

The sight was overwhelming.

An enormous castle stood before him, bathed in the colors of the setting sun as the sentinels on the walls lit torches against the coming night. The fanged portcullis lifted and Lor grabbed him by the tunic, pulling him through the gatehouse and following Luther as they headed toward an oddly small keep given the size of the fortress.

Bane couldn't help but feel intimidated.

"How long have ye been here, Lor?" he asked quietly.

Lor's gaze was on the keep. "I've been a trainer for about a year," he said. "But I was at the Cal before that for many months."

"Ye said that ye came here so they could teach ye tae fight so ye could seek vengeance."

"Aye."

"Did ye?"

Lor looked at him then. "Aye."

"Then ye dunna regret yer decision tae come here?"

Lor shook his head. "Luther was right when he said that it could change yer life," he said. "It has changed mine. If ye let it, it'll change yers. But ye must be dedicated, Bane. The Cal must have all of ye, so if ye're serious about committing yerself tae fight, then make sure ye can give everything."

They were nearing the door. "I remember the first time ye came tae the Sticky Wick," Bane said. "Ye were dirty and beaten. I know that look because I have it, too. The look of a man with nothing at all. I'm sorry I dinna make a friend of ye. I suppose we both could have used one."

Lor smiled faintly. "I dunna think I was ready for it," he said. "A man must have a mindset for friendship just like anything else. Make sure yer mindset is learning and obedience from now on. The Cal willna accept anything less."

With that, Luther shoved the door open and Lor pushed Bane in front of him, following Luther into the dim interior that smelled heavily of incense. It was dark inside with the only light coming from a window capturing the last strains of sunset and the blazing fire in the hearth.

A man with flowing silver hair and swathed in pristine white robes sat in a large chair in front of the hearth, glancing up when Luther and Lor entered. He noted his two men but he was particularly interested in the tall, well-built man between them.

He looked Bane over with intense silver eyes.

"Is this the one?" he asked.

Luther nodded. "This is Bane Morgan, my lord."

"Welsh?"

Both Luther and Lor looked at Bane, who realized he was meant to answer. He shook his head.

"Clan Morgan, m'laird."

"A Highlander."

"Aye, m'laird."

The man turned back to his hearth, sipping dark-red wine from a crystal cup. In fact, everything about the room was luxurious, from the furs on the stone floor to the heavy tapestries that covered the walls.

This was a man with money.

"I find that Highlanders can be the fiercest fighters of all," the man finally said. "But they tend to be single-minded. Intelligence is not their gift, although Lor has proven to be an exception to that rule. He's from the Highlands, also."

Bane looked at Lor, who nodded. Bane's focus returned to the man in the fine robes. "I have a good mind, m'laird, and I use it," he said. "I make a decision and I stand by it."

"Why have you sought the Ludus Caledonia?"

"Because I want tae earn money tae buy my lady's freedom."

That seemed to bring the man's interest and he stood up, setting his wine aside. "Who is this lady?"

Bane wasn't honestly sure how much to tell him. Given that Lady Currie came to the Ludus Caledonia to buy lovers, this man probably knew her, if not her modest lady-in-waiting. He seemed to be the one in charge and Bane didn't want to start off on the wrong foot, so he decided to keep Lady Currie to himself.

For now.

"She is the lady I wish tae marry, m'laird," he said quietly. "She is working off her father's debt, and it is my intention tae pay it off and marry her."

The man smiled, though it was without warmth or humor. "A noble enough goal, I suppose," he said. "And you want to make the money here?"

Bane nodded. "I'll fight until I drop, m'laird. I'm strong and I'm fearless. Where I come from, they used tae call me the Highland Defender."

The man cocked a bushy, silver eyebrow. "Used to? They do not call you that any longer?"

"I've not seen them in a few years, so I have no way of knowing."

"Why did you leave?"

"Tae seek money and opportunity, m'laird."

The answer seemed to satisfy the man. He turned back to his

wine. "If Luther and Lor have brought you here, then I assume you are worthy of what we can provide you," he said. "My name is Clegg de Lave and all that you see belongs to me. I am the god, the master, the mother, and the father of everything at the Ludus Caledonia. Do you understand so far?"

"Aye, m'laird."

He gestured to the men standing on either side of him. "And you have met your escorts."

"They introduced themselves, m'laird."

Lor spoke up. "The truth is that Bane and I know of each other, m'laird," he said. "We were both patrons of the Sticky Wick at the same time, though we were not friends."

Clegg nodded. "I see," he said. "Have you told him of the Ludus Caledonia yet?"

Lor shook his head. "That is yer privilege, m'laird."

Clegg went to pour himself more wine without offering it to anyone else. "Luther and Lor are *doctores*, or trainers here at the Ludus Caledonia," he said. "I have modeled my guild after the ancient gladiatorial schools of Rome and it runs quite efficiently. We accept only the most dedicated men and expect strict obedience. Anything less and we shall reduce you in status to a servant and you can work off what you have cost me before you are sent on your way. Resistance to discipline results in severe punishment. Am I making myself clear?"

Bane nodded. "Aye, m'laird."

Clegg sipped on his wine. "This castle is the heart of my complex, the Ludus Caledonia," he said. "That is the term for everything you see—the castle, the village, the arena. The arena is called the Fields of Mars and it is both our training facility and our entertainment field. Wealthy lords pay a good deal of money to gamble on our fights."

"Is that how I will earn money, m'laird?"

Clegg nodded. "In part," he said. "When you are raised in

rank from a *novicius*, or novice, to a *tiro*, which is a professional fighter, you are eligible to win purses. But know this: you are an investment to me. I will invest money into your training and your housing, and in return, you will swear fealty to me and you shall fight for me. The usual duration of the oath is seven years, and I will expect you to hold to that oath. If you cannot wait that long, then you are free to leave now. I will not waste any further time on you."

But Bane shook his head. "I was told of the seven years," he said. "I was also told that I can bring my wife here tae live with me."

"That is true."

"Then I shall buy her freedom and she will come tae live with me while I serve ye," he said. "Mayhap it is strange for a man tae be driven by emotion tae something like this, but until I met Lucia, I was directionless. I had no hope. She has changed that. She has given me the will tae regain what I have lost."

"What have you lost?"

"Myself."

It was an unusual answer, one that had Clegg's interest, but he didn't press. He simply lifted his hand. "Each man has his own motivation," he said. "I will not question it. But understand something else about the Ludus Caledonia. Men come here to be trained so they may secure positions in big armies. Some of the lords who come to watch the bouts do so in order to find strong warriors for their ranks. If a lord is willing to buy out the remainder of your contract, then you shall serve a new master until such time as the contract is finished. Whether or not you wish to continue serving the man after that will be up to you, but you will swear fealty to him if the price is right. Do you understand?"

"I do, m'laird."

"And you have no hesitation?"

"Nay, m'laird. But I have one more question, if ye please."

"Ask."

"Do ye sell the champions tae women for the right price? Tae service them, I mean. Is that part of the training, too?"

Clegg's expression was almost amused. "The Ludus Caledonia follows the Roman customs in every way," he said, lifting his hands. "In ancient times, it was not considered unseemly for a rich patroness to pay for the services of a champion. We continue that tradition. It is simply another way to make money."

"Then ye sell men like…"

Clegg held up a finger, cutting him off. "I do not sell men," he said firmly. "A man has his own free will. If he chooses to accept the money of a patroness, that is his choice. Some women pay extremely well. As much as the fight purses in some cases. But I do take half of the money. Why shouldn't I? Everything at the Cal is to make money, Bane. That is the heart of our existence."

That clarified the situation for Bane. In the back of his mind, he had thought of Lady Currie and other rich women who came to the Ludus Caledonia to satisfy their lusts and was concerned he'd be forced into that situation.

For a brief moment, he had even considered it. It would be a way to make money faster to buy Lucia's freedom. But no sooner had he entertained the thought than he cast it aside. Though he hadn't known Lucia intimately, there was no possibility he would be disloyal to her in that sense. Not even if it meant buying her freedom sooner. He was meant for her and her only, body and soul.

"Thank ye for being honest, m'laird," he said.

"And you are satisfied?"

"I am."

"Then let us delay no longer."

Clegg returned to his table and produced a contract that had been carefully written on parchment. When he handed the quill to Bane, he signed his name. He stood there a moment, staring at the ink, feeling as if he'd just signed his life away. As Clegg sanded the ink, Luther spoke to Bane.

"Now your education begins," he said. "Put your right hand over your chest."

He was making the motion, indicating for Bane to do the same. Once Bane put his hand over his chest, Luther spoke the fateful words.

"Repeat after me," he said. "'I faithfully swear to do all that is commanded of me, all that is required of me, and all that is asked of me.'"

Bane's aptitude for memorizing things had never been good, as the priests who taught him to read and write could profess. Still, he tried.

"'I faithfully swear tae do all that is commanded of me, all that is required of me, and all that is asked of me,'" he said.

"'May I live to both fight and protect my brethren. May God smile upon me and grant me courage so that I may not fail myself or those around me.'"

Bane wasn't sure he could remember the words in order, but he tried. "'May I live tae both fight and protect my brethren. May God smile upon me and grant me courage so that...'"

"'I may not fail myself or those around me.'"

Relieved, he finished the oath. "'I may not fail myself or those around me.'"

When Bane was finished, Clegg spoke softly. "Thus it is spoken," he murmured. "Thus shall it be done. Now you are a *novicius*, Highland Defender. Let us see if you can live up to your name."

"I will try, m'laird."

Clegg's gaze lingered on him. "Remember something, Bane."

"M'laird?"

"The motto of the Ludus Caledonia is *Hominibus Gloria*—'In men, there is honor.' See that you keep it."

"Aye, m'laird."

The oath Bane had taken had been the *Fionnadh Fuil*, or the Blood Oath, of the Ludus Caledonia. With that oath, he had become part of something that was far bigger and far more brutal than he could ever have imagined. He'd come to the place to earn money, but what would happen in the days and months to come would far exceed that hope.

It would define him.

The education for the Highland Defender had begun.

CHAPTER THIRTEEN

IT HAD BEEN OVER A MONTH SINCE LUCIA HAD SEEN BANE.

Not knowing where he was or what he was doing made every day a venture between hope and despair. Sometimes the angst was so bad that she could hardly concentrate, and for what she was doing these days, she needed her concentration.

All of it.

It had been a month of hell.

Tynan had told her about Bane's visit and the message he bore. That gave her some hope that he hadn't abandoned her but was simply off looking for work. Part of their last conversation had revolved around the Ludus Caledonia and the possibility of making money, but she didn't honestly believe he'd go there. Surely, he'd find something else that didn't involve bloody combat.

Whatever he found didn't really matter to her as long as he was a man of his word. He said he'd return for her, and she clung to that belief. As it stood, she wasn't getting any closer to working off the debt.

Quite the opposite.

Since that day that Colly had overwhelmed her in the kitchen and threw her in a locked chamber, only to be released when Lady Currie demanded it, she had been on her best behavior. After her conversation with Laird Currie, she tried doubly hard to behave. She didn't want to jeopardize any chances of finally being released from her servitude.

But she prayed for the day that Bane would return.

If he returned…

The passing weeks had seen more than simply her semi-imprisonment and Bane's disappearance. Lady Currie had taken ill over those weeks and although Lucia hadn't been privy to the details, there were whispers of a miscarriage for Lady Currie. No one really knew for certain, of course, except the physic who tended her and probably Colly, but Lady Currie was in bed for that entire month before she was finally encouraged to rise and take exercise.

If the woman has a son, it will not be the laird's.

That's what Lucia had told Bane.

Perhaps any miscarriage, in that case, had been a blessing.

Winter was in full force and as Lady Currie walked the chambers and stairs of Meadowbank to regain her strength because of the poor weather outside, Lucia remained tucked into a small chamber that was used for sewing and dressing. All she'd done during the month was sew garments for Lady Currie, including the Roman garb she'd requested. It had turned out splendidly, with beautiful embroidery on the hem and neckline in red silk.

Even now, Lucia was working on a pink garment for Lady Currie because her last encounter with Colly had emphasized one thing—no matter what, Lady Currie would always side with Colly, which meant the old woman had the true power at Meadowbank.

Perhaps that wouldn't have mattered so much to Lucia before she met Bane, but now that she had hope for her future, she wanted to remain in one piece, waiting for the day when he would come and take her away from all of this.

Ironic how the man had made her less combative.

"Lucia?"

Shaken from her thoughts, Lucia looked up from the sewing in her hands to see Tynan's mother standing there. When their eyes met, Amy smiled timidly at her.

"Lady Currie wishes tae see ye," she said. Then she lowered her voice. "I do believe she wants tae leave Meadowbank tonight. I heard her speaking tae Colly."

Lucia's brow furrowed. "Leave it?" she repeated. "And go where?"

"The Ludus Caledonia."

Lucia set down the sewing. "That again," she said softly. "I'd hoped she'd forgotten about it. I suppose it was a foolish hope, after all."

Amy nodded as she came into the chamber. "She seems determined tae go back," she said quietly. "Poor Lucia. Forced to escort the woman tae that horrible place."

Lucia felt sorry for herself, too, but she caught the pitiful expression on Amy's face and she smiled, patting the woman on the hand as she stood up. "There is one thing I like about it."

"What?"

"Colly willna come."

Both she and Amy chuckled as they left the tiny chamber and headed into the small corridor that would take them into Lady Currie's large chamber. Lucia still had her sewing in her hand because she wanted to show Lady Currie that she had been working hard like a good servant would.

She didn't want to give the woman any cause to doubt her, no matter what Colly said.

Lady Currie's chamber smelled of fresh rushes and smoke as she entered. Servants were spreading the fresh rushes they'd collected all over the floor, giving the air that sharp scent of pine.

In fact, Lady Currie was sitting up in a lovely robe, looking healthier than she had in weeks. When she saw Lucia enter with the pink confection in her hands, she immediately perked up.

"What have you brought me, Lucia?" she demanded. "Hurry, bring it to me!"

Lucia hurried it over to her, completely ignoring Colly, who was standing at a nearby table and mixing something in wine. Lucia presented Lady Currie with the pink silk, and the woman gasped in delight.

"How divine!" she said. "For me?"

Lucia smiled, holding it up so the woman could get the full

view of it. "'Tis a surprise, m'lady," she said. "But I'm nearly finished with it so ye can wear it tonight if ye'd like. It's a sleeping gown."

Lady Currie was beside herself with delight. "It's beautiful," she said. "But where did you get the fabric?"

Lucia let the woman take it from her so she could inspect it. "When I negotiated with the merchant for the other fabric I bought for ye, I had him include the pink because I knew ye'd like it," she said. "Are ye pleased, m'lady?"

Lady Currie nodded enthusiastically. "Ever so much," she said. Then she held it up to Colly. "Did you see, Colly? See what Lucia has made for me."

Colly had the wine in her hand as she made her way over to Lady Currie. Lucia dared to look at her at that point, seeing that she was eyeing the garment with disdain.

"Ye will catch a chill in it," she said. "It isna warm enough for ye."

Lady Currie's enthusiasm was not dampened. "It will be warm enough," she said. "It's so beautiful. That was very thoughtful of you, Lucia. Would you not say so, Colly?"

Colly looked at Lucia with the same contempt she always did. "She's simply trying tae make up for the terrible things she's done."

Lady Currie frowned. "That is not very nice of you, Colly. You must learn to be more forgiving."

Colly didn't say anything as she handed the wine to Lady Currie. Lucia watched the old woman, visions of throwing that wine on the pink gown filling her head. But the gown remained unscathed as Lady Currie took the wine and drained half the cup almost immediately.

"Well done, Lucia," she said. "I am eager to wear the gown tonight after we return from the Ludus Caledonia. I want you to come with me."

Lucia nodded. "Aye, m'lady."

"You will wear the amber silk, and I shall wear the glorious Roman costume you made for me." She turned to Amy, who was standing behind Lucia. "Amy, I want you to do my hair in the Roman fashion. Lots of braids and curls. I want to look like a queen tonight. I am sure those at the Cal are wondering what has become of me."

The thought of going to the Ludus Caledonia had Lady Currie moving faster than she'd moved in a month. She was calling for a bath and sending her servants into a frenzy. Lucia took the pink gown and headed back to the little sewing room to put the finishing touches on it so Lady Currie could wear it later that night.

All the while, however, a singular thought was rolling through her head.

The Ludus Caledonia.

Lucia realized that she wasn't entirely resistant to going because thoughts of the place brought about thoughts of Bane. She was quite eager to see if he had, in fact, gone to the Ludus Caledonia. Perhaps he would be there and she would have a chance to see him, to know he was all right. Lady Currie always looked over the new recruits, and if he was there, he was probably among them.

But that also brought another thought to mind.

Lady Currie liked her pick of fine, young men and Bane would stand out in a crowd. He was wildly handsome. If she wanted to purchase Bane's services, the money would be great. Lucia had never seen a warrior turn down Lady Currie, and she assumed that the men weren't given any choice.

What if she chose Bane?

The horror of that thought was almost more than she could bear.

CHAPTER FOURTEEN

IT WAS A BLEAK, FROSTED WINTER MORNING THAT BANE FOUND himself fighting in.

If one could call it fighting. It was fighting like he'd never done in his life.

Repetitive exercises took the instinct out of a battle. Being expected to take a blow and not defend oneself had him frustrated. For the fighting Bane had done his entire life, he'd depended on an innate sense of self-preservation coupled with moves his father had taught him. He could use a short sword and a mace better than most, but all he was given for training at the Ludus Caledonia was a *gladius*, a small but sturdy wooden sword.

He hated the damned thing.

His forty-three days at "the Cal" had been nothing like he'd expected. He was back to the bearded, unhappy man he'd been during his days in Edinburgh. For the first week, the *novicius* did nothing but run up and down the hills surrounding the Ludus Caledonia. That had transitioned into running with the *gladius* and a heavy wooden shield before they were finally taken into the arena to begin training with other training groups.

Bane was in Lor's troop, and Lor was assisted by a big Englishman named Galan. One of the first exercises Lor and Galan had them do was fighting against a *palus*, or a post. Bane thought it was all ridiculously stupid, but he went along with it, much to Lor's amusement. Lor seemed to know exactly what Bane was thinking but he never chastised him. He encouraged him and spoke to him of tactics and blind spots, things Bane already knew about. At least, he knew most of it. There were a few things Lor taught him that he'd never heard of before. Lor may not have chastised him for his know-it-all attitude, but a big brute with piercing blue eyes did.

Axel was his name.

Axel von Rossau was from Saxony and he'd been Clegg's *ianista*, or manager, for many years. Axel was tough but fair, at least when he was feeling particularly benevolent, but Bane's frustration at the slow pace of the training had him paying more attention to Bane than most of the other recruits.

As Bane found out, that wasn't a good thing.

On this icy morning, the four *novicius* troops were in the arena and Bane was coming to wonder why. There weren't normally more than two troops in the arena at any one time, and as he soon found out, they'd all been gathered for a purpose.

They were going to use what they had learned—against each other.

It was an exercise of sorts, to pit men from different troops against one another to see what they'd learned. Each troop was standing in a corner of the arena, watching the bouts that were going on in the middle. Four, six men at a time went at it. All men were eager fighters, but some were better than others. Rumor had it that there were fights that night and the trainers were looking to see if there were any *novicius* who might be ready to fight in a preliminary bout.

Then it became Bane's turn.

But he wasn't pitted against any *novicius*. For him, Axel brought out a warrior who had been with the Ludus Caledonia for a few years. The man was a *tertiarius*, a fighter at the top of the game. These were men who fought for money and prestige, hoping a great lord would offer them a position.

They were ruthless.

Bane didn't know the man, but he'd seen him around the complex. As Axel called forth the fighters, including Bane, Lor quickly took him aside.

"The man ye're tae fight against is the one they call the Eagle," he said. "He's been part of the fight guild for years, but he's been at one of Clegg's other guilds, the Ludus Hadrian. We havena seen him at the Cal until recently."

Bane glanced at his opponent. "He's short."

Lor shook his head. "Dunna let his stature fool ye," he said. "He's shorter than ye are, but he packs a punch. Axel is pairing the two of ye because he thinks yer pride will prevent ye from making a truly great fighter."

Bane looked at him curiously. "What do ye mean?"

"Because ye believe training is beneath ye," Lor said. "We've all seen it. That's why Axel wants tae pair ye with the Eagle—so he can cut ye down tae size. Underestimating him is the worst thing ye can do. They call him the Eagle for a reason. He'll come at ye like a bird of prey, and it'll be over before ye realize what happened. He likes tae use leverage against his opponents, so watch out for him getting too close tae ye. He'll destroy ye if he can."

Bane shook his head confidently. "He'll not destroy me."

Lor could hear the man's pride and he wanted to shake him. "Listen tae me," he said, hazard in his tone. "I had pride when I came tae the Cal, too, and it nearly got me killed. Know when a man is trying tae help ye, Bane. There's a reason why they call Magnus Stewart 'the Eagle.'"

Bane simply nodded to appease Lor, but he had no intention of showing any caution in the face of a man who was shorter than he was. Bane was quite tall, about four inches over six feet, and this man was probably three or four inches shorter.

Enough that Bane considered him inferior.

Axel was motioning to him and he moved away from Lor, taking his wooden *gladius* and his shield with him.

He was going to clip the Eagle's wings and be done with it.

As Bane approached, he looked over his opponent from head to toe. The man was wearing leather breeches, boots, and nothing more. Absolutely nothing more, and given the icy winter conditions, it was ludicrous. He was quite muscular, however, a fine specimen of male form, but Bane didn't give that any consideration. So what if he had muscles; Bane had them, too.

And he intended to use them.

So far, the fights that morning had involved groups, but as Bane came to a halt several feet away from his opponent, Axel waved off the other combatants who were gathering to fight. It was clear that this row was going to be a two-man event. He stepped between the pair, motioning them to move closer to one another, which they did so reluctantly.

"Magnus," he said in his heavy Germanic accent, "meet the Highland Defender. At least, that is what he told us he used to be called. Mayhap you can put that name to the test."

Magnus grinned, but without humor. "Gladly."

Bane sensed a distinct challenge and it raised his hackles. "Eagles dunna live very long," he said, running his finger along the edge of his dull wooden sword. "And they tend to eat the leavings of other animals. They're scavengers."

Axel had to bite off a guffaw as he stepped back from the pair. Magnus's smile turned genuine. "Indeed, they are," he said. "And they pick the bones of their enemies."

"Of which, I am sure, they have many."

"Mayhap they do. But eagles always come out on top. Shall we?"

"At yer pleasure."

When it became clear that the giant ego was about to go up against the immovable pride, Axel spoke before the battle could commence. "Since these are friendly bouts, no intentionally cutting a man down or drawing blood," he said pointedly. "Avoid injuring each other if you can. First man who falls to the ground is the loser."

The words weren't completely out of Axel's mouth before

Magnus was flying at Bane. Literally. Bane saw legs going up in the air, and he took a powerful kick to the head before he could raise his arms to defend himself.

The lights went out.

⚭ ⚭ ⚭

Bane wasn't quite sure how long he'd been staring at the stone ceiling.

In fact, he wasn't even sure how he got here.

Suddenly, he sat bolt upright, realizing he was in the holding area that was next to the arena. It was a massive chamber cut into the side of the hill, and it was where the competitors gathered before the fights, cool caverns that reeked of smoke and sweaty bodies. But the swift motion of sitting up quickly had the world rocking and someone was pulling him back down to the bench he was lying on.

"Lie back," a woman said. "Ye've got a nasty lump on yer head, so lie still."

Looking up, he saw a beautiful woman with red curls tied at the nape of her neck and skin like cream. She was holding a cold compress against his head.

He blinked.

"What happened?"

The woman lifted the compress and wrung it out in a bowl. "Ye tangled with the Eagle," she said. "Do ye not remember?"

He thought a moment before realization dawned. "Christ," he muttered. "I remember…something. What did he do?"

"He kicked ye in the head."

Bane thought on that for a moment. Then he started to laugh, ironic and embarrassed laughter when he realized he'd been made a fool of. All of that confidence he'd displayed had cost him. A hand went up, feeling the bump on the side of his head.

He'd never felt so stupid in his entire life.

"Lor warned me," he said. "I suppose I should have listened tae him."

"Aye, ye should have," the woman said. "My husband is usually right about such things."

"Ye're Lor's wife?"

"My name is Isabail."

In all the weeks he'd been here, he'd never met his trainer's wife. She never came around the men, which was probably wise considering how pretty she was. Bane sighed heavily, wincing when she put the cold compress back on.

"Well," he said, "'tis a hard lesson learned. I should have paid closer attention."

"Tae who? My husband or the Eagle?"

"Both."

Isabail fought off a smile. "If it's any consolation, Magnus was punished for doing what he did."

He looked at her curiously. "He was?"

"Aye," she said. "From what I understand, he dinna wait for Axel tae signal the beginning of the fight. He went off on his own before anyone told him tae and caught ye off guard."

Bane lay there a moment longer, trying to remember the details of what had happened and being unable to. He remembered listening to the big Saxon speak on the rules of the engagement but nothing after that.

The Eagle had a hard strike.

"How long have I been unconscious?" he asked.

"Not too long," she replied. "Lor asked me tae tend ye while he's gone, but he needs tae return soon because I must return tae my bairn."

"Ye have a child here? At the Cal?"

She nodded. "Niko," she said. "Has Lor not told ye about his son?"

Bane sat up slowly, politely handing the compress back to Isabail. "Nay," he said. "We've not spoken of much other than having tae do with training, though we did know of each other before all of this."

"Where?"

"In Edinburgh."

Isabail nodded but was prevented from replying further when Lor entered the area. When he saw that Bane was sitting up, he made his way over to the man, looking him over. He held up a hand with two fingers raised.

"How many fingers am I holding up?" he asked.

"Two," Bane mumbled. "One for the Eagle's victory and the other for my stupidity."

Lor grinned. "At least ye've not lost yer humor," he said. Then he looked to his wife. "Thank ye for tending him, love. I'll take over."

Isabail stood up, handing the compress over to her husband. "Next time, warn him that Magnus doesna like tae follow rules, either," she said. Her gaze moved to Bane. "I hope I dunna see ye again with a bump on yer head."

"I hope not, either," Bane said. "And ye have my thanks, Lady Careston."

As she headed out of the chamber, Lor handed the cold, wet sponge back to Bane. "Keep it on the lump," he said. "The Eagle kicked ye hard."

Bane raised the soggy compress to his head. "Go ahead and say it," he said. "Ye warned me but I dinna listen."

Lor sat down on the bench, eyeing Bane. "It sounds as if I dunna need tae say it," he said. "But the next time I tell ye something, it would be wise for ye tae listen. I'm not speaking tae hear the sound of my own voice."

"I know," Bane said, feeling ashamed. "In fact, I dunna think I've listened tae ye much since I came here."

Lor fought off a grin. "That happens sometimes," he said. "Especially with men who have fought before. They think they know everything."

Bane grunted. "I thought I did," he said. Then he looked at Lor. "I'll be honest with ye. Ye told me ye never had any battle experience before ye came tae the Ludus Caledonia. I've had years of battle experience, of facing real battles, so it's not been easy for me tae take orders or advice from ye."

Lor leaned back on the bench. "I realize that," he said. "Ye dunna want tae take commands from a man who's never faced a battle."

Bane was looking at his feet. "'Tis true," he said. "What do ye know about combat? I mean when a man's life is at stake. Mayhap ye're a great trainer of men, but a fighter?"

"Do ye want me tae fight ye and show ye what I'm capable of?"

"Dunna."

The voice came from the entry to the chamber, and they both looked over to see Isabail still standing there. She'd made it out into the yard beyond the chamber but no further because something in their conversation brought her back.

Her gaze was intense as she returned to Bane and her husband. "Is that what it'll take tae convince ye that my husband knows what he's talking about?" she asked Bane. "A fight? Because I can tell ye from experience that he's a great warrior. Mayhap he's never faced an actual battle, but he's had plenty of fights on his own, fights he has won decisively. I was raised in the Highlands, Bane. I was raised with a father and two brothers, and I held a pike in my hand before I could walk. I've had more battle experience than my husband, but battle experience doesna always make a great warrior. I've seen Lor fight a man twice his size and win using his wits alone. Dunna challenge my husband, Bane. Ye would be very sorry."

Bane took another look at Isabail, tall and long-legged and beautiful. "Ye were a warrior?"

She nodded. "I led the lads of our village in many a skirmish, but when I married Lor, I gave that up. Where he goes, I go, and I wouldna say that if he were an ordinary man. What he has is something all men wish they had, so ye'll not discount him. He's a man of great wisdom."

Lor reached up, taking her hand and giving it a squeeze to quiet her. It was clear that she was fiercely protective over him. But Bane met her gaze before silently nodding, just once, to acknowledge her words. Whether or not he agreed with them was another matter, but he did her the respect of not arguing with her. Isabail turned for the chamber door once more and was nearly through it when she heard Bane's voice again.

"Ye should know I have a history of not listening," he said. "I do what my instincts tell me tae."

Isabail paused by the door. "Are yer instincts always correct?"

He looked at her before shaking his head. "Nay," he said. "They told me tae disobey my father a couple of years ago when the English were waging war on the border, when Berwick was sacked. I thought I had the opportunity tae ambush English knights, and as it turned out, they were waiting tae ambush the Scots. I took thirty men with me. Six survived. That was the last time I disobeyed my da, and now…now I'm here, trying tae find that warrior I lost. I was called the Highland Defender once. My biggest fear is that he's gone and I'll never find him again."

Isabail came back into the room. "Is that why ye came tae the Cal?"

He lifted his big shoulders. "Partly," he said. "But I mostly came tae earn money tae buy my lady's freedom. She's a servant in a fine house, working off the debt of her father. If I can pay off the debt, we'll be free tae marry."

Isabail smiled, coming to sit on the bench next to Lor. "Ye came here for a woman?" she said. "That's very sweet. What's her name?"

"Lucia."

"That's a pretty name."

"She's a beautiful lass. I...havena known her very long, but that doesna matter. What we have is what all men hope for. I miss her a great deal."

Isabail looked at Lor before replying. "Bane," she said, "I'm going tae say something tae ye, so I hope ye'll listen because I mean tae help ye. Ye made it tae the Cal, which is a great accomplishment, but if ye dunna listen tae Lor and the other trainers, ye'll fail and ye'll never make any money tae help yer lady. Getting kicked in the head by the Eagle is only the beginning."

Bane looked at her, the light in his eyes suggesting he knew that now. He knew his arrogance was only going to cost him. "'Tis difficult tae listen when ye've always been the one giving the orders."

"Not anymore," Isabail said firmly. "Ye've been in many a battle and I understand that, but fighting in battle is different from what ye do here at the Cal. If ye want tae make money, then ye must listen and stop thinking ye know everything."

"She's right," Lor spoke up. "I've been watching ye for several weeks now, Bane. Ye think the exercises we make ye do are beneath ye, but ye do them because ye must. Still, I've noticed that even though ye dunna want tae do them, ye put yer entire effort intae them. Ye give them everything ye have, and that tells me that ye're a man of character. But there's also a restlessness about ye. That's something that will cause ye trouble here."

Bane took a deep breath. He was being chastised, however gently, and he knew he deserved it.

What they said made sense.

"I know," he said. "I suppose my bout with the Eagle made me realize that. Lor, ye've been patient with me and ye're a good man for it. Isabail, I thank ye for yer honesty. Lor's a fortunate man tae have a wife like ye."

Isabail grinned. "I tell him that every day," she said, standing up yet again and heading for the door. "I'd like tae hear more about Lucia when my husband isna putting ye through yer paces. We'll talk again, Bane. If ye take our advice, ye'll be here a long time and ye'll earn yer money."

Bane snorted softly. "I hope so," he said. "I intend tae buy Lucia's freedom as soon as I can and bring her here tae live. I'd be grateful if ye'd be a friend tae her."

"I would like that."

Isabail left the chamber, this time for good, heading out into the waning day. Lor's gaze was on the door as if he could still see her there, the expression on his face suggesting his great love for her.

But he pulled his gaze away, turning to look at Bane, who was sitting there with his head hung. Lor felt a good deal of pity for the stubborn Scotsman, mostly because he had been nearly the same when he'd first come to the Ludus Caledonia.

Sometimes, it was difficult for a man to accept help even when he wanted it.

"Let me speak with Axel and see if he'll let ye fight tonight," he said. "We have a few novice bouts. I think the Eagle cheated ye out of a chance tae prove yer worth."

Bane looked at him, surprised. "Ye'd do that?"

"I would, but dunna fail me. If ye do, it'll be the last time I do ye a favor."

Bane nodded, understanding that he and Lor were at some kind of precipice. Bane's pride had caused him to fail before and he knew it, so he wasn't about to let it get in the way this time. He very much wanted to prove that he was capable of fighting for money, and this was the exact opportunity he'd been looking for.

"I swear tae ye that I willna fail ye. Not this time."

Lor believed him.

CHAPTER FIFTEEN

IT WAS A FULL SCHEDULE AT THE LUDUS CALEDONIA.

That's what Lady Currie was told as soon as they arrived at the torchlit venue. Hundreds of torches lined Caelian Hill, the warrior village to the south, and the Fields of Mars. As Lady Currie's fine carriage rolled in, one of the guides at the Ludus Caledonia explained that there were four preliminary *novicius* bouts before the main events took place.

"Did you hear, Lucia?" Lady Currie said excitedly. "There will be many fights tonight. New men to see!"

If Lucia hadn't known better, she'd swear that Lady Currie was drooling at the prospect. More than a month away from her favorite entertainment had the woman twitching with glee, and all of the wine she'd imbibed from her personal flask on the ride from Meadowbank had her drunk.

It made for a loud and dramatic combination.

On this night, Lucia and Amy, Tynan's mother, were the only maids permitted to accompany Lady Currie to the Ludus Caledonia for her triumphant return. She was wearing the exquisite Roman-style garment that Lucia had made for her, her hair done up in curls and braids that emulated the hairstyle from the Roman vase that Lucia had taken inspiration from for the garment. Amy had copied it down to the last curl.

The carriage pulled into an area north of the warriors' village where other carriages and horses were parked and there were men to help them disembark. Lady Currie exited first, followed by Amy in a red dress that had been loaned to her by Lady Currie, and then Lucia in an amber silk that Lady Currie had given her last year. It was faded but still serviceable but, most important, it didn't outshine Lady Currie.

That was critical.

There was great excitement in the air as the patrons flocked to the arena for a good seat. Lucia and Amy followed Lady Currie as she charged toward the Fields of Mars, determined to sit down in the very first row so she could observe the fighters close up. That was her usual position for the best view.

"Lucia," Lady Currie said to her as they walked briskly toward the arena. "I am hungry, so find the men selling food and hot wine. I want some before the battles begin."

That was Lucia's usual job. She usually ran all over the place, looking for the food vendors, the men who sold hot wine, and hunted down the officials when Lady Currie found a warrior she wanted a closer look at. At the moment, Lady Currie was heading over to the staging area next to the arena that was in full view of the spectators.

It was where she would look over the stock.

As Lady Currie and Amy headed over to the staging area, Lucia went on the hunt for the food vendors, but she was also hunting for someone else.

Bane.

Since their last conversation had been about the Ludus Caledonia, she found herself hoping that he was here. She wasn't sure if she believed it, but there were great crowds and new recruits, so it was a very real possibility that he might be among them.

She hoped to find out.

Spectators were pressed up against the iron fence that lined the top of the staging area, which was several feet below. Lady Currie was at one corner of it, standing with an official from the Ludus Caledonia, who was pointing out to her the men below. Undoubtedly pointing out newcomers.

With Lady Currie occupied for the moment and so many people gathering around, Lucia dared to push through the crowd around the fence so she could peek down into the yard below.

It was full of men.

In fact, it was quite full of men preparing for the bouts. She pressed her face between the bars, searching for Bane's familiar form. She didn't see him right away, which discouraged her, but she told herself that simply because he wasn't below didn't mean he wasn't at the Ludus Caledonia. It just meant he wasn't fighting.

She had to hold firm to that thought.

Reluctantly, she pulled away from the iron fence and went on the hunt for the food vendors. The Ludus Caledonia was more crowded than usual, with great groups of men and even women moving about. There was a warriors' village off to the southwest and she could see the small cottages, all lined up. Tendrils of smoke snaked into the air from the cooking fires.

It was possible that Bane was in the warrior village, but she knew it wouldn't be safe for her to walk around and look for him. She didn't want to be mistaken for a harlot.

Therefore, she headed to the area where the food vendors were. Tables were lined up and she found a vendor selling meatballs made from ground meat and ginger and boiled in beef broth. They were then seared over an open flame and placed on a stick. Lucia purchased two of those for Lady Currie. There were also little pork pies, some other kind of skewered meat that looked rather suspicious, and pies that were made from brains and eggs, which she avoided since Lady Currie wasn't fond of organ meat.

With her bounty of meatballs and pork pies, she found the hot wine vendor and purchased a bladder of the stuff. With her hands full, she began to make her way back toward the Fields of Mars, but her trek was interrupted as some of the men from the warrior village were brought out to the arena.

Pausing with hot food in her hands wasn't ideal, but Lucia had to wait until the men passed before she could continue. The pork pies were seriously burning her hands and she shifted them, impatiently waiting for the men to pass. But the moment she looked up from the pies in her hands, she recognized one of the men as he walked on the far end of the group.

He was bearded and shaggy, but there was no mistaking him. She'd seen him in that state once before, in a dirty alleyway in Edinburgh. He walked with the grace of a stalking cat, power in his movements, grace in his limbs.

Her heart lurched.

"*Bane!*"

He heard her. Bane had been looking ahead, not paying attention to the spectators, but the sound of a familiar voice had him urgently scanning the crowd. The moment he spied Lucia, his eyes widened with shock. Shoving men out of the way, he rushed to her but a sharp word from Galan, the English trainer, stopped him.

"Move along, Morgan," Galan boomed. "Straight ahead."

Bane couldn't come any closer to her, but the expression on his face told Lucia he was very close to disobeying the command. He was as surprised as she was. Therefore, she started to walk on the fringe of the group of men, holding her food and wine, tears stinging her eyes as Bane, too, began to walk at a proper distance alongside her. Moving forward, each one trying to pretend that there was no great reunion to be had.

It was almost too much to bear.

"Ye're here," Lucia said, her voice hoarse with emotion. "Ye're really here!"

Bane nodded. "My angel," he muttered with satisfaction. "I have been waiting for ye. I knew ye'd come at some point. Ye're here with Lady Currie?"

She nodded, so eagerly that her hair came undone from its braid. "Aye," she said. "She has been ill. It's our first visit in over a month."

Bane was trying very hard not to move closer to her, fearful he would get in trouble if he did. But, God, he wanted to reach out and grab her.

"Did ye receive my message?" he asked as quietly as he could.

"From Tynan? He told me."

Bane shook his head. "I paid the man at the Sticky Wick tae send someone tae tell ye that I'd gone tae the Cal. No one told ye?"

"Nay."

Bane couldn't hide his exasperation. "I'm sorry," he said. "I paid the man tae get a message tae ye. Ye must have thought I'd run off and left ye."

She smiled faintly, shaking her head. "Nay," she said softly. "I had faith. I'd hoped ye were here. It was the very last thing we spoke of."

"It was something I was serious about," he said. He paused a moment, looking her over as much as he dared. "God, I've missed ye. Ye have no idea how much I've missed ye."

"And I've missed ye," she said fervently. "So very much."

They were nearing the gates that led down to the staging area and Bane glanced up ahead, almost in a panic when he realized his time with her would soon be cut short. "Are ye well?" he asked. "Tynan told me that Colly—"

She cut him off, knowing what he was going to say. "I am very well," she said quickly. "Please dunna worry. I'm restricted tae the house and all I do is sew. Truly, I'm fine. Ye needna worry at all."

The group of *novicius* had come to a halt while the big iron gates were opened. Knowing their time was at an end, Bane dared to move closer to her.

"I have a cottage at the end of the warrior village," he murmured. "If ye can find me when this is over…I'll look for ye. If not, I'll see ye the next time ye come. And…Lucia?"

"Aye?"

"I've never said this before tae anyone, but I've been thinking about it and ye need tae know that I…"

"Move on, Morgan," Galan said as he came up, putting himself between the pair. "Move along. No fraternizing with the spectators unless they pay for it."

Lucia stood there, crestfallen, as Bane was pushed along by a big brute who spoke like a proper Sassenach. Before Bane was herded through the gate, he mouthed words to her over the heads of the others.

I love ye.

At least, that's what Lucia thought he said. She couldn't be sure, but it certainly looked like it to her. Perhaps it was wishful thinking.

But she didn't think so.

She stood there a moment as Bane disappeared through the gate, feeling tremendous joy and tremendous sadness. She was walking on air and felt like crumpling in tears, all at the same time.

He loved her.

But the Ludus Caledonia had him.

Taking a deep breath to steady her composure, she headed back into the crowd, on the hunt for Lady Currie.

⚶ ⚶ ⚶

Clouds rolled in before the bouts could begin, and by the time they started, a dusting of snow was beginning to fall.

Since the Ludus Caledonia ran their gambling entertainment all year round, they weren't worried about a light snowfall. The games went on, rain or shine. In fact, much of the snow was melting as soon as it hit the ground, which made for slippery conditions for the men in the arena.

The games began with an announcement and the roar of the crowd. It was a bloodthirsty lot who thrived on the thrill of one man injuring another and the sport of an excellent conquest. The cheering was going on all around Lucia as she sat with Lady Currie and Amy in the very first row of the arena, off to the left side where men entered from the staging area.

That gave Lady Currie a firsthand look at all of the men coming into the arena and she had her pick. She didn't cheer when they entered but watched with the intensity of a hunter spying prey.

She was also intensely jealous of the other women who had come for the exact same purpose. There was a sense of urgency about her, to get to the most handsome men first, so she made sure to sit right by the entrance to the arena so she could see them first.

The fights began.

The initial bout was a disappointment because neither man was handsome. As Lady Currie commented, they both looked like old goats. One was more advanced than the other and he ended up breaking the arm of his opponent. The fight was over quickly.

The second bout saw a man who was a potential prospect. He was tall, sinewy, and blond, and she eyed him with great interest as he fought bravely against a man who was trying to take out his legs. The blond man deftly avoided his opponent's clumsy attempts and finally ended up putting the man in a choke hold and causing him to faint. Once the opponent fell to the ground, the fight was over, but Lady Currie was still looking at the blond warrior.

"What's his name?" she asked Lucia.

Lucia leaned in to her. "I believe they called him Warenne, m'lady."

"Warenne," Lady Currie repeated slowly. "Very nice. We must remember him."

Lucia nodded, making a mental note. Often, Lady Currie had four or five men she wanted to look over, so Lucia was responsible for helping her remember exactly whom she wanted to see. As Lady Currie muttered something to Amy, several servants ran onto the arena floor and raked up the dirt, smoothing it over for the next bout.

Lucia was looking at the crowd and at a mother and two daughters who always came to the Ludus Caledonia to pick over the men just as Lady Currie did. They were always richly dressed, with lots of jewels, and they came with guards.

But they were also unattractive and heavily rouged. At least Lady Currie was pretty. One of the daughters caught sight of Lucia looking at them, and she stuck her tongue out belligerently. Since Lucia wasn't going to back down from a painted moppet, she stuck her tongue out at her, too. They were engaging in the mutual exchange of silent insults when the next two combatants were brought out.

The roar of the crowd distracted Lucia. She turned with disinterest to the field only to see Bane emerge with another man.

Her heart immediately went into her throat.

My God, she thought. *He's fighting!*

Bane had a wooden shield and a sword of shiny steel, and he moved out into the arena, his gaze moving out over the top of the lists. Lucia was certain he was looking for her but she didn't want to do anything that might catch his attention. Somehow, she didn't think it would go well for her if he acknowledged her, so she prayed he had sense enough to realize that. She'd told him before that Lady Currie was jealous, and she had no idea what her lady would think if she knew that Lucia knew one of the men on the arena floor.

More than knew him.

Loved him.

Aye, she could admit it. She wasn't sure when she'd started loving him, but she knew she did. It seemed as if she always had. He was everything she never thought she would have and here he was, serving in a fight guild to make enough money to pay off her father's debt.

He was doing it for her.

"Look at him, Lucia," Lady Currie said, interrupting her thoughts. She was pointing at Bane. "I've not seen him here before. He must be new."

Lucia's heart sank. She sighed faintly, feeling the sickening certainty that her mistress had spied Bane. Of course the woman would have; he was tall and strong and handsome. Why wouldn't she notice him?

It was Lucia's greatest fear realized.

"He...he must be new, m'lady," she said carefully. "I've not seen him here before, either."

It was the truth. Lady Currie's gaze followed Bane as he moved, a lascivious cast in her eyes.

"Oh, he's quite tasty," she said. "What is his name? Did they say?"

Lucia shook her head. She also wanted to wring Lady Currie's neck. "Nay, m'lady," she said, feeling the powerful strains of jealousy herself. "They've not announced him. Look at his opponent. He is very nice, too."

Lady Currie looked to the man Lucia was indicating. He was short but very muscular, built spectacularly. In spite of the icy weather, he was wearing little more than breeches and boots, making his build all the more obvious.

"He *is* nice," she agreed. "Both of them are. I want to know their names, Lucia. Listen closely."

Before Lucia could respond, the big Saxon who usually announced the fights came forth, shouting above the buzz of the crowd and announcing men known as the Eagle and the Highland Defender.

The crowd roared.

As soon as the Saxon stepped away, the fight began.

The shorter, muscular man went on the attack right away, and it was all Lucia could do not to cover her eyes. Swords were flying faster than she could imagine, the dull thud of metal against the shields as Bane and the man known as the Eagle went after each other with a vengeance.

It was brutal from the beginning.

Though Lucia wanted to look away, she couldn't. Morbid fascination had her watching every move Bane made. She could see in an instant that his history as a warrior was true; he knew exactly what he was doing. His moves were intuitive. He was fast, he was strong, and he was sure-footed, even in the mud that the light snow had created.

Once, he slid as he went on the attack and ended up on his knees, but it was enough to undercut his opponent, who took a shield to the jaw that sent him reeling. Lucia almost cheered but caught herself before she could expose her excitement.

But watching the fight, she'd never been prouder or more excited about anything.

Bane was truly a warrior to watch.

"Look at him, Lucia," Lady Currie said, breaking into her thoughts. "The big warrior, I mean. Look at the way he moves. Such power."

Lucia found herself struggling again. "Aye, m'lady."

"I must know his name."

"Shall I go and ask, m'lady?"

Lady Currie shook her head. "Not yet," she said. "I suppose the other warrior is very fine, too, but something about the taller one…"

She trailed off and Lucia dared to look at her. It was a mistake; the woman was virtually licking her lips with glee. Lucia looked away quickly before she said something she would regret.

The fight lasted longer than most fights did, even the professional bouts. Bane and his opponent slashed away at each other for quite some time until his opponent lost his shield or, more correctly, threw his shield. It flew up at Bane's face, and as he ducked to miss being hit, his opponent slashed him with his sword. The blade cut along the left side of Bane's torso, immediately drawing blood.

The crowd screamed with glee.

Bane didn't let the blow go unanswered. Using his shield, he managed to hit his opponent in the head, causing the man to falter.

As he went down, Bane came down on him, but his opponent managed to get his sword up, pointing it right at Bane's throat. Had Bane not stopped when he had, he would have impaled himself on the upturned blade. Realizing he was in a precarious position, he had no choice but to drop his weapon and lift his hands.

The crowd roared.

Clearly surrendering, Bane backed off, but as he did, his opponent suddenly leapt to his feet and threw a knee into the side of Bane's head. The blow sent him face-first into the mud.

The crowd erupted in a chorus, making sure their disgust with the illegal move was known. At this point, men rushed the field, pulling Bane out of the mud so he wouldn't suffocate as the big Saxon grabbed Bane's opponent by the back of the neck and forcibly removed him from the arena. Lucia watched in horror as Bane was dragged half-conscious from the arena. Beside her, Lady Currie bolted to her feet.

"Hurry," she said, pushing at Lucia. "Find an official and ask him about the one who was injured. And the blond from the first bout, too."

Lucia was sick to her stomach, but she complied. With Lady Currie behind her, pushing her, they climbed the steps to the top of the arena and headed over to the iron fence that overlooked the staging ground.

Lucia was particularly concerned with Bane and how badly he was injured, and Lady Currie's lust for the man threatened to undo her completely. She was so upset over it that by the time they reached the staging ground, she was trembling. She was also slowing down, which caused Lady Currie to rush around her and head straight to one of the guards from the Ludus Caledonia who was guarding the gate.

He knew her on sight.

"Lady Currie," the man with the heavy French accent said. "We have not seen you here for some time. How may I be of service?"

Lady Currie smiled prettily. "Where is Sir Clegg?" she asked. "I wish to speak with him."

The man seemed to know what she wanted, so he unlocked the gate and ushered her and Lucia inside. Since Lady Currie had been here so many times, she knew exactly where to go. Lucia followed her along a path that was laid with tile, a path that would lead them directly to the private viewing box of Sir Clegg de Lave.

From this lavish and private box overlooking both the staging ground and the arena beyond, the owner of the Ludus Caledonia could watch everything. It was a structure built on the edge of the gully that contained the Fields of Mars, one that had big arches instead of walls so there was a great view from all angles.

In the winter, however, those arches were fitted with shutters and curtains that were now closed up against the gently falling snow except for two of them, directly overlooking the staging area and the arena.

An enormous fire roared in the hearth near lavish couches and a table with fine wine decanters and a spread of delicacies. A man with flowing silver hair was standing in one of the open arches, heavily wrapped against the cold. When he noticed Lady Currie, he came away from the arch.

"Ah," he said pleasantly. "Lady Currie. It is always a pleasure to see you."

Lady Currie smiled brightly. "And you, Sir Clegg," she said. "I was wondering if I might ask a question about a couple of your new novices."

Clegg nodded, sensing money to be made. He always made a great deal of money from Lady Currie when it came to his fine, young warriors and this was, after all, a business.

"Of course," he said. "Come and sit with me. Let us drink warmed wine and speak about those men you are interested in."

Lady Currie giggled. "I am rather obvious, aren't I?"

Clegg smiled, displaying yellowed teeth. "I like a woman who knows what she wants," he said as they moved toward the fine couches. "Let me guess. You want to know of the two that were just in combat."

Lady Currie nodded. "In particular, the one who was injured," she said. "Tell me of him."

Clegg's bushy eyebrows lifted. "Ah," he said. "The Highlander. That is Bane Morgan. He is an excellent fighter."

"And his opponent?"

"Magnus Stewart, another Scotsman. They call him the Eagle."

"I heard," Lady Currie said with a hint of impatience. "And in the first round there was a tall blond. Who was that?"

"A young Englishman named Warenne de Soulant," he said. "Which one would you like to meet?"

"Bane."

Clegg shook his head. "He was wounded from what I saw, so I do not believe he'll be good company for you," he said. "What of Magnus? Or Warenne?"

Lady Currie was unhappy that he'd rejected her first choice and she wasn't shy about it. "But he didn't look too badly injured," she said. "Bane, I mean. Where is he?"

Clegg grinned. "He has been taken to his cottage, I would imagine, to be tended by the physic," he said. "A wounded man will not be of much use to you and your needs, my lady, so choose another for tonight. When Bane heals, I will introduce you."

Lady Currie didn't press him, but she was still unhappy. "Very well," she sighed sharply. "Warenne was nice-looking. Do you have any others?"

"I do."

"Will you show me?"

Clegg nodded. "Come out to the balcony, and we shall inspect the men in the staging area below."

Lady Currie nodded, eager to take a good look. Lucia, still

standing back by the door, watched the woman as she moved swiftly to the big balcony that gave a supreme vantage point. But she also knew that, from this point forward, she wasn't needed. Lady Currie had Clegg's attention, and it would be through Clegg that she would find the evening's companionship. Sometimes Lucia followed her for lack of anything better to do, but sometimes she didn't. Sometimes, she went back to the carriage to wait in the dark and cold.

But tonight…she wasn't going to go back to the carriage.

She had another destination in mind.

"M'lady?" she said before Lady Currie could become too involved in her inspection. "Do ye require me? I can wait for ye elsewhere if ye wish."

Lady Currie waved an impatient hand at her. "Go back to the carriage," she said. "Find Amy and the two of you can wait for me. I do not know how long I shall be, so do not ask."

Lucia simply nodded, eager to be gone. In little time, she was out the door and back through the iron gate. The warrior village was to the south and she stood there a moment, remembering what Bane had told her.

I have a cottage at the end of the warrior village. Come find me when this is over.

She intended to.

CHAPTER SIXTEEN

THE WARRIOR VILLAGE WAS SURPRISINGLY UNGUARDED.

Since tonight was a game night, people were wandering in and out of the village even though there were at least four guards that Lucia could see. But the guards were gathered in a bunch in conversation, and they completely ignored the people going in and out.

Lucia used that to her advantage.

Bane had said he was at the end of the warrior village, which she took to mean the opposite end. She scurried down the narrow avenue that ran between the neat cottage rows, trying not to slide in the slush that had developed from the snowfall. As she neared the end of the row, she saw the big Saxon emerge from one of the cottages.

Quickly, she hid against another cottage, staying out of sight but hearing the Saxon speak to someone, telling him to remain still and do what the physic demanded. She sank back against the wall as the Saxon walked past her, heading back to the arena, but something told her that he was speaking to Bane.

It was just a feeling she had.

Quickly, Lucia made her way to the cottage, hiding in the shadows and waiting for the physic to depart. Because of the stone, she couldn't hear what was going on inside and the wait became an impatient one. She was worried about Lady Currie, wondering if the woman had indeed found a young warrior to spend her time with or if she'd given up and had gone back to the arena. In which case, she would be looking for Lucia.

That concerned her.

Still, she didn't want to leave before finding out if Bane was all right.

Fortunately, she didn't have to wait too much longer. The door to the cottage opened again and slammed back against the hinges. She could hear footsteps crunching on the slushy ground before peering around the corner and seeing a man walking away.

Carefully, she made her way up to the cottage door.

Lucia stood there a moment, putting her ear against it and hearing nothing. Whoever was inside was alone because she didn't hear any movement whatsoever. Very quietly, she knocked on the door.

"Bane?" she whispered loudly. "*Bane?*"

It took a moment, but she finally heard an answer. "Lucia? Is that ye?"

She shoved the door open, coming face-to-face with a pale Bane as he struggled to sit up in bed. His wound hadn't needed stitches, but his entire torso was tightly wrapped and she slammed the door, rushing to him and pushing him back on the bed.

"Nay," she said. "Dunna strain yerself. Lie down."

Bane did, but it was clear that he was surprised to see her. His hands went up, grasping her by the arms even as she laid him back on the bed.

"Ye found me," he said, a smile on his lips. "Did ye see the fight?"

"Of course I did. Did ye not see me right in the front row with Lady Currie?"

He sighed faintly as she checked his bandages. "I looked for ye but the fight started so quickly that I dinna have a chance," he said. "I'm sorry I lost. I would never intentionally shame ye."

She stopped fussing and looked at him. "Is that what ye think? That ye shamed me?"

He closed his eyes, feeling the drag of the pain potion the physic had given him. "I'm ashamed of myself," he said softly. "I dunna blame ye if ye are."

Lucia stared at him for a moment. "I'm not sure how ye can

even say that," she said softly. "Bane, ye came here tae make money tae pay off my father's debt. It was a great and noble gesture. Do ye really think I would be ashamed of anything ye did? If ye do, then ye dunna know me very well. I'm never ashamed of a man who gives an honest effort in anything he does."

He met her eyes. After a moment, he reached out to touch her cheek gently. "Then I am ashamed of myself more than I ever was," he murmured. "I dinna stop tae think that I would slander yer character by thinking ye might be ashamed. 'Tis only that I want tae always be a victor in yer eyes. I always want ye tae be proud of me."

Her concern turned to warmth and she sat next to the head of his bed, her arm across his shoulders. "I *am*," she assured him. "For a man tae do what ye've set out tae do, for a woman ye havena known very long… Of course I'm proud of ye. There's something between us that was forged strong from nearly the moment we met. I felt so much pity for ye because ye seemed so…defeated. I wanted tae help ye, so I did."

He had his arm up in such a way that his right hand was on her head, gently stroking her hair.

"I know," he said. "But I told ye before that ye gave me hope. Now ye've given me purpose. *Ye're* my purpose, Lucia. The men from the Ludus Caledonia tell me that they can change my life and I want tae do that, but only if ye're a part of it. The hope, the change, the future…they mean nothing without ye."

Lucia was deeply touched by his words. "After this time apart, ye've not changed yer mind?"

Bane didn't know why he felt indignant about that question. He also felt sad, as if somehow he'd caused her to mistrust his motives. Even though the physic had given him a potion for the pain that was making him sleepy, he abruptly sat up, wincing when his wound pulled. He sat on the edge of the bed, looking down at Lucia as she sat beside him.

"I've not changed my mind," he said firmly. "I realize that everything I've done seems like a rash decision but I assure ye, there's nothing rash about it. I dunna make foolish decisions, so it wouldna matter if we spent two weeks apart or two years. I would never change my mind about ye. Is that in any way unclear?"

Lucia shook her head slowly. "It is clear."

"Then I dunna want tae hear doubt in yer voice again."

"I promise. Never again."

As he looked down at her, he felt guilty for being stern with her. He knew how abrupt all of this looked. He'd barely known the woman a week before he was making life-changing declarations.

But he meant every word.

He wanted her to know that.

Reaching down, Bane pulled her to her knees, cupping her face in both of his big, battered hands. His lips moved to her cheek, gently, his nose inhaling the scent of her skin. There was something about smelling her that drove him wild. The hands on her cheeks began to caress her, feeling her silken flesh against his fingers. It had been years since he'd tasted a woman he wanted to taste, and the feel of her, the scent of her, was overwhelming. His lips began to move along her jawline.

Lucia felt his hot, gentle kisses and her body began to tremble. His touch had an intoxicating effect and she could feel herself surrendering as his mouth moved across her chin. He was close to her lips, but he didn't kiss her mouth; instead, he continued across her jaw to her other cheek.

It was titillating, gentle, and passionate as his kisses moved across one eye and then the other. Lucia quivered, feeling every kiss like a thousand pinpricks of joy, waiting for the magic moment when he would claim her lips with his own.

Bane was moving in that direction and the more he tasted, the more his control was lost. She was warm and delicious, better than he had ever tasted in his life. He didn't realize until he touched her how starved he was for her flesh. Finally, he slanted his mouth hungrily over hers, his hands entwining in her hair to hold her fast against him.

In his grip, Lucia gasped at the delight of his touch. She was wildly aroused by it. It felt like the most natural of things, his lips against hers, his hands in her hair. She knew she could learn to love it. Her arms snaked around his neck and she pulled him close.

Her response to him fed Bane's lust. He removed his hands from her hair and wrapped his big arms around her body, pulling her up against him and trying to be mindful of his wound. It ached, but not as much as the ache in his heart for Lucia. His tongue licked at her lips, silently encouraging her to admit him, and she timidly opened her mouth. He invaded her with his tongue, tasting her sweetness and losing himself completely.

Lucia held on to him tightly as he flipped her onto her back, laying her on the small bed and covering her with his enormous body. His arms, massive strong things, were around her but she could feel his hands moving, caressing her, exploring her back and her torso. She was relishing everything about it when his hand began to move across her belly, up toward her breasts.

Lucia could feel him getting closer, finally stroking the underside of her right breast. As exciting as it was, it was also intimidating. If she let herself go, she knew there would be no end to their passion. It would go on until he took her innocence. When he moved to enclose her breast in his palm, she put up a hand and stopped him.

"Bane," she murmured, tearing her mouth away from his. "I dunna think… Someone might come in and catch us."

Bane had been far gone with passion. But as she spoke, he came to his senses enough to realize he was moving toward intimate places. He further realized that he fully intended to bed the woman. There was no question in his mind. But as he pulled back and gazed into her beautiful face, his ardor cooled.

"Forgive me," he whispered. "I shouldna have taken such liberties but… Lucia, I canna explain what I feel for ye. All I know is that…that I love ye, my angel."

Lucia sighed at the sound of his words, feeling them ring a chord within her. "When ye were going intae the arena, I thought that's what ye said tae me."

"It was."

Reaching up, she touched his face. "I've never had anyone tell me that, not even my da," she said. "I…I dunna know what tae say."

He fingered a strand of chestnut-colored hair. "I told ye that I love ye and I want tae marry ye. Tell me ye'll at least give me the opportunity tae earn yer love in return."

His vulnerability was apparent. This big, strong warrior had a tender side. Leaning into him, she sweetly kissed his cheek.

"I dunna need tae," she whispered. "Ye already have it. I canna explain it, Bane, but whatever feelings have grown between us are something stronger than I've ever known. As if it was meant tae be."

A smile flickered on his lips. "I feel the same way."

Lucia returned his smile before kissing him gently, twice. "I wish I could stay and talk tae ye all night, but I'm afraid Lady Currie may be on the prowl," she said. Then her smile faded. "Bane, she saw ye tonight. She even went tae Clegg de Lave tae ask about ye. I told ye that she comes tae the Cal tae find men tae pleasure her, and I fear now that she's seen ye, she'll try tae buy yer favors. What will ye do?"

The warmth in his eyes faded and he sat up, gingerly, pulling Lucia up with him. "I'll refuse, of course," he said. "It was one of the questions I asked Sir Clegg. I wanted tae know if I had any choice in the matter if a woman tried tae buy me. He told me that men have free will in such matters, so I'll refuse. 'Tis as simple as that."

"But she'll offer ye a good deal of money. Mayhap more than a fight purse."

"It doesna matter. I belong tae one woman, my angel—ye. There is no one else."

She was greatly relieved to hear him say that. Swinging her legs over the side of the bed, she stood up and smoothed at her skirt.

"Let me go and see tae Lady Currie," she said. "If she's busy with someone, then I'll return tae ye. But if not, I'm sure we'll return tomorrow night. I'll see ye then. Oh—and there is something else I forgot tae tell ye. I spoke with Laird Currie, and he told me that my debt is nearly paid. He said another two pounds should be enough."

Bane appeared pleasantly surprised. "Is that all? Then it shouldna take too long tae get the money together."

"He said he would release me if he could. He's going tae speak tae Lady Currie about it again."

"Even better. Then we can marry and ye can come tae live here with me."

She looked at him, confused. "But why here? Why would ye stay?"

He sighed faintly, dreading what he was about to tell her. "Because I gave an oath that I'd stay for the full term," he said. "They know I'm here tae earn money tae buy yer freedom, but they also told me that they expect a vow from me if they're tae train me and provide me with opportunity."

She understood, sort of. "But how long?"

"Seven years."

Her eyes widened. "*Seven* years? We must stay here for seven years? Bane, that's as bad as being forced intae servitude with Lady Currie. When will our lives become our own?"

He could see that she was getting upset and he put his arms around her, pulling her into a warm embrace. But he also knew that she had a point.

"Mayhap it willna be a full seven years," he said soothingly. "I dunna want ye tae worry over it. One day at a time, my angel."

She nodded but she wasn't comforted. She was gravely concerned over a seven-year commitment. "If ye say so."

"I do." He kissed her on the head before standing up wearily, his hand on his wrapped wound. "Now, I'll escort ye from the camp. Ye'll not walk alone around here."

She shook her head and tried to push him back onto the bed. "I can find my way," she said. "Ye needna worry about me. I can take care of myself."

He acted as if he didn't hear her. There was a tunic hanging on a peg near the door and he pulled it on, grunting with the pain the movement caused him.

"Dunna be ridiculous," he said. "I'll escort ye and no argument."

She stood her ground. "If Lady Currie sees us together, I'll pay the price. Is that what ye want?"

His eyes narrowed. "She'll not see us. I'll walk ye tae the edge."

"But—"

"Shut yer yap. The first thing ye need tae learn is not tae argue with me."

"Is that so?"

"'Tis."

She scowled at him a moment longer before losing the fight against a grin. Rolling her eyes, she threw open the cottage door.

"Very well," she sighed sharply. "Come along, then. Ye're the walking wounded, but who am I tae tell ye tae stay in bed?"

He grabbed her as she headed out the door, snapping her back against him as his big arms went around her.

"Ye're the woman I belong tae," he murmured. "Ye're the woman who has given me my life back. Ye're everything tae me. Does that answer yer question?"

Lucia relished his embrace one last time for the night. "It does."

"Good."

True to his word, Bane walked her to the edge of the village before seeing her off as she headed back toward the arena.

Lucia found Lady Currie still with Clegg, still discussing the new recruits, but as the evening wore on, it became apparent that Lady Currie was pouting because Bane Morgan had been denied her. She finally ended up with the blond *novicius* named Warenne, whom she took back to her carriage.

With Lucia and Amy waiting outside the carriage, it was quite obvious what the pair was up to.

Chapter Seventeen

"Ye sent for me, m'laird?"

Lor was standing in the doorway of Clegg's grand viewing box with its odd smells and rich furnishings. Clegg, wrapped up in furs against the cold, waved him in.

"Come, Lor," he said. "Come in and close the door, although that seems ridiculous considering I've got two wide-open bays from which to watch the games that let the cold air in. Tonight, it was worth it, however."

"What do ye mean?"

"The Highland Defender against the Eagle."

Lor grinned. "It was quite a match."

Clegg nodded firmly. "Indeed, it was," he said. "I expected a show from the Eagle, but the Highland Defender was a surprise. The man has a great amount of skill."

"He does, m'laird. He told us that he was a great warrior for his clan, and we have seen that he was telling the truth."

"He was," Clegg said. "How has he been in training? I heard that he and the Eagle became acquainted this afternoon."

"That is true," Lor said. "Up until then, Bane had behaved as if training was beneath him."

"I know," Clegg said. "Axel told me. You know he likes to cut down men with that kind of attitude."

Lor nodded. "Aye, he does. And he did it effectively when he paired Bane with the Eagle. I think that was Bane's first taste of defeat and, surprisingly, he seems tae have taken it tae heart."

"He's a proud man."

"He is, m'laird." Lor paused a moment before continuing. "I had a long talk with him this afternoon about it and discovered there's something more behind that pride. It seems that he disobeyed a command and ended up getting men killed. That seemed tae destroy something in him. He hopes tae find it again here."

Clegg lingered on that thought as he went to pour himself more hot wine. "He's not afraid to hold a sword."

"Not at all," Lor said. "I dunna believe his battle confidence was lost, but something else. Mayhap confidence in himself, in his own judgment. That may be why he seems so prideful. He doesna want us tae see his weakness."

Clegg took a sip of his hot wine. "From what I saw tonight, he has no weakness. He's an excellent warrior, and to be truthful, I am not sure we can teach him more than he already knows."

Lor shrugged. "Possibly," he said. "But he dinna come here tae learn tae fight. He came tae make money."

"I remember. He wants to buy his lady's freedom."

"He does," Lor said. "And he fought admirably tonight, as ye said. It was quite a bout."

"Very exciting. We made a good deal of money on it, I'm told."

"Then pit Bane against the Eagle again tomorrow night. I'd wager tae say the gambling pools will be high with a rematch."

"But Bane was injured tonight."

Lor shook his head. "I saw the wound and I dunna believe it was too terrible. I've seen worse."

"I am pleased to hear that, but I'd rather have time to advertise such a rematch to guarantee a large crowd," Clegg said. "Tonight was just a foretaste. We'll move the Eagle and the Highland Defender up to a major bout."

"With a big purse?"

"Indeed."

Lor grinned. "Good," he said. "But meanwhile, it might be a good idea tae test Bane again tae make sure his fight against the Eagle wasna an accident. The true test of skill will come the second time around."

Clegg nodded. "Excellent idea," he said. "If he's up to it, let him fight tomorrow night. I will tell Axel to pin a small purse on the bout and see if the lure of money drives the Highland Defender even harder."

Lor agreed. "My guess is that it will."

Clegg grinned with a mouthful of wine-stained teeth. "Care to wager on that, Lor? Do you have enough faith in your Highland Defender to place money on him?"

"I do."

"Good. But do not tell Isabail. I do not wish to rile the mother of my godson."

Lor laughed softly. "Nor do I," he said. "It will be our secret, m'laird."

"I hope Bane is as good as you think he is."

Lor's smile faded as he thought on the prideful, stubborn, and somewhat mysterious Highland Defender.

"So do I, m'laird," he said quietly. "So do I."

△ △ △

Bane was just falling asleep when there was a soft knock on the door. Thinking Lucia had returned, he quickly sat up.

"Come," he said.

The door creaked open but the person entering was not Lucia. It was the warrior called the Eagle.

Magnus Stewart shut the door quietly behind him and faced Bane.

"Well?" he said, looking Bane over. "Will ye heal?"

Bane eyed the man, clearly mistrustful of him. "It seems so," he said. "What are ye doing here?"

Magnus rested his fists on his narrow hips. "I came to see how ye were," he said. "It was a brutal fight between us. Much longer than usual. Ye're good, Defender. Where did ye learn tae fight?"

Bane wasn't entirely sure if the man was trying to be friendly or simply nosy. Perhaps both. Or perhaps he was even trying to determine if Bane was too weak to continue fighting. In any case, Bane wasn't comfortable with the man in his cottage. The door had a lock on it and he should have used it, but thinking that Lucia might come back, he hadn't bothered.

Now he was regretting that decision.

"I'm from the Highlands," he said. "We learn tae fight when we are born. And ye?"

"Near Stirling," he said. "But I, too, learned tae fight young. Not many hold out against me."

"Nor me."

Magnus continued to stare at him. Then he cracked a smile. "I'll admit something tae ye," he said. "It was a miracle I was able tae pull the blade on ye at the end. I thought for sure ye were going tae cripple me."

Bane thought that sounded suspiciously like a compliment. "Ye like tae kick a man in the head, don't ye? Ye've done it tae me twice. There willna be a third time."

Magnus's smile faded. "I've learned tae strike hard and strike fast."

"How long have ye been with Clegg and his fight guilds? I hear there's more than one."

Magnus nodded. "There are five," he said. "Besides the Ludus Caledonia, there is the Ludus Hadrian, the Ludus Antonine, the Ludus Trimontium, and the Ludus Valentia."

Bane had no idea there were more than two guild locations, and his eyebrows lifted in surprise. "That many?"

Magnus shifted on his big legs. "Some are larger, some are smaller. The Ludus Caledonia is the largest, and the Ludus Valentia is the smallest." He moved away from the door, going to the only stool in the cottage, and planted his body upon it. "And in answer tae yer question, I've been here a little over three years."

Bane was starting to relax a little in the man's presence. It seemed to him that the man simply wanted to talk. "Has it been worth it tae ye?" he asked. "Knowing what ye know now, I mean. Would ye do it all over again?"

Magnus nodded without hesitation. "I'm richer than I could have ever imagined," he said. "I have a place where I belong, where I can make my way. 'Tis more than most men can say."

"Ye dunna mind fighting like this for a living?"

Magnus cocked his head thoughtfully. "Being Scots, we are expected tae fight," he said. "We fight the Sassenachs, each other… It is in our blood. Why *did* ye come here, Defender?"

Bane avoided the question. "I havena been here as long as ye. There is a lot tae learn."

"How long have ye been here?"

"Little more than a month."

Magnus's eyebrows lifted. "And ye fight like that? God's bones, lad, ye've got talent. In fact, they have games where men fight in pairs. I'll pair with ye anytime."

Bane was mildly flattered. He found himself taking a second look at the man, thinking he wasn't so short after all. And he had good taste in warriors.

"If there's a chance tae win a purse, I'll do it," he said.

Magnus eyed him as if sensing something in that statement. "Do ye need money, then? Is that why ye're here?"

"Aye."

"Why do ye need money?"

Bane sighed faintly; he supposed it was no great secret why he'd come. "Tae buy my lady's freedom," he said. "She's a servant in a great house, working off a debt."

Magnus stood up from the stool. "'Tis as good a reason as any," he said. "So ye have a noble streak, do ye? Buying a woman's freedom?"

Bane scratched his head. "I dunna know about that, but I want tae marry her and the debt must be paid before I can."

"Good," Magnus said as he moved for the door. "That'll make ye fight harder than most if ye're fighting for a reason. I suppose I came tae see ye because no man has lasted as long as ye have against me. Now I know why."

Bane watched him lift the latch. "And ye intend tae use it against me somehow? Is that why ye came—tae discover my weakness?"

Magnus simply smiled, a genuine gesture. "From what I see, I'm not sure ye have any weaknesses. That makes ye interesting… and dangerous."

It occurred to Bane that Magnus had really come to inspect the competition—*him*. There wasn't any animosity, but there didn't seem to be any trust, either.

Simply an honest appraisal.

"Mayhap," Bane said. "But the next time, ye just might be getting kicked in the head instead of me."

Magnus chuckled as he quit the cottage, closing the door behind him. Bane stood up and went to the door, throwing the bolt because he didn't want any more surprise guests. Magnus's visit had been odd, but not entirely unexpected in the grand scheme of things. The man had fought someone who impressed him, and he wanted to inspect him. Fair enough.

But what Magnus didn't realize was that Bane had inspected him, too.

Next time, there would be no mistakes.

With that thought on his mind, Bane lay back down again, physically and mentally exhausted. He was still hoping Lucia would return to him, but as the minutes dragged on, he had to accept that it was less of a possibility. Just as he closed his eyes and settled down for sleep, there was a knock at the door.

His eyes opened, staring at the ceiling in frustration. *Again?* With a grunt of effort, Bane swung his legs onto the floor and stood up, staggering his way over to the door.

"Who comes?" he demanded.

"Lor," came the muffled reply.

Curious, Bane unbolted the door. Lor was standing on his stoop, looking at him with concern.

"Are ye well, lad?" he asked.

Bane nodded. "I'll be fine."

"Did I just see Magnus leaving yer cottage?"

"Ye did."

"What did he want?"

Bane shrugged. "He came tae see if I was well," he said. "I think he came tae discover for himself if he'd badly injured me."

"He dinna try tae smother ye?"

Bane gave him a lopsided grin. "Nay," he said flatly. "He made no move against me."

Lor seemed satisfied. "Good," he said. "The man is a bit... questionable. I wanted tae make sure he dinna try tae harm ye."

Bane shook his head. "He dinna," he said. "But that's not tae say I wasna on edge with him. He's unpredictable and that makes him more dangerous than most."

"Ye've met him twice in battle. Unpredictable is where he begins. No one knows where he ends."

"What do ye know about him?"

Lor shrugged. "As I told ye, he's come from another fight guild, so he hasna been here long."

"I know that. But what do ye know about *him*?"

"Him?" Lor repeated thoughtfully. "He keeps tae himself, mostly, but Clegg told me that he's the bastard of a Scottish prince."

That brought surprise from Bane. "Magnus?"

"Aye," Lor said. "I dunna know more than that. But it seems strange tae me that a royal bastard would choose a life like this."

"I suppose he's got tae earn his way somehow."

"Or mayhap he was forced intae earning his way."

"Ye mean his sire refuses tae acknowledge him?"

"Possibly. All I know is that when I see him fight, there's anger there. Can ye not see it?"

Bane rubbed his head. "Aye. I can feel it, too."

Lor smiled weakly. "Do ye feel it enough that ye willna be able tae fight in a bout tomorrow night? Sir Clegg liked what he saw. He'll let ye fight for a purse tomorrow if ye feel well enough."

Bane's eyes widened as he forgot all about Magnus. "He will?" he said, shocked. "But I dinna think *novicius* could fight for a purse."

"Not usually," Lor said, amused by the look on Bane's face. "But ye did so well tonight that he'll make an exception. Can ye do it?"

"Of course I can. I could move mountains if there was money involved."

Lor grinned. "Good," he said. "Sleep well tonight, and tomorrow we'll see how that wound fares."

Bane looked down at his wrapped torso. "It wasna deep enough for stitches," he said. "If I keep it wrapped, it should be fine."

Lor had a twinkle in his eye as he patted Bane on the shoulder and left him standing there in his doorway. Bane watched the man go, suddenly not so tired. The prospect of fighting for a purse tomorrow night had him excited.

This was what he'd come for.

The first step toward securing Lucia's freedom.

He didn't think he'd be able to sleep, but he was wrong. The moment he lay back down on his bed, an exhausted sleep claimed him.

His dreams had visions of plucking the feathers from a certain royal eagle.

Chapter Eighteen

Bane was back fighting again tonight.

The only good thing about coming to the Ludus Caledonia two nights in a row was the fact that Lucia got to see Bane again. Clearly, the wound on his torso from the previous night wasn't a factor that hindered him because as she sat in the front row of the arena yet again with Lady Currie, Bane was in the very first bout and he looked strong and healthy.

Even so, Lucia was so racked with nerves that she was trembling, and beside her, Lady Currie was breathing heavily at the sight of the warrior she was beginning to obsess on.

The woman hadn't worn the Roman gown this time. She'd dressed in a wine-red silk that Lucia had made for her some time ago, one that was cut low so that her bosom would show. It wasn't very warm in this icy weather so she wore a heavy fur wrap with it. She'd dressed carefully that afternoon, primping and powdering, putting perfume on her breasts and on her thighs.

Lucia had been in the chamber when she'd dressed, watching Lady Currie as she prepared herself for what she hoped would be a night with the warrior they called the Highland Defender. That's what she'd told Colly, who frowned but wisely kept her mouth shut.

The main reason Colly wasn't allowed to go to the Ludus Caledonia was because she was old and frumpy, and Lady Currie didn't want to hear her judgment. She wanted companionship that wouldn't dispute her wants, and she also surrounded herself with pretty young women so the warriors would have more incentive to look in her direction.

That was why Lucia and, at times, Amy were permitted to go.

They were bait.

Therefore, as Lucia sat next to Lady Currie and watched Bane stretch out his shoulders, she knew that Lady Currie was focused on Bane and she hated the woman for it. She'd never felt such anger or jealousy in her life and it was difficult to suppress it, but exposing her feelings would open Pandora's box.

She knew that.

Therefore, she bit her lip when Lady Currie stood up and waved to Bane as the man stretched himself out.

"Look at him," Lady Currie said, waving her hand like an idiot. "He is not looking over here. Why is he not looking over here?"

Lucia was watching Bane as the man twisted his torso, somewhat gingerly. "He seems focused on the fight, m'lady," she said. "Mayhap ye shouldna distract him. If he is wounded again, ye'll not have the chance tae see him tonight."

Lady Currie immediately sat down. "Good thinking," she said. "I *do* intend to see him tonight. Sir Clegg cannot tell me that the man is wounded again, for clearly he is not."

"He's also not fought yet tonight."

Lady Currie appeared worried. "You are right again," she said. "God, I hope the man does not get hurt again."

Lucia dared to glance at the woman, but Lady Currie was focused on her prey across the arena floor.

Lucia prayed for strength to get through the evening without throttling her.

It was true, however, that Bane hadn't looked in her direction, for which she was grateful. He seemed focused on what he was doing, stretching out his muscles and preparing for the coming bout, which turned out to be against a very big and barbaric-looking opponent they called the Thistle, presumably because he was hairy-looking.

But that wasn't the case.

Once the fight started, Lucia realized it was because the man had a prickly temperament. There was no rhyme or reason to his actions; he simply came at Bane with a roar and swinging a club. Everything about him was edgy and abrupt. As the crowd screamed in excitement, Bane simply stayed out of the man's way until he exhausted himself.

It didn't take long.

When the Thistle was winded, Bane swung into action. With the broad side of his wooden shield, he hit the man in the jaw so hard that the force lifted the Thistle up and sent him flying backwards onto his arse. The crowd roared in approval as Bane pounced, using his shield to press against the man's face when he was down, effectively smothering him. The Thistle fought and kicked, trying to move away from the shield in his face, but Bane was merciless.

He was in for the kill.

But the rules stated that once a man was down and clearly disabled, the battle would be over. The Thistle wasn't getting up on his feet anytime soon, so the field marshals called the fight.

Still, Bane remained on top of the Thistle.

The big Saxon who officiated the fights was forced to come out onto the field to break up the brawl, followed by a muscular blond man who was quite handsome. Lucia watched with great concern as the pair went to Bane and his opponent, literally pulling Bane off the man.

But Bane had bloodlust in him. He was the victor and he fed off the thrill. He threw his arms up to the crowd, who screamed their adoration for him. They cheered their champion and Lady Currie was on her feet, waving her white kerchief like a flag.

Lucia, thinking that Lady Currie might be displeased if she sat there and did nothing, also rose to her feet and clapped hesitantly as Bane soaked up the adulation of the spectators. He was walking by the front row of the stands, from one end of the arena to the other, being congratulated as he went. Men shook his hand

and patted him on the shoulder. Some even slipped him coinage. Lucia watched with wide eyes as he moved in front of her and Lady Currie.

He didn't even look at them.

Lady Currie was thrilled that he was so close and she reached out, tucking her kerchief into the neckline of his tunic as he came near. But Bane ripped it out and tossed it onto the ground as he walked past, causing Lady Currie to shriek in outrage.

"Did you see what he did?" she demanded. "How rude! I will have him whipped for that!"

Lucia was standing alongside Lady Currie, looking after Bane with a worried expression on her face. "Mayhap he dinna want it tae get wet, m'lady," she said. "He's sweaty... It would soil yer kerchief."

Lady Currie was furious. "He threw it on the ground," she said, jabbing a finger at it. "It is filthy now. I shall see Clegg about this right away. I will not stand for this insult!"

Bane was just leaving the arena floor as Lady Currie bolted from her seat and practically ran up the stairs that led out of the arena. Only Lucia had come with her tonight, so she was the only one following the woman as she marched over to the gate that guarded the entrance to Clegg's viewing box.

The guard at the gate greeted her by name but told her that Sir Clegg was busy with someone else inside his private box. That didn't sit well with Lady Currie. She demanded to be announced, and when the guard wouldn't comply, she shoved him out of the way and yanked the gate open. The guard, who was not permitted to put hands upon any woman, and especially not a steady customer like Lady Currie, simply stood back in surprise as Lady Currie marched down the tiled walkway and into Sir Clegg's private box.

In fact, Lady Currie didn't care that Clegg was occupied with business. It never occurred to her that she wasn't the most important person at the Ludus Caledonia. She barged into the viewing box as Clegg and another man stood in one of the archways with a clear view of the field. When Clegg looked up and saw her, his brow furrowed in displeasure.

"Lady Currie," he greeted. "I am occupied at the moment. Would you please excuse—?"

Lady Currie cut him off rudely. "I will *not* be put off," she said. "Do you know what just happened? Your insolent and arrogant Highland Defender insulted me deeply, and I demand satisfaction."

Clegg's irritation turned to concern. "What did he do?"

Lady Currie was so angry that her forehead was peppered with sweat. "He won his bout, and being a gracious lady, I gave him my favor," she said. "He tossed it onto the ground and stomped on it. What right does that man have to show me such disrespect?"

Clegg, who had watched the astonishingly good match with Bane and the Thistle hadn't seen that part of it. Lady Currie had offered for Bane last night but had been denied, and here she was back again, now demanding satisfaction for an insult dealt by the man.

Clegg had seen women like Lady Currie all of his life— demanding, spoiled, used to having their way in everything. Lady Currie was used to men falling at her feet and Bane hadn't done that. Now she was furious and embarrassed. Unless Clegg wanted trouble on his hands, or worse—losing a high-paying customer—he knew he needed to placate the woman.

Even though he really didn't like her.

"Sometimes, men in the heat of battle do things they would not normally do," he said evenly. "Did he say anything to you?"

Lady Currie fumed. "Nay."

"Did he look at you?"

"Nay."

Clegg smiled. "Then clearly he did not know you gave it to him," he said. "You must understand that men have a sort of blood madness when they are victorious over another man. There is something that temporarily drives them to do things they would not normally do. In this case, Bane did not see that it was you. He did not know it was you who had given him the favor. If he had, I am certain he would not have removed it."

Lady Currie was cooling down at his logical explanation. "I suppose," she said. "I guess…I would agree that he did not know it was me."

Clegg was quite comforting. "You see? There is nothing to be angry over. In fact, I shall summon him immediately and he can apologize to you personally. Would you like that?"

Now Lady Currie was completely cooled off and, in fact, enticed by the thought of finally meeting the mysterious Highland Defender. "You called him Bane?"

Clegg nodded. "His name is Bane Morgan," he said. Then he indicated the nearest cushioned couch. "Please, sit. I will have him brought to you."

A smile spread across Lady Currie's face as she turned toward the silk-cushioned couch to await the delivery of the man she'd been trying to know for two days. Clegg went to the man he'd been speaking with when Lady Currie so rudely interrupted them and lowered his voice.

"Bring Bane here," he said. "Tell him why so he is prepared."

Lor had been that man. He and Clegg had watched Bane's fight together to assess his performance and were speaking of it when Lady Currie barged in. He eyed the woman on the couch.

"Bane has a woman, m'laird," he muttered. "I know Lady Currie and I know what she wants. It is unfair tae put Bane in that position."

Clegg grunted. "We make a good deal of money from her, so I will not deny her the chance to meet him," he said. "Tell Bane he is expected to apologize to her, but beyond that, I expect nothing from him as long as he is polite about it. If he is to decline her offer, then he had better explain why. Meanwhile…meanwhile, send Warenne to me as well. If one man denies her, mayhap the comfort of another man will satisfy her."

Lor nodded and headed out of the chamber, out into the icy night that was beginning to fog over. Clegg went to sit with Lady Currie, making sure she had warmed wine and making small conversation as they waited for Bane's appearance.

In truth, Clegg wasn't looking forward to it.

⚭ ⚭ ⚭

"I *what*?"

"Ye must apologize," Lor said steadily. "Bane, I know it seems ridiculous, but part of being a warrior with the Cal is also being an ambassador between the Cal and the patrons. Without the patrons, there is no fight guild. It is imperative that ye never show anger or irritation toward one of them. Ye must always be polite, even if ye dunna want tae be. Lady Currie is furious because she believes ye slighted her."

"I did."

Lor sighed heavily. They were standing in the staging area below Clegg's viewing box, and Bane was only now coming down off of his battle high. Lor could see from the look in Bane's eyes that he was quite serious about insulting Lady Currie.

That made little sense to Lor.

"But why?" he asked. "What do ye have against the woman? Do ye know her?"

Bane eyed him, debating how much to tell him, but he opted for all of it. He liked Lor; he was coming to trust the man. He knew that whatever he told him would remain in confidence. For Lucia's sake, it had to.

He forced himself to calm.

"There's a woman with Lady Currie," he said quietly. "Did ye see her?"

Lor thought back. "I think so," he said. "Briefly. My attention was mostly on Lady Currie. Why do ye ask?"

"Because that is my Lucia. That's the lady whose freedom I intend tae buy."

Lor's eyes widened in surprise. "She serves Lady Currie?"

Bane nodded. Then he started to look miserable. "It was Lucia who first told me about the Cal and how the fighters earn money," he said. "She's the entire reason I came here. I knew even before I came here that Lady Currie uses this place like her own personal stable of men, and it did occur tae me that she might take a fancy tae me. Now I'm faced with a problem. I will refuse anything she offers, Lor. I willna service the woman like a whore."

Lor stared at him a moment before puffing out his cheeks. "God's bones, lad," he said. "I'd say ye have a problem. She wants ye badly from what I can see."

"Clegg said I could refuse her."

"Ye can. But what about yer lass?"

"Lady Currie doesna know about me and Lucia," Bane said. "For Lucia's sake, we need tae keep that secret at all costs. She says that Lady Currie can be jealous, and if the woman knows Lucia and I are fond of one another, it could go badly for Lucia."

"True enough. But I canna imagine how she must feel, watching her lady lust after the man she loves."

"Nor I," Bane said, sighing heavily. "Lucia is a decent woman with a good heart, yet she's forced tae serve a woman with the morals of a bitch in heat. Do ye know she's been coming tae the Ludus Caledonia for as long as she's been serving the House of Currie? She tells me how much she hates this place, but Lady Currie forces her tae come. And Lady Currie's old husband... He remains at home. Surely the man must wonder what goes on with his wife nightly."

Lor shook his head in a sorrowful motion. "What man would let his wife wander and not care?"

"A man who has lost his direction in life, I would think," Bane said. "A man who doesna realize the shame his wife brings upon him. We're fortunate, ye and I, Lor. Fortunate that the women we love are true and good. I've come tae see that those are rare qualities in a woman."

"'Tis a pity yer Lucia is forced tae associate with a woman like Lady Currie."

"Which is why it is important I make as much money as I can, as quickly as I can."

Lor understood. "'Tis a bind ye're in," he said. "Clegg should know, however. He is the only one who can truly discourage Lady Currie if she's on yer scent."

"He willna tell her?"

"He willna if ye ask him not tae."

Bane hesitated a moment before nodding his head. "Very well," he said. "If I dunna have the opportunity tae tell him, ye have my permission to do it."

Lor didn't envy Bane his situation. "Can I make a suggestion, then?"

"I wish ye would."

Lor was clearly hesitant, but he forged on. "The lady has already had quite a bit tae drink," he said. "She'll pay a good deal of money for ye, and ye said ye needed tae make money quickly, so consider taking her money and plying her with drink until she falls unconscious. That way, ye'll have yer money without having tae touch the woman. Clegg doesna much like her, but she pays well for what she requires."

Bane considered that, but only for a moment. He shook his head. "I canna do it," he said. "I canna give her hope that I'll accept her money in exchange for my company. She might expect it nightly, and I can only get her ragingly drunk so many times before she'll want something more. But more than anything, I canna do that tae Lucia. Money or no money, it would be cruel tae her."

"I understand," Lor said. "'Twas only a thought, given the circumstances."

"It wasna a bad thought, but I canna bring myself tae do it. Not even for the money."

Lor shrugged. "Then come along. Ye might as well face this now and get it over with."

There was nothing more to say on the subject and Bane simply nodded, letting Lor take him by the shoulder and guide him toward the staircase that led up to Clegg's private box.

The closer he came to Lady Currie, the angrier he became. He desperately didn't want to do anything to create havoc for Lucia, but he was furious that Lady Currie had her eyes on him. He wasn't about to become the woman's stallion. Even if Lucia had never existed, he still wouldn't have been interested.

Calm, lad, calm!

The door opened into Clegg's private domain, and the heat from the blazing hearth was like a slap in the face after the chill conditions outside. Lor entered first, followed by Bane. The moment Bane entered, his attention went straight to the couch where Lady Currie was sitting and Lucia was standing. For a split second, his gaze fell on Lucia and all he could see was fear in her expression.

That only fed his rage.

Lady Currie was on her feet.

"Do you know who I am?" she demanded. "If you do not, then you should."

"Bane, this is Lady Currie," Clegg said, gaining control of the conversation over the irate lady. "She passed you her favor after your bout, and she says you threw it to the dirt. I have assured her that you did not do it intentionally, that you simply didn't realize whose it was."

The way he was looking at him made Bane realize that Clegg was trying to defuse the situation. The lady was angry, and Bane was angry, and the woman's spoiled manner wasn't helping things.

But Bane knew he had no standing in this situation. He knew he couldn't do or say anything that might provoke the woman. His was a position of submission. Not only did he want to protect Lucia, but he would not shame Clegg or Lor, who had gone out of their way to accommodate him in all ways.

He had no choice.

"I...I dinna know," he said, his gaze moving from Clegg to the irate Lady Currie. "I dunna even remember what happened, m'lady. I was still in the heat of battle."

Surprisingly, Lady Currie folded immediately. No argument, no demands for an apology that she'd made earlier. She simply smiled and made her way over to him, inspecting him from head to toe.

"No harm done," she said, looking at him rather flirtatiously. "Your name is Bane?"

"Aye, m'lady."

"Where are you from?"

"The Highlands, m'lady."

"You're new here."

"New enough, m'lady."

As he stood there, Lady Currie walked a circle around him, inspecting him from every angle. Bane kept his gaze straight ahead, staring at a wall in the distance, though he could see Lucia in his peripheral vision. It took everything he had not to look at her, fearful that her expression might weaken his composure. He knew this must be upsetting her greatly. He could only imagine how he would feel were the roles reversed and it was she standing here, being looked over by another man.

He would kill the man.

Therefore, he simply stared straight ahead as Lady Currie finished her inspection.

"Clegg," she finally said, "I would like to speak with Bane alone, if you please."

That wasn't the usual process when it came to Lady Currie and her lovers. Usually, she bargained with Clegg and he sent the man to her. Therefore, Clegg wasn't certain why she wanted to speak to Bane alone.

"My lady, all business is conducted through me, as you know," he said. "If you have something to say, then you will say it to me, as usual."

Lady Currie's gaze was on Bane. "I simply want to speak to him, not conduct business," she said. "I will bargain with you when the time comes, but I wish to speak to him first. May I?"

Clegg shook his head. "Not alone," he said. "If you wish, you may go to the other end of the chamber, but you will not go out of my sight. Everything stays right here until a bargain is struck."

That wasn't what Lady Currie wanted to hear but she didn't argue. With a grimace of displeasure, she moved to the other end of the chamber, crooking a finger at Bane for him to follow. Bane did, but he kept a distance from her. With Clegg and Lor and Lucia on the other end of the large chamber, Lady Currie and Bane came to a halt at the far end and faced one another.

Lady Currie smiled coyly at him.

"I wanted to speak to you first since you are new and since you seem to have a certain something that most others here do not," she said. "You have not been here very long, have you?"

Bane shook his head. He also spoke loudly enough that the others could hear him. "A little over a month, m'lady."

"Have you had many encounters with rich women?"

"I dunna know what ye mean, m'lady."

Lady Currie's gaze moved over him in a most unnerving fashion. "In ancient times, rich women paid handsomely to be serviced by the best gladiators," she said. "I know that because Clegg has told me and so has my husband. It was a way for the gladiators to make money and it was also viewed as a sign of prestige. You have not been aware of this?"

Bane was looking over her head, staring at the wall again because he didn't want to look her in the face. "I am aware, m'lady."

"Good. Because I shall make Clegg an offer for your company tonight."

He did look at her then. "I must respectfully decline, m'lady."

Her smile vanished. "Why?"

"Because I have a wife."

Her mouth popped open in outrage. "That means nothing to me, *novicius*. I am offering a good deal of money for you."

"And I respectfully decline, m'lady."

Lady Currie was more outraged by the second response. She abruptly turned away from him, marching straight to Clegg.

"You should tell this fool what his duties are, de Lave," she snarled. "He has a duty to keep your well-paying patrons happy, or is he too stupid to know that?"

Clegg had seen this coming. He knew what Lady Currie was going to offer and he knew what Bane was going to say because when he'd first come to the Ludus Caledonia, he'd made a point of asking if he could refuse to be bought by rich customers.

Therefore, he had been prepared for this moment.

"Lady Currie, our warriors are given a choice in matters such as this," he said patiently. "I believe there have been one or two men who have refused you, so this is nothing new. If Bane does not choose to accept your money, then there are many others who will. You need not go away disappointed."

Lady Currie was gearing up for a fight. "I do not want any others," she said. "May I speak with you privately, Clegg?"

Clegg was already exhausted just looking at her. But he was a businessman and, above all, he had to be gracious. Even to spoiled tarts like Lady Currie. He nodded patiently.

"Of course," he said, looking to Lor, who was still standing over by the door that led down into the staging area. "You and Bane will leave. Lady Currie and I have business to attend to."

Lor nodded, motioning to Bane, who gladly followed him from the chamber. Lucia, still standing over by the couch, also fled. She didn't even ask permission. In fact, she was close to tears and didn't want Lady Currie to see her state, so leaving the situation was the best thing she could do. She knew Lady Currie wouldn't miss her.

She had to find Bane.

CHAPTER NINETEEN

WHEN BANE RETURNED TO HIS COTTAGE, LUCIA WAS WAITING for him.

She was sitting in the dark on his bed, and when he entered and closed the door, bolting it, she startled the hell out of him. In fact, he was about to grab her by the throat when he realized it was her, and then all he could do was pull her into a crushing embrace.

He'd never been so glad to see anyone in his entire life.

"I'm sorry, my angel," he murmured. "I'm so sorry ye had tae see that. I would have spared ye if I could have."

Lucia clung to him. "It wasna yer fault," she said. "I knew what Lady Currie would do. It dinna make it any easier tae watch."

Bane lifted her off the ground and took her over to the bed, setting her down upon it. He stood there a moment, looking down at her, feeling emotions roll through him like the surge of the sea. He was feeling so much that it was difficult to decide what, exactly, he was feeling at all. Everything was muddled.

He was muddled.

"Two pounds," he muttered. "Laird Currie said it would take two pounds tae buy yer freedom?"

Lucia looked up at him fearfully. "Aye," she said. "That's what he said. Why do ye ask?"

Bane shook his head, exasperated. "Because that woman is going tae hound me, I know it," he said. "I can see it in her eyes. She's not used tae being denied. Mayhap I can borrow the two pounds tae buy yer freedom and then work it off. Somehow, I must get ye out of Meadowbank and do it quickly."

"Lady Currie *isna* used tae being denied," she said miserably. "I warned ye."

He stopped pacing and looked at her. "Ye know her," he said. "What will she do now? She's speaking tae Clegg and I dunna like it. What's she saying?"

Lucia could only shrug. "I dunna know what she's saying, but I can guess," she said. "She's trying tae force him tae command ye tae accept her offer. Will he?"

Bane was cooling off a little. Now he was more fearful. "I dunna think so," he said. "He told me I could deny her. I canna imagine he'd go back on his word."

"Then ye're safe, at least for tonight," she said. "But I suspect we'll be back tomorrow night and she'll try again."

"I'll deny her again."

Lucia watched him, feeling greatly comforted by his staunch resistance. There had never been any doubt, but he was almost rabid in his opposition. It was a gesture that proved everything he'd said to her—his devotion, his love. She was deeply touched by it.

They had a bond that no one, not even Lady Currie and her money, could break.

"Bane," she said softly. "Sit down. Sit down and be calm."

She was patting the bed next to her and Bane looked at it, looked at her, and realized just how agitated he was. His times with her were so few and far between that he didn't want to ruin them with his anger. Smiling weakly, he ran his fingers through his dark hair and sat heavily beside her.

For a moment, they simply looked at one another, drawing strength from the sight and presence of each other. For a brief and shining moment, things were calm between them. They were together.

That was all that mattered.

"Ye let yer beard grow back," Lucia said, reaching up to finger the bush that wasn't particularly neat. "Have the rodents moved back in?"

He laughed softly when he remembered one of the first conversations they'd ever had about him shaving off his beard and destroying a home for vermin.

"If ye dunna like it, I'll shave it off," he said. "I havena given it much thought."

She smiled because he was, stroking the exposed skin on his face. "Beard or no beard, it doesna change who ye are," she said. "This is how ye looked when I first met ye."

"I was a man in turmoil."

"I know. Ye still are, only now for different reasons."

He nodded, sighing heavily as he pulled her against him in a comforting embrace. He kissed the top of her head.

"I know," he muttered. "Ye canna imagine how I just want tae run away right now and take ye with me. We can go someplace and be free, together."

She had her hand on his chest, patting him gently. "We *will* be together and free, someday," she said. "But not now. The time isna right. Ye've given yer oath tae the Cal, and even if we wanted tae leave, there's something tae be said for honor. Ye canna break yer oath."

He sat back against the wall, drawing her with him. "Nay," he said after a moment. "Sir Clegg and Lor have been good tae me. They've been more than fair. I wouldna betray them like that. But that doesna mean I canna dream of the day when all of this is behind us."

Lucia didn't answer for a moment, thinking of that day as well. "I heard ye tell Lady Currie that ye had a wife."

"I do."

"Not officially."

"In my heart, mind, and body, it is official. I dunna need a priest tae make it so."

"Nor I."

"Do ye mean it?"

"Of course I do."

"I've been waiting my whole life tae hear that, Lucia. But only from ye."

It was a sweet thing to say, a tender moment that touched Lucia deeply. When his head dipped down, his lips brushing against hers, she responded readily. He had eased her, made her feel loved and wanted, and she realized that she was ready to give herself over to him completely because, come what may, she had already given her mind and her heart over to him.

Bane's lips slanted over Lucia's gently at first, reacquainting himself with her taste before growing bolder with his attention. His kisses became more forceful, his tongue licking her lips, and she opened her mouth in silent invitation.

There was no restraint this time, no hesitation in what they were doing. As Bane coaxed her awakening desire, he began to carefully remove her from her clothing. Lucia didn't fight him. In fact, she helped him. She yanked at the ties that held her dress together. She was so caught up in the haze of passion that she hardly realized when he loosened the gown enough to slip it off her shoulders. She became aware only when she felt it slide off her buttocks and onto the dirt floor.

Bane pushed her back onto his tiny bed and removed his clothing in nearly the same motion. When he covered her with his body, the feel of his hot flesh against hers was more than either of them could bear. In fact, Bane could hardly hold himself in check. He'd never been more aroused in his life and the feel of her, the scent of her, was intoxicating. He suckled her neck and her earlobe, feeling her tremble beneath him as his hands moved down to her belly, stroking the soft flesh before moving to a soft breast and gently cupping it.

Lucia gasped with surprise at the sensual intrusion, but Bane kissed her passionately to distract her. It wasn't long before Lucia settled down and enjoyed the attention as he kissed a blazing trail down her neck, onto her chest, and took a hard nipple into his mouth.

Lucia squirmed with delight, utterly at his mercy as he wedged himself between her legs, parting her thighs with his knees. She was overwhelmed, feeling every sensation roll through her as his kisses moved from one breast to the other, tasting and touching, while his fingers moved to the warm, moist folds between her legs.

Young and nubile, her body knew what it needed even if her mind did not. She was slick and ready for him. Bane finally brought up her knees and carefully entered her.

The first thrust brought a sting of pain, but Lucia didn't utter a sound. Her eyes were closed and her back arched, and Bane thrust again, feeling her tight, wet body draw him in. Gently, he began to plunge into her to loosen her body to receive all of him.

It was a magical moment.

Beneath him, Lucia's hands gripped his forearms as he braced himself. Bane had never felt such arousal as he did when she clutched him with her soft hands. He watched her as he made love to her, slightly elevated from her body so he could watch. Her full breasts jarred every time his body thrust into hers, and the sight of it drove him to a quick release as he spilled himself before he could control it.

But he wanted Lucia to feel what he had experienced, so he stroked her wet folds with his fingers as he continued to thrust into her, feeling her release mere seconds later. She had been so highly aroused that it hadn't taken much effort. Her body convulsed and the sounds of her gentle gasping filled the cold, dark air.

It was beauty beyond measure.

Bane's mouth fused with hers again, kissing her with all the adoration and lust he felt for her. The woman was embedded in every fiber of his being, a part of him as he could have never imagined. The experience of their first coupling had been one of the greatest moments of his life, knowing that this woman was made for him and him alone.

There was no doubt in his mind.

When the heavy breathing eventually faded and their bodies relaxed, he pulled her into a snug embrace as he lay there, staring at the ceiling.

"Are ye well?" he whispered. "I dinna hurt ye, did I?"

Lucia was burrowed against him. "Nay," she said. "But now I realize something."

"What?"

"I know why Lady Currie is so anxious tae do…*this*. It all makes sense now."

Bane started to laugh, his body shaking gently. "But not with everyone."

"Nay, not with everyone. Only with ye." She paused a moment. "I have a confession tae make, Bane."

"What is it?"

"When I first took ye tae Meadowbank, do ye remember when I barged intae the cottage while ye were taking a bath?"

He thought back. "Aye," he said. "Ye were embarrassed."

She grinned. "A little. But I caught a glimpse of yer naked arse and I liked it."

"Do ye still like it?"

"Better than before." Her smile faded as she looked into his eyes. "I love ye, Bane Morgan. I'll love ye until I die."

"And I, ye."

He kissed her forehead, pulling her closer if such a thing was possible. As he cuddled with her, feeling her body relax as she began to doze, there was a knock at the door.

"Bane? Bane, are you in there?"

Lucia's head shot up so fast that she clipped him in the chin. "It's Lady Currie!"

Terror filled the air. Bane was on his feet in a flash, pulling her off the bed. "Get under the bed," he whispered urgently. "Hurry!"

Lucia dropped to her knees, rolling under the small bed as

Bane shoved a coverlet in after her. But he was mindful to reply to the woman just outside his door.

"What do ye want?" he boomed.

There was a pause as he tucked the coverlet in and around Lucia to shield her from all angles. "I want to speak with you, please," Lady Currie said, muffled.

With Lucia covered, Bane moved for the door but he realized he was stark naked. Quickly, he grabbed his breeches from the bottom of the bed where he'd kicked them off and yanked them onto his body. He was fastening the ties as he unbolted the door and opened it.

The door cracked open to reveal Lady Currie standing there, wrapped up in her finery and smiling politely at him. He looked around outside to see if anyone had accompanied her, but she appeared quite alone.

"How did ye find my cottage?" he asked warily.

She maintained her polite smile. "I gave one of the camp guards a coin and he told me," she said. "May I come in?"

"Nay. State yer business, please."

She struggled to keep the smile on her face. "I was hoping we could...speak."

That's not what she wanted from him. Bane could see that from the look on her face. She was trying very hard to throw an alluring look in his direction, saying she wanted to speak with him but meaning she wanted something far more.

"I thought ye were speaking with Sir Clegg," he said.

She shook her head. "As strange as it sounds, he would not take my money for you," she said. "He told me he would stand by your decision. I am, therefore, appealing to you directly. Won't you let me in?"

"It is late and I am weary, m'lady."

"*Please?*"

He sighed faintly. What was it he'd told Lucia? *The woman is going to hound me.*

Already, it was starting.

"M'lady, I dunna know how much plainer I can be," he said. "I am not trying tae insult ye, but I have a wife and I am faithful only tae her. I dunna want yer company, but I am sure there are a dozen other men who would gladly entertain ye. Even if ye dunna understand, I would ask that ye respect my decision. I willna change my mind."

The smile on her face vanished. "Then you are a fool," she hissed. "Do you have any idea how much money I have at my disposal? I could make you a very wealthy man, Bane."

"My honor is worth more than money, m'lady. Please go."

Embarrassed and angry, she backed away from the door. "This is not over," she said defiantly. "I always get what I want, Bane. Do not forget that."

"In this case, m'lady, ye shall not get me."

She growled unhappily and turned on her heel, marching back the way she had come. Bane watched her until he was certain she wasn't going to turn around and charge back to him. Closing the door, he threw the bolt again before heading to the bed.

"Ye can come out now," he said, pulling up the coverlet he'd stuffed around her. "Did ye hear that?"

Lucia poked her head out, extending her hand so he could pull her all the way out. Standing up, she brushed the dirt off her legs and arms, grasping at her shift on the ground where Bane had tossed it.

"I heard," she said unhappily, pulling her clothing on. "I've seen her do this, Bane. She'll pick at ye and hope tae break ye down."

"Then she's in for a big disappointment."

Lucia smiled sadly at him, sad for the entire situation. Theirs would have been such a happy circumstance were it not for Lady Currie's interference.

Something told Lucia that it was only going to get worse.

"I must go," she said. "If she's in a state, she'll probably want tae leave early, so I must be ready tae leave, too."

He knew that but he was still disappointed that she had to leave at all. "Someday, ye'll not have tae leave me," he said, helping her secure the ties on the back of her dress. "There will be a day when we willna have tae worry over Lady Currie and her tantrums."

"I know," she said, turning to face him. "But that time is not now. But someday."

Reaching out, he smoothed at her mussed hair. There was so much he wanted to say to her but he wasn't sure where to even start.

"I'm going tae beg or borrow those two pounds," he finally said, cupping her face in his big hands. "I canna stand that ye must live with that...that woman and her nurse who beats ye. I canna stomach any of it, Lucia. I want ye tae come here and live with me. That's the only thing in the world I want right now."

She could see the turmoil in his face. "As do I," she said, her hands on his. "Somehow, I dunna feel whole knowing I have tae leave ye. I feel as if something is missing in me."

He smiled faintly. "*I'm* missing. But not for long, I swear it."

"I believe ye," she said, standing on her toes to kiss him sweetly. "And I look forward tae that time more than ye know. But for now...I *must* go."

He was reluctant to let her go and Lucia had to pull herself away from him, as difficult as it was. He grabbed her and kissed her one final time before finally releasing her, and she headed out into the icy night, leaving behind a man that she was aching for.

As she'd told him, she felt as if she were leaving a piece of herself behind.

But for now, they had little choice.

Fortunately for Lucia, she made it back to Lady Currie's carriage about five minutes before Lady Currie herself joined her, upset and frustrated that the warrior she wanted as a companion didn't want her.

As the carriage lurched along the darkened road home, Lady

Currie abruptly fell silent. When she spoke again, it was without the recent agitation.

There was a frightening amount of calm.

"Lucia," she said thoughtfully, "Bane Morgan thinks he has beaten me, but that is not true. I told him I always get my way and I shall."

"Aye, m'lady," Lucia said.

Lady Currie turned to her. "Do you know how?"

Lucia shook her head. In truth, she was terrified to hear it. "Nay, m'lady."

Lady Currie smiled. To Lucia, it looked like a horrific, nasty gesture. There was no warmth to it, only evil.

"Warriors at the Cal are purchased to lead armies," she said. "If Bane will not allow me to purchase him for my pleasure, then I will purchase him for Meadowbank's insignificant little army."

Lucia didn't understand what she meant and wasn't sure she wanted to. "M'lady?"

Lady Currie's face lit up. "Don't you see?" she said excitedly. "If he serves Meadowbank's army, then he serves *me*."

Lucia still wasn't clear. "He would answer tae ye and Laird Currie."

Lady Currie began to laugh. Peals of sweet and sinister laughter. "Nay, Lucia, you don't understand," she said. "If he serves me, then I can command him to do whatever I wish him to do. If I want to command him into my bed, then he cannot refuse. He is bound by his oath to obey and a man of honor would never break his oath. *Now* do you understand?"

Lucia did and she was horrified. It was worse than she could have imagined. "I…I think so, m'lady."

Lady Currie was still cackling over what she perceived as a coming victory. She pulled out her personal flask, which was empty, before digging around in a basket that Colly had sent along, which had more wine in it. She drank deeply.

"We shall return tomorrow, and I shall make an offer that Clegg cannot refuse," she said. "By tomorrow night, Bane Morgan will be mine."

Lucia didn't know what to say. In truth, she was afraid to speak. She turned her attention to the small window in the cab of the carriage, watching the dark landscape pass and feeling an inordinate amount of apprehension.

A man of honor would never break his oath.

It was very possible that, on that technicality, Lady Currie could very well back Bane into a corner.

Would he be forced to obey?

A bad situation was about to get worse.

CHAPTER TWENTY

"As I have said many a time, Husband, Meadowbank is without a fine warrior," Lady Currie said. "You have ten soldiers and one old sergeant in command, but he is not a great warrior. He's just an old soldier, and he is drunk most of the time. But I have found a great warrior I believe we should retain. With everything valuable we have within this house, I should think you would want at least one man who is highly skilled to protect us."

Laird and Lady Currie were in Laird Currie's cluttered solar. Laird Currie was listening to his wife rattle on this morning, thinking it unusual that she was up so early. But in hearing her speak on a warrior that caught her eye at the Ludus Caledonia, he was coming to understand why she was up at this hour.

She wanted something.

The only time she ever spoke to him was when she wanted something.

The woman was prattling on about this great fighter she had discovered, but Laird Currie wasn't giving her his full and undivided attention. He was looking for something on his bookshelf, haphazardly stacked with books and clutter and dust.

"Did you hear me?" Lady Currie demanded when he didn't answer her quickly enough. "We must have greater protection here at Meadowbank. *I* must have greater protection. I have found such a man, and for the right price, he shall be ours."

"I hear ye, my dear," Laird Currie said, turning to look at her with a dusty book in his hand. "What would ye have me do?"

Lady Currie was back to smiling pleasantly. "Give me money to purchase him, of course," she said. "I believe he makes the Ludus

Caledonia a good deal of money when he fights, so they will want a high price for him."

Laird Currie scratched his head in thought, reaching into his pocket and pulling forth one of his rats. He held the little beast as he moved away from his bookshelf, heading to the great table in the chamber that was so terribly cluttered. As he shuffled across the room, lost in thought, Lady Currie sighed heavily.

"Greer, do you understand me?" she said sternly. "I am trying to gain some quality protection for Meadowbank. The least you could do is cooperate. This warrior is relatively new to the Ludus Caledonia, which means they haven't spent a good deal on his training yet. However, he could make them a good deal of money over the life of his oath there. I've heard that the good ones will make the Cal twenty pounds a year or more. If we pay them sixty pounds sterling for him, I am sure they will take it."

Laird Currie reached his table and, still clutching the rat, seemed to be fumbling for something on the tabletop.

"My dear, we have plenty of soldiers," he said. "I dunna see how one more will make a difference."

Lady Currie pointed to the shelves and all of their expensive items. "If we were ever robbed, you would lose years' worth of income," she said. "All you have are ten drunkards to guard us. You know what I say is true. Those men spend more time drinking than paying attention to their duties. Every night when I go to bed, I bolt my doors and pray we are not robbed in the night."

"And ye believe this great warrior will help protect us?"

"I know he will."

Laird Currie didn't seem interested in what his wife was telling him, but he knew better than to argue. She would peck at him until she got her wish, so he waved a hand at her as if to shoo her out of his solar.

"If ye feel strongly about it, then do as ye wish," he told her. "Go, now. I'll have the money for ye before ye leave for the Ludus Caledonia tonight."

"How do you know I am going tonight?"

"Because ye go every night."

Considering Lady Currie rarely spoke to her husband, the subject of the Ludus Caledonia had her uncomfortable. She lived her life and he lived his, and they rarely crossed paths.

"It is a welcome respite from the monotony of this place," she said. "I refuse to spend my life boxed up in this…this *tomb*."

"And ye find distraction at the Cal?"

"You know I do."

Laird Currie put his rat down on the tabletop, petting the little beast before it scurried away. He busied himself with a piece of vellum that was in front of him, picking it up and pretending to examine it. But all the while, he had something on his mind, something that his selfish wife had failed to notice.

Behind those dark eyes, he was calculating.

"I am glad," he said after a moment. "I suppose it is exciting, though it has been years since I last attended a game there. Is Sir Clegg still in good health?"

"He is."

"He has bought many fine pieces from me over the years, ye know."

"I know."

"I consider him a friend."

"I *know*, Greer."

"Ye missed going tae the Cal for about a month, so I was told."

That caused Lady Currie to falter. "I was…ill," she said. "Had you come to visit me, you would have known."

He chuckled weakly, but it was without humor. "I am not in the habit of visiting a woman, not even my wife, when she is ill with another man's child," he said. "Dunna let it upset ye, my dear. I've known all along. But there is something ye should know, too—any child ye bear will be my heir. I need a son and since ye will lay with everyone but yer husband, I'll claim any child ye give birth tae as my own. So remember that when choosing those who will lie betwixt yer legs—make sure he's strong and intelligent. I should like those qualities for a son since I dunna have those qualities in a wife."

By the time he was finished, Lady Currie was red in the face. She stood over by the door to the solar, twitching with anger as Laird Currie continued to shuffle through the contents of his table as if he didn't have a care in the world.

"I must look for a father for my child elsewhere since my husband is a shriveled shell of a man," she hissed. "I must find a real man to produce a son."

He glanced up at her. "I wish ye well," he said. "I'll have yer money for ye later. Mayhap it'll buy ye the man ye want."

Lady Currie departed in a huff, slamming the solar door behind her. Laird Currie stood there a moment, remembering the first woman he'd married, the fair Iris, and lamenting the tumor that had claimed her life. Had he known then what he knew now, he would not have married again so he could have a son. At least, he would not have married Blanche Ireby. It had been a dreadful mistake.

Unfortunately, it was one he had to live with.

⚜ ⚜ ⚜

Lucia was in her sewing room, working on a vibrant orange silk for Lady Currie that she planned to wear when spring came. Lucia had been embroidering flowers and bees all around the neckline, a detailed project that took focus and skill, but all the focus in the world couldn't help her today.

Not after everything that had happened the night before.

Even now, she knew Lady Currie was with Laird Currie, making demands of the man. And she knew what the demands were— Lady Currie intended to purchase Bane from the Ludus Caledonia so he could take charge of Meadowbank's tiny group of soldiers. But it wasn't because Lady Currie wanted Bane's fighting skill.

It was because she could command the man to bed her if he served her husband.

That had been the grand scheme she'd come up with. As long as Bane was at the Ludus Caledonia, he could refuse her advances. But if she purchased his contract, he could refuse nothing.

Lucia's hands were shaking even as she thought about it. It was all Lady Currie could speak of last night as they returned from the Ludus Caledonia. Lucia had spent a night of turmoil, thinking of Bane's body against hers and the importance of their intimate encounter, but Lady Currie's horrible plan threatened to ruin the joy she was feeling. When she should be focused on her love for Bane, she was focused on her conniving mistress.

It was a hellish situation she found herself in.

"Lucia?"

A little voice broke her out of her train of thought, and she looked up to see Tynan standing in the doorway with a tray in his hands. She smiled weakly.

"Come in, Tynan," she said. "I've not seen ye lately. Where have ye been?"

The little boy entered the room, setting the tray down on the corner of a table that wasn't covered with fabric or needles or thread.

"Angus has been teaching me about the horses," he said. "I can work in the stable someday."

Lucia set her sewing down in her lap. "There's a good lad," she said. "It'll do ye well tae learn as much as ye can about many things."

Tynan nodded. Then he pointed to the tray. "Mam told me tae bring ye this. She said ye need tae eat."

Leave it to Amy to pay attention to Lucia's moods. It was true that Lucia hadn't eaten much over the past few days. There had been too much on her mind. She smiled at her friend's concern.

"I'll thank her for watching over me," she said.

She peered at the contents of the tray, which contained cheese, bread, and a full cup of wine. The food didn't hold any allure, but the wine did. Picking up the cup, she downed half of it in two big swallows, feeling the warmth course into her belly.

Tynan was watching her closely.

"Lucia?"

"Aye?"

"Are ye worried?"

She looked at the boy, smiling. "About what?"

Tynan lowered his voice. "About m'lady," he said. "About… everything."

"What's 'everything'?"

"Ye know," he said. "*Bane*. He said he'd come back for ye. Dunna worry because I know he will."

Lucia's smile faded and she set the cup down. Reaching out, she pulled Tynan very close to her so she could whisper in his ear.

"Tynan, I want ye tae listen closely," she murmured. "Can ye do that?"

He nodded eagerly. "Aye."

"Ye must never, ever mention Bane's name here at Meadowbank," she said. "Never speak of him, not even tae me. And if ye ever see him here, ye must never acknowledge that ye know him. Can ye do that?"

Tynan frowned. Bane was his friend and Lucia's words were confusing, but he nodded. "Canna I even talk tae him?"

Lucia shook her head. "Nay," she said. "M'lady might hear, and if she does, she will do terrible things. Or Colly will. We must never speak of Bane again. I know ye dunna understand why, but ye must trust me. Please?"

The boy nodded solemnly. "Aye."

"Ye must tell Angus, too," she said softly. "He's not tae speak of Bane or let on that he knows him, and he's tae make sure no one else does, either. There are a few servants who saw Bane when he worked here, but mostly the men from the stables. Make sure Angus tells them not tae speak of Bane at all. Can ye do that?"

"Aye, I can."

"Good. 'Tis very important."

"I'll tell him right now."

Her smile returned and she pinched him gently on the cheek. She was about to pick her cup up again when Lady Currie was suddenly in the doorway.

"Lucia," she said sharply. "Come with me. And bring the orange silk you are working on."

Lucia was on her feet, garment in hand as she quickly followed Lady Currie into her warm, fragrant chamber. She wondered with horror if the woman had heard her speaking to Tynan about Bane, and she braced herself for what was surely to come. Lady Currie was in a snit and surely Lucia was going to take the brunt of it. She caught sight of the boy dashing for the stairs as she swept into Lady Currie's chamber.

"Is the orange silk ready for me to wear tonight?" Lady Currie demanded. "Let me see it."

Lucia held it up to her. "I'm not finished with the embroidery, m'lady," she said. "It is very delicate work."

Lady Currie looked at the beautiful embroidery all along the neckline. "Aye, it is," she said, her crisp manner softening as she inspected the stunning work. "It is quite lovely, Lucia."

"I am sorry it is not ready tae wear yet, m'lady."

Lady Currie handed the dress back to her, taking a deep breath before plopping down on a cushioned bench at her dressing table.

"You did not know I wanted to wear it tonight," she said. Then she snorted ironically. "I did not even know I wanted to wear it. Forgive me for being sharp with you, Lucia. It has been a trying day with Laird Currie."

Lucia was coming to realize that the woman hadn't heard her conversation with Tynan and relief swept her.

"May I get ye something, then?" she asked. "More wine? Something tae eat, mayhap?"

Lady Currie was staring at herself in her big, polished glass mirror that had come all the way from London. "Nay," she said, sinking into melancholy as Colly rushed in from another room. Having heard her mistress's voice, she had come running. "Nothing to eat. But I do want to wear something beautiful tonight to the Cal. What do you think I should wear?"

Before Lucia could answer, Colly interjected. "If ye're going tae the Cal tonight, ye should rest before ye go, lamb," she said. "Lie down and I'll rub yer head. Ye like that."

But Lady Currie waved her off. "I do not want to lie down," she said. "I want to dress beautifully. Like a bride. Lucia, what do you think about the pale-blue silk?"

Lucia knew the dress. "It is very thin for this cold weather, m'lady," she said. "Unless ye wear the ermine with it. Ye'll freeze if ye dunna."

Lady Currie flicked her hand at her. "Bring me the blue silk and my ermine cape," she said. "I will wear those tonight. We are going to the Ludus Caledonia, and we must be dressed like queens."

Lucia was moving to the massive wardrobe in Lady Currie's chamber, one of three that held her expensive clothing.

"Is there something special tonight, m'lady?" Lucia asked.

Lady Currie was looking at herself in the mirror. Staring at herself, really. Picking up a brush, she began to stroke her soft, red hair.

"Special? Aye," she said after a moment. "I have Laird Currie's agreement. We are going tonight to purchase Bane Morgan's contract for Meadowbank."

Lucia had the doors of the wardrobe open wide, closing her eyes at the realization that Lady Currie planned to execute her scheme sooner rather than later. "I see, m'lady," she said, trying not to sound distraught. *God, this can't be happening!* "The laird... agreed with ye, did he?"

Lady Currie nodded. "He did," she said. "I was able to convince my stupid husband that we need an experienced warrior, and he told me that he would give me the money. Tonight, I will purchase Bane's contract from Clegg, and he will become mine to do with as I please."

Lucia's hands were quivering as she pulled forth the blue silk. So much rage and horror was bubbling up inside of her that she was sickened by it, struggling not to reveal her true feelings. She knew what would happen if Lady Currie knew of her relationship with Bane. She knew the woman would put her through hell.

But the situation had become so much more than Lady Currie purchasing Bane.

Now there was also the matter of those two pounds for her freedom.

Even if Bane purchased her freedom, she'd be right back where she was—living under Lady Currie's roof while Lady Currie ordered Bane to pleasure her. And Lucia would have to stand by and watch it happen. Servants were not permitted any free will; they did as they were told. By purchasing Bane, Lady Currie removed the protection of the Ludus Caledonia, the protection that had given him free will to deny Lady Currie's propositions.

But no more.

Once his contract was purchased, Bane would have to submit to Lady Currie like everyone else.

"Hurry up, Lucia," Colly snapped. "M'lady wishes tae be dressed immediately."

Lucia realized that she was daydreaming, thinking of the murky future of both her and Bane at the hands of Lady Currie. As she took the dress over to the rack where it would be hung and inspected for any spots or flaws, she eyed Lady Currie as the woman brushed her hair.

"M'lady," she said hesitantly, "have ye considered that the man will bring his wife here tae live at Meadowbank? He told ye that he was married."

Lady Currie stopped brushing and looked at her. "I never told you that."

Lucia only realized that as Lady Currie said it. It was true; she'd never told Lucia, in all of her scheming and planning, that Bane was married. Quickly, Lucia hastened to clarify how, exactly, she knew that.

"I know ye dinna, but I heard him tell ye that when we were in Sir Clegg's private box," she said, which was the truth. "He told ye that he had a wife."

Lady Currie went back to brushing her hair. "As if that will stop me," she snorted. "He can bring his wife, and I will put her to work in the soldiers' barracks. She can be of use to the soldiers while her husband becomes my personal comfort-giver."

It was a rather brutal thought, even for Lady Currie. Usually, the woman wasn't so nasty, but it was clear that jealousy had her in its grip when it came to Bane. The more the man refused her, the more obsessed she became over him.

And she didn't want any competition.

"Mayhap ye'll be lucky and he willna bring her at all," Lucia said. "It would be better if she dinna come if that is the fate ye have consigned for her."

Lady Currie chuckled, but not in a nice way. She stopped brushing her hair long enough to pour herself a large cup of wine from the pitcher that was always on her dressing table.

"Then she'll do well to let me have her husband," she said, taking a long, satisfying gulp of the red liquid. "Hurry now, Lucia. I want to dress and go early to the Cal so I may make the offer to Clegg. I want to make sure I offer for the man before anyone else does. I saw how those whores at the Cal were looking him over. You know the ones I speak of: that hideous mother and her equally hideous daughters. They want what I want, but in the end, *I* shall have him."

Lucia began the process of hanging the dress and smoothing

it out, laboring to focus as Colly summoned Amy and the woman began to fashion Lady Currie's hair. The chamber became a hive of activity once again, as it so often did when Lady Currie dressed for a visit to the Ludus Caledonia.

But this time, there was something more to it.

The stakes were about to escalate.

CHAPTER TWENTY-ONE

"BANE?"

It was a gentle winter's afternoon. Bane was sitting outside his cottage in the warrior village, smoothing the *gladius* he'd been using since he'd arrived at the Ludus Caledonia. He'd used it so much that splinters were coming out all over the place.

Glancing up when he heard his name, he could see Lor and Isabail approaching. Isabail was carrying their toddler son on her hip, a little lad with his mother's red hair and his father's green eyes.

Bane smiled weakly at the pair.

"Well?" he said. "Am I fighting tonight?"

Lor lifted his big shoulders. "I've not yet heard," he said. "I came tae ye about something else."

"What?"

"Lady Currie came early today," he said, lowering his voice. "I saw yer lady, Lucia, with her. They were heading intae the keep of Caelian Hill."

Bane lowered the sword, looking at Lor curiously. "Why did they go intae Caelian Hill?"

"That's what I wanted tae know," Lor said. "Axel and I followed them because he saw them arrive, too. It's no secret that Lady Currie wants ye badly, so we assumed she'd come tae speak with Clegg about ye again."

"And? Did she?"

Lor nodded. "Axel and I slipped in after them and listened from the shadows," he said. "'Tis no secret I dunna like Lady Currie. She's spoiled and bold. The more ye deny her, the more she wants ye. In fact, she wants ye so badly that she offered Clegg sixty pounds sterling tae buy yer contract."

Bane's eyebrows lifted in surprise. "Sixty *pounds*?" he repeated. "Are ye certain?"

"I heard it myself."

"But I'm not worth that much. No man is."

Lor grunted unhappily. "She thinks ye are," he said. "I dunna know what Clegg has agreed tae because I left before he answered. I thought I should warn ye that it's possible he'll take her offer. The Cal is a business, Bane. If someone offers enough money for ye, Clegg will take it, regardless of his personal feelings."

Bane's jaw began to flex as that possibility settled. In fact, he could feel a creeping sense of unmitigated horror at the very thought.

"But I'm not even fully trained," he said. "I've given my word that I will stay with the Cal for seven years. I've not even been here for two months. Why would Clegg take money on a warrior who hasna earned his worth?"

"I have a theory about that, Bane," Isabail said, bouncing her restless son. "I saw Lor when he came out of the keep, and he told me everything. I dunna know if Clegg will take the offer, but I have an idea why Lady Currie made it."

Bane was disgusted, furious and disgusted. He set the sword aside. "Because she's mad?" he snapped softly. "She's mad and she is fixed on me like a hunter fixed on prey."

"The lady *is* a hunter," Isabail agreed. "She's hunted ye and failed, so she's become resourceful. Now she's going tae buy ye. If she buys yer fealty, ye're sworn tae her and she can command ye tae do whatever she pleases."

Bane's head snapped up. "Is *that* it? She will command me tae do what I have refused tae do? I'll still refuse tae do it. I'll not touch her and I'll not let her touch me."

"If she buys yer contract, ye may not have a choice," Lor said softly.

Bane's anger was rising. He stood up, pacing in a small circle, pounding a balled fist against his open palm.

"Lucia told me that Laird Currie said that it would only take two pounds tae pay off her da's debt," he said. "I made some money in my most recent fight, but it's not nearly enough. If I had two pounds, I'd buy her freedom and I'd bring her here tae live with me so she's away from that…that *witch* of a woman."

"Bane, if Lady Currie buys ye, then ye'll be taking Lucia back tae her home," Lor pointed out. "Dunna ye see? Lucia would be the one in danger. I've seen Lady Currie coming tae the Cal for the better part of a year. She is jealous and spoiled, and I have a feeling she'll not take kindly tae ye marrying her servant. Do ye know what I mean?"

Bane did. In truth, he hadn't thought of it that way. Wearily, he rubbed at the back of his neck, trying to think of a way out of this mess.

"Lor, ye and Sir Clegg have been good tae me," he said. "I have every intention of fulfilling my oath, but I will not swear an oath tae a woman who simply wants tae buy a stallion tae service her. That's no honorable life for a warrior."

"I know," Lor said quietly, extending a small leather pouch to him. "Issie and I have been talking and we're going tae give ye the two pounds. Ye should take it, pay off her debt, and run. No one would blame ye, Bane. This is an impossible situation for everyone."

Bane looked at him in shock as he reached out to take the pouch, which jingled with coinage. "Ye…ye would give me the money?"

"Aye."

Bane looked back and forth between Isabail and Lor, stunned by their offer. He peered into the pouch to see that there were, indeed, several silver coins presumably amounting to two pounds.

He finally had the money he'd set out to earn for Lucia's freedom. Not by earning it, or stealing it, or begging or borrowing it… but by friendship.

By people wanting to help him.

"I dunna know what tae say," he said. Then he sat back down on the rock where he'd left his *gladius*. "Ye have tae understand… I've spent so much time accepting the guilt and responsibility of the men I killed all those years ago, of disobeying my da's command, that the day I met Lucia was the day my life unexpectedly turned around. She was kind and generous tae me and I fell in love with her. She means more tae me than ye'll ever know. And now the two of ye…offering tae help me. I suppose I still have trouble thinking I deserve any help from anyone. Ye canna know what it means tae me. I'll pay it back, I swear it."

Lor didn't have time to respond. As he opened his mouth, a voice came out of the shadows.

"Ye'll have tae take yer lass and hide her, Bane." Magnus abruptly appeared, coming out from between two cottages and heading toward them. When he saw their puzzled and perhaps indignant expressions, he held up a hand to ease them. "Sorry, but I was walking on the other side of these cottages and heard everything. I canna remain silent on this because I've seen similar situations at the Ludus Antonine. Rich women hounding men who dunna want their money, for whatever reason. Bane, I've been seeing Lady Currie since I've been at the Cal and she has purchased herself some studly companionship, but with ye…it seems she wants all of ye, not just a piece of ye."

Bane cocked an eyebrow. "Then ye know?"

"I think everyone does," Magnus said. "There's a certain gate guard tae Clegg's box who has made sure tae spread the tale of Lady Currie and her demands for ye."

Bane's face darkened. "Damn the man."

Magnus nodded, but he didn't want to get off the subject, so he lifted his hand to beg for patience while he finished. "If the lady has come tae buy ye as easily as if she would buy a prize stallion, then ye need tae run," he said. "Forget about yer oath tae the Cal if that means ye have tae accept a lady's dishonorable offer. Take yer woman and run. Hide until this passes."

Bane glanced at Lor and Isabail, uncertainty in his expression, before returning his focus to Magnus. "I have nowhere tae hide," he said. "I suppose I could take her back tae my clan in the Highlands, but I havena been home in a long time. I'm not sure I'm welcome there any longer."

Magnus folded his big arms across his chest; he had a very regal appearance, a man who had fine bloodlines. Bane remembered what Lor had said about him: *he's a royal bastard*. Bane could see it. There was something about him that was refined and noble, and his suggestions were surprisingly realistic.

Take yer woman and run.

Perhaps that statement emphasized just how serious the situation was.

"Is that what ye would do?" Bane asked. "Knowing what ye know now, ye'd still run away?"

Magnus nodded faintly. "Ye've only been here a short while, but I've seen enough," he said. "Ye never needed tae be trained as a warrior, Bane. Ye already knew how tae fight. Ye said yerself ye only came tae make money. 'Tis true ye gave yer oath, but Lady Currie doesna have honorable intentions when it comes tae buying yer services. She wants a stud, not a warrior."

"Let her buy ye and then run off afterward," Isabail said quietly, watching the men turn to her. "It would serve her right. Let her pay sixty pounds for a man who's going tae run off. Clegg would have her money and she'd be out not only the sterling, but the man she bought in the first place."

Lor looked at his wife, puzzled. "What are ye saying, Is?"

Isabail looked straight at Bane. "If yer lady serves Lady Currie, then ye'll have tae go tae Lady Currie's home tae get her," she said. "Why not make it easy and let Lady Currie buy ye? It'll put ye intae her house and hold, right where ye need tae be tae take yer lady and leave."

"I have a better idea."

The four of them turned to see Clegg approaching with Axel behind him, emerging from between a pair of cottages much as Magnus had done. Since the cottages were so closely packed, it was an easy thing to overhear a conversation, even one as clandestine as this. Clegg and Axel walked up to the quartet, but Clegg's attention was on Bane.

"M'laird?" Bane asked, somewhat warily. "I'm sorry if ye thought we were being subversive. We were simply discussing the situation with Lady Currie."

Clegg was wrapped up in his usual fine robes, looking somewhat out of place in the dirt and filth of the warrior village. But his gaze was intense.

"I know," he said, glancing at the group. "I heard what you were speaking of, and I think it is an excellent idea."

"Which idea, m'laird?" Bane asked. "We've been discussing several."

Clegg shook his head. "The *only* idea as far as I am concerned," he said. "Letting Lady Currie buy you and then going to Meadowbank to collect your young lady who serves there. Lor told me that your young woman serves Lady Currie."

"She does, m'laird."

Clegg's intense gaze lingered on Bane. "Lady Currie did, indeed, come to the Cal to buy you," he said quietly. "Sixty pounds sterling, which is an enormous sum for a warrior. You understand that I could not refuse that, Bane, but it was with a purpose in mind. It wasn't strictly business."

Bane looked at him, torn between outrage and curiosity. "Then ye accepted her offer?"

"I did. But I have a reason."

"What *is* the reason?"

Clegg turned to Axel and extended his hand. Axel produced two large leather pouches, jingling with coins, and heaved them both into Clegg's arms.

"This is what she paid me," Clegg said. "Or, I should say, what her husband paid me. You see, I know Greer Hume-Currie. I have for years, since before he ever married Blanche Ireby. That's Lady Currie's real name, you know. Greer deals in fine goods and I have purchased many things for my collection from him—Roman coins, vases, rings. Greer is a very nice man who married a viper. I do not like Lady Currie. I never have. She shames her husband daily with her ventures here to the Cal to fornicate with my warriors. But I took her money because I want you to do something for me."

Bane was quite intrigued. "If I can, m'laird."

"You can and you will," Clegg said, handing the heavy leather pouches of coinage that amounted to sixty pounds sterling to Bane. "You will return with Lady Currie to her home of Meadowbank. You will return Greer's money to him, and then you will take your lady and flee. Go wherever you wish, but just go. That way, Greer gets his money back, you have your freedom, and Lady Currie gets nothing. And that's the way I want it."

Bane stared at him in shock when he realized that Clegg agreed with Isabail's suggestion. "Ye want me tae run?"

"I do. Do you have any money of your own, Bane?"

"The purse from my bout with the Thistle."

"Good. It should be enough. But there is one more thing."

"Anything, m'laird."

"Stay away for a while, just long enough so that thoughts of you will cool in Lady Currie's mind," he said. "Then I want you to return here to fulfill your oath to me."

Bane would do anything for Clegg. He'd just made it so Bane could keep his honor, marry Lucia, and punish Lady Currie all at the same time. What *wouldn't* he do for the man?

"I'd be happy tae return if ye truly want me, m'laird," he said. "It would be an honor tae continue as a warrior."

But Clegg shook his head. "Nay," he said. "Not as a warrior. As a trainer. There is nothing more we can teach you, Bane. But I think there is a good deal you can teach our new recruits. It is a position I am offering you, and you will, of course, bring your wife with you. Will you do it?"

Bane was stunned. He looked around, to Magnus and Lor and Isabail and even Axel. They were all looking back at him in varied degrees of warmth and approval. This little family at the Ludus Caledonia that had somehow adopted him, too.

They wanted him.

Bane could hardly believe it.

"Ye…ye want me tae train men?" he managed to ask.

"I do," Clegg said. "Will you come?"

Bane was truly overwhelmed. "Two months ago, I was living in the gutters of Edinburgh," he said, feeling a lump in his throat. "I had no hope, no future. Then I met Lucia. She gave me hope again. I came here because of that hope, because I wanted tae earn money tae buy her freedom. But never did I imagine I would find friends here, people willing tae help a man they dunna even know very well. But ye've given me a gift I never expected tae receive—a gift of friendship. Will I return here tae teach? I canna imagine a greater honor, m'laird. I'll return, and gladly."

Clegg smiled at him. "Then it shall be done," he said. "Now I must return to Lady Currie and tell her we have struck a bargain. And, Bane…when you return that money to Laird Currie, make sure you tell him it is with my compliments."

"I will indeed, m'laird."

"Above all, remember our motto—*Hominibus Gloria*. In men, there is honor. And there is honor in you."

With that, Clegg turned away and headed back to Caelian Hill with Axel on his heels, leaving Bane standing there with the others, stunned by what had just happened. He was still trying to take it all in. Bane finally turned to Lor.

"It looks as if I am going tae Meadowbank tonight," he said.

Lor nodded. "We'll miss ye, but we'll look forward tae yer return."

Bane smiled weakly, looking between Lor and Isabail and even Magnus. "I came here tae make money," he said. "I found much more than that. I'll be back, ye can believe it."

"Good," Lor said. "If we dunna see ye before ye leave, then Godspeed tae ye, wherever ye may go. But should ye need anything…ye know where tae find us."

Bane reached out a hand, taking Lor's and squeezing it strongly. "Ye have my thanks, Lor," he said, looking to Isabail and smiling at her. "Both of ye have my thanks. I promise I'll pay ye back for the money ye've given me for Lucia. I'll pay ye back every pence."

Lor squeezed his hand in return, taking his wife and child and heading back toward the small cottage they shared. Magnus was left standing there, watching everyone walk away. But he lingered.

"If ye find ye are not welcome when ye return tae the Highlands, then go to a place called Blackwood House in Stirling," he said. "My mother lives there. Tell her I sent ye and she'll give ye shelter."

Bane looked at him seriously. "That is very generous," he said. "Given that I've nearly killed ye twice, that's a very gracious thing tae do."

Magnus chuckled. "Is that how ye remember our battles?"

"Dunna *ye*?"

Magnus's laughter grew. "I think I kicked ye in the head harder than I thought."

"Ye dinna kick hard enough tae knock over a pile of sand."

Magnus crowed. "Keep telling yerself that, Bane," he said. "I canna wait for ye tae return so we can kick each other again."

He walked away, chortling, leaving Bane standing there with a grin on his face and a warmth in his heart that he couldn't begin to describe. In what should have been one of the most terrible moments of his life, all he could feel were hope, friendship, and anticipation for what the future would bring.

But first, he had to survive his round with Lady Currie.

Not only did he intend to survive, he intended to win.

PART THREE

HIGHLAND DEFENDER

CHAPTER TWENTY-TWO

Meadowbank

MEET OUR NEW WARRIOR.

That's what Lady Currie had proudly exclaimed to Colly and the rest of the house and hold of Meadowbank on a crisp, cold morning. All except for Laird Currie. He wasn't anywhere to be found, but the other inhabitants of Meadowbank found themselves looking over a very big man dressed in leather and mail. He was big and rough-looking, with a bushy beard and hair that needed to be groomed.

But Colly knew she'd seen him before.

There was something about him that seemed familiar, though she couldn't put her finger on it. She watched the man stand like a stone as Lady Currie pawed all over him, finally leading him away so the drunk sergeant in charge of Meadowbank could show the man around. The last Colly saw, Lady Currie was following from behind as the old sergeant took Bane on his rounds.

So that's the warrior from the Cal, Colly thought. Lady Currie finally had what she wanted.

But Colly couldn't shake the notion that she'd seen him before. She returned to the house, to Lady Currie's chamber, and snapped at the maids who were cleaning the room. No one ever cleaned to Colly's satisfaction. Lady Currie had spent the night at the Ludus Caledonia, finding lodgings in cottages reserved for special guests, before returning the next morning with Lucia and the enormous warrior, and Laird Currie had yet to show his face.

The man was a ghost in his own home.

But that was of no concern to Colly. In her opinion, the old man was useless and would hopefully die soon, leaving the entire estate to his beautiful, young wife. All of that lovely money would go right to sweet Blanche and, consequently, to Colly as well.

Life would be much easier when that blessed event happened.

Meanwhile, Colly sat at Lady Currie's dressing table, drinking what was left of the woman's wine and stuffing herself on the sausages that had been brought for Lady Currie's morning meal. She would eat them all and then blame it on the servants, which she had often done.

As Lucia entered the room with a fresh dress for Lady Currie to change into once she returned to her chamber, Colly thought she might even blame the missing sausages on Lucia. After all, the girl had claimed to have lost sausages once before, but the truth was that she had probably eaten them and blamed robbers.

Sausages…

Colly suddenly sat up straight, setting aside the cup of wine. It occurred to her now just where she'd seen the warrior. He was the same man Lucia said had saved her from the sausage thieves, the one she'd brought back to Meadowbank to work in the stables. That man had been clean-shaven, however, and the truth was that Colly hadn't gotten a good look at him. Still…it was possible that Lady Currie's new warrior and Lucia's protector were one and the same.

That made for a very interesting situation.

Colly watched Lucia as the woman cleaned Lady Currie's day dress, brushing at it with a fine horsehair brush. Little Lucia had been much better behaved since their encounter in the kitchens when Colly had brained her and locked her up for a day to teach her a lesson. It had been a show of force and it had worked. The lesson had been learned because Lucia had been much better mannered since then.

Even so, Colly just wanted the girl gone.

Lady Currie listened to Lucia and valued her opinion, and Colly was threatened by that relationship. She wanted to be the only one Lady Currie valued. Perhaps the arrival of Bane Morgan was just the excuse Colly needed to get rid of Lucia once and for all. She knew that Lady Currie would not want Bane's attention diverted from her, and if she knew the man had an eye for Lucia, or at least a history with her, she would surely send the young woman away.

Colly rather liked that plan.

Finally, she could be rid of the Symington wench.

Farewell, Lucia…

⚜ ⚜ ⚜

"What do you think of my humble home, Bane?" Lady Currie asked, her hands looped through Bane's elbow. "We can certainly use your expertise on our safety. I think we are too relaxed, while my husband does not seem to share that opinion."

Bane's face was like stone as he and Lady Currie departed the gatehouse of Meadowbank, crossing the small bailey as they headed for the house. When he'd worked here before, he'd made it up into the bailey a few times, but not enough to really study it.

Now he could. It was a busy place, with trade stalls to the east along with a small troop house for the soldiers. It wasn't a military fortress by any means, as he'd already known, and the massive stone walls were perhaps its greatest protection.

But he didn't much care.

He wouldn't be here long enough to.

"This is yer husband's house, m'lady," he said after a moment. "I should like tae meet Laird Currie and discuss it with him."

"Discuss it with me."

"He is yer husband, m'lady, and laird of the home. That is men's business."

Lady Currie was trying very hard not to become angry with him. He'd been like this since she purchased his contract from Clegg—stiff, unfeeling, unemotional. The man had ice water running through his veins, but she was determined to warm him.

She didn't give up easily.

"I suppose you are correct," she said. "It is men's business, but I am interested in men's business. Don't you think that ladies should be curious about a man's business?"

"Not if it doesna concern her, m'lady."

"The safety of Meadowbank concerns me, Bane." When he didn't respond, she tried another tactic. "We shall share a morning meal together, and you may tell me of your great plans for the manse."

"I would prefer ye show me where I am tae sleep," he said. "I have some organizing tae do before I assume my duties."

Lady Currie liked that idea even better. She could take him straight to his bedchamber, which happened to be next to hers, and surely she could loosen his harsh stance from there.

It was time to show the man who was in command.

"Of course," she said. "Come with me."

She led him into the manse itself, the big gray-stoned edifice with three floors. She completely bypassed Laird Currie's solar, even though they walked right past it, and headed up the spiral stairs to the next level.

This was where her chamber took up one entire side of the manse. There were four other chambers on this level, and she took Bane to the chamber next to hers, throwing open the old oak doors to reveal a sparsely furnished room. There was a messy bed, a table, and little more. It was where Colly slept, but she was going to relocate the old woman starting today.

"I will have this cleaned immediately," she told him. "I will have fresh straw brought in for your bed and a fire started in the hearth. Is there anything else you require?"

Bane walked into the chamber, looking around and realizing that someone else already lived here, but clearly, Lady Currie didn't see that as a problem. He turned to her.

"I would rather sleep with the men," he said. "Sleeping in the house isna a good location for the man in charge of the safety of Meadowbank. I will sleep with the soldiers. It is where I belong."

He started to walk out but she quickly shut the doors, preventing him from leaving. "You will sleep where I tell you to sleep," she said in a low voice, standing in front of the doors to block him. "I am in command now, Bane, and you will do what I tell you to do. You will sleep here."

Bane had a feeling this entire morning had been coming to this.

After a tormented ride to Meadowbank, trying not to look at Lucia as she sat across the carriage from him, he'd been forced to keep company with Lady Currie since his arrival. The woman had gripped him tightly through every move they made, from their arrival into the bailey until this very moment. She was clingy and possessive, and Bane was losing patience by the second.

But he had something he had to do before he told the woman off.

Those sixty pounds sterling were in a trunk that Clegg had provided him, a trunk that also contained his skimpy belongings and was now sitting in the foyer of the manse. Sixty pounds sterling that he fully intended to deliver back to Laird Currie this very day.

He wasn't going to spend one more moment here than necessary.

"M'lady, do other soldiers sleep in the house?" he asked.

She frowned. "Of course not."

"Then why me?" he said. "Ye purchased my contract from Clegg and told him it was because ye wanted a seasoned warrior tae protect Meadowbank. If ye want me tae do my job, then I must be near the gatehouse. I must be where my duties are focused."

Lady Currie's smile was gone. "I want you in the house with me," she said. "Is that so hard to understand?"

"I understand," Bane said. "But just because I chose not tae bring my wife tae this place doesna mean I'm ripe for the picking. I am here tae assume control of yer soldiers and nothing more. *Nothing* more."

Lady Currie's pleasant demeanor snapped. "It was wise of you to leave your wife back at the Cal," she said. "It would not have been enjoyable for her here, Bane. She would not have been able to sleep in the same chamber with you, in any case."

"I left her behind for that very reason. I suspected ye would view her as yer competition when, in truth, there *is* no competition."

Lady Currie's jaw hardened. "You are sworn to me now," she growled. "You must do as I say, and I say I want you in this chamber. Is that clear?"

"Who paid for my contract?"

"I did, you fool!"

"Where did ye get the money?"

"From my husband!"

"Then he is the one who bought my contract. Not ye. 'Tis Laird Currie who will have the final say in where I sleep. Let us ask him."

Lady Currie was so angry by this time that she was grinding her teeth. "You serve the laird *and* lady of Meadowbank," she said through clenched teeth. "*I* am the lady of Meadowbank and I demand you serve me."

"I shall serve ye loyally, m'lady. But only as a warrior and nothing more."

"Ye'll do as I say!"

"Or what?"

Her mouth popped open in outrage. "I'll have you whipped!"

"By whom?"

"I have ten soldiers that will do my bidding!"

"There are ten soldiers tae do yer husband's bidding and mine. Ye're not in the chain of command, Lady Currie."

Lady Currie was positively enraged. She growled angrily,

balling her fists. "We shall see what my husband has to say about this!"

Bane nodded readily. "I agree," he said. "Let's see what yer husband has tae say about ye commanding a warrior tae do anything more than his duties *as* a warrior. I'm not a whore, m'lady. If ye paid for my contract with that on yer mind, then ye wasted yer money."

Lady Currie wasn't finished. She was wearing the pale-blue satin with the ermine robe over it against the cold and she immediately tossed off the ermine, exposing a dress that was far better suited for warm temperatures. Dramatically, she grabbed her full breasts.

"You will never see anything better than what I have to offer, Bane," she said, fondling herself in the hopes of arousing him. "My skin is soft and sweet, far better than anything you have ever tasted. All you need to do is take what you wish. I will not resist."

Bane sighed heavily, clearly unimpressed. He walked up to her, gazing down at her impassively as she clutched herself. She had such hope, such expectation on her face, that when he reached out and grasped her by the arms she believed that she'd finally broken through to him. For just a split second, her joy was obvious.

But it was not to be.

Bane grasped her by the arms, lifted her up, and moved her away from the door. As Lady Currie stood there with her hands still on her breasts, Bane opened the door and quit the chamber. He could hear Lady Currie screaming in anger as he walked down the corridor toward the stairs.

But the noise had brought out the servants, wondering why Lady Currie was yelling. Bane could see heads popping out from open doorways, including Lucia's. He saw her just beyond the stairwell, looking at him with shock and fear on her face. He was so glad to see her that it was all he could do not to run to her.

Instead, he pointed in the direction of the stable yard.

CHAPTER TWENTY-THREE

LATER THAT NIGHT, WITH TYNAN ON THE LOOKOUT FOR LADY Currie, Lucia slipped out of the manse and ran into the stable yard. Moving swiftly, she ran straight for the stables, rushing inside only to find Bane and Angus talking quietly in one of the stalls. When Bane looked up and saw her, he came out to greet her.

"My angel," he murmured, sweeping her into his powerful embrace. "God, it's good tae finally see ye alone."

Lucia's arms were around his neck. "It is," she agreed. "We've not had a moment alone since the Cal. Bane, why did ye agree tae come here? I canna believe ye would agree tae come with Lady Currie when ye know—"

He cut her off gently, kissing her to silence her. "I have a plan," he said quietly. "Ye dunna think I'd come here blindly, do ye?"

She eyed him curiously. "A plan? What plan?"

Bane knew she wasn't privy to his reasons for coming, the plans he'd made with Lor and Isabail and Magnus and Clegg. She didn't know any of it, so surely she thought he must have lost his mind. Quickly, he pulled her into the stall as Angus, grass in his teeth as usual, wandered out.

"Where is Angus going?" she asked. "He's not going tae tell anyone we're here, is he?"

Bane pulled her down onto the hay. "He's going tae watch for any sign of Lady Currie or anyone else," he said. "I told him tae pretend he doesna know me. Did ye tell Tynan not tae know me?"

"Aye. But others saw ye the first time I brought ye here. They might give ye away."

He shook his head quickly. "Angus has told them not tae. Seems no one likes Lady Currie, so they're willing tae keep the secret."

Lucia felt a little better. "I hope so," she said. "I know Lady Currie never saw ye so we dunna want her tae know ye're the man that Colly said I was fornicating with."

"What *about* Colly? Did she recognize me?"

Lucia shook her head. "I dinna know," she said. "I'm not entirely sure she ever got a good look at ye, so ye may be safe."

"We can pray for small mercies," he said. His gaze drifted over her, drinking in the sight of her. He felt whole again when she was in his arms. "But it willna matter if she did or not. We're leaving tonight, for good."

Her eyes widened. "We *are*?"

He nodded, kissing her hands. "Aye," he said. "Lady Currie paid sixty pounds sterling for me, but Clegg gave it all back tae me with specific instructions—I'm tae return it tae Laird Currie and leave this place with ye."

Lucia was bewildered. "*Return* it tae Laird Currie? I dunna understand. *Why?*"

He could see that she wasn't following him. "Listen tae me," he said with quiet urgency. "It seems that Clegg and Laird Currie are old friends. Clegg doesna like Lady Currie. He feels that she brings shame upon her husband with her behavior, which she does. Clegg has given me the money Lady Currie paid for me tae return it tae her husband, but he wants us tae flee Meadowbank after I do. That way, Laird Currie has his money returned tae him and Lady Currie is left with nothing. Ye're safe, I'll be safe, and Lady Currie will be sorely disappointed."

Lucia's hand was over her mouth in surprise. "Sir Clegg has done this for ye?"

"For us," he said softly. "Better still, when this situation is over, Clegg has asked me tae return tae the Cal as a trainer of men. A *doctores*. Lucia, he's offered me a position there. A position of honor with people I respect."

Lucia was starting to understand. She smiled at him, thrilled to hear what had transpired. "Is it true?" she gasped. "Bane, that's wonderful news. I'm so very proud of ye."

His smile faded as he looked at her. "Are ye?" he asked. "It's been so long since someone has been proud of me. Ye canna imagine how long, my angel. 'Tis good tae hear it."

Her smile broadened. "Of course I'm proud of ye," she said. "It seems that a good deal has happened since the last time I saw ye."

That was an understatement. "Very true," he said. "But good things. Except for Lady Currie and her lewd intentions, all good things. But in the end...mayhap everything happened the way it should. Had Lady Currie not set her cap for me, I would still be at the Cal, still trying tae earn money for yer freedom. Who knows how long it would have taken?"

Lucia could see his point. "I suppose," she said. "I simply canna believe that so much good has come from this. What do ye intend tae do now?"

Bane released her from his embrace. "Now I intend tae seek Laird Currie and return his money and pay off yer debt, so I want ye tae pack whatever ye need and be ready tae leave right away. Will ye do that?"

Lucia could hardly believe what she was hearing. "Aye," she murmured. "Oh, Bane...I can hardly believe it. I'll finally be leaving this terrible place."

He kissed her gently. "I intend tae take ye out of here before the evening meal, so we must hurry. We'll leave as soon as I give Laird Currie his money back."

"But what about the two pounds for my da's debt?"

Bane grinned. "Lor loaned it tae me," he said. "He and his wife. I'll pay back every pence and then some, so Laird Currie will receive exactly sixty-two pounds for my freedom and for yers. I have all of the money with me in the trunk I brought."

Lucia was so anxious that she took him by the hand and began dragging him toward the stable entry. "Laird Currie's solar is by the manse entry," she told him. "He's always there. There is no other place he'll be. Go in through the front of the house, and it'll be the first doors ye see. Great, carved doors."

Bane nodded. "Give me an hour and meet me back here. We'll leave from the postern gate where no one is watching."

They had just reached the doors and Lucia turned to him, throwing her arms around his neck forcefully enough to knock him off-balance.

"I canna believe this is happening," she said. "I'll be here in an hour. But be kind to Laird Currie... He's a nice man. What his wife does tae him is cruel beyond measure."

Bane cocked an eyebrow. "Then mayhap he'll easily take his money back and wish us well."

"Without his wife finding out before we've left."

That was the unknown factor in all of this and Bane knew it. All of this had to be done without Lady Currie becoming wise to it. That's why he wanted to get it over with so quickly. The sooner they were out of Meadowbank, the better for them both.

"Be discreet when ye pack yer things, my angel," he said quietly. "The last thing we want is Lady Currie becoming wise tae what is happening."

Lucia nodded solemnly. "I will be very cautious," she said, moving for the stable door. "I'll see ye soon."

He nodded, blowing her a kiss as she slipped from the stable and out into the cold winter's day. He wisely waited a nominal amount of time before departing himself, taking an entirely different path and heading for the foyer of Meadowbank where his big trunk awaited. Locked and solid, so no one could steal the contents.

Laird Currie was soon to be in for a surprise.

Colly could see that Lady Currie was in a snit.

She'd known the woman her entire life, so when Lady Currie's mood shifted, Colly was alert to it. Moreover, it hadn't taken a genius to figure out that the woman was upset because she'd heard her screaming, like everyone else at Meadowbank, in a manner that suggested she'd been grossly displeased or insulted.

Or both.

Colly poked her head out of Lady Currie's bower in time to catch a glimpse of the big warrior making his way down the stairs, leaving Lady Currie so angry that she was kicking the table in Colly's chamber.

Colly, of course, had no idea why Lady Currie was in her chamber, only that she was. Timidly, she entered, watching Lady Currie kick the table until the leg buckled. Even then, she kicked some more, growling and bellowing.

Colly stood by the door in fear.

"M'lady?" she said hesitantly. "Can I help with anything?"

Lady Currie wasn't finished with her tantrum. She kicked the buckled leg until it broke from the table, which fell forward and clipped her foot. Howling, she hobbled over to the bed and sat heavily, rubbing her injured toes.

"I purchased his contract for Meadowbank," she said angrily. "I am the lady of Meadowbank, am I not?"

"Ye are, lamb."

"And everyone here must obey me."

"That is true."

"Even the soldiers."

"Aye, they must." Colly came into the chamber and quietly shut the door so they'd have more privacy. "What happened with yer new warrior, lamb? What did he say tae make ye so angry?"

Lady Currie looked at her. "He did not *say* anything," she said. "But he refused to... He refused everything I asked of him."

Colly frowned. "He canna do that," she said. "Ye're the lady of the house."

"He says he only answers to my husband because it was my husband's money that purchased his contract. Have you ever heard anything so outrageous?"

"Nay, lamb."

"He says he has a wife and he must be faithful to her. What rubbish!"

She was shouting by the time she was finished. Colly had a feeling that was why Lady Currie was so angry, that this warrior she seemed to be obsessed with saw no attraction in her.

But Colly was sly and conniving. That was something inherent to her. So was the desire to ease Lady Currie in any given situation. When the woman was hungry, she fed her. When she was angry, she soothed her. She had an idea of how to soothe her *and* force the new warrior to Lady Currie's will all in the same breath.

Grasping a stool, she pulled it up to the bed and sat down next to Lady Currie as the woman rubbed her foot.

"I think I know why he willna bend tae yer will, lamb," she said quietly.

Lady Currie snorted. "That is no secret," she said. "I already told you that it was because of his wife."

"I think I know who the wife is."

Lady Currie glanced at her in disbelief. "How would you know who his wife is? You've not been to the Ludus Caledonia with me."

Colly shook her head. "I dunna have tae go there tae know," she said. "I believe his wife is here at Meadowbank."

"Here? You've gone mad."

"I believe his wife is none other than Lucia."

Lady Currie stopped rubbing her foot. "Lucia?" she repeated, perplexed. "*Our* Lucia?"

Colly nodded firmly. "I'll tell ye why I think so," she said. "Do ye remember a couple of months ago when Lucia brought a man here tae Meadowbank, a man she said saved her from the assault when she lost yer sausages?"

By this time, Lady Currie's rage had cooled and she was looking at Colly warily. "I remember," she said. "The same man you said she was fornicating with."

"The man who tried tae beat me when I discovered it."

"I remember that," Lady Currie said. Then her eyes widened. "Are you telling me that Bane was that man?"

"Think about it, m'lady," Colly said, grasping her wrists to emphasize her point. "When was the first time ye saw Bane at the Cal?"

Lady Currie was trying very hard to put the pieces of the puzzle together. "Just a short time ago."

"But ye never saw him before I caught Lucia fornicating."

Lady Currie shook her head. "Nay," she said. "Clegg told me that he was a new recruit."

"There ye have it," Colly said. "Mayhap he and Lucia have planned this all along. He went tae the Cal just so ye would pay attention tae him. Mayhap they even wanted ye tae bring him here."

"But why? He's refused me since I first saw him. Why would he want to come here?"

"Tae be with Lucia, of course!"

Lady Currie's mouth popped open. "He did not bring his wife with him," she said. "He told me he left her at the Cal because he did not want to bring her here. But what if she was *already* here?"

Colly nodded firmly. "Now ye understand, m'lady. No doubt the warrior and Lucia are planning something terrible. Mayhap they plan tae kill ye and the laird!"

Lady Currie looked at her with both fear and shock. "Is it true?"

Colly patted her hand. "Before ye do anything, let me speak with Lucia," she said. "I can force her tae tell the truth. She might not tell ye because she doesna fear ye, but she fears me. I know I can force her tae tell me everything."

Lady Currie was clearly bewildered by it all, realizing that her new warrior and one of her maids could possibly be married. Had they set a trap for her? She never would have believed it of Lucia, but Colly seemed convinced.

"Are you certain he was the same man Lucia brought here?" she asked. "Lucia has never been disloyal to me, Colly. I find this all quite shocking."

Colly stood up, pulling her to her feet. "I will find out," she said confidently. "I want ye tae return tae yer chamber and wait for me. I am going to find Lucia and get the truth out of her."

Lady Currie allowed Colly to lead her to the door. "Colly, if this is all true, then I understand why Bane has refused me, but Lucia… Why would she not tell me she had married the man? Why keep it a secret?"

Colly opened the chamber door. "Because she is a deceitful liar," she said. "I have been telling ye for two years that Lucia is not someone ye should have around ye. When she confesses the truth, ye must dismiss her. Better still, send her tae another house far away. Mayhap ye should send her tae yer father's house where she can scrub the floors from dawn to dusk. Send her far away so that ye will have all of Bane's attention. With his wife gone, surely he will submit tae ye."

Lady Currie liked that idea a great deal. Had she finally found the key to Bane's submission? She nodded as if, finally, she had hope in the situation.

"Speak with Lucia and come to me when you are finished," she said. "If the woman is guilty, then you will bring her to me. I want to hear it from her own lips."

"I shall, m'lady. Not to worry. Colly will tend tae everything."

"Make sure you get the answers to your questions. Do not let her be evasive."

"I willna, lamb. I promise."

As Lady Currie disappeared into her chamber, Colly felt great satisfaction. Whether or not Lucia was guilty wasn't the issue.

Colly intended to wrangle a confession from her one way or another because this was what she'd been waiting for.

Hoping for.

Lucia was finally going to fall.

CHAPTER TWENTY-FOUR

THE DOORS.

Bane stood before enormous oak doors that had been carved into figures from Celtic mythology. Fantastic creatures were on the panels along with warriors bearing great muscles and great weapons. They were quite intricate and he stood there a moment, inspecting them, before softly rapping on the door.

The knocks reverberated throughout the foyer.

He was holding the chest that Clegg had given him, and it was quite heavy. When no one answered his knock, he tried again, louder this time. As he wondered if Laird Currie was even in the chamber, he began to hear shuffling on the other side. A bolt was thrown. Slowly, the door creaked open and an old man with long, white hair appeared.

"Who are ye?" he asked. "What do ye want?"

Bane wasn't sure how to answer that except with the truth. "Sir Clegg de Lave of the Ludus Caledonia sent me," he said. "Are ye Laird Currie?"

The old man blinked as if startled both by the answer and the question. "Clegg has sent ye?"

"If ye are Laird Currie, he has."

The old man hesitated for a split second before moving aside, opening the door to admit Bane. "Aye," he said. "Clegg de Lave *truly* sent ye?"

Bane moved into the chamber, which turned out to be a vast and magical place that smelled of dust and smoke. It was quite cluttered, filled to the rafters with books and treasures that Bane couldn't even begin to guess about.

There were also rats.

He saw several of them gathered on a messy table, looking at him with their beady rat eyes. "Aye, he did, m'laird," he said, eyeing the rats. "My name is Bane Morgan. I've come with a message."

Laird Currie came around to stand in front of him, watching him as he set the heavy chest onto the floor. "I've not seen Clegg in a year," he said. "Is the man well?"

"Well, m'laird."

"What message does he send me?"

Bane looked at the old man, *really* looked at him. He remembered Lucia telling him that Laird Currie was much older than his wife and he could see that it was the truth. He was old enough to be her grandfather. He was tall and thin, with stringy white hair and an odd cap on his head. He appeared rather odd in general, but Bane also remember that Lucia told him of the old man's kindness.

Already, he felt pity for the man and the life he was relegated to with a frisky young wife.

"It is a long story, m'laird, so I'll beg yer patience while I tell it," he said after a moment. "First—may we bolt the door? We dunna want any interruptions."

Laird Currie scurried over to the doors, throwing the big bolt that more than likely would have stopped a herd of stampeding cattle. It was enormous. He rushed back over to Bane.

"It must be important if I am bolting doors," he said.

"It is," Bane said. "It is easiest if I start from the beginning. I am the warrior yer wife purchased from the Ludus Caledonia."

Laird Currie never changed expressions. "Are ye, now?" he said as if very interested in that fact. "Ye must be a great warrior."

Bane shrugged. "There was a time when men called me the Highland Defender," he said. "I've seen my share of battles."

"Ye look it. Ye're a big lad."

Bane snorted. "Big enough, I suppose," he said. "M'laird, I'm not sure how much ye know about the situation, so forgive me if

I'm blunt. I know of no other way than tae be truthful. Yer wife dinna purchase my contract so I could protect Meadowbank. She purchased me tae be her lover."

The old man nodded. "She chose well," he said. "I told her if she was tae buy a father for my son, then he should be strong and intelligent."

Bane frowned. "Then ye know why she did this?" he asked. "Ye told her tae?"

Laird Currie lifted his slender shoulders. "She would do it with or without my encouragement," he said. "Since ye're being honest, so shall I. The truth is that I married a harlot, Bane. The woman spreads her legs for everyone but her husband. But the thought of it stopped vexing me long ago. I'm being punished for being selfish enough tae marry a young lass who only wanted my money. That's my private purgatory."

Bane was relieved to know that Laird Currie wasn't in on his wife's purchase of a lover. He'd been worried for a moment. But he could see that the old man was simply acknowledging the situation, not endorsing it.

"Then…then ye have no feelings about it, m'laird?" he asked.

Laird Currie threw up his hands in a gesture of resignation. "She does as she pleases," he said as he planted himself on the nearest stool. "My mistake was in thinking she'd be happy married tae a man who only wanted a son from her. I suppose it's not an easy life for her. Would I rather she not go tae the Cal and fornicate with the warriors there? Of course I would. At least, I did. But I stopped caring long ago. As I said, my punishment is being married tae a lass who pays men tae pleasure her. 'Tis a shameful thing."

Bane's pity for the man deepened. "Would ye be open to seeking some vengeance on her? Vengeance for shaming ye, I mean."

Laird Currie looked at him sharply. "What do ye mean?"

Bane bent over, using a big iron key to unlock the chest. He flipped open the lid and pulled out two big leather pouches. He set them both down heavily on the table as Laird Currie looked on in astonishment. Rising from his stool, he pointed at the purses.

"Those…" he hissed. "I sent those with my wife last night."

"I know."

"She used them tae pay for a warrior…tae pay for *ye*."

"She did."

Laird Currie looked at him with his mouth hanging open. "What are ye doing with them?"

Bane's eyes glimmered. "I am returning them tae ye with Clegg's compliments," he said. Then he reached into the chest again and pulled out a smaller leather pouch, setting it onto the table with the others. "And that purse contains two pounds. That is from me, tae purchase the remainder of Lucia Symington's debt. She said ye told her it would be two pounds for the debt tae be paid in full."

Laird Currie was clearly confused. "Lucia? Why would ye pay for Lucia?"

Bane could see that the old man was bewildered and possibly even shaken by everything he was being told. It was a great deal to absorb. He gently grasped the old man by the arms and directed him back to his stool.

"I want tae marry Lucia," he said softly. "I want tae pay off her debt and take her away, tonight. M'laird, I'm sure ye know how they treat her here. She is beaten and mistreated, and I willna stand for it any longer. The money is for her debt, and if ye require more, I promise I'll send it tae ye. But I am taking her away tonight, no matter what. This way, the money yer wife paid for me is returned tae ye, Lucia's debt is returned tae ye, and yer wife will be without the man she purchased purely for her pleasure. That's the vengeance I speak of, m'laird. Painless, but the message is clear."

Laird Currie stared at him, digesting what he'd been told. His gaze eventually moved to the table again where the three pouches sat, pouches that his rats were beginning to sniff.

"'Tis overwhelmed I am," he said, fingering the leather purses. "When life turns against ye... It was easier tae hide in my solar and pretend this was my only world. The place that had been my home my entire life was no longer my home. It was no longer happy. But this...this gives me hope, lad. Clegg will never know what he's done for me."

Bane smiled faintly at the old man. "And me," he said. "Clegg is a good man."

Laird Currie looked at him. "Is that how ye met Lucia? When she visited the Cal with Lady Currie?"

Bane shook his head. "When I saved her from robbers."

Laird Currie sensed there was a story behind that but he didn't ask. He was more concerned with what the future held.

"She's a good lass," he said. "I knew her father. He was a servant but he was also my friend, and when he died, she came tae Meadowbank of her own free will tae work off the debt I'd incurred in paying for a physic for him. Did she tell ye that?"

Bane nodded. "She did."

Laird Currie turned serious. "Take her away from here, Bane," he said. "Ye're right when ye say she was mistreated here. Ye've paid me more than enough for her debt, so take her. The lass deserves a better life than what she's had at the hands of Lady Currie."

Bane was greatly relieved to hear that Laird Currie wasn't going to give him a fight. "Thank ye, m'laird," he said. "I will do all I can tae make her happy."

"Good," Laird Currie said. "Her father would have wanted that. Mayhap it's the last gift I can give a man who meant something tae me. Until now, I've failed when it came tae the care of his daughter. But I'll fail no more."

Bane smiled. "Nor will I," he said. "But I do have a favor tae ask ye, m'laird."

"Anything."

"We'll need a horse," he said. "Ye've a fine stud in the stables, and I'm told ye never ride him. Could I borrow him? Just tae get where I'm going, of course. I'll send him back tae ye when I can."

Laird Currie waved him off. "He's yers," he said. "The horse is growing fat for want of use, so take him and welcome. If I tried tae ride him, I'd probably end up on my head."

Bane was truly appreciative. With a lingering expression of gratitude to Laird Currie, he took his possessions out of the chest, few as they were, and quit the chamber. Laird Currie had his money returned and Lucia's debt was paid. Everything was working out, just as he'd planned.

Quickly, he made his way back to the stables to prepare the big, fat, white horse with the gloriously long mane and tail. When he told Angus that Laird Currie had given him the beast, Angus was more than happy to help him prepare the animal for travel.

Time was growing short.

Lucia was packing and he had to be ready.

Chapter Twenty-Five

THE LITTLE SEWING ROOM WHERE LUCIA DID ALL OF HER WORK was also her sleeping chamber.

It was a tiny interior chamber with no windows and only a door. The way the second floor of the manse was configured, it was built into the curve of the stairwell. It had a small hearth and a transom built over the door for ventilation, but in all, it was a small and dingy chamber. It had been Lucia's home for the past two years and she was glad to be rid of it.

When Lucia had first come to Meadowbank, she'd brought everything she owned in the world in a little reed basket—two extra shifts, a broadcloth dress, a comb, hose, shoes, and little more. But her two years at Meadowbank had changed that situation dramatically—Lady Currie had been generous in giving Lucia her castoff clothing, so Lucia had accumulated quite a wardrobe of nice dresses.

Her favorites were an amber silk, a blue brocade, and two dresses of the exact same style, one in unbleached linen and one in a dark-green wool. But those were dresses strictly reserved for the visits to the Ludus Caledonia. For her chores around the manse, she wore a standard shift with a broadcloth skirt and leather girdle. All of those possessions, new and old, went into a satchel with a torn corner that Lady Currie had given her.

Lucia was able to shove a good deal into the old satchel, including shoes and combs and soap. Everything she would need to start a new life with Bane. She was careful in packing things, never leaving the satchel sitting out in the open for all to see. At the moment, it was sitting under the bed.

As she promised Bane, she was being discreet.

It was a good thing, too, because when her back was turned, the door to her chamber pushed open, almost gently, and Colly stood in the doorway. Glancing up, Lucia could see the expression on the woman's face, grim and focused as she stood there.

Immediately, Lucia's defenses went up.

"Does m'lady need me?" she asked. "I heard her earlier...yelling. Is she better now?"

Colly stepped into the chamber. "She's still quite upset," she said as she closed the door quietly. "Lucia, we must talk."

With the door closed, Lucia fought off a creeping sense of fear. "Why did ye close the door?" she asked. "Open it, please. I dunna want tae be in a closed room with ye."

Colly didn't open the door but she didn't advance, either. She simply stood there, looking Lucia over in an appraising manner.

"Did ye think I wouldna notice?" she asked.

"About what?"

"The warrior Lady Currie brought from the Cal," Colly said. "It's the same man ye brought here tae Meadowbank months ago, the one ye said saved ye from the sausage thieves. The one who almost killed me."

So the old hag *had* noticed. That answered the question that had come up between Lucia and Bane. But Lucia wasn't prepared to confess anything. Bane looked different enough now with his beard and clothing that she could say the old woman had made a mistake. Colly couldn't prove otherwise because she knew Bane would never admit to it, either.

Therefore, Lucia had to take a stand.

"They do look a bit alike," she said evenly. "The man I knew... He was clean-shaven and dressed in rags. Lady Currie's warrior has a beard and wears fine clothing."

"That makes no difference," Colly snapped, already becoming frustrated that Lucia wasn't telling her what she wanted to hear. "I'm not blind, Lucia. It *is* the same man."

Lucia shrugged, trying to keep her end of the conversation calm. "If it is, I'm unaware."

Colly sighed sharply. "Ye've always been a liar," she said, trying to provoke her. "Ye're lying now. Why can ye not tell me the truth?"

"Ask the man yerself if ye dunna believe me."

"I'm asking *ye*," Colly said, her voice becoming stronger. "Ye may as well confess because I know it's him. I've told Lady Currie and she knows it's him, too."

"She never saw the man that was here before. How can she know it's the same man?"

Colly was growing agitated. "Because I say it is," she said. "But there's more that ye've lied about. Lady Currie's warrior told her that he had a wife. I can only assume that's ye. Are ye married, Lucia, and ye never told us?"

"I'm not his wife."

"Ye're lying!"

"And ye're imagining things that arena there. Ye have a touch of madness, Colly. Ye always have."

That was all it took for Colly to charge.

Unfortunately for the old woman, she didn't move very swiftly. That gave Lucia time to dodge out of the way. Colly crashed into the wardrobe, ramming her shoulder into it as Lucia moved to the door. Just as she opened it, Colly charged again and slammed it shut, narrowly missing slamming it on Lucia's hand.

"What do ye want from me?" Lucia demanded, her fear taking hold now that Colly was clearly intent on hurting her. "I told ye I am not his wife. I told ye it is not the same man. What more do ye want from me?"

Colly picked up a small three-legged stool and wielded it like a club. "I want the truth," she snarled. "Ye've been a thorn in my side since ye arrived at Meadowbank, and that is going tae end today. I'll beat the truth out of ye."

She came at Lucia with the stool raised over her head. Lucia ducked behind her sewing table and Colly brought the stool down on the tabletop, sending everything scattering. Thread, needles, fabric—everything went flying, including a big pair of iron scissors that Lucia used to cut fabric. As Lucia ducked underneath the table, she picked up the scissors from the floor.

She had to protect herself.

Just as Lucia came out from under the table, Colly swung the stool again, clipping Lucia in the shoulder. She screeched, lurching to her feet and running to hide behind the wardrobe because Colly was blocking the door.

"Tell me the truth!" Colly boomed. "Tell me the truth or ye'll regret it! Ye and the man are conspiring against Lady Currie, are not ye? Ye've brought him here as part of a terrible plan!"

Lucia had the open wardrobe door in front of her, a shield from Colly and her stool, but the woman was slamming the stool into the wardrobe door, battering Lucia on the other side.

"Go away!" Lucia roared, clutching the scissors like a dagger. "I've done nothing wrong!"

Colly was beating on the doors, splintering them with the strength of her blows. She may have been old, but she was surprisingly strong.

"Ye were going tae kill Lady Currie, werena ye?" she shouted. "Tell me the truth, ye little chit! *Tell me!*"

The stool managed to take out a chunk of the door, sending splinters into the side of Lucia's face. Gasping, she pulled out two big ones, leaving small wounds on her jaw.

"Ye're mad!" she screamed. "Get out of here and leave me alone!"

Colly wasn't listening. Fury was feeding her, making her irrational. When the stool disintegrated in her hand, she tossed it aside and yanked open the battered wardrobe door, revealing Lucia cowering on the other side.

What Colly didn't see were the scissors in Lucia's hand. She didn't see them until she grabbed Lucia by the neck and Lucia brought up the shears.

By then it was too late. Lucia plunged the scissors into Colly's neck and blood erupted. The old woman emitted a gurgling cry, grabbing the hilt of the scissors as she toppled over onto Lucia's bed. She lay there, twitching and trying to speak, pulling at the scissors that wouldn't come free. But it was no use; death was imminent. Sightless eyes gazed up at the ceiling as she breathed her last.

Lucia stood there, hands on her mouth in horror as she realized that she had just killed the woman. It had all happened so fast. But she knew, without a doubt, that Colly had meant to kill her, so she'd had little choice but to defend herself. Years of contention between the two of them, and Colly's impulsive brutality, had built to this point.

The door to her chamber was closed but Lucia knew that others had heard the fight. There was no way they could not have. Shaking with fear, she knew that she had to leave immediately. Lady Currie would be devastated about Colly's death, and she would turn her grief against Lucia, even if the woman had acted in the effort of self-preservation. Punishment would be swift and severe, no matter if it had been justified.

Therefore, she had to go.

Now.

With trembling hands, Lucia pulled her satchel out from underneath the bed and sealed it up. Colly was lying on her bed, with blood now starting to drip onto the floor, so Lucia tossed a blanket over the woman and covered her up. She didn't know why she did it; she wasn't thinking clearly. It wasn't as if the blanket could cover up the increasingly widening pool of blood.

Lucia cracked the door open to see who was out in the corridor. She could hear voices, but she couldn't see anyone. Surprisingly, the corridor seemed vacant. Silently, she slipped through the door, closing it so quietly that it didn't make a sound. With her satchel in hand, she headed for the servants' stairs that were directly across from her chamber, taking the darkened steps to an alcove on the first floor.

From there, she bolted for the stables.

☘ ☘ ☘

The horse was spirited, no doubt. Even putting the saddle on the animal had it jumping around as Bane labored to secure it. Angus and Tynan were standing by, watching Bane wrestle with the horse.

"Are ye going tae ride him, Bane?" Tynan said excitedly, trying to avoid hooves that were as big as his head. "Does he have a name?"

Bane grinned at the enthusiastic child whom Angus had evidently been training in the ways of the stables since Bane had left.

"I dunna know if he has a name," he said. "Angus? Do ye?"

The old man had a half-chewed piece of green grass hanging from his lips. "When Laird Currie purchased this horse, he named it after the immortal steed owned by the Roman god of war," he said. "His name is Aethon."

Bane looked at the animal. It was white with a hint of gray, which made it look silver. Its mane was dark gray, as was its tail, giving it a striking appearance.

"Aethon," he said. "I like it. What say ye, Tynan?"

The boy nodded eagerly. "It's magical."

"Aye, it is."

"Where will ye take the horse, Bane?"

Bane looked at the child, hearing something wistful in that tone. The little boy had attached himself to Bane when he'd been here the first time, and now it was as if he'd never left. Tynan adored Bane. Truth be told, Bane loved Tynan, as well. He was going to be sad to leave him behind.

"Far away," he said quietly as he finished securing the saddle. "Have ye been tae the Highlands, lad?"

Tynan shook his head. "I've only been here."

Bane came away from the horse. "The Highlands are a place of beauty and magic," he said. "There are big mountains of the greenest green and lochs of the bluest blue. 'Tis a beautiful place."

"Will ye take me there sometime?"

"If yer mother allows it."

Tynan left his post by the horse, coming to stand in front of Bane. "I dunna want tae work in a house like my da did," he said. "I want tae fight, like ye. Will ye let me fight with ye?"

Bane smiled, mussing the boy's straw-like hair. "That is up tae Laird Currie," he said. "When ye're old enough, mayhap I'll ask him if ye can come with me tae the Highlands and learn tae fight. Would ye like that?"

Tynan's face lit up. "I would!" he said. "Can Mam come with me?"

"If Laird Currie says so."

Tynan was delighted with the prospect of learning to fight with Bane. He picked up a horse brush and began to dance around, trying to brush the horse, but the animal was skittish and didn't want a dancing boy near him.

Bane finally had to put a big hand on Tynan's shoulder to settle the lad down, and he stopped wriggling long enough to brush the horse's left front leg and part of his torso. Bane watched the boy for a moment before turning to Angus.

"When I'm gone, ye'll watch out for him, willna ye?" he asked quietly. "He's a good lad. I worry about him here and how much they work him."

Angus chewed on his grass as he looked over at the child eagerly doing his task. "That's why I brought him intae the stable," he said. "He's too young tae scrub floors and work the kitchens. He's smart, too."

"I know."

"He doesna belong here. Bane, did ye mean what ye said? About taking him with ye?"

"I never say anything I dunna mean."

Angus seemed relieved. "Good," he said. "Come back for him and his mam soon. Take them both with ye, away from Lady Currie and her nurse. That woman is the devil."

Bane knew that but refrained from agreeing. He was simply glad they were finally able to leave it all behind. His belongings were tied onto the back of the saddle, and he took a few steps toward the open stable door, looking up into the sky. It was nearing dusk. Lucia should come around soon. He was just turning away from the door when something in the yard caught his attention.

Lucia was approaching.

Bane tucked in behind the open door, watching her as she practically ran across the yard and darted into the stables.

That was when he realized she was sobbing.

"Lucia?" he said, rushing to her and grasping her by the arms. "What's wrong? Why are ye weeping?"

"We have to run," she gasped. "Bane, we must leave *now*!"

He looked at her with great concern, seeing dark droplets on her shoulder and hand. It didn't take him long to realize it was blood. His eyes widened.

"Bleeding Christ," he hissed. "Are ye hurt? *What* happened?"

She wiped at her eyes. "Colly attacked me," she said. "She said she recognized ye. She tried to force me tae confess…something. I dunna even know what she wanted before she attacked me with a stool. She was trying tae kill me so I stabbed her with my scissors. I had no choice!"

She was off on a crying binge and Bane pulled her against him, holding her tightly as the news settled in.

The old nurse was dead?

"God," he finally hissed. "Where is she?"

"In the manse," Lucia wept. "Bane, we must run! We must leave before Lady Currie discovers her!"

Bane understood the situation for what it was—critical. Even if Lucia had killed in self-defense, she was a servant and the magistrates would not look kindly upon her. If Lady Currie pushed hard enough, Lucia could be severely punished.

She might even be executed.

Not now, he thought in a panic. *We've come too far tae see it all slip away now. God, not now!*

Leaving Lucia sobbing by the door, he rushed to the horse and unfastened the tethers. "We must leave," he said to Angus and Tynan, who were standing there in shock. "If they come looking for us, deny ye ever saw us. 'Tis the only way ye'll not be held accountable in this, so deny everything."

Angus nodded firmly. "No one would bother a silly old man," he assured him. "Get along, Bane. Take the lady and go."

Bane didn't need to be told twice. As he ran to the entry where Lucia was standing, leading Aethon behind him, Tynan scampered after him.

"Bane!" he cried. "Will ye still let me fight for ye?"

Bane turned to the child, who looked as if he were losing his best friend. He smiled at the lad. "Ye know I will," he said. "When ye're older, I'll come for ye. Do ye believe me?"

"Aye."

"Then be a good lad. Be strong for yer mother."

Tynan nodded, furiously wiping at his eyes so his tears would not be seen as Bane grasped Lucia by the hand and, together, the two of them rushed across the stable yard to the postern gate, which was unmanned and unwatched.

Slipping through the gate, they mounted the horse and took off toward Edinburgh, leaving the heartache, death, and destruction of Meadowbank behind them.

Forever.

CHAPTER TWENTY-SIX

THE POUNDING ON HIS DOOR WAS FRANTIC.

Laird Currie was sitting at his cluttered table, counting out every single piece of silver that Bane had brought back to him. He was putting them into neat little stacks, at least those that were more uniform and could be stacked, but the rest of them ended up in a pile.

He'd deduced that everything was there. Every single pence.

And then the pounding on the door.

He could hear a voice on the other side, begging him to open it. He knew it was his wife, so he let her pound a little while longer before he decided to answer. Throwing the heavy bolt, he pulled open the right-hand panel.

Lady Currie was standing there, her pale face streaked with tears.

"She's dead!" Lady Currie blurted out. "She's dead and Lucia killed her!"

Laird Currie didn't even raise an eyebrow. "Who is dead, my dear?"

"Colly!" Lady Currie sobbed. "Colly is dead and Lucia killed her. *Murdered* her. Now Lucia is nowhere to be found and I need your men to go and look for her because Bane is nowhere to be found, either!"

The woman was hysterical. There were several servants standing behind her, all of them weeping and carrying on because their mistress was. All but one of them. Laird Currie recognized Amy, the woman who so ably dressed Lady Currie's hair. He knew her because, years ago, Amy's husband used to serve him. But Amy wasn't shedding a tear. She stood there quietly, watching Lady Currie weep without reacting.

Strange, indeed.

"Calm yerself, my dear," Laird Currie said to his wife. "Tell me what happened and why ye think little Lucia killed Colly."

Lady Currie had a kerchief in front of her face, weeping into it. "Because Colly suspected that Lucia was in league with my new warrior," she said, not even bothering to catch herself as she personally claimed Bane by saying *my new warrior*. "Colly said that Lucia and Bane were plotting against me. She went to Lucia to force her to tell the truth, and Lucia killed her for it!"

"Force her tae tell the truth? How was she tae do it?"

"However she could! Beat her, frighten her—any way she could!"

"So she threatened Lucia?"

"I am sure she did, but Lucia deserved it!"

"And ye say that Lucia killed the woman?"

"She *murdered* her!"

"Was it possible that she was defending herself from Colly?"

Lady Currie's mouth opened in outrage. "Never! Lucia murdered her, and that is all there is to it!"

Laird Currie was starting to piece together what could have happened. He didn't need anyone to explain that to him, knowing what he knew of Colly and the way she liked to slap the servants around. She was big and brutish, and Lucia was half her size. But his wife would never admit such a thing. Therefore, he looked at Amy, standing stoically away from the other servants, and motioned to her.

"Ye, there," he said. "Ye're Amy, are ye not?"

Amy perked up as she became the focus of attention. "Aye, m'laird."

"Yer husband was Robert."

Amy nodded quickly. "Aye, m'laird," she said. "He used tae help Colm Symington. He would bring ye wood for yer fire and do other jobs around the manse."

"I remember him well," Laird Currie said. "He became sickly a few years ago. A sickness in his lungs that killed him."

"Aye, m'laird."

"He was a good man."

"Thank ye, m'laird."

"What do ye know of this whole situation with Colly and Lucia? Did ye hear anything?"

Amy looked at Lady Currie as the woman sobbed, clearly hesitant to speak. "I…I heard shouting," she said. "I heard banging. Colly went in tae Lucia's chamber and shut the door."

Laird Currie pondered that. "Banging and shouting," he said. "Was it Colly or Lucia?"

"Both, m'laird," she said. "Colly was screaming about a confession, and Lucia told her tae go away."

"I see," Laird Currie said. "Amy, I will ask ye a question and I want a truthful answer."

"Of course, m'laird."

"Has Colly ever beaten ye?"

Amy froze, fearful of replying, but after a moment she lowered her gaze. "Aye, she has, m'laird."

"And have ye seen her beat other servants?"

"Aye, m'laird."

"What does this have to do with anything?" Lady Currie demanded, suddenly not so tearful. "Colly has my permission to discipline the servants. There is no crime in that."

Laird Currie looked at her. "My dear, Colly was a brute who took delight in beating the servants for the slightest misstep," he said. "Ye think I dunna know that, but I do. The day she came here with ye is the day she started slapping my servants around as if she had the right. She seemed tae have a particular dislike for Lucia, or so I've heard. Colly wasna a saint. She was a nasty, brutal woman."

Lady Currie looked stricken. "She…she was no such thing!"

"Aye, she was," Laird Currie said. "I let it go on and shouldna have. I should have put a stop tae it back then, but I was a coward. I retreated intae my solar and let the fools run my house and hold."

"That's not—!"

"Wait," Laird Currie said, putting up a hand to silence her. "I'm not finished. Based on the history of Colly and her delight in inflicting pain on others, 'tis my guess that Lucia was defending herself against Colly, who was twice as big. And ye thought it was a good idea for that woman tae interrogate Lucia over some imagined plot? Did it not occur tae ye that Colly merely wanted an excuse tae beat the lass?"

Lady Currie was beside herself with horror. The man had no sympathy for her; that was clear. Her tears were gone, replaced by an astonishing sense of guilt and disbelief.

"That is not true!" she insisted. "Colly was always faithful to me. She only did what she felt was in my best interest."

Laird Currie sighed heavily and shook his head. "My dear, Colly did what she had tae do in order to strike fear intae everyone around ye," he said. "She raised ye, so I understand yer loyalty tae her, but she was a selfish hag who wanted nothing more than tae control everyone around ye. And she succeeded."

Seeing that the tide of judgment had turned against her, Lady Currie lashed out. "Lucia killed her," she said. "I want justice for Colly and I shall have it!"

"Not here," Laird Currie said, surprisingly firm. "Lucia is gone from this place. Her freedom has been purchased so she has left Meadowbank for good, and ye'll forget about any justice for Colly. It seems that Lucia is the one who delivered justice for everyone here at Meadowbank by doing away with the woman. Now bury the old cow and be done with it. I willna hear anything more about it."

Lady Currie could hardly believe her ears. "But what about Bane?" she demanded. "I paid sixty pounds for the man and—"

"And I have the money back," Laird Currie cut her off. "Clegg returned it tae me and Bane has his freedom. We're old friends, Clegg and I. It seems that he doesna like ye very much. Ye go tae the Cal every night like a dog in heat and shame yer husband, and he's had enough. So have I. From now on, ye'll keep tae yer chambers. Ye'll have an escort whenever ye leave the manse, and ye'll never go tae the Cal again."

"But—!"

"Ye'll be a good and proper wife and stay home where ye belong," he continued, to shut her up. "If ye dunna obey me, I'll lock ye up and throw away the key. I've had enough of yer behavior, my dear. Yer days of doing as ye please are finished, and if we have a son, it'll be from my loins, as it should be. Is this in any way unclear?"

Lady Currie looked as if her husband had physically struck her. She stared at him, wide-eyed and pale, wanting very badly to respond but knowing she hadn't the grounds to do it. Greer Currie had finally called her out for her horrific behavior, and there wasn't a priest, bishop, magistrate, or king in the land that would side with her.

And she knew it.

The reign of Lady Currie was over.

"You cannot cage me," she finally hissed. "You cannot do that to me!"

Laird Currie eyed her pointedly. "I am yer husband and I can do as I wish," he said. "Now go back tae yer chamber and stay there. If I want ye, I'll send for ye. Otherwise, stay there and behave yerself because if ye dunna, my wrath will be swift."

Sniffling, embarrassed, and horrified, Lady Currie glared at the man as she turned for the stairs that led to the upper floor. She didn't dare argue with him, but Laird Currie knew it was only a matter of time before she tried.

And she *would* try.

Of that, he had little doubt.

He watched her as she headed up the stairs, followed by her shocked servants. When he caught sight of Amy bringing up the rear, he called to her.

"Amy," he said quietly. "Come here."

Amy did, trotting over to him. He eyed her for a moment.

"Do ye like working for my wife?" he asked.

Amy hesitated before finally shaking her head. "If there was something else I could do here at Meadowbank, m'laird, I would do it."

"There is," he said. "Ye can serve me. I've had no one since yer husband and Colm Symington left me. Would ye dust my solar and bring me hot wine when I ask?"

Amy beamed. "I would, m'laird," she said. "I have a son—Robert's son—who would be very good in service tae ye, as well. He would be very happy tae."

"Good," Laird Currie said, turning back for his solar. "Bring the little lad, too. Ye can both serve me. Does the lad play chess?"

Amy shook her head. "Nay, but he's very bright, m'laird," she said. "Ye can teach him."

Laird Currie paused, a smile on his lips. "I'd like that."

"I think he would, too, m'laird."

As it turned out, Tynan beat Laird Currie with his very first game.

The old man couldn't have been happier.

PART FOUR

HOMINIBUS GLORIA

Chapter Twenty-Seven

Falkirk

It was very late and Aethon, for all his spirit, had tired quickly. He was a hot and sweaty mess, snorting his exhaustion as Bane and Lucia rode into the small village of Falkirk. It had been a long ride and the horse was understandably spent.

After her strenuous day, Lucia had fallen asleep against Bane's back. He could feel her, limp and boneless, as they rode along. Both of her arms were around his waist and he held her hands at his belly to keep her from falling off, but when they stopped at a livery on the edge of town, he finally had to wake her. She groaned.

"My arms," she muttered. "They feel as if a thousand pins are sticking them."

He grinned as he dismounted the horse, pulling her off behind him. Her satchel fell to the earth because it had been on her lap, held between them as they'd ridden along, and she bent over to pick it up as she shook out her arms.

"Did ye sleep well?" he asked as he handed the exhausted horse over to the livery owner. "The horse isna exactly smooth in its gait."

Lucia clutched her satchel to her, covering her mouth as she yawned. "I never felt it," she said. "I suppose I was too weary tae care."

He reached out, taking her by the elbow. "Just a little while longer, and I'll find ye a good bed for the night."

He took her out into the crisp night. There were torches lit throughout the town, and the smell of cooking fires was heavy in the air.

"Where are we going?" she asked.

He pointed straight ahead. "Tae the church," he said. "That's

St. Andrew's. When I came down from the Highlands, I passed through this very town, so I knew the church was here. I'm going tae marry ye."

She looked at him in surprise. "Now?"

"Now. Unless ye have any objection."

Lucia shook her head, unable to keep the smile off her face. "Nay," she said. "I...I suppose with everything that's happened, I'd nearly forgotten."

"I havena."

She giggled. Taking her hand, Bane led her down the darkened street, heading for the small parish of St. Andrew's. To their right, a broad but short avenue ended in a two-storied tavern. Beams of light emitted from the windows, and they could hear the soft hum of laughter and conversation. But they continued on until they came to the church, which was mostly dark at this hour. Only a few torches among the arches gave forth light into the night.

Bane rapped on the church door.

"Do ye suppose the priests will marry us at this hour?" Lucia whispered.

"Why not?" Bane said. "I have money with me. I'll pay them well."

"Ye do? Where did ye get it from?"

"It's the purse I earned at the Cal. That was the only money I dinna give tae Laird Currie because I knew we would need it."

The mention of Laird Currie brought back the horrors of the day at Meadowbank, something Lucia was trying desperately to forget. Her mood sank, no matter how hard she tried to fight it.

"Do ye think Laird Currie will send his men after me?" she asked. "Bane, I wouldna have killed the woman if I'd had another choice, but she came at me and I knew she meant tae kill me."

He could see her distress and he pulled her into his strong embrace. "Ye did what ye had tae do. Ye mustna feel guilty for that."

"She attacked me!"

"I know, my angel."

Lucia drew strength from his arms, feeling his power around her. Nothing in the world had ever made her feel so safe. "Do ye think we've been followed?"

Bane released her, cupping her face in his big hands. "I dunna think Laird Currie would send anyone after us," he said. "He knows Colly beat ye. He knows what the woman was capable of. I'm sure he knows ye were only defending yerself."

"Do ye really think so?"

"I do."

That comforted Lucia immensely but she was still sad, still fearful. She smiled weakly at him just as the door to the church lurched open and a man in rumpled woolen robes stood there, candle in hand as he looked at the pair curiously. Bane immediately dropped his hands from Lucia.

"We've come tae see the priest about a marriage," he said. "We wish tae be married."

The priest yawned. "Now?"

"Now."

"Can ye not come back on the morrow?"

"We canna. We must be married tonight, if ye please."

The man looked back and forth between them. He studied Lucia for a moment, frowning. "Why is the lady distressed?"

Bane looked at Lucia, whose expression of sadness and fear hadn't yet left her. Realizing that, she smiled brightly at the priest.

"She's not distressed," Bane said, pointing to her smile and offering his own. "See? Neither one of us is distressed."

The priest was still looking at Lucia. "Is he forcing ye tae marry him, lass?"

Lucia shook her head firmly. "Not at all. I want tae marry him, Father. I swear it."

"Where's yer family?"

"Dead."

As the priest debated about the odd situation, Bane took out his leather purse and planted two silver coins into the priest's hand.

"There," he said. "*Now* will ye marry us?"

The priest looked at the money, at Bane, and then motioned for them to wait at the door of the church. As Bane and Lucia stood there, looking at each other curiously, the priest returned with a pair of sleepy acolytes, and right there at the door of the church, Bane and Lucia were married by a priest who spoke the blessing quickly so he could return to his bed. It wasn't much, but it was what they'd asked for.

Lucia didn't remember much of the blessing itself. All she remembered was the look in Bane's eyes as he gazed at her. It was full of joy and warmth and love. All of those things flowed in and around her, filling her veins with something more than she could have ever imagined. But the one thing she felt more than anything else was hope—

Ye give me hope, Lucia. Hope that life can be good again.

For them, it finally was.

☰ ☰ ☰

The busy, noisy tavern on the dead-end avenue was called the Copper Kelpie, and it was filled to the rafters with people on this cold night.

Bane wouldn't have cared so much if it was only him. He could have found a warm corner to sleep in. But he had his wife with him, and he would do everything in his power to secure a bed for her for the night.

He wasn't beyond playing on sympathy for it.

The tavernkeep was a big man with an eye missing who listened to Bane tell a story of his rushed wedding and how all his wife wanted in the entire world was a bed and a fire for the night. Fortunately for Bane, the man's wife overheard him and she offered them the only chamber they had left, which was a small attic room where the servants slept.

Bane took it, and happily so.

He and Lucia retreated to the chamber, which was up a tiny flight of stairs. It amounted to nothing more than a dusty little room with a small window, a brazier of hot coals to stave off the chill, and two beds that were hardly big enough for children to sleep in. While Bane went downstairs to commandeer a meal, Lucia dragged the mattresses from both beds onto the floor next to the brazier so they could sleep next to the heat. By the time he returned with a full tray, she was sitting on the mattresses, waiting for him.

"What's this?" he asked. "Why are we on the floor?"

Lucia pointed to the timber-and-rope bed frames shoved up against the wall. "Because ye canna fit in those," she said. "Besides…I want tae sleep next tae ye. 'Tis my right now, after all."

He grinned as he sat down on the floor, putting the tray on the mattresses. "Good thinking, Lady Morgan," he said. Then he paused, looking at her with an expression that relayed a heart that was full to bursting. "God, that sounds like music tae my ears. *Lady Morgan*. I never thought words could sound so sweet."

Lucia flushed, smiling bashfully. "Ye must say it every day, several times a day. I want tae hear it as much as possible."

He laughed softly, taking her hand and lifting it for a tender kiss. "I promise I will," he said. Then he lowered her hand and focused on the tray, handing her a full cup of warm wine. "I've paid for a good deal of food. I hope ye're hungry."

Lucia was. She sat in front of the tray, cross-legged, inspecting the contents. "It looks like some kind of pies?"

Bane pointed. "An eel tart, stuffed eggs, bread, butter, and stewed apples."

Lucia jumped in. The tart was delicious, as were the eggs, and she and Bane ate heartily as he spoke about the friends he'd left behind at the Ludus Caledonia and how he planned to return as soon as he could.

All the while, Lucia listened with a smile on her lips.

"For a place ye'd never heard of before, it has certainly become important tae ye," she said. "Ye speak about it as if ye've been there most of yer life."

He conceded the point. "I went there tae earn money tae pay for yer freedom, but I found much more than that."

"Friends?"

He nodded. "Mostly," he said. "Even the one they call the Eagle. His real name is Magnus, and even he has become something of a friendly acquaintance. But it's more than that… When I went there, I told Lor that I was hoping tae find myself again."

"What do ye mean?"

"I mean the man I lost when I killed those lads near Jedburgh," he said quietly. "That man was confident and courageous and reckless. Afterward, he was crippled with guilt for what he'd done, and he lost everything he thought he was."

"And did he find himself again?"

He nodded. "I think so," he said pensively. "I feel as if I'm on the right path. This journey north is part of it."

"Oh?"

He nodded, slowing his movements as he thought on what the future would hold. "We're going home tae the village of Ledmore, where my family has lived for generations. I'm going home tae face my father, which is something I should have done in the beginning. I know that now."

Lucia was listening intently. "But ye did face him after that terrible event," she said. "Ye said that he sent ye home."

Bane grunted softly. "He sent me home because I refused tae admit that I'd been wrong, Lucia," he said frankly. "I was convinced I'd been right, and given that I couldna see my own faults, my da had no choice but tae send me home so I wouldna get myself killed. He did right. I want tae tell him that."

He was more at ease speaking on his father than Lucia had ever seen him. She leaned forward, eyes glimmering.

"Tell me about yer da," she asked softly.

Bane smiled as memories came flooding back to him about a man he'd not remembered in some time. "Arch Morgan is his name," he said. "Arch is short for Archer, my grandmother's family name. He's a big man, like me. In fact, people say we look just alike, but the way we behave—that's where the lines are drawn."

"What do ye mean?"

"My da is much more deliberate in his decisions," he said. "He thinks things through. I dunna. I charge in, and by the grace of God, I've not gotten myself killed. My da never understood that in me, although I know he told others that I would grow out of that impulsive behavior."

"Have ye?"

He looked at her, chuckling. "A little," he said. "I still charge in. I'm a man of action and I always will be."

"Will ye tell yer da that when ye see him?"

Bane's smile faded. "Not at first," he said. "At first, I'll tell him I love him. Then I'll tell him the rest."

"When will ye tell him about me?"

He reached out, pulling her over onto his lap with one hand and pushing the food tray out of the way with the other.

"Right away," he said, wrapping his muscular arms around her. "I never had any brothers or sisters, so I'm sure my da will be very happy tae know I've married well."

"Well?" she repeated. "Dunna tell him that. I havena a cent tae my name."

He hugged her, kissing her cheek. "I dinna mean money," he said. "I meant everything else. Ye're what my heart has been waiting for. I thought that when I first met ye, and that hasna changed. My love for ye has grown deeper every day."

Lucia wrapped her arms around his neck, kissing him sweetly. But when he moved in for something more lusty, she stopped him. Rising from his lap, she went to bolt the door. Stirring the brazier, she moved to douse the spirit candles, two by the bed frames and another on a small table by the door. The chamber was warm and dim, shadows from the glowing coals dancing on the walls as she stood beside the two mattresses where he sat and removed her blood-speckled dress.

It fell in a heap on the floor. In only her shift, she sat down beside him again and kissed him tenderly on the cheek. She gazed at his masculine beauty, memorizing every line of his face, and her eyes glimmered warmly as he studied her in return.

No words passed between them. They weren't required. When Lucia reached out to touch his neck, he closed his eyes, relishing the sensation of her warm hand. Her fingers moved upward, feeling the stubble of his face and tracing the cleft in his chin. When he reached out to touch her in return, she pushed his hands down. This was her moment. She wanted him to feel her emotions based solely on her touch.

She wanted him to know how much she loved him.

Bane groaned softly.

"Ye're going tae be the death of me, lass."

She smiled. "What do ye mean?"

His eyes rolled open. "Because all I can think of at this moment is making love tae ye and ye willna let me touch ye."

With a grin, she launched herself at him, putting her face in the crook of his neck as they fell back together on the straw mattresses. His arms went around her as they settled down by the brazier, facing one another.

"So much has happened," she murmured. "Today was a day of days and now we find ourselves going home. *Yer* home. Ye know I've never had a proper home? Not in my entire life."

"That will change," he said confidently, releasing her long

enough to pull his tunic over his head. When Lucia saw what he was doing, she pulled off her shift without hesitation. When his breeches were in a pile on the floor, he quickly gathered her into his arms again, his heat against hers.

"Trust me, my angel," he said. "Ye'll have everything I can provide for ye and more."

Her naked skin against his, Lucia was giddily content. "But where?" she asked. "Ye'll return tae the Cal tae train men for some time. Is that where we'll have our home? Or do ye intend tae stay in the Highlands?"

He smoothed loose strands of hair away from her face. "I hope tae return tae the Cal soon," he said. "Going tae Ledmore—that is simply tae make peace with my da."

"But ye dunna intend tae stay?"

"I dunna know," he said honestly. "I'll know more when we arrive. But I do know one thing—wherever I go, ye'll go. We're family, now and forever."

"I've never really known a family," Lucia said softly. "My da served at Meadowbank while I lived with my aunt. For years, it was that way. I can remember dreaming of my own family someday, with ten children around me and a handsome husband. It may seem like a silly dream, but once, it was mine."

"It isna a silly dream," he said. "But ten children…"

She laughed. "How many did ye have in mind?"

"One tae start with, I suppose."

"And then?"

"As many as God will give us."

She wrapped her arms around his neck, her gaze melding with his. "Then let us start now."

"Now?"

Lucia was resolute. "Why not?" She touched his cheek, smiling in response to his surprise. "Can ye imagine anything better than children tae carry on yer name?"

No, he really couldn't. They'd never spoken of children, but she was making her wishes known. Truth was, he'd never thought of children at all until this very moment. Now, a son to carry on his name seemed like the best gift he could possibly receive.

A legacy he'd never thought he would have.

"A son," he said softly. "It seems like a dream tae even think such a thing."

"It could be a lass. Would ye be disappointed?"

"Never."

Lucia gazed at him, feeling the pull of emotion overwhelm her. She brushed her lips against his. "Then give me yer son, Bane Morgan," she breathed against his mouth. "Give me the honor of bearing yer child."

He growled, pulling her tight against him and plunging his tongue into her mouth. Lucia wrapped her legs around his hips, feeling his arousal push at her. Bane's hand was at her breast, his lips against her forehead as he whispered words of desire.

With every kiss, every word, the fire in her loins grew and she thrust her pelvis forward, capturing the tip of his seeking manhood. Bane groaned as he finished what she had started by thrusting into her hot, waiting body.

The first full thrust rocked her. Lucia gasped with pleasure, holding fast to him for support as he thrust into her again and again.

"Do it harder, Bane," she said breathlessly.

Her words of lust lit a fire in him that could not be controlled. He pounded into her welcoming body, determined to make this time last longer than he had the last time. He wanted to enjoy every move, every touch, every emotion.

Lucia groaned with pleasure beneath him, lifting her pelvis to meet his. She savored the heat he was creating within her, remembering how Bane had so deftly given her release with his expert touch. But she simply couldn't wait. Reaching up, she pulled his mouth to her swollen lips.

"Make me feel as ye did at the Cal," she whispered. "The heat... the feelings, Bane. Let me feel them again."

"In time," he whispered.

With that, he took firm hold of her hips and rolled onto his back, still joined to her body. Lucia gasped with the unexpected move as she ended up on top, straddling him. Bane grinned wolfishly, his hands moving to her breasts.

"Make yer own feelings, my angel." He thrust his hips upward, impaling her on his body. "Move yer body against me, like this."

Hair in her face, Lucia looked bewildered, but Bane moved again, thrusting into her from his position beneath her until she caught on. Rising on her knees, she plunged her body down upon him again and again, biting her lip in delight when he groaned.

"Do ye like this?" she asked.

He could only nod his head, closing his eyes to the glory of the moment. She smiled at his reaction to her; it made her feel powerful. Her rhythm became steady, and in little time, Lucia felt the ripples of release rolling through her body. Beneath her, Bane could feel the contractions and he clutched her body against his as he released himself deep.

For a moment, neither of them had the strength or will to move. Lucia remained straddled over his hips, feeling the last of his climax die away. She was exhausted, but in a good way. She was his wife now and the closeness she felt to the man was more than she could verbalize. He was part of her, and she was part of him, until the end of time.

As he said...they were a family.

Finally, she lay down upon him and his big arms went around her, holding her close. His gentle touch, his hand tenderly caressing her hair, told her that he was feeling the same way she was.

Warm...content...

Loved.

When morning came, she was still in the exact same position, curled up on Bane's chest.

It had been the best night of her life.

CHAPTER TWENTY-EIGHT

THE JOURNEY NORTH TO LEDMORE HAD TAKEN MUCH LONGER than Lucia had imagined.

It was winter, which meant the weather was vicious at times even though Bane had assured her that it was a mild winter in the Highlands from his experience. Given the fact that she had spent her entire life either at her aunt's home in Selkirk or at Meadowbank, a journey of this magnitude was overwhelming.

The path was not easy, nor was it swift. At times, the weather turned sour and they were forced to seek refuge. Once, when they reached the village of Killiecrankie, a snowstorm blew in and they spent five solid days bunking with a farmer and his wife. That hadn't been too terrible, in truth, as the couple was more than happy for the company and Lucia spent those days helping the farmer's wife and playing with their small children.

It had magical moments.

Bane had watched his new wife playing with the children, thinking that she would make a wonderful mother and falling in love with her more every day. The storm eventually cleared and they continued onward, traveling through a winter-white land as they moved deeper into the Highlands.

In spite of the winter beauty, the truth was that it was very cold. Bane had purchased furs from a trapper in the town of Dunkeld that Lucia had sewn together to make two very fine cloaks. That was the same place where he'd also purchased a mare for Lucia to ride since the burden of two people on Aethon was heavy.

Wrapped in their fur cloaks and riding separate horses, Bane and Lucia made better time through the Highlands, sometimes covering fifteen miles a day if the weather wasn't too horrible.

Aethon had settled down admirably and was an excellent traveling horse, and Lucia's mare was sturdy and comfortable.

All things considered, the journey, though long, wasn't as bad as it could have been. Bane made sure to stop every night and find his wife a bed, even if that bed was a warm stable with clean straw. He did his very best to ensure Lucia was comfortable, and she was appreciative of his efforts. It seemed that the man she'd first met, who seemed incapable of taking care of himself, was very good at taking care of others.

The man she'd first met in that dank, dirty alley no longer existed.

The Highland Defender had returned.

When their journey finally came to the seaside village of Ullapool, Bane informed Lucia that his home of Ledmore was a mere two days away, and she was thrilled to realize they were nearing the end of their journey. But Bane didn't seem too excited. In fact, he seemed subdued.

They had used some of the last of their coinage to rent a room in Ullapool at a tavern called the Queen's Ax. It sat on the edge of town, next to the main road, and the window of their chamber overlooked that road and the massive loch beyond. They'd arrived at sunset and Bane had a hot bath brought to Lucia, who sat in the dented copper tub until the water cooled off and she was forced to get out.

As she dried off in front of the fire, Bane climbed into the cool water and bathed with the soap she'd brought from Meadowbank, the *savon d'Alep* that reminded him so much of her. He kept trying to splash her with the cold water, causing her to squeal. She finally moved out of firing range, braiding her damp hair in the warmth of the fire.

"Stop throwing water at me or ye'll be very sorry," she said. "I willna be so nice tae ye and let ye use my soap."

He grinned as he washed the soap from his hair. "I was thinking of shaving my beard for ye, but I'll rethink that if ye're going tae be cruel."

She snorted. "Cruel, am I? Consider it a favor I'm doing ye because ye smell like one of those sheep we passed on the road. Ye look like one, too, with that fuzzy face."

He laughed quietly as he began to froth up his beard with the slimy soap. "A man has a right tae smell as he pleases," he said. "Ye've not complained before."

"I am now."

He cocked an eyebrow at her. "Fickle wench," he said. Then he pointed at his satchel. "Can ye find my razor? Be cautious, it's sharp."

Carefully, Lucia felt around in his satchel until she came across the razor he kept wrapped up in canvas. It was the same razor that Tynan had brought him at Meadowbank those months ago. Pulling it forth, she handed it to him, butt-end first. Bane sat in the water, looking into it, until it stopped moving enough that he could use it as a mirror.

"So ye decide tae shave that off now," Lucia said. "Why? It keeps yer face warm."

He took off a whole strip on the left side of his face. "Because my da will have a difficult enough time recognizing me without this forest growing on my face," he said. "Besides...I thought ye'd rather have a clean-shaven husband."

She was back over at the fire, brushing out the ends of her braid. "I will admit that yer whiskers are bristly like horsehair," she said. "Sometimes when ye kiss me, my face is raw from it."

"I know," he said, rinsing off the razor and waiting until the water calmed again. "I can see how red yer skin is all over yer body after we've fornicated."

She frowned. "Do ye have tae call it that? That's what Colly called it and—"

He shushed her gently. "I'm sorry, my angel," he said. "I willna use that word again. I will simply say that we're doing the devil's dance."

She looked at him in horror. "*What?*"

"Belly bumping?"

Lucia burst out laughing. "Nay! Bane, that's terrible!"

He pretended to ignore her as he shaved the right side of his face. "I've heard it called beating the guts. Is that better?"

"Stop this instant!"

She was laughing so hard that she could scarcely breathe, which brought out the naughty boy in him. "We'll call it docking the boat. Ye're the dock and I'm the—"

"Enough!" Lucia was far gone with laughter, hand over her mouth. "Ye're a terrible, terrible man. How dare ye say such things about…*that*. Something we do that's an expression of our love."

He was grinning as he looked at her; it was such an adorably dastardly grin. "And it means the world tae me," he said, sobering. "I was only jesting, my angel. It's good tae see ye laugh."

She was still chuckling. "And ye," she said. "I dunna think we've laughed enough. We need tae laugh more."

"And we shall," he said, washing the remainder of the suds from his face and rubbing his hands over his cheeks and chin. "I'll think up more names tae call dipping my wick, and I'll make ye laugh until ye cry."

Lucia was torn between screeching and laughing until he put up his hands in surrender. "I know," he said. "Ye said *enough*. I'll stop. Now—how does my face look?"

Lucia went over to her mischievous husband, inspecting his cheeks. "Very clean," she said. "Ye look like the man I fell in love with."

He beamed. "Good," he said, splashing around again and causing her to move away from the tub. "Tomorrow, my da will actually know who I am. I hope…I truly hope he's glad tae see me."

He climbed out of the tub and she grew serious. "He will be, willna he?" she said. "Surely a man would be glad tae see his own son."

Bane took the same drying linen she had used, damp from her, and began to rub his big body down with it. "My da is a man of calm and reasonable temperament," he said. "I've not thought much about him until I met ye and forced myself tae remember things I'd tried hard tae forget. I realize that I miss my da very much. I'm eager tae see him."

Lucia could see the strain on his face, the strain of longing for a loved one. Standing up from the stool she'd been sitting on, she gently pushed him to sit on it as she took the drying linen and began to dry his hair.

"Tell me about yer village," she said. "Ye were born there, werena ye?"

Bane closed his eyes as she gently buffeted his head, remembering the place where he'd lived most of his life. It seemed like so long ago.

"Aye," he said. "Ledmore is the small village. But the place where I was born is a tower that has been in my family for two hundred years. Latheron Tower has four floors and is built with thick walls and little windows. I was born on the second floor and my mother, Valery, passed away shortly thereafter."

Lucia put the towel aside and picked up her comb, pulling it through his thick brown hair. "Who raised ye?"

"My da," he said. "I had uncles who had wives, but they were busy with my cousins. No one had time for me, but I dinna mind. My da and I were close when I was young."

She continued to comb. "But that changed after Jedburgh."

"Aye."

She cocked her head thoughtfully. "He probably thinks ye've just run away," she said. "What I mean is, he couldna think ye were dead, could he? Surely, he thought ye've run off and will return any day."

Bane shrugged. "Possibly."

He sat there for a few moments, enjoying her attention, letting her comb his hair until she teasingly made an attempt to braid it and he'd had enough. He stood up and went to find his clothing.

"I'm going tae go tae the common room and bring us back some warmed wine," he said. "Is there anything else ye'd like?"

"Can I come with ye?"

"If ye dress in something proper, ye can."

She looked down at the sleeping shift she was wearing. As Bane pulled on his leather breeches and not one but two heavy tunics, she quickly donned the dark-green wool that Lady Currie had given her. It was tight around the bust but flowing everywhere else, with sleeves that were long enough to wrap her hands up in. It was warm and comfortable, and Bane took her hand as they headed down into the common room of the bustling tavern.

Given that snow flurries had started again, the tavern was full. People were piling in from outside, finding any space available to stay warm. The hearth was low and wide, and it gave off an enormous amount of heat into the small, stuffy room.

Bane moved for the kitchens. He had been very frugal on their way north, but they'd come down to their last few coins and he was going to have to see about earning more money before they could travel back to Edinburgh and the Ludus Caledonia. Were it just him, he wouldn't have worried because he could have slept anywhere or eaten whenever the opportunity presented itself, but he wouldn't do that to Lucia. She had changed his whole perspective on travel.

She had changed his perspective on life.

"Bane?"

He heard his name and it had not come from his wife. Puzzled, not to mention on his guard, he quickly turned to the source and saw three men sitting at a nearby table, looking at him in shock.

He knew their faces.

They were sitting by the kitchens, huddled around a small table with a broken leg, and the moment he recognized them, his eyes widened in astonishment.

"Hamlin?" he gasped. "And Dougal, and little Ramsey? Christ, lads, is it really ye?"

Suddenly, Lucia was pushed out of the way by a mob of men rushing her husband. She would have thought they were attacking him except for one thing—they were hugging him instead of producing weapons. They were crowing happily instead of screaming in anger. The one that had called Bane by name was kissing her husband on both cheeks, clearly glad to see him.

And Bane seemed very glad to see them as well.

"Lads, let me introduce ye to my wife," Bane said, reaching out to grasp Lucia by the hand. He pulled her against him tightly. "This is my wife, Lucia. Angel, these are men I hold most dearly. These are my cousins Hamlin, Dougal, and Ramsey Morgan. Their fathers are my father's younger brothers."

The men looked at Lucia with warmth and curiosity and, truthfully, a good deal of surprise. Hamlin was big and dark, like Bane, while Dougal had bushy red hair. "Little" Ramsey wasn't so little; he was quite tall and dark, but he was also very young. She smiled politely.

"I am very happy tae know ye," she said.

Bane didn't even let them reply to her before he was making demands. "What are ye doing here?" he asked. "'Tis a cold winter's night for ye tae be so far from home."

The one who had called Bane by name, Hamlin, still wasn't over the shock of seeing him. He pulled Bane down into an empty chair at their table. Lucia ended up on Bane's lap because there were no more chairs.

"We're heading tae Inverness," Hamlin said. "The winter has been bad tae the north, and we've had sickness move through the village. Do ye remember old Keltie?"

Bane nodded quickly. "The apothecary," he said. "He's still alive, is he? The man was ancient when I was a lad."

Hamlin agreed. "That he was," he said. "Do ye remember how a-feared we were of him? I was afraid tae look at him lest I turn tae stone."

Bane snorted. "We all were," he said. "But he's a knowledgeable man. Is he sending ye intae Inverness?"

Hamlin nodded. "He is," he said. "We've a list of medicines tae purchase tae help the sick. But no more talk of us. Bane, *where* have ye been, lad? We dinna see ye again after Jedburgh and we thought ye were dead."

Bane quickly sobered. He knew this would come up when he reached Ledmore, and rightly so, but it seemed that he wasn't as prepared as he'd thought to answer for his actions. He loved Hamlin like a brother; they'd grown up together. Dougal and Ramsey, too. He didn't want them to think poorly of him.

He sighed faintly.

"I did what I shouldna have done," he said quietly. "After the ambush with the Sassenachs…I couldna face what I'd done. Ye were there, Hamlin. Ye know what I'm talking about. I couldna return tae Ledmore and face those women and children, knowing I'd killed their sons and fathers and husbands. So…I ran away. I'm ashamed of myself, but that's what I did."

Hamlin didn't seem surprised by the confession. "But it wasna yer fault," he said quietly. "We all had a hand in the decision. Ye werena alone in it, lad."

"But I'm the one who disobeyed my da," Bane said. "All of ye looked tae me as yer commander and I led ye astray. It was stupid and reckless. It was my pride that did it, I suppose. I brought shame on my da and I just couldna face it."

Hamlin reached out, putting a hand on Bane's arm. "No one blamed ye," he said. "Ye never let us tell ye that. Ye disappeared before we could."

Bane shook his head, unwilling to be forgiven. Not yet, anyway. "I thought it would be best if I left. Hamlin, I never had the chance tae tell ye I was sorry I got yer brother killed. If I could have given my life for his, I would have."

Hamlin smiled wryly. "Cauley was charging against the Sassenachs before ye ever gave the command," he said. "He would have done it with or without ye, Bane. Ye take too much credit for my brother's foolishness. Ye're not tae blame."

"While I appreciate that, I was with Cauley when he drowned," Bane said quietly. "I tried tae swim with him, but he panicked. I couldna save him and save myself, too, so I chose myself. Hamlin...I hope ye can forgive me."

Hamlin's smile turned real and he took Bane's hand. "I forgave ye the moment it happened," he said. "I wish I could have told ye that before ye ran."

Bane appreciated his mercy. It did much to help him deal with the guilt he'd carried since that time. "Ye're a good man, Hamlin," he said, looking to the other men at the table. "The two of ye, as well. I've missed ye all."

Hamlin squeezed his hand. "We've missed ye a great deal," he said. "No one knew what had happened tae ye, least of all yer da. The not knowing...it ate at him, Bane. He was convinced ye hated him."

Bane shook his head, feeling his guilt return. "I dinna want tae shame him," he said. "Mayhap if everyone thought I was dead and gone...the object of their hatred would be gone. It wouldna reflect poorly on my da."

Hamlin hesitated before speaking. "Ye should know something, Bane," he said. "Yer da took the blame for the ambush. He told everyone that he ordered ye tae take the men. No one but those of us who survived know the truth, and Uncle Arch swore us tae secrecy."

Bane's eyes widened in shock. "Christ," he muttered. "Did he really take the blame?"

"He did."

"Damn the man… He shouldna have done that. It was *my* fault!"

Hamlin shook his head. "It wasna anyone's fault," he said. "That's what I was trying tae tell ye. Ye were in command of a group of hotheaded Albannach who would have gone even if ye hadna disobeyed yer da. Uncle Arch knew that. That's why he took the blame."

Bane wasn't happy about that at all. He sat there, his brow furrowed with distress, unable to articulate what he was feeling. So many emotions were running through his mind, not the least of which was horror.

"I canna let that go on," he said. "That's why I returned, lads, tae see my da and tae apologize tae him for what I did. Tae tell him that there hasna been a day since that the guilt of it hasna consumed me. I'll tell everyone in Ledmore who will listen that it wasna his fault at all, it was mine. I canna let him accept responsibility for something that wasna his fault. How is he, anyway? Ye said there was sickness in Ledmore. Is my da well?"

Hamlin glanced at Dougal and Ramsey, who didn't seem able to meet his eyes. With a heavy sigh, he answered Bane's question.

"Uncle Arch was one of the first tae get the fever, Bane," he said. "That was about two months ago. He was strong, but in the end, the fever claimed him. I'm so sorry, lad. He's gone."

Bane sat back in his chair, staring at Hamlin. He could feel Lucia's hand seek his, squeezing it, but she wisely kept silent. She didn't say a word. Bane didn't say a word, either. He couldn't. He simply sat there as the news sank in.

Tears formed in his eyes.

His father was gone.

"How…how long ago?" he asked hoarsely.

Hamlin's expression was full of sympathy. "A little over a month," he said. "My da has taken over as the clan chief. Bane,

Uncle Arch fought hard until the end. Ye should know that. And he never stopped loving ye, lad. I dunna think he ever gave up hope that someday ye might return."

Bane swallowed hard as tears streamed down his cheeks. The pain of grief was too much to bear.

"I did return," he whispered. "But not in time. Christ…not in time."

"But ye're here now," Dougal spoke up. "At least ye came when ye could."

Bane dropped his head, staring at his lap, struggling to process the death of his father. The man he loved most in the world, the man he'd betrayed so badly. The guilt was consuming him, guilt that he'd let his father die without apologizing to him, without telling him that he loved him.

God, he'd been so stupid. He'd stayed away, wallowing in self-pity, uncaring of the effect it was having on his father. He'd only been thinking about himself.

Now, he was only thinking about his father.

I'm so sorry, Da…

"Thank ye for telling me," he finally said, wiping at his face. "Thank ye for giving my da comfort in the end. I know he loved ye, Hamlin. He looked at ye as another son."

Hamlin smiled weakly. "My da and I were with him when he passed," he said. "He wasna alone, Bane. We were there."

That threatened Bane's composure again, but he fought it. There would be a moment for him to weep unashamedly for his father, but now wasn't the time in a room full of strangers. When he was alone with Lucia, he would grieve his father properly.

"And I thank ye for it," he said. "It means a great deal tae me."

As Hamlin nodded, Dougal spoke up again. "We thought ye were dead, Bane," he said. "Mayhap this isna the right time tae say this, but Uncle Andrew is now clan chief. That title rightly belongs tae ye, as Uncle Arch's son."

Bane looked at him. That was very true, something that didn't even occur to him until Dougal said it. Immediately, he shook his head.

"Nay," he said firmly. "I dunna want it. I dunna deserve it. Uncle Andrew will make a fine chieftain. But not me."

Hamlin frowned. "But it is yer legacy, Bane," he said. "It belongs tae ye."

Bane continued to shake his head. "Hamlin, I'll ask ye a question and I want ye tae answer truthfully. Is the village at peace now?"

"Aye."

"Are the people happy?"

"Aye, for the most part."

"And they respect Uncle Andrew as the chieftain?"

"They do. Very much."

"Then I've no right tae disrupt that," Bane said, raising his voice. "I came home tae see my da and make peace, not insert myself where I havena been for over two years. Let Uncle Andrew be the chieftain. He has earned it. Me… I've not earned anything. Let things lie."

Hamlin looked at Dougal and Ramsey, who weren't quite sure how to react. "Bane," Hamlin said, "ye canna legitimately refuse yer inheritance. It belongs only tae ye."

"I can refuse it if I'm dead," Bane said. "Ye said yerself that everyone thought I was dead. Well, let them keep thinking that. There's no reason for me tae return tae Ledmore and upset everyone's lives. Ye'll not tell anyone that ye've seen me, do ye hear? I'm dead tae ye, too."

Hamlin could see what he was doing even if Dougal and Ramsey couldn't. The man knew that returning after a long absence and assuming his legal rights would only shake up Clan Morgan. He was sacrificing his legacy for the sake of peace in the clan. And perhaps because he truly didn't feel worthy of it, too.

It was a difficult choice that only a man of honor would have made.

"Are ye sure that's what ye want, Bane?" he asked.

Bane looked at Lucia for the first time since sitting down at the table. A smile played on her lips as she returned his gaze, a smile of warmth and love and encouragement.

"'Tis yer decision," she said softly. "I'll stand by ye no matter what ye do."

He gave her a gentle squeeze, mulling over the situation, his options, his wants. "I promised ye a home," he said. "Latheron Tower is a fine home."

"Is it what ye want?"

He thought on that. "Would ye be angry if I said I wanted tae return tae the Cal?"

She shook her head. "Of course not," she said. "Yer friends are there. A new life is there. 'Tis a grand thing tae have a place like that waiting for ye."

Her reasoning made his decision for him. Bane turned to his cousins.

"Aye," he said firmly. "It's what I want. Please dunna tell Uncle Andrew that ye saw me. He doesna need that burden on him, 'tis difficult enough tae be the chieftain. Let him think what my da thought…that I'm dead and buried somewhere. It'll be easier that way."

Hamlin was grieved by the decision, but he understood. "Ye realize that when my da passes on, I'll become the chieftain."

"And a fine one ye'll be, Hamlin. I know ye'll make me proud. But do something for me, please."

"Whatever ye want."

"Where is my da buried?"

"In the little churchyard next tae St. John's Church," he said. "Ye can see it from Latheron."

Bane knew the church well. He'd spent a good deal of time

there as a child, having his knuckles rapped by the priests because he wouldn't pay attention to their teachings. Reaching out, he took Hamlin's hand.

"When ye return home, will ye go tae my father's grave and tell him that ye found me?" he asked, his voice cracking. "Will ye tell him that I'm happy? Tell him I've married a woman who has shown me what it means tae love. Tell him…tell him that I know he'd be proud of the man I've become and that I love him very much. Will ye do that for me?"

Hamlin's eyes filled with tears. "I will," he said. "He was always proud of ye, Bane. Did ye not know that?"

Bane was struggling with his composure again. "I wish I could have heard him tell me," he said. "I wish I could have earned it. He deserved better than I gave him, Hamlin. I'll spend the rest of my life living the way I think he would have wanted me tae."

Hamlin sniffled, giving Bane's hand a squeeze before releasing him so he could wipe his face. "Dougal," he said gruffly. "Make yerself useful. Go get us some warmed wine. We'll make it a night of celebrating the return of a brother."

As Dougal and Ramsey went to gather the requested drink, Lucia stood up from Bane's lap.

"I'll leave ye with yer menfolk," she said to Bane. "I'm a little tired, anyway. I wouldna be very good conversation."

Bane smiled at her, appreciating the fact that she wanted to give him time alone with his cousins. Time to speak on things to soothe his soul, to bring closure to a part of his life that needed it. He kissed her hands.

"I'll join ye later," he said.

She patted him on the cheek as she turned to Hamlin. "It was very nice tae meet ye, Hamlin," she said. "Mayhap we will see each other again someday."

"I hope so, Lady Morgan," Hamlin said.

With a final smile to her husband, Lucia retreated to their

chamber, giving her husband the private time with his cousins that he so badly needed. Running into them at the tavern had been fortuitous in so many ways; it had been cathartic to Bane in a sense. Perhaps Hamlin told him something he didn't want to hear with the death of his father, but in the end, it put Bane on a different path.

A path to a new life.

The Ludus Caledonia was a large part of that new life, a place where Bane could start fresh and new, where there was no past hounding him. Only a future that would unlock his potential. Lucia didn't care about a home of their own that he had promised her, at least not now. She was content to return with him to the Ludus Caledonia, a place she knew very well.

The past month had given her a good perspective on what had happened at Meadowbank and why. Bane had convinced her that she wouldn't be punished for killing Colly in self-defense because he was quite certain Laird Currie would not allow it. That gave her the confidence to return with Bane to the Ludus Caledonia, knowing that, come what may, he would protect her from harm. He would protect her from anything Lady Currie could throw at her.

Bane was not only the Highland Defender—he was her defender, too.

A giant among men.

As Lucia finally found rest on the mattresses on the floor, feeling the delicious heat from the brazier, her thoughts turned to the future and what would come for her and Bane. For whatever happened, it would be with Bane by her side, for all time. She'd been married to the man for nearly a month, and already it seemed as if they had always been together.

She couldn't imagine her life without him.

Had Lucia not taken that shortcut in Edinburgh and suffered the attack of sausage thieves, she would never have met the man who had come to be her purpose for living. That defeated wretch of a man she had shown kindness to had been an angel in disguise.

Bane had called her his angel once, and he continued to call her that to this day. But the truth was that he was *her* savior.

Her love.

When Lucia finally drifted off to sleep, it was with dreams of the Ludus Caledonia.

Dreams of home.

EPILOGUE

Year of Our Lord 1487
July

"WATCH OUT FOR HIS FEET," LOR MUTTERED INTO BANE'S EAR. "I told ye that the last time and ye dinna listen."

It was a warm, dusty day over southern Scotland, with a brilliant sun hanging in the pale-blue sky.

And Bane had made a terrible mistake.

He and Lor had been working with a group of *novicius* in the Fields of Mars when Magnus, who was in the holding area next to the arena, challenged Bane to a fight. Bane would have refused except Magnus was smirking at him in a mocking manner, one that had Bane accepting before he'd even stopped to think about it.

Now he was stuck.

The group of *novicius* had been moved into the lists which, unfortunately for Bane, also included his wife and Isabail this morning. They were sitting about halfway up the arena, in the shade for the most part, watching their men train new recruits. Now they'd be watching a rematch between Bane and Magnus, who was strutting over on the other side of the arena, pointing his finger at Bane and laughing.

Bane liked Magnus well enough. In fact, they'd become good friends since his return to the Ludus Caledonia three months ago. Magnus was arrogant but loyal and wise when he settled down enough to display those characteristics. Rumor had it that Clegg was getting ready to move him to another fight guild, the Ludus Antonine in Glasgow, because it was becoming extremely popular and the moneymaking potential was great. Magnus didn't particularly want to go, but as a career warrior, he went where he was told.

Therefore, Bane might not get another chance to best the man.

"He'll not get those feet anywhere near my head," Bane said confidently. "If he tries, I'll break his toes."

Lor snorted, turning away from Bane but catching sight of someone else entering the arena. Galan, who used to help him train *novicius* but had since moved on to become the trainer of his own group, was emerging from the staging area with two shields and two wooden swords.

Lor came to a halt.

"What are ye doing here?" he called.

Galan smiled broadly. He was big, strong, and handsome, and there had been a time when Lady Currie, long ago, had noticed him. But he'd refused her just as Bane had, only she hadn't pursued him nearly as hard. He'd slipped away unscathed.

"I thought we might team up against the Highland Dimwit and the Chicken," Galan said, watching Bane laugh and Magnus's feathers ruffle. "I'm sorry. I meant the Highland Defender and the Eagle. My apologies."

Magnus's eyes narrowed. "I'm going tae stick my talons in ye, Galan."

Galan laughed loudly, tossing a *gladius* to Lor as he came near the man. "You can try," he said. Then he looked at Bane. "Get over there with your teammate, Defender. You're not welcome on this side of the arena at the moment."

Grinning, Bane took his *gladius* and his wooden shield and headed over to Magnus, who was clearly disturbed by the change in game plan.

"Damnation," Magnus muttered. "It seems that I willna have the chance tae kick ye in the head again."

Bane smirked. "Ye never had the chance tae begin with," he

said. "I know yer tricks. And so do Lor and Galan. They'll be expecting it from ye, but they willna be expecting it from me."

Magnus looked at him, surprised. "Ye think ye can get that big body of yers up in the air tae take someone's head off? I would sincerely like tae see that."

"If ye dunna start acting like ye're on my side, we are going tae lose this battle."

Magnus shrugged. "I'm on yer side," he said. "But ye'd better let me do the kicking. I'll take Galan. I never did like that Sassenach. Can ye take down Lor?"

"I can try."

"Ye dunna sound confident."

"Then ye take Lor and I'll take Galan."

Magnus shook his head. "I'll keep Galan," he said. "With Lor, it's a matter of catching the man off guard. They dunna call him the Lion of the Highlands for nothing."

Bane had heard that nickname for Lor when he'd first come to the Ludus Caledonia last year. It suited the big blond warrior who was quiet and efficient until he had a reason to roar. Then he was unstoppable.

"As I said, I'll try," he said after a moment. "If I take him down first, I'll help ye with Galan."

Magnus frowned. "What makes ye think I'll not take that bloody Sassenach down first?"

"Care tae wager?"

"Gladly. Six silver marks."

"Afraid, are ye?"

Magnus's eyes opened wide at the challenge. "Ten marks, ye foolish man."

Bane chuckled. "Ye're not a very good team player."

Magnus huffed at him, grabbing his *gladius* and shield, preparing to take the field. He and Bane were just starting to move forward when Axel and Clegg appeared on the arena floor, followed by some of the other *doctores* that trained other groups of warriors.

Luther was there, followed by trainers Milo Linton and Wendell Stanhope. Both Milo and Wendell were fixtures at the Ludus Caledonia, training the more advanced warriors. When Bane and Magnus saw the group turning out, they came to a halt.

"This is an event," Clegg said, grinning at Bane and Magnus, and Lor and Galan. He waved the men closer to him. "I saw this coming about from my viewing box above, and I highly encourage this type of combat, but remember that the men you are training are watching you. If you fail miserably, you will lose their respect. Do you understand that?"

All four men nodded and Clegg continued. "Therefore, no dirty fighting," he said. "Magnus, I am speaking to you. Once a man has fallen, he is out of the fight. This will go to the last man standing, so make it good and try not to dismember each other. Remember our motto—in men, there is honor. Be honorable. And there is something more to consider."

As Clegg delved into how this should be a lesson to the other men on technique in battle, Lucia and Isabail were watching from high in the lists. They spent most of their mornings together these days, cleaning, washing, talking, and sewing while Isabail chased around her toddler son, Niko.

Lucia didn't do much chasing, but she did watch everything Isabail did, for in three months she would have her own son to consider. Rosy and round with pregnancy, she felt marvelous most of the time, and even Bane had a hard time keeping up with her energy. But it was a wonderful time in their lives, and they'd spent the past three months happy and content at the Ludus Caledonia.

It really was like a family, with Lor and Isabail and Niko, and everyone else who had made such an impact on their lives. It was an exceptionally close group. Even now, Lucia and Isabail sat together with Niko between them, watching with interest the happenings in the arena.

"So they're truly going tae fight one another?" Lucia asked.

Isabail nodded, holding on to Niko as he tried to climb down to the next row of seats. "Aye," she said. "'Tis good practice for them and their men get to see examples of how tae fight in the arena."

Lucia leaned back, rubbing her gently swollen belly. "Have ye seen them fight each other before?"

"A few times. They dunna do it too often. I think they're doing it this time because Magnus challenged Bane."

Lucia grinned. "Bane loves Magnus, but sometimes he wants tae pluck the Eagle's feathers. That's what he's told me."

Isabail started to laugh. "Magnus need it," she said. "He hasna been at the Cal long, but long enough take make himself an important and annoying figure around here. And he knows it."

Lucia thought back to the days when she first saw the Eagle. "I remember when he first came," she said. "He's quite handsome. I know that Lady Currie thought so, but her focus was on Bane. A time I'd rather forget. At least, some aspects of it."

Isabail glanced at her as she wrestled with her son. "Lor says Lady Currie hasna returned since she purchased Bane last year. Have ye seen her since?"

Lucia shook her head. "Nay," she said. "But Laird Currie has been here a few times. I've seen him, and he and Bane have become close. Bane said that Clegg is glad to see his old friend out and about again."

"But what happened tae Lady Currie?"

Lucia's gaze was on her husband in the distance. "Laird Currie sent her back tae her father, or so Bane tells me," she said. "He said that she was living in a wine barrel, drunk from morning tae night, so Laird Currie sent her back tae her father with only what she came with when she married him. He's cut her off from his money completely. Bane says her father is a tyrant and has locked her in the vault, but who knows if that is really true. She's gone and that's all that matters."

"I'm sure it's a relief tae ye."

"More than ye know, lass."

Down below, the fight abruptly commenced, cleaving any further conversation. Lor and Galan were caught off guard by a ferocious attack from Bane and Magnus, and Lucia ended up on her feet, cheering loudly for her husband as he went after Lor with a vengeance.

Beside her, Isabail was also on her feet, holding Niko on her hip and explaining to the lad that his father was fighting a terrible man. Lucia heard the comment, laughing softly, but it didn't dampen her excitement for the fight.

Bane was quite a warrior.

But so were Lor, Galan, and Magnus. Lor regained his equilibrium and countered Bane's powerful tactics, and the fight continued all over the arena floor. The *gladius* pounded on the wooden shield, one after the other, the sounds of heavy blows reverberating off the stone lists.

Even the *novicius* were getting into the mood and they, too, began to cheer their *doctores*. At one point, however, Magnus got too close to Galan and managed to get his feet up, kicking Galan in the head.

Down he went.

Unfortunately for Magnus, that caused both Lor and Bane to turn on him, and he soon found himself fending off two powerful warriors. Magnus was an excellent fighter, and a professional one, but Bane moved in behind him and Lor attacked from the front, and it was Bane who ended up tripping him.

Magnus went down to the roar of the crowd.

Even Lor cheered, standing over Magnus and telling him just what he thought of his brutal tactics, but it gave Bane the ability to approach Lor from behind because he was distracted with Magnus.

Down Lor went.

With three men down, Bane was the winner. He threw up his arms as he approached the lists, encouraging everyone there to cheer for their champion. He was laughing as he did it, arrogantly soaking up the adoration as his wife screamed and whistled wildly for him. He pointed to her, acknowledging her cheers, as both Lucia and Isabail laughed uproariously about it.

They laughed even harder when Lor and Magnus came up behind him, lifting him into the air and tossing him onto the dirt. By then, it became a dog pile as Clegg and Axel stepped in to stop it before someone was unintentionally injured.

The great fight between the *doctores* and Magnus had come to a satisfying conclusion.

Galan was helped out of the arena by Luther and Milo, while the *novicius* came down out of the lists and gathered in a big group. Axel discussed the bout they'd just witnessed and asked the men what they had learned from it.

Lucia and Isabail had come down to the edge of the arena, watching and listening. Lucia couldn't help but reflect on the times she had sat at the edges of the arena, watching the bouts between half-naked men as Lady Currie drooled. It was something she had hated, and a place she had hated, but now...

Now she loved everything about it.

The Ludus Caledonia had become her home.

But the afternoon was beginning to wane, and soon the arena would need to be prepared for the coming fights that evening. When Axel was finished with his teaching moment, Bane and Lor broke up the group of *novicius* and sent them back to their cottages. When the men dispersed, Bane and Lor headed for their wives.

Niko screamed when he saw his father, running to Lor, who picked him up and tossed him in the air, listening to him shriek in delight. As Lor and Isabail headed off, Bane went to Lucia, hugging her gently and putting his hand on her rounded belly.

"How is Mattox?" he asked.

She laughed softly. "So today it is Mattox?" she said. "Yesterday, it was Alex."

"I've changed my mind."

"Ye've changed yer mind a hundred times."

Bane turned her for the arena exit. "Naming my son is very important," he insisted. "It must be the right name."

"Alex was a nice name."

He shook his head. "Too common," he said. "He must have something unique and unusual, like my name."

"Where did ye get yer name, anyway?"

"It was my mother's family name. In my family, the men are usually named after the mother's family. My father was named for his mother's family."

They began to mount the steps that would take them out of the arena. "My mother's family name was Hayes," Lucia said. "I like the name Hayes Morgan."

Bane cocked his head. "Nice enough," he said. "I shall consider it."

"Do I not get a say in this?"

"Ye can name the lasses. I'll name the lads."

She twisted her lips unhappily. "Is that so?"

"'Tis."

She broke into a grin, shaking her head at her stubborn husband as they came to the top of the arena and began heading for their small cottage that was located near Caelian Hill. It was a bigger cottage, with three rooms, and it stood alongside Lor and Isabail's larger cottage.

With their family growing, Clegg had moved them away from the rank and file of the warrior village, which Bane appreciated. It was one kind gesture in a long line of kind gestures that Clegg had made for them since they had discovered Lucia's pregnancy. The only caveat Clegg demanded was that he be named the child's godfather, to which they had readily agreed.

The sun was sinking low in the sky as they neared Caelian Hill, but as they did so, Lucia suddenly came to a halt. When Bane looked at her curiously, she pointed toward Caelian Hill.

Laird Currie's carriage was parked alongside the curtain wall.

Interested at the appearance of the old lord, they shifted course and headed toward the carriage. The door to the cab suddenly popped open and Laird Currie emerged, moving with more vigor than either Lucia or Bane had ever seen. When Laird Currie saw Bane, he waved a hand at him.

"Bane!"

His voice was surprisingly robust, and Bane left Lucia to jog toward the old man.

"M'laird," he greeted pleasantly. "'Tis good tae see ye. I dinna know ye were coming tonight."

Laird Currie took Bane's hand warmly. Truthfully, the old man looked marvelously well. There was color in his cheeks that hadn't been there before, and he'd gained weight. He no longer looked like a frail old man, but a healthy specimen for a man his age.

"I know," Laird Currie said. "'Twas a sudden decision, but I've come early because I wanted tae see ye. Clegg said ye'd be coming out of the arena soon, so I waited for ye."

"Oh?" Bane said. "Why did ye not come tae the arena? Ye would have seen a good fight."

The old man shook his head. "I dinna come tae see the fights," he said. "I came tae see *ye*. I've brought ye something."

Bane looked at him curiously. "What's that?"

Laird Currie continued to hold Bane's hand. "First, I must say something," he said. "I'm glad for the life ye've found here for ye and Lucia. Colm would be very happy tae know how well ye've taken care of his daughter. Even though ye both ended up at a place like the Ludus Caledonia, I've never seen her happier."

By this time Lucia had walked up, smiling when she heard Laird Currie's last few words. "Thank ye, m'laird," she said. "I've never *been* happier."

"Good," Laird Currie said. "Now that I've got ye both here, I'll say what I came tae say. Bane, ye've asked me about Tynan a few times, and I've told ye that the lad was well."

Bane's warm expression vanished. "God," he hissed. "Dunna tell me that has changed. Nothing has happened tae him, has it?"

Laird Currie quickly shook his head. "Nay, lad, he's well. But Tynan told me something once, something ye promised him. He said ye'd teach him how tae fight when he got older. Did ye mean it?"

Bane nodded. "Of course I did. With all my heart."

Laird Currie smiled as he let go of Bane's hand and turned for his carriage. "I want ye tae teach him, too," he said. "He's a smart lad. If he stays at Meadowbank, the best he can hope tae be is my majordomo. Or mayhap he'll be in charge of the stables. He's a good lad and he deserves more opportunity than I can give him. Amy has given her permission, so I came tae ask him if ye'll take him now. He wants tae come with ye, Bane. Will ye take him with ye and give him the opportunities that I canna?"

With that, he opened the door and Tynan spilled out, falling to his knees because he'd been leaning against the door, listening. But the moment he saw Bane, he bolted to his feet and ran at the man, who took him in his arms and held him tightly.

"Bane!" Tynan wept. "Bane, can I stay with ye? Please?"

Bane hugged the lad before gently setting him to his feet. Bane looked him over, seeing that he'd grown taller and fatter since he'd last seen him. But the straw-like hair was still the same; that just made him laugh.

"My, my, lad," he said, putting his hand on the boy's head. "Ye've grown up behind my back. Look how big ye are."

Tynan smiled hugely, displaying two front missing teeth. "I serve Laird Currie now," he said. "Me and my mam. And I play chess!"

"Is that so?" Bane said, stroking his chin as if impressed. "Then ye can teach me."

"I will if ye teach me tae fight!"

Everything about Tynan was enthusiastic and happy. Bane couldn't get over how healthy the boy appeared. Like Laird Currie, the boy had blossomed without the weight of an unhappy household hanging over him. That was clear with both of them.

Bane looked at Laird Currie.

"And his mother approves?" he asked. "The lad would have tae remain here with me, ye know. He couldna go home frequently tae see her."

Laird Currie nodded. "But I can bring her here when I come," he said. "She can visit him then. I have a confession, Bane... Amy and I... Well, she's the woman I should have married. I dunna know why I never considered her, but I should have. She's meant the world tae me."

Bane smiled at Laird Currie admitting his affections for a servant, but the man's healthy appearance was now coming to make some sense. Finally, he had someone who genuinely cared for him and it showed.

"I hope she's a good companion tae ye, m'laird," he said, returning his focus to Tynan. "As for the lad... If it's agreeable tae my wife, I'm happy tae keep him here and train him."

Lucia opened her arms to Tynan, who immediately hugged her tightly. "Of course I'm agreeable," she said. "Tynan and I are old friends. He's most welcome."

Bane put his arm around her shoulders as she held Tynan. "Even with our own bairn on the way?"

"Think of what a wonderful older brother Tynan will be tae Mattox."

"Or Henry."

"Another change?"

Bane simply laughed, but the situation with Tynan was settled. Laird Currie watched the exchange, knowing he'd made the right decision and happy for it. As Lucia bent over and picked up the boy who was very nearly as tall as she was, Laird Currie reached out to Bane.

"I will admit something to ye," he said. "I've been coming tae the Cal since ye left Meadowbank, hoping ye'd return someday. When ye did, I wanted tae make sure ye were happy and settled before I brought up the subject of Tynan. I know he's too young tae train now, but a place like this will give him a better life than I can give him. He'll learn tae fight, and he'll learn the ways of men. And he'll learn it all from ye. I canna imagine a better teacher."

"Nor I," Lucia said, squeezing Tynan tightly. "Bane has found a new life here, as have I. I thank ye for that, Laird Currie. Without ye…we wouldna know such happiness. We owe ye everything."

Laird Currie waved them off. "And ye've both changed my life, as well, so the feeling is mutual," he said. For a moment, he faced Tynan, smiling at the boy in a way that suggested he was going to miss him very much. "Well, lad, ye finally have Bane and Lucia. I know yer mother will miss ye, but she's happy for ye tae find something better. Dunna disappoint her. Be the very best ye can be at whatever Bane chooses tae teach ye."

Tynan nodded firmly. Then he ran at Laird Currie, hugging the man tightly. "Thank ye, m'laird."

Laird Currie was growing emotional. He hugged the boy before pushing him away, sniffling as he returned to his carriage. Hand on the door, he turned to the three of them, standing there.

"Be happy, all of ye," he said tightly. "I know I will be."

With that, he climbed into his carriage and the driver snapped the reins, moving the horses forward. Bane and Lucia and Tynan stood there, waving at him, as the carriage made a big circle and headed out the way it had come.

"He's a good man," Lucia said. "My da always thought so."

"So do I," Bane said. Putting his arm around Lucia's shoulders, he kissed her on the temple. "It seems as if we're well on our way tae those ten bairns ye wanted."

Lucia laughed softly, reaching out to take Tynan by the hand. "I think we're going tae need a bigger cottage."

It turned out to be a prophetic statement.

In early October, after two days of labor and two of the longest days of Bane's life, Lucia delivered twin boys, healthy and screaming. Greer Colm Morgan and his brother Archer Clegg Morgan would grow up to be great and powerful warriors, just like their father.

As Bane looked into the faces of his newborns on the night they were born, he realized that the infants represented what he'd been searching for all along. Glory didn't lie in victory or power or even money; it lay in the heart. It lay in the two sleeping infants in his arms and in his willingness to understand what was important in life.

Who was important in life.

Home, for Bane, wasn't in the tiny Highland village of Ledmore. He'd left that long ago. It was in a big, dusty fight guild where he and Lucia were loved and accepted for who they were. It was the home, and family, they had always dreamed of.

Arch Morgan would indeed have been proud.

Keep reading for an exclusive sneak peek
at the next book in Kathryn Le Veque's
thrilling Scots and Swords series

HIGHLAND LEGEND

Coming July 2021
From Sourcebooks Casablanca

CHAPTER ONE

The Month of August
Year of Our Lord 1488
Edinburgh, Scotland
The Ludus Caledonia

HE COULD SEE HIM ACROSS THE ARENA FLOOR, THROUGH A haze of dust that seemed to conceal just how badly injured his opponent was.

But no amount of dust could dampen his bloodlust.

It was time to go in for the kill.

His heart always started pumping in a moment like this. It had been a long, drawn-out fight with a hairy brute from Saxony known as *Der Bär*, or the Bear. He'd been brought to the Ludus Caledonia, the premier fight guild of Scotland, by an arrogant Saxon lord who was positive he could make a wagonful of money on the fights.

His warrior against a *rudiarius*—the Cal's top warrior.

Magnus Stewart was that warrior. Known as the Eagle, he watched the Bear pace on the other side of the arena known as the Fields of Mars. He could hear the roar of the crowd, men who also had bloodlust now that they knew the Bear was wounded. A wounded bear could be a dangerous thing, but Magnus was confident he could deliver a blow that would end this match.

Truth be told, he was becoming weary.

But not weary enough.

He was going to skin that bear.

The field marshals, having checked upon the condition of the Bear to ensure he could continue, were satisfied that the man could withstand more pounding. On the opposite side of the arena, Magnus was pacing, anxious to move, anxious to win yet one more fight in a long line of fights that had seen him emerge the victor.

And to the victor went the spoils.

He was ready.

The field marshals signaled for the bout to continue. It was a surprisingly warm August afternoon. As the last vestiges of golden rays beat upon Magnus's bronzed skin, he approached his injured opponent. He began to circle his opponent, preparing to deliver what was his signature move.

A kick to the side of the head.

One blow to the Bear's already damaged skull and the man would be no more.

The Bear, however, wasn't stupid. He tracked Magnus as the man skirted him, walking circles around him then reversing course in an attempt to disorient him. Magnus had the ability to block out the world around him when focused on a target, one of the gifts that made him such a great warrior. He was a true hunter. Even now, all he could see in this vast arena full of people was the man in front of him.

It was time to end this.

The Bear roared and the crowd roared along with him. Magnus used that moment to make his charge, knowing that the Bear would hear the roar of the crowd and more than likely be distracted by it. He rushed the man as fast as he could run and that was very fast indeed. His feet were light, his muscular legs pumping, and as he got within about ten feet of the Bear, he suddenly went airborne.

The Bear, who had been expecting a head-on charge, was unprepared when Magnus used the man's own chest as leverage against a vicious kick to the skull.

The Bear fell like a stone.

The crowd in the arena went mad. They cheered their champion as Magnus threw up his arms, signifying his victory. Money began to rain down into the arena as people threw coins to signify their appreciation. Since this happened frequently, Magnus had two servants he trusted who would run out onto the field and collect the money that had been thrown at him. They would collect every last coin for him and he would give them a cut.

Tonight's haul would be a big one.

The crowd screamed and cheered for him for at least five minutes, which only fed his indomitable pride. His record for the longest cheering was twelve minutes, but tonight, he didn't feel like soaking up their adoration for too long. He had already had three bouts today, ending with the Bear, so he was ready for some good food, some good wine, and hopefully some good companionship.

He knew that particular kind of companionship, the female kind, was already clamoring for him at the gates that led from the public area into the staging area because that was where the wealthy matrons gathered.

He expected a long line and much bidding tonight.

Waving to the crowd one last time, he made his way to the exit of the arena floor, where other fight guild warriors were applauding him. He did not acknowledge them because, frankly, they were not of his class. The only ones he really respected were men he considered his equal, and those were few. But he could see those men standing just inside the staging area, and they were not cheering.

They were laughing at him.

Lor Careston, a *doctores*, or trainer, was the first one Magnus made eye contact with. Big, blond, and a brilliant tactical fighter, Lor simply stood there and shook his head.

"Do ye ever do anything different?" he asked drolly. "Is it always yer finishing move tae kick a man where he thinks?"

"Of course it is," Magnus said, untying the leather gloves on his hands. "By the time I kick him there, he is thinking about kicking *me*, so I must deliver the death blow."

Lor was a quiet one for the most part, but he loved to poke holes in Magnus's pride. It was in good-natured fun, however. Magnus knew he had Lor's admiration and friendship. The man standing next to Lor, however, was another matter because, at one time, Magnus and the man were both colleagues and opponents.

He made eye contact with Bane Morgan. Muscular, handsome Bane used to be competition for the ladies' attention until he married last year. Women still looked at him and cheered for him, but there was no woman for Bane except his wife, which made Magnus appreciate him all the more.

Less competition for women's attention.

"And what does the great Highland Defender have tae say about my bout?" Magnus demanded. "Did ye not see how perfect it was?"

Bane, whose fight guild nickname was the Highland Defender, knew the man was looking to have his ego stroked.

He would not oblige.

"It was decent," he said.

Magnus was insulted. "Better than anything ye've fought in yer life," he said. "'Tis understandable for ye tae be envious of me. 'Tis all right, lad. Someday, ye may fight as well as I do."

Bane started laughing, looking to Lor and rolling his eyes. Bane and Magnus had been on many tandem teams because, surprisingly, they worked well together and they were undefeated before Bane retired to become a *doctores*. Still, Magnus liked to poke at Bane, as brothers would roast one another.

And it was most definitely a brotherhood.

The last of the trio of men was another *doctores* who had Magnus's respect, although he'd rather die that admit it. Galan de Lara and Magnus had suffered their share of bouts with each other, and Magnus had the edge with victories. Unlike Lor and Bane, Galan was English. That meant he was the butt of insults, more than most, and he greatly frustrated Magnus from time to time.

Even so, their bond was strong.

"And ye, Sassenach," he said to Galan. "Tell me how great I am. I would hear yer praise."

Galan sighed heavily. Like Lor and Bane, he found great annoyance with Magnus, but the man was pure greatness. They all knew it. Magnus knew it. It was a game between them after nearly every bout, with Magnus demanding recognition and the *doctores* refusing to give it to him.

But tonight was different.

They had a little surprise for him.

"You were magnificent," Galan said. "In fact, you were so magnificent, that Lor and Bane and I have chosen the most beautiful woman in the arena for you tonight."

Magnus looked at them in surprise. "Is this true?" he said, surprised. "Where is she?"

Galan pointed into the holding area. There was a three-storied structure that comprised the north wall of the area—the bottom levels were for the competitors while the very top level, complete with a large stone balcony, was the private viewing apartment of the owner of the Ludus Caledonia, Clegg de Lave.

Clegg, however, was away from the Ludus Caledonia this night. He and one of his senior *doctores*, Luther Eddleston, were off visiting other fight guilds. That left his private rooms empty, but not for long.

That's where the *doctores* had the surprise waiting.

"There," Galan said. "In Clegg's apartment. Take the private stairs so the women waiting at the gates overlooking the holding area do not see you."

Magnus's emerald gaze looked up at the third floor of the building, envisioning the beauty who would surely be waiting for him. A seductive smile crossed his lips, but he refused to heed their advice about taking the private stairs.

He paraded across the holding area floor for all to see.

Women were screaming at him from above, since the holding area was down below, sunk into the same hillside that the arena had been carved out of. Magnus looked up at the throng, blowing kisses, flexing his biceps, and he had women fainting at the sight.

Behind him, Lor and Bane and Galan followed, watching the spectacle with the greatest amusement. Magnus was great; he *knew* he was great. He wanted to make sure everyone else knew that he was great, so the man never did anything subtly or secretively.

It was part of his charm.

And then came the garments.

It was usual every time Magnus pranced around after a bout. Women started throwing pieces of clothing over the iron fence that separated them from the holding area. Scarves would come raining down in a flutter of perfumed material. They almost always smelled heavily of perfume.

Next came the hose—fine silk hose would hit the floor of the holding area with a thud because women had stuffed coins into them. Magnus pointed to some of the warriors standing around to pick up the hose, snapping at them when they wanted to keep the money. He would snatch the hose and the money away from them.

Holding his booty of coin-filled hose, Magnus looked up at the women lining the fence to see that half were screaming and half were crying. That was usual. He paused, blowing more kisses up to the crowd, and one young woman was so overcome that she vomited. Chunks of the stuff fell through the fence and landed near Magnus, who eyed it with some disgust and decided to end his cavalcade of worship. If the crowd was beginning to spew in excitement, it was time for him to exit.

Until the next time.

He decided to take the private stairs, after all.

Leaving his friends down in the holding area, Magnus took the steps two at a time. He was sweaty and dirty from his bouts in the arena, but he knew that Clegg's private apartment had a bathing area. The viewing rooms had floor to ceiling doors that opened up to a private balcony, the same balcony that the stairs led up to. As he hit the balcony, he was quite curious to see the woman his friends had chosen.

Beautiful, they'd said.

He might even permit her to bathe him.

When he reached the top of the steps, the door into the private rooms was open. He stepped in, his dirty sandals against the tile floor that Clegg had brought all the way from Rome. In fact, everything at the Ludus Caledonia reflected the Romans and their architecture, all the way down to the beautiful robes that Clegg wore, like a great patriarch.

Even the chamber itself reflected that love of ancient Rome— beautiful columns, tile, glass. It was lovely. There were tapestries on the walls, silks on the cushioned couches, and great bowls of incense that burned all day and all night. Magnus expected that the woman would be waiting for him, but he didn't see anyone as he entered. He was halfway into the chamber when he saw movement on one of the couches.

"Ye must be Magnus."

Magnus froze. The voice was low and raspy, not at all sweet and delicate-sounding, and he turned his head to see a pile of silk moving on one of the couches. A delicate, age-worn hand came up, removing the veil from a head that was covered in soft, white hair.

The woman revealed herself fully. She wasn't simply old; she was ancient. He could see that she'd been lovely in her day, but that had been long ago. She wasn't exactly the raging young beauty that his friends had lauded.

And they'd known it all along.

Magnus knew in an instant that he'd been fooled.

"So ye're tae be my companion this evening?" he asked evenly. "Ye must have paid a high price."

The woman nodded as she sat up. She was well dressed, in velvet and perfume, and he could smell the sweet scent where he stood. There was something graceful about her, in fact, in the way she moved. In her time, she must have been most alluring.

But it didn't change the fact that she was old enough to be his grandmother.

"I did," she said. "I paid the *ianista* handsomely. I can see it was worth every penny."

Had Magnus not been so shocked at his rather ancient company, the situation would have been laughable. His gaze drifted over the woman, her fine clothing and surprisingly shapely figure for her age. But her statement made him realize that not only were his friends in on the joke, but so was the manager of the Ludus Caledonia, Axel von Rossau.

He was certain they'd done it to teach him a lesson in humility he'd not soon forget.

"Of course I'm worth every penny," he said after a moment, moving in her direction. "Let us come tae know one another, sweetheart. What's yer name?"

"Mary," the woman said, her features lighting up with joy. "Lady MacMerry of Whitekirk Castle. My dead husband was Lord Whitekirk. Surely ye've heard of Merry Whitekirk."

Magnus had. He may have presented the image of a man only interested in money and victory, but the truth was that he was much deeper than that. It was a trait he kept well-hidden. His father, Hugh Stewart, Duke of Kintyre and Lorne, was the king's youngest brother and a prince of the Scottish royal family. Magnus had been born out of wedlock to a lady-in-waiting to the duke's wife.

But being a royal bastard wasn't information that Magnus spread around.

In fact, royal blood had been a curse in Magnus's case, but it also meant he kept abreast of the politics of Scotland. He was a sharp and astute man, and he knew who the enemies of the crown were. MacMerry had most definitely been an enemy.

Therefore, he was careful in his reply.

"What does it matter if I have or have not?" he asked, a twinkle in his eyes. "All that matters is that ye have the money and I have the time. Let's have a drink before I wash the grime from my body."

He was already moving for Clegg's elaborate sideboard, brought all the way from Constantinople. Upon it sat a full pitcher of wine and cut glass cups. Magnus set down the coin-filled hose he'd been carrying, the ones he'd collected from the staging area floor, and poured two full measures. He handed one cup to the old woman, who was gulping it down before he even took the first sip of his own.

He watched her drink, wondering what he was going to do with her. He wasn't one to bed anything other than young and beautiful women, but he supposed a good lay was a good lay. Maybe a woman of Mary MacMerry's age might have more experience than most.

Perhaps he'd even learn something.

"More, love?" he asked, picking up the pitcher again. "Let's drink tae our good health and tae the sovereignty of Scotland."

Mary eagerly took another drink. "'Tis fine wine, indeed."

Magnus refilled her cup even though it wasn't quite empty. "It is," he said. "The finest wine for the finest women. Tell me, Mary—how did ye come here? I've not seen ye before."

Mary was nervous. Magnus hadn't noticed that before. He could see that her hands were trembling as she downed her wine.

"I've been here before," she said. "I've seen ye fight many a time. Ye're the prettiest man I've ever seen. A beauteous lad, ye are."

Magnus grinned, flashing straight and white teeth. "And ye've never wanted tae meet me before now?"

Mary shrugged. "There are a hundred women waiting for ye every time I come," she said. "I paid well tae have ye tae myself tonight because I've come with a purpose."

"Oh?" he said, sipping his wine. "What is that?"

Mary took another gulp of wine that drained her cup. Oddly, she wasn't as confident as she had been when he'd first entered the chamber. She seemed nervous and…forlorn. It was difficult to describe, but he knew that he was starting to feel some pity for her.

He filled her cup again.

"Tell me, Mary," he said. "Why did ye come?"

She took another big drink before looking at him. "I came tae be with ye," she said. "And I'll give ye something in exchange."

"Of course ye will. Money."

She shook her head. "Something better," she said. "I have no heirs. When I pass, Whitekirk Castle will return tae the king and I dunna want him tae have it."

"I canna help ye, lady."

She nodded eagerly. "Ye can," she said. "Instead of money, I'll make ye my heir. I'd rather have Whitekirk go tae a fighter than go tae the bastard on the throne. Will ye take the castle instead of money?"

Magnus almost started laughing. If the woman knew who he really was, she would not have made such an offer. It certainly wasn't an offer he had expected.

At first, he wasn't sure what to say, but the royal bastard in him who had been denied everything from birth wasn't afraid to speak up. It was the entire reason Magnus had become a fighter for profit—he had to work for everything he ever had and ever would have. He'd been born illegitimately, held captive for years with the understanding that his father wanted nothing to do with him, before finally being released and having nowhere to go. Therefore, he'd learned to take money where he could get it.

Including accepting a castle from an old woman with no heirs.

"Are ye certain about that?" he said. "It seems like a high price tae pay, even tae me."

"I've no one else. Will ye accept?"

He eyed her a moment as if deliberating, but it was all an act. If she was serious, then he'd be foolish to pass it up.

"Of course," he said. "I wouldna want ye tae go tae yer grave fearful of leaving yer property behind. But tell me again so there are no misunderstandings—are ye *sure* ye want me tae have it?"

The old woman nodded. "I do," she said, downing most of her second cup of wine. "And dunna worry—I've no relatives tae contest my wishes. I'll find a Serjeant-at-Law and have him witness my signature on my will. But I only know ye as the Eagle, love. What's yer name?"

"Magnus Alexander Albert Hugh Stewart."

The long name sank into her wine-soaked mind and she gave him a startled expression. "Stewart?" she repeated. "Like the king?"

"Not like the king."

It was a lie, but she didn't question it. She accepted his answer and settled down quickly, finishing off her cup of wine. She was well on her way to becoming drunk and with the next measure of drink, Magnus watered down the wine significantly. He didn't need a drunken old woman on his hands.

"Well and good yer not related tae the king," she said. "I dunna want Whitekirk tae fall tae a relation."

"Ye worry too much," he said, avoiding a direct answer to her statement. "Tell me about yer family. Where do ye come from?"

It was a distraction. He wanted to get her talking, hoping she might forget that she'd come to bed him. In fact, the wine was making her chatty and Magnus feigned interest when she spoke of her childhood as a lass in Blackness and how Harry MacMerry—as that was truly his name—came courting.

After her third full cup of wine, Mary lay her head back on the couch and stared up at the ceiling. She'd stopped talking and was now simply staring up into space. Magnus watched her carefully, wondering if she was about to pass out, when she quietly spoke.

"I like ye, Magnus," she said. "Ye listened tae an old woman talk about herself, and most men wouldna do such a thing."

Magnus propped his elbows on his knees, folding his hands and resting his chin upon them as he watched her.

"I want tae know about the woman who is tae give me her castle," he said. "If ye truly want tae make me yer heir, then I should know about ye."

She didn't reply for a moment. She just kept staring up to the ceiling. But then, her head came up and she looked at him.

"Ye know that yer friends put me in this chamber as a joke, don't ye?" she asked softly.

It was a strange change in subject, but not entirely unexpected in hindsight. She was sharp for her age and even she saw the irony of their situation. As if a man of Magnus's stature would really want a woman of her advanced years.

He didn't hesitate in his reply.

"I know."

"And ye still are willing tae go through with it?"

"Are ye still willing tae give me yer castle?"

She cocked her head thoughtfully. "I've a suspicion that yer friends like tae play jokes on ye," she said, avoiding his question. "I got that sense from them because they were quite gleeful tae put me here. Am I wrong?"

"Ye're not wrong."

"Then they've done this kind of thing before?"

He fought off a grin. "We've done many things tae each other all in the name of the friendship."

"They dunna sound like good friends."

"They're the best I've ever had."

"Do ye want tae seek revenge on them?"

He was intrigued at the suggestion. "Always," he said. "What did ye have in mind?"

"Give me one of those coin purses ye were carrying when ye entered the chamber and I'll tell ye."

He snorted; he couldn't help it. "Are ye saying ye'll help me for a price?"

She nodded, a smug grin on her face. "I'm sure ye have no intention of bedding me. But I'll help ye get revenge on yer friends just the same."

"Why?"

"I told ye. Because ye've been kind tae me and I like ye. And this was a nasty little joke they wanted tae play on ye."

She may have been tipsy, but she wasn't stupid. In fact, her dark eyes were glittering with surprising lucidity. He snorted.

"Very well, Mary MacMerry," he said. "What did ye have in mind?"

"Money first. Then I'll tell ye."

Magnus stood up, going to the table with the wine on it, and collected one of the coin-filled hose. He weighed a couple of them and, selecting the lighter one, handed it over to Mary. She snatched it, feeling the weight, before tucking it into the purse on her belt.

"Follow me," she said.

Up she came from the couch, moving with surprising agility considering the wine she'd ingested. There was a sleeping area in a sectioned off corner of the apartment, back behind a massive screen with a scene depicting ancient Rome painted upon it. Mary headed straight to the bed.

It was a big piece of furniture, with a carved wooden frame, and she braced her hands on the end of the bed. She silently gestured, making quick motions as if to shove the bed right into the wall, but she was doing it in a rhythmic motion. Magnus quickly understood what she meant and with a grin, he put his hands on one of the four end posts.

If his friends thought they'd pulled a joke on him, they were about to learn differently.

He was about to turn the table on them.

Magnus and Mary started ramming the bed into the wall regular rhythm, as a man would when making love to a woman. The banging bed was accompanied by loud grunts on his part, as if he were genuinely bedding the woman and having a good time doing it. His grunts were peppered with high-pitched gasps from Mary, mimicking cries of pleasure.

They went on for an hour.

A solid hour of the bed bumping, of his loud growls of pleasure, and of her female shrieks. It was the performance of a lifetime. They only stopped because Magnus was becoming weary, especially after having fought three bouts that night, so he ended the spectacle with rapid thumps against the wall and then a high-pitched scream from Mary.

After that, there was dead silence.

At least, silence to anyone listening in from the outside, but by then, he and Mary were nearly doubled over with laughter. Magnus could just see the shocked faces of Lor and Bane and Galan as they realized their arrogant friend had not only taken the bait but had used it. By the sounds emitting from the apartment, he'd had a good time of it, too.

After he and Mary rested a few minutes, they went on to bed bump for another half-hour that would certainly impress his friends. They were going to know that their trick on him had failed spectacularly. But soon, Magnus's exhaustion got the better of him and they ended their brilliant performance for the night.

It had been glorious.

In the quiet of pseudo afterglow that followed, Magnus went

to bathe as Mary ate the food that had been brought up earlier. Magnus joined her once he was clean, taking the time to eat and chat with the clever old woman he was genuinely coming to like. They passed the hours until it neared dawn and the Ludus Caledonia was shutting down for the night. Patrons were leaving on horseback or fine carriages, and warriors were retreating to their cottages, so Magnus finished up his food and stood up from the table.

"Time tae leave, m'dear," he said. "'Ye've been a grand companion this night, but 'tis time for ye tae go home."

Mary was groggy. She had been sitting at the table for the last hour, her eyes half-lidded from wine, food, and exhaustion. She stood up, weaving dangerously, as Magnus draped her with the shawl that was tossed over a chair. She smoothed at her white hair, but he ruffled it, making it a wild mass of silver. Mary looked as if she'd spent all night being pleasured by a virile warrior and when she realized why he'd done it, she cast him a reproachful look.

Naughty lad.

He simply smiled.

Magnus wanted to make sure her disheveled appearance matched the screaming she'd done earlier and once he was satisfied that she appeared properly pleasured, he directed her towards the entry that led out into the common areas of the Ludus Caledonia.

"Ye have a carriage, I assume?" he asked as he escorted her to the door.

Mary nodded. "Aye."

"Good," he said. Then, he lowered his voice and leaned down to her. "If ye dunna look as if I've taken advantage of ye all night, no one will believe the performance we just gave, so look properly weary, will ye?"

Mary nodded quickly, leaning against him as if she could hardly stand. Magnus threw open the door and began walking her out to the area where the carriages usually waited. His gaze scanned the area, immediately spying Galan and Axel, the enormous Saxon manager of the Ludus Caledonia. He could see that they were trying to stay out of sight, but everyone made eye contact, so there was no use in trying to hide.

He could see the pair smirking in the torchlight.

That only made Magnus give the old woman a squeeze.

"There, now, m'lady," he said for all to hear. "Ye had quite a night. Go home and rest and I will see ye another time."

Mary was pretending to have difficulty with her balance, but she managed to spy her carriage. She pointed to it and Magnus turned her in that direction.

"Did we have a good time, then?" she asked loudly.

Magnus nodded confidently. "The best time ye've ever had."

"Was I good?"

"Ye were excellent. And so was I."

That was enough for the nosy ears around them. Magnus took her right up to the carriage. The driver was there, an old man who took Mary from Magnus and practically lifted her into the open carriage. When the driver returned to his seat, Mary crooked a finger at Magnus.

He moved closer.

"I'm sorry for ye, my beauteous lad," she said. "But there's something ye must know."

"What?"

"Yer friends will have the last laugh, after all."

He frowned. "What do ye mean?"

"I mean that I never paid them for the chance tae be with ye," she said. "They paid *me*. It was all part of the joke. When ye paid me tae help ye get revenge upon them, I was paid twice. Dunna be angry, lad; there's not much opportunity for a woman my age tae make good money."

A creeping sense of realization filled him. "I see," he said. "They paid ye tae trick me."

"They did."

"And Whitekirk?"

She sighed heavily. "It willna belong tae ye, sorry tae say," she said, reaching out to pat his cheek. "And my name isn't Mary MacMerry. That's what I meant by yer friends having the last laugh. Ye did well, but in the end, the victory is theirs. Better luck next time, Magnus."

The carriage pulled away, leaving Magnus standing there with his mouth open. A split second of shock was followed by the acute awareness that he'd been duped all the way around. He loved his friends at the Ludus Caledonia, the only real friends he'd ever had, and they'd spent the past year playing pranks on one another as part of the bond of their brotherhood, but this one…this one was a master stroke.

He had to admit, it had been brilliant.

A crafty old woman in need of money and their plan had been perfect.

As more carriages began to pull away beneath the pewter skies of the breaking dawn, he turned to see Galan and Axel waving at him, rejoicing in his humiliation. Lor and Bane had probably already gone to bed, with wives who were waiting for them, but Galan and Axel didn't have any female baggage.

They had the freedom to stay up all night, reveling in the Eagle's humiliation.

It had been the biggest one yet.

Even Magnus appreciated the very clever prank. To prove how un-humiliated he was, he waved back at them and even bowed, as if to acknowledge that they'd wholly tricked him. It was a gesture of respect, but beneath it, he was already calculating his revenge.

Surely, they had to know he would come for them, and he would.

When they least expected it.

CHAPTER TWO

Edinburgh

"I WANT SOMETHING THAT WILL MAKE THEM THINK THEIR GUTS are all coming out through the one small hole in their arses, but I dunna want tae truly hurt them. I just want them tae think they're dying."

Two days after his bout with the faux Mary MacMerry, Magnus was bent on revenge. He was completely serious as he delivered his request to a wool-swathed apothecary, the most reputable one in all of Edinburgh. The shop was called The Seed, run by two brothers who were nearly as old as Scotland herself.

At least, that was the rumor. They were quite old, and identical twins, and some said they'd found the very secret to immortality. But Magnus didn't want their secret of life.

He simply wanted something to make his friends ill.

The old apothecary tried not to look too shocked or too confused.

"Ye want tae make them...*ill*?" he asked.

Magnus nodded. "For a day or two," he said. "As a joke, ye see. They saddled me with a... Well, it docsna matter. I need tae punish them but not hurt them. I want everything they've eaten tae come out from the top and the bottom. What can ye sell me that will do that but not harm them?"

"Ye want a cleanse?"

"If that will expel everything from their innards, I do."

The old man with the yellow beard was beginning to understand. He didn't seem confused any longer, but rather disapproving of what he was being asked for and the purpose for which it would be used. However, given that he'd seen this man before, once in the company of the owner of the Ludus Caledonia and a few other times on his own, he didn't press him further. He wanted to get through this without any trouble from the muscular warrior, so he turned back to his shelves of glass phials.

Each little bottle held mysterious or expensive ingredients. There had to be hundreds of the phials lining the shelves of the shop. Most contained what was called a "simple" ingredient, meaning that it was only one element. But others had multiple ingredients, or "compounds," which were mixed for a specific purpose.

The old man went to a particular area of the shop, peering up towards the top shelf, lined with dusty glass bottles. Pulling forth a small ladder, he climbed the rickety rungs and plucked one of the bottles from the top shelf. With the glass carefully cradled in one hand, he returned to Magnus.

The phial was filled with silver pellets. Removing the stopper, he plucked one of the pellets and held it up to Magnus.

"Steep this in wine a few hours," he said. "Have yer…friends drink the wine without the pellet in it. It will have the desired effect without injuring them."

Magnus took the silver bit out of his hand, holding it up to the dim light of the shop to get a better look at it.

"What is it?" he asked.

The old man was already turning away from him, returning the bottle to its proper place.

"It is called tartar emetic," he said. "It is used tae purge foul humors. Careful ye dunna give yer friends too much or it will kill them."

Magnus didn't want to do that. He just wanted to get back at them for the old whore trick.

"I let it soak just a few hours?" he clarified.

"Just a few and no longer."

"And it willna kill them?"

"If ye use it properly, it shouldna."

That was good enough for Magnus. He inspected the silver pellet a moment longer before tucking it into his purse and pulling forth two silver coins. Handing those over to the appreciative apothecary, he was just turning for the door when a group of women blew in.

Magnus couldn't see them very well because of the bright sunlight coming in through the doorway behind them, but he could see their shapes. He could smell the perfume. As they came deeper into the shop, he realized that he recognized the woman in the lead.

A bolt of shock ran through him.

She was well-dressed and elegant, and Magnus knew her well, but she reminded him of a time in his life he'd rather forget. For a moment, he wasn't sure what to do and his moment of indecision cost him, for the woman locked gazes with him and she, too, registered great surprise.

"Magnus?" she gasped. "Magnus, is that you?"

Magnus nodded, realizing that he could not run now. He took a deep breath to steady himself as his heart began to pound.

"Aye," he said. "Greetings, Lady Ayr."

The woman shuffled over to him in a flurry of fine fabric and strong perfume, her expression filled with delight.

"Oh, it *is* you," she said in her clipped English accent. "What a magnificent stroke of luck to find you here, Magnus. I've not seen you in years."

That was very true. Not since he'd had been her husband's hostage. He'd spent most of his life in captivity before being released, cast off into the world to fend for himself. Those were the years that Magnus tried to pretend never happened, but seeing Agnes Stewart, Duchess of Ayr, brought back that which he hadn't thought of in quite some time.

Seeing her face brought back the old, familiar hatred.

"It has been many years, m'lady," he said, feeling uncomfortable. "If ye will excuse me, I've business elsewhere."

"Magnus, wait," she said, putting her hand on his arm to stop him. She looked him over appraisingly. "Do you not have a moment to spare me? My, you *have* grown. When I last saw you, you had only just become a man and my husband finally found peace with your father. What a glorious day that was, your release. To tell you the truth, I had begun to look on you as one of the family. You had been with us for so long, I felt as if I had raised you and I was sorry to see you go."

I doubt that raising your children means keeping them locked up and punished at the slightest infraction, he thought bitterly. Lady Ayr wasn't a terrible person, at least not as terrible as her husband, but she had been guilty of ignorance. She was slightly daft, and silly, and hardly noticed the things that went on around her. The more Magnus looked at her, the more those terrible memories filled him.

The more he was bombarded by things he had tried hard to forget.

He had been so young when he'd been taken hostage by Ambrose Stewart, Duke of Ayr. The man was a cousin to his father, Hugh Stewart, Duke of Kintyre and Lorne, youngest brother of James, the King of Scotland. Hugh was a man with a rebellious streak in him. At least, that was the general consensus from the royals when others called him a true loyalist to Scotland. When Hugh had fallen afoul of his brother in a sloppy coup attempt, Ambrose had stepped in to take Hugh's bastard son hostage to ensure Hugh's good behavior.

And that's how Magnus had spent his entire life up until his release seven years ago. He had been treated adequately or poorly within the household of the Duke of Ayr, depending on his father's behavior.

It had been a horrible way to live.

"Aye, it was a long time," he said. It was all he could manage. "Please excuse me, m'lady. I do have pressing business elsewhere."

This time, Agnes let him go. "Of course, Magnus," she said, watching him head for the door. "I shall tell my husband that I have seen you and that you look well. We are staying at Trinity House in town. You remember the place? To the north, near the sea. Please visit us when you have the time to do so."

Her last words were called out to him as he quit the shop, a shouted invitation he would never accept. But just as he rushed through the doorway and onto the street, he plowed into a small body in his path. He hadn't even been watching where he was going and he heard a feminine yelp as he knocked a woman into the gutter.

In his current mood Magnus would have kept going, leaving the woman on her backside, had she not been in his way. But she was, and if he took another step, he would step on her. Therefore, he was forced to stop out of necessity, annoyed that she was blocking his exit. He sidestepped her and reached down to pull her to her feet, purely as a courtesy.

He didn't know why he should show any courtesy, because he wasn't the courteous type. Or polite when it came to women in general. Other than natural male urges or a way to make money, he'd never had any use for them. But the moment he pulled the woman to her feet and looked into her eyes, something changed.

Magnus found himself looking into a face that could only be described as angelic. The startled eyes gazing at him were large and bottomless, a pale shade of brown he'd never seen before. Her nose was pert, her mouth lush and generous, now popped open in surprise. There was a strange magic to the moment, a buzzing in his ears that shut out everything else around him.

Suddenly, he didn't feel like running off.

"My apologies, m'lady," he said. "I dinna see ye."

She was trying to brush off her beautiful dress. It was pale green, perhaps silk because it was so fine, with yellow edges around the neckline and at the bottom of her belled sleeves. Now, it had the addition of dirt from the avenue and Magnus took his eyes from her face long enough to realize that she was quite dirty as the result of his handiwork.

"No wonder," she said in an accent that was not Scots. "You were moving so quickly, it is a wonder you waited for the door to open at all. Why not take it right from the hinges?"

She was scolding him.

He deserved it.

"Had it not moved aside fast enough, I would have," he said defensively, crouching down to brush the dirt from the bottom of the hem. "If I've ruined yer dress, I'll pay for it."

She continued shaking out the dress, looking for any real damage. "It is not my dress," she said. "It belongs to the Duchess of Ayr. She will not be pleased if you've ruined it."

She was shaking the dress around so much that he stopped trying to brush the dirt from it. Standing up, he studied her for a moment, coming to think there was something oddly familiar about her now that he'd had a good look.

He'd seen those eyes somewhere before.

"Are ye a lady for the duchess?" he asked.

She nodded, now brushing her left sleeve. "I am," she said, taking more time to look at him than at her dress. "No harm done, I suppose. But be careful the next time. The next lady you shove into the gutter may not be as gracious as I am."

"What's yer name?"

She stopped brushing, annoyed at the question. "That is none of your affair," she said. "Go on with you or I shall call for a guard."

He shook his head. "Ye misunderstand," he said. "I...I think I've seen ye before."

ACKNOWLEDGMENTS

An author's journey is never a solitary endeavor, and I've had a lot of help along the way, advised and assisted by generous people who have left a lasting mark on me.

It takes a village!

To my partner in crime and general all-around good guy, Scott Moreland. None of this would have been possible without your support, your advice, your honesty, and your occasional meltdown. You push me to be a better writer.

To my author-sisters, women who inspire me every day to be the very best I can be. Each one has contributed something to my life—friendship, advice, direction, wisdom—Tanya Anne Crosby, Eliza Knight, Barbara Devlin, Christi Caldwell, Kerrigan Bryne, Hildie McQueen, Violetta Rand, Susan Stoker, Amy Jarecki, my de Wolfe Pack authors, Melissa Storm, and so many others who have been with me through this journey. You have all contributed something along the way, and I can never fully express my gratitude.

To agent extraordinaire, Sarah Elizabeth Younger, who believed in me and worked her tail off to help me achieve a life-long dream.

To Deb Werksman, "THE" editor extraordinaire who made sure that dream came true.

To my mother and father, Bill and Sylvia Bouse, and my brother, Bill Bouse, who have watched all of this happen from the fifty-yard line and have been an endless source of encouragement (and astonishment!).

And, of course, to my husband, Rob, the real knight in shining armor in all of this.

Lastly, to my readers, without whom none of this would be possible.

ABOUT THE AUTHOR

With over one hundred published novels, Kathryn Le Veque is a critically acclaimed *USA Today* bestselling author, a charter Amazon All-Star author, and a number one bestselling, award-winning, multipublished author in medieval historical romance.

Kathryn is a multiple award nominee and winner, including winner of *Uncaged Book Reviews* magazine's Raven Award for Favorite Medieval Romance and Favorite Cover. Kathryn is also a multiple RONE nominee for *InD'Tale Magazine*, holding the record for the number of nominations. In 2018, her novel *Warwolfe* was the winner in the romance category of the Book Excellence Awards and a finalist for several other awards. Kathryn's books have also hit the *USA Today* bestseller list more than fifteen times.

In addition to her own published works, Kathryn is president/CEO of Dragonblade Publishing, a boutique publishing house specializing in historical romance, and President/CEO of DragonMedia Publishing, a publishing house that publishes the Pirates of Britannia Connected World series. In July 2018, Kathryn launched yet another publishing house, WolfeBane Publishing, which publishes the World of de Wolfe Pack Connected series (formerly Kindle Worlds).

Kathryn is considered one of the top Indie authors in the world with over two million copies in circulation, and her novels have been translated into several languages.

Kathryn loves to connect with her readers. You can find her on Facebook @kathrynlevequenovels, on her website at kathrynleveque.com, on Twitter @kathrynleveque, and on Bookbub for her latest and greatest novels.